the CURSE

Part I

Georgi Velkov

Typeset in Dante MT Std

Editing, design, typesetting and publishing by UK Book Publishing

www.ukbookpublishing.com

ISBN: 978-1-915338-02-0

the
CURSE
Part I

Chapter 1

Family dinner

Teela Fehrenberg was standing in front of the door to her two-story house that was lined from almost all sides with windows. She wiped the soles of her boots on the doormat, the words 'Welcome to the Fehrenberg family' printed across it, and proceeded to open the rosewood door. She hung her coat and took off her shoes, running a hand through her long brown hair.

"I'm home," she announced to whoever was listening. "Is anyone here?"

A tall, blonde woman jumped out of the kitchen, almost startling Teela, carrying a saucepan and a wooden spoon in her hands. A ruby liquid was splattered across the spoon's surface.

"Try this, sweetie," the woman said.

Teela inched closer to the wooden spoon, her lips tasting the tomato sauce.

"It's good, Mum," she stated. "But a piece of advice for future reference."

Teela's mother shoved the spoon into the saucepan.

"Easy on the jumping out," Teela giggled. "You can give people a heart attack!"

"It's not my fault you're not prepared for my entrance." The older woman smiled.

"What are you on about again, Perventia?" called out an approaching male voice from the hallway, that must have been Teela's father.

"Nothing, Pattery," Perventia responded. "Teela claims I'm startling."

"I didn't say that *exactly...*"

"Doesn't matter," Perventia interrupted her. "Come – let's eat!"

Perventia started dragging her daughter to the kitchen, which was located several steps away from the front door, living room and the hallway Pattery had emerged from. Pattery followed them. In the kitchen, Tiffany – one of Teela's sisters – looked like she had been waiting for them, seated on a chair next to the vast wooden table in the living room. It seemed as if she had come out of nowhere.

"You came home, at last!" Tiffany exclaimed, sighing.

"I didn't know you were waiting for me," Teela said, positioning herself on the chair next to Tiffany's.

"Of course we were waiting for you!" Tiffany cracked a smile. "You know the family tradition – we always dine together!"

"A great tradition if I do say so myself," Pattery pointed out while taking his place on the far end of the vast wooden table, his bronze hair glistening in the fading rays of sunlight.

The kitchen table was littered with various culinary achievements, courtesy of Perventia – a fresh emerald salad, the tomato sauce Teela had tasted not two minutes ago, several different types of cheese such as parmesan, rainbow cheddar, brie and gouda, a few pizzas, pasta Bolognese, garlic bread, balsamic-glazed steak rolls, chicken with lemon and spicy spring onions, chicken saltimbocca with crunchy pea salad, hasselback tomato caprese, mineral water, freshly squeezed apple and orange juices, red and white wines, a huge chocolate cake, vanilla biscuits, and chocolate pudding. She had really outdone herself.

Teela smiled – she knew her mother Perventia had always considered herself a devoted chef, and she took great pleasure in providing delicious meals for her family. Often, she had made so much food that it was hard for Pattery, Teela, Tiffany, and Perventia herself, to climb the stairs up to their bedrooms. In these instances, a lot of food was left untouched, saved for later.

"Do you think it's enough?" Perventia asked them worriedly, while she was pouring the tomato sauce into four different glass cups for the present members of her family.

"You're joking, right?" Teela asked her. "There's enough food on this table to feed the whole town!"

"I'm completely serious, Teela!" Perventia sounded as if she was almost reprimanding Teela. "If you get hungry later, I would be to blame!"

"Per," her husband Pattery said warmly. "It's more than enough. Now sit back, relax, and enjoy these delicious treats with us."

Perventia looked at Pattery, her frown betraying her uncertainty, but took her seat at the opposite far end of the table, nevertheless.

Pattery poured some white wine into his and Perventia's glasses and stood up from his seat, raising his glass in the air. He was dressed in an expensive-looking charcoal shirt and jeans – it was clear he had prepared for the family dinner.

"A toast," he announced. "To our family."

Teela and Tiffany had just filled up their glasses with white wine, following their father's example. The two young girls were allowed to drink, but only a glass, and only at official family occasions, such as this one.

"For our ordinary family!" Teela rose from her seat, waving her glass in the air proudly.

Teela noticed Perventia and Pattery exchanging dubious looks, upon hearing the word *ordinary*.

"A toast to this family – even with not all the members present," Teela uttered, her voice turning down an octave.

Perventia and Pattery Fehrenberg had three more daughters – Pacifika, Kayla, and Klacifia. They had left their family house long ago, due to constant fights with their family about a specific subject. A subject that Teela and Tiffany had no idea about. The three older Fehrenberg sisters hadn't even spoken to their family for years.

"A toast!" Perventia also joined the praise with her glass, standing up from her seat.

"To our ordinary family!" Tiffany proclaimed as well, following her mother's example.

Perventia and Pattery exchanged dubious looks once again when they heard that word – '*ordinary*'.

The four of them clinked their glasses together and took sips of the wine. The remainder of the evening was occupied with dining on the delicious treats and engaging in various discussions amongst the members of the Fehrenberg family.

The reason for the hesitant looks, exchanged between Perventia and Pattery Fehrenberg, was a complicated one. Their family was harboring secrets and profound mysteries that were yet to be revealed.

Challenges lay ahead for this family – things that don't happen every day. But, for the time being, the Fehrenberg family – at least to the uncomprehending eye – appeared as the typical middle-class family, with its ordinary life and ordinary problems.

But was the Fehrenberg family *really* ordinary? Or was there more beneath this family's appearance?

Chapter 2

The Book and The Curse

Teela and Tiffany Fehrenberg had just gotten home from school, having closed the front door behind them. The two girls found their parents – Pattery and Perventia – sitting on the couch in the living room, visibly nervous, their hands and legs shaking violently. Both of them had their gazes set on a huge book with metallic front and back covers, open on the small glass table in front of them. There was also a padlock, attached to the front cover.

Teela and Tiffany left their school supplies on the star-patterned kitchen counter and started for the couch. Teela, and she also suspected Tiffany, expected the same old – their mother cooking a delicious dinner and their father solving a crossword or working on one of his newest novels. When Teela and Tiffany reached the couch, however, their parents looked up from the strange-looking book to their daughters. Teela couldn't help noticing that the cheeriness in her mother's eyes had untraceably disappeared, and her father seemed tenser than usual.

Suddenly, Perventia stood from the couch, caressing Teela and Tiffany's faces and enveloping them in a tight embrace.

"What's going on, Mum?" Teela asked, beginning to worry.

"Sit," Perventia instructed, and the two girls sat opposite their father on two tall wooden chairs that were taken from the vast wooden dining table, located mere centimeters away from them. Perventia resumed her place next to her husband on the soft couch.

"It's time for us to tell you," Perventia added. "We've put it off long enough, wanting for you to have a normal childhood, but there's no other way."

"Tell us what?" Tiffany asked, with Teela picking up on the suspicion, and rising alarm, present in her voice.

Perventia flashed a silver key out of her jeans' front pocket and placed it inside the book's padlock. She twisted it momentarily after, and the sizable book sprang open with a slight thud when the front cover hit the glass. Tiffany and Teela saw that it was composed of hundreds upon hundreds of pages, most of them containing a combination of text and pictures, reeking of old, probably due to storage. The two girls inched closer to the odd item. Teela scanned it, trying to make out the text. The book was written in old-fashioned English and the handwriting was relatively understandable, but due to some of the letters being twisted in an odd cursive, Teela could only make out the words *'witches', 'curse'* and *'death'*.

"What is this?" Teela almost giggled. "Some children's book?"

"I wish it was," Pattery stated, tension obscuring his tone.

"This is our family book of shadows," Perventia started, seemingly calmer now. "It has been in our family for generations, hundreds of years."

"Okay," Tiffany replied unsurely. "What does that have to do with us? It must be one of the old books we keep in the attic!"

"No. No!" Perventia said firmly. "This book is different! Listen to me, this book is from the past, but it can give predictions and statements about the future. Do you understand?"

Teela and Tiffany nodded simultaneously. Teela was still not entirely convinced.

"This book was created in the year of 1692, during the 17th century, when the witch trials in Salem began. It was written by two men under the names of Sarvit Fehrenberg and Mour Klauzer."

"Wait a minute," Teela interrupted her mother. "This man Sarvit has the same surname as our family, and Mour's surname is identical to Kastilius and Kasteron's!"

Kasteron and Kastilius Klauzer were Teela and Tiffany's schoolmates. A year ago, Teela had started dating Kasteron and they were still going strong to this day. They had a one-year age difference, with Teela being the youngest member of the Fehrenberg family at 16-years-old. The Klauzer family lived on the opposite side of the street to the Fehrenberg family. Similar to the Fehrenberg family, the Klauzer family also had five children – but all males. And Teela knew from Kasteron that just like her family, three of their children weren't living at home with the rest of them.

"That's right, Teela," Perventia confirmed with a nod. "Sarvit Fehrenberg is one of our ancestors and Mour Klauzer is one of the Klauzer family's."

"Even if that is even remotely true, what do *we* have to do with *them*?" Tiffany asked. "They must be long dead and gone by now – why dwell on the past?"

"Because the past, Tiffany," Pattery joined the conversation, "has a vital role to the present and to be more specific – what is about to happen to our family real soon! This book," Pattery said, pointing at the item, "tells the tale of a curse that looms over our family and the Klauzer family. A curse that a powerful witch by the name of Feever and her relatives cast over us. A curse that will be very difficult to run away from!"

"What are you on about, you guys?" Teela refused to believe what she was hearing. It all seemed a bit too much, a bit too sudden. "Things such as curses and witches don't exist!"

7

"I want to desperately believe in that statement too!" Perventia said. "I want to believe in that more than anything else in the whole wide world." A pause. "But that's not a possibility! The Curse is a fact – a fact that will soon commence!"

"Sarvit and Mour were cursed by the witch Feever and her family," Pattery added. "We don't know the exact reason – The Book hasn't revealed that yet." He looked at both of his daughters, their faces scrunched up in denial. "But we *do* know that the curse they cast will soon be fully upon us!"

"You're joking, right?" Tiffany asked, a note of faint hope in her voice.

"We're dead serious," Pattery said. "Sarvit and Mour have put together this book to aid the people that will fall victim to The Curse – in this case, that's us! The Curse is set to start in the 21st century and will affect the descendants of Sarvit and Mour. They hadn't wanted their descendants to perish without giving them a fair chance and a head start to fight! That's why they'd written this book and passed it onto their kids – their kids passed it onto their kids and so on and so forth. This book is now in our possession and we mustn't ever lose it – if Feever ever gets her hands on it, we'd all be lost!"

Teela and Tiffany had fallen dead silent. Teela didn't know whether to believe all she'd just heard, or not.

"Okay, let's say for a second that all this is true to some extent," Teela agreed reluctantly. "How is it even remotely possible that *this* book could fall in the hands of a witch that lived more than three hundred years ago? And what does this *curse*, that you're all so afraid of, entail?"

"I'm glad you asked, Teela." Perventia smiled, for the first time in a good while. "The answer is quite simple, actually. The Curse consists of the following…" Perventia started narrating as if she knew the text by heart – probably with The Book as the source. "'*The descendants of Sarvit and Mour are going to be killed one by one* on a random basis by the witch Feever. Every three weeks, Feever is going to pay a visit to Sarvit and Mour's descendants and claim a victim'." A slight pause. "Our job, as your parents, is to protect you from this vicious witch and find a way to somehow stop this curse – even though the chances for the latter are slim, to put it mildly!"

At this, Teela and Tiffany shared an alarmed, wide-eyed glance. Teela started breathing heavier than usual.

"Feever is not dead!" Pattery added to Teela's horror. "When she cursed the two families she cast some sort of spell, making herself sleep for more than three hundred years. That time is nearly up and the witch will soon awaken, and I have no doubts she would want to continue what she started!"

"That all sounds like an extract from a science-fiction film!" Teela laughed, and then, just a moment later, she heard the loud clank of her mother's fist on the rectangular glass table, The Book shaking as a result. That made Teela shut her mouth for a moment, startled by her mother's sudden outburst, especially since she had always been so positive and cheerful. For the first time, the realization dawned on Teela that the situation must have been serious if her mother was behaving that way.

"This is no laughing matter, children," Perventia reprimanded them, for a second time that day. "This is the reality!" As if in an afterthought the blond woman added – "We also need to inform you that Sarvit and Mour also possessed a witch inheritance, just like Feever!"

"So you're saying that our family and the Klauzer family are witches?" Tiffany had just then drawn the conclusion, which Teela had already come to. "Feever is also a witch? A witch, who's going to miraculously come back from the dead to hunt us down? A witch, who is hell-bent on destroying our family, having cursed us for reasons unknown? All of us are destined to die by her hand? Killed one by one, like a pack of wild animals?" Tiffany's questions poured out like a fountain. Tiffany was one year older than Teela and Teela was aware that meant she naturally had a protective nature over her baby sister, their three older sisters having left home a long time ago.

"But what's the connection between the Salem witch trials, Feever, and us?" Teela demanded. "Feever had probably been at the heart of the trials – they must have been directed at her! Why did she curse *us* then?"

"Sarvit and Mour must have done something – I don't know what, exactly!" Pattery responded. "Something that must have harmed Feever, or her family. Feever must have figured it out, and decided to take her revenge by cursing their whole family lines!"

"So you're saying that Sarvit and Mour were the bad guys?" Teela inquired again.

"There were no bad or good guys!" Perventia stated, a bit too firmly. "Just three families trying to escape the Salem witch trials. During the 17th century, everyone had been suspicious of everyone, brother had turned against brother, father against child, wife against husband. No one trusted anyone – even their loved ones! People were living in fear. The three families must have been found suspicious of witch deeds, trying to survive by any means necessary! Sarvit and Mour must have done something to anger Feever and her family – all of this, however vague, is described in The Book."

It seemed that all four of them had momentarily forgotten about the old, but at the same time luxuriously looking, item that lay spread out on the glass table between them. The silver covers attracted the sun rays, streaming through the kitchen windows.

"But we can't really blame them, seeing that if they hadn't done what they did, I doubt all of us would be sitting here right now, safe and sound, *existing*! *There were no bad, or good guys* – just three families, all affected by the Salem witch trials, in one way or another," Perventia said.

"So, we're all witches, who are soon to be hunted by another witch, named Feever, having cursed our line of heritage because of something Sarvit and Mour had done?" Tiffany summed up the conversation.

"Yeah, that's just about it," Perventia confirmed, and lay back against the couch, sighing in relief.

Teela looked at her parents for a few seconds. She supposed she knew where their relief was coming from – they must have kept that secret for years. Now, it was out in the open – and there was no turning back. "Another question," Teela added. "This whole thing about The Curse and us falling victims to Feever; when does it commence, exactly? And what are *we* going to do about it? *I*, personally, have no intention of just sitting around on my butt, waiting for Feever to arrive!"

"It starts in a week," Pattery answered. "The solution is one – we run! We take The Book with us and together with the Klauzer family, we pick up the rest of our family members! And one more thing – your older sisters and the three eldest children of the Klauzer family already know all that!"

"Is that why they left and don't live with us anymore?" Tiffany asked. "Because they know everything you just told *us*?"

Perventia nodded. "They wanted to be away from us and the knowledge, living their last peaceful moments to the fullest! That's why your father and I were arguing so much with your sisters over the years – because they refused to accept reality, refused to accept the possibility that their life may end abruptly!"

"But we *are* going to try and stop all that, right?" Teela asked hopefully.

"We will do the absolute best we can!" Perventia assured her. "We will fight to the last breath!"

Pattery added, "Later on – we don't know when, exactly – you will all develop certain magical abilities that will enable you to defend yourselves against Feever. You can also cast certain limited spells before unlocking your power. It's all in The Book – there are hundreds of spells and suggestions to guide you toward finding your powers. I assure you, my girls, you won't be alone! You may feel scared at the beginning, but you *will* eventually learn to stand up to Feever, and build your confidence in your abilities!"

Pattery smiled at Teela and Tiffany warmly. And with that specific smile, he somehow gave Teela, and she supposed Tiffany too, the hope that this *curse* would be handled somehow.

"The Book has everything we need," Perventia informed them. "That's why it's so important to keep it safe and away from Feever's grip! It will keep *you* safe, and guide you toward the path of becoming fully-fledged witches. As long as The Book is with us, we would never be defenseless against Feever and whatever she has in store for us! That witch bitch wants to hurt our family? We will push back triply as much!"

There was a determined fire, crackling in Perventia's eyes, and Teela somehow knew that it would not be so easily snuffed out. Tiffany and Teela smiled at their parents warmly, having already fully believed their story, their hopeful smiles evident.

"And that random basis that you mentioned?" Teela said. "There isn't a way to know who's going to be the first one to go, is there? Or the next, for that matter?"

"I am not yet sure about that," Perventia answered.

~~~~~~~~~~

Both families were determined to face Feever and whatever tricks she had up her sleeve. She was one – they were 14. How hard could it be? They had precisely a week to prepare for leaving, because after this period had passed, The Curse would commence. The Fehrenberg family and the Klauzer family had to run with every ounce of strength they possessed.

The starting point had been set – that signified all the members of the two families finding out the truth.

And that had just taken place.

Chapter 3

Families gathering

The next day, the Fehrenberg family called the Klauzer family and the two families decided to get together for a meeting, intending to compose a plan for fleeing their hometown – Kasterfainz – as soon as possible. The meeting took place in the Fehrenberg's family house.

Teela and Kasteron were seated on the couch, their fingers intertwined. Tiffany and Kastilius sat next to them. Kasteron and Kastilius were the only two of the Klauzer family's five sons who lived with them.

Pattery, Perventia, and Kastilius and Kasteron's parents – their mother Berventy and their father Brouzenvert – paced around the living room nervously, their gazes directed at their children.

"We've got a week to gather our luggage and run far away from this town!" Berventy stated, her voice cracking like fragile glass. "A *week!*"

"We need to be long gone by the time Feever arrives – the first place she's going to look for us is our homes, I'm sure of it!" Perventia added.

Teela Fehrenberg could only imagine what it must have been like for her mother – preparing to leave her current life behind in favor of one on the run, always looking over her shoulder.

"Don't forget we need to pick up the rest of our relatives," Tiffany voiced out a reminder as if they'd forgotten. "They are also a part of all this!"

"Yes, we will do that," Pattery confirmed with a nod.

Brouzenvert looked at his children, Kasteron and Kastilius, letting out a slight sigh. "I hope you all know that we won't be able to stay in one place for too long. Feever is wicked and she will search for us wherever we go. That's why we cannot possibly afford to stay rooted!"

Kasteron and Kastilius nodded affirmatively, Teela and Tiffany following their example.

"When do you think we should set off?" Perventia turned to Berventy and Brouzenvert. "What should we take with us? Where will we stay? What are we going to eat?"

Teela felt the edges of her mouth altering into an involuntary smile – even at a time like this, her mother thought about whether her children would be fed.

"As soon as possible!" Brouzenvert said. "I say we give ourselves two days to gather everything we need – mostly essentials! The Book being one of the most important items!"

"And then we will pick up the rest of our children," Berventy said.

The other members of the two families were between 20 and 30 years of age. Only Tiffany, Teela, Kasteron and Kastilius were between 16 and 17. Kasteron was almost 18. Kastilius was the youngest son of Berventy and Brouzenvert, the same age as Teela.

"Then we run as fast as our feet can carry us!" Perventia almost commanded. "We will stop rarely, probably at hotels – but for no more than a day or two."

Teela still couldn't believe that all those fantasy tales were *actually* happening. Just last week, Kasteron was all she thought about, juggling her existence between her ordinary school life and her ordinary problems. And then bam – out of nowhere, just yesterday, she had learned about a curse, looming over her family, created by a witch, named Feever, who was hell-bent on exacting her revenge for something that had happened more than 300 years ago, by eliminating Teela and her family one by one?

She turned to her boyfriend Kasteron, pulling him close to her. A second later, their lips locked in a passionate kiss. Out of the corner of her eye, Teela saw Kastilius averting his gaze, as if he were disgusted by them and what they were doing.

"The Book is a vital item that we should take with us!" Perventia said. "If we don't take it, we would all be dead!"

"We know." Berventy frowned.

Teela knew Perventia was just repeating knowledge they all already knew. But she sensed Berventy couldn't blame her at the same time – both of the families were nervous about the fact that in a week their lives would be irrevocably changed forever.

"So the plan is set – you all got it?" Brouzenvert asked the seven of them. There was no room for mistakes. "In two days, we start running away from this town; we need to be ready by then, okay?"

"Okay," confirmed the four children and the rest of the parents simultaneously.

After the plan was constructed, Berventy, Brouzenvert, and Kastilius decided to head home and get some rest, but Berventy added that they didn't know when they would have such an opportunity again.

"You go on ahead," Kasteron advised his parents and his brother. "I will be over later."

Considering that the Klauzer family lived just on the opposite side of the street to the Fehrenberg family, there was no issue in Kasteron staying over at Teela's.

Chapter 6

A problem with a witch

Teela came back home from school, her mind throughout the day entirely occupied by memories of the previous night with Kasteron. It was simply magical, and Teela couldn't have asked for a better first time. After hanging up her coat and leaving her backpack beside the front door, Teela entered the closely located kitchen, finding her mother Perventia with a huge backpack, slung across her shoulders, and her father Pattery, holding a similar-sized duffel bag.

"What is going on?" Teela asked them, the worry in her voice evident. They both seemed on edge, seconds short of trembling.

"Feever is early!" Perventia answered.

"How do you know?" Teela said.

"I just feel it, honey; I can't really explain it."

"We need to flee. *Now!*" Pattery almost ordered. "Last night the museum burned down with two police officers found dead at the scene."

"What? *What?*" Teela frantically started questioning them. "We had *a week*, remember? And how do you know it was her?"

"It's too much of a coincidence to just ignore. I guess Feever decided to surprise us!" Pattery said and handed another duffel bag to Teela he had retrieved from the floor. "Take this."

Teela did as she was told, without asking any more questions.

"Where the hell is Tiffany?" Perventia asked, her forehead creasing in concern.

"Upstairs!" Tiffany's voice could be heard from the second floor of the house, above the staircase.

"I'll go get her!" Pattery said and started heading up the stairs when he froze on his spot.

Teela averted her gaze in the direction he was looking at and felt her limbs freezing too. Through the back door's window, she could see a woman standing in the backyard. Even though Teela knew the woman in question was, in fact, much older, she looked no more than 30 years of age, dressed in an expensive-looking onyx-blue dress. Something told Teela that this was indeed the legendary Feever. The witch was standing, rooted to her spot, looking at them through the back door's window. Teela caught a glimpse of the pure malice, raging in her eyes.

"Run, run, run," Perventia whispered in Teela's ear, and the two of them ran for the star-patterned kitchen counter, which was just a few meters away, crouching low below it. Teela heard her father Pattery starting to jog up the stairs, to pick up Tiffany. Teela and her family were aiming not to make a single sound, but she had no doubt Feever had seen them already.

~~~~~~~~~~

Feever tilted her head back slightly, her eyes closing shut. In a matter of mere seconds, another three Feevers separated from her body, identical to the original. They started walking toward the house, soon circling it from all sides, except for the original, who raised her head to see an interesting exchange between two members of the Fehrenberg family.

"Tiffany!" Feever heard Pattery hissing in the second floor's hallway, through an open bedroom window. "Down, down!"

Then, Feever saw the figures of Pattery and Tiffany lowering themselves to the ground, escaping her line of sight. The original Feever, who had begun walking around the house, toward the front door, thrust her hands up in the air, two pistols appearing out of nowhere. Because her copies were linked directly to their creator, Feever knew they now had guns in their hands too.

"That thing," the original Feever said. "Seemed interesting. All credit goes to my friends at the museum yesterday!" Her lips formed into a smile.

~~~~~~~~~~

"We need to get the fuck out of here!" Perventia told her daughter Teela, both of them still crouched under the counter. Perventia didn't usually swear but there was a first time for everything.

"What about Pattery and Tiffany?" Teela asked. "And Kasteron?"

"I believe they're going to find a way," Perventia claimed. "I hope we can all make it to the pickup truck by the time Feever's done shooting." Perventia showed her nose from below the counter slightly, only to see through the kitchen window, a few Feevers walking past. One of them, a copy, or maybe even the original, stopped in front of the kitchen windows.

"You *hope*?" Terror crept into Teela's voice.

"Just stay down!" Perventia said and was glad when Teela followed her instructions.

~~~~~~~~~~

"You, my dears," said the original Feever, now standing in front of the rosewood door. "You've got a problem with a witch!"

Feever tapped her temple with her index finger and her X-ray vision turned on, exposing the layout of the spacious two-story house. She turned toward the kitchen to see the first duplicate, standing in front of the kitchen's windows, raising the two guns. She pulled the triggers of both guns at precisely the same time and bullets shattered the windows, flying through the kitchen, destroying cupboards, sofas, framed photos of the Fehrenberg family, in their path. The scene looked like a literal rain of bullets.

Satisfied with the outcome so far on this side, Feever moved on to observe the handiwork of the second copy, which was positioned below Teela's bedroom window. She pulled the triggers after her comrade had opened fire first, littering the space with bullets. Sadly, for all Feevers involved, there wasn't anyone in there to hurt.

Feever saw the third and last copy standing below Tiffany's bedroom window, where Tiffany and Pattery were hiding. The copy initiated her own rain of bullets, showering the two Fehrenberg family members with debris, but never quite hurting them properly. The three copies were soon finished with their shooting.

Now, it was their motherboard's turn.

~~~~~~~~~~

"Run fast through there." Perventia motioned Teela to the back door with a hand, having seen there wasn't a Feever standing there. Once they were outside the house, one of the copies, positioned in front of the kitchen, noticed them almost immediately, lifting her pistols in the air. Perventia and Teela, however, swiftly escaped her attack by ducking as low as possible, dodging the bullets. The two of them soon reached the pickup truck, parked in the driveway a few meters away from the kitchen.

Chapter 7

Another family gathering

The Fehrenberg family's pickup truck pulled over after about an hour, on a secluded section of the highway, leading out of Kasterfainz. The road was surrounded by a small meadow, an even tinier water fountain and several benches. The dusk soon threatened to fall, and the atmosphere was so dead-quiet, it was a miracle that the Fehrenberg family had even found this precise spot.

Tiffany heard Perventia killing the engine and then saw her stepping out of the front side of the truck. Pattery was just making his way down from the back compartment, next to Tiffany, when Perventia almost jumped on top of him in ecstasy, kissing him affectionately. Tiffany smiled – it was nice to know that after all these years, her parents still had the hots for one another.

"Relax," he said with a smile, but he clearly didn't want Perventia to stop.

"I thought Feever got you." Perventia's eyes filled with tears, and Pattery pressed her against him in a tight hug.

Tiffany and Teela got out of the back and front compartments of the truck, respectively, and smiled upon seeing each other. Then, they walked toward their parents.

"Well," Tiffany uttered, a certain joy in her tone. "We survived Feever's first attack!"

Perventia stepped away from Pattery for a minute, in order to embrace both her daughters.

"Perventia," Pattery addressed her, Tiffany sensing the sudden alarm in his voice. "The Book? You took The Book, right?"

"Of course I took The Book!" she answered. "It's in the truck – I placed it there before Feever attacked, when we were getting ready to flee."

Tiffany's gaze suddenly averted to the tiny meadow, her eyes refusing to believe the sight. For the first time in *years*, she was seeing one of her older sisters – Klacifia – who was now walking toward them from the meadow, her long chestnut hair glinting in the fading rays of sunlight. Teela's hair was shorter than her sisters', but it had a similar color – just two shades darker. Klacifia was five years older than Teela and four years older than Tiffany.

~~~~~~~~~

"KLACIFIA!" Perventia exclaimed happily upon seeing one of her other daughters and started smothering her with hugs. Perventia and Pattery had let Pacifika, Kayla, and Klacifia know about the start of The Curse and knew that they *would* see them again. But it was still a shock seeing your child after all the years of no communication.

Perventia whipped her head around at the sight of tires, scraping against cement. In another pickup truck were Berventy, Brouzenvert, Kastilius and Kasteron. When Kasteron emerged from the vehicle, Teela made a beeline for him, almost jumping on top of him, giving him endless kisses – just as Perventia herself had done to Pattery just a few minutes earlier. Perventia smiled, seeing that upon impact the young lovers crumbled to the ground and laughed, but didn't stop kissing.

Berventy, Brouzenvert and Kastilius headed toward Tiffany, Perventia, Pattery, and Klacifia.

Next to Perventia, Klacifia looked like she was inspecting her surroundings. "Where are the others?" Klacifia asked. "Kayla and Pacifika should have been here by now!"

"The same applies to Brouzun, Morven and Marisii!" Berventy added worriedly. The three men Berventy mentioned were the rest of the members of the Klauzer family, Kastilius and Kasteron's older brothers.

"We all agreed to wait for each other on this exact spot!" Brouzenvert noted, the nervousness in his voice evident. "But so far only Klacifia's arrived."

"What if something went wrong?" Berventy's hands shook vigorously, her voice following suit.

"Hey," Perventia said softly and took Berventy's hand in hers. "They *will* come! They all know this is the rendezvous point – nothing will go wrong, okay?" Perventia smiled warmly, trying to comfort her friend. Berventy Klauzer returned the smile and nodded.

An hour passed, then two, but there were still no signs of any more family members arriving. The present members were all expecting Pacifika, Kayla, Brouzun, Morven and Marisii to emerge from somewhere any minute now. They were all living far away from here, but they had been notified of the meeting spot.

So why had only Klacifia appeared? Feever had awoken from her slumber sooner than expected and the two families hadn't even all gathered in one place yet.

The dawn officially fell, enveloping the empty road from all sides – and there was *still* nobody even approaching.

"You all know what we need to do," Brouzenvert suddenly said.

"We can't leave without them, Bronz," his wife Berventy said.

"If they wanted to meet us so badly, they would have been here already!" he said, his tone rising a notch, Perventia sensing the tension building up. Teela and Kasteron had just returned from their make-out session, to witness Brouzenvert's frustration erupting from its confines. "If they're late, *they* would have to find a way to locate us somehow!"

"Brouzenvert, calm down!" Pattery reprimanded him, earning a look full of disdain from Brouzenvert.

"Don't tell me to calm down!" Brouzenvert said even louder now. "You're doing fine – most of your kids are with you already. But *I* am still missing three of my sons! Feever could have already captured them for all we know. So don't you *dare* tell me to calm down!"

Brouzenvert snatched away from Berventy's arms, breaking the intended embrace, angrily heading for the Klauzer family's vehicle. He climbed inside, slamming the door loudly after him. *This whole curse is clearly taking a toll on him,* Perventia thought.

~~~~~~~~~

The Curse was affecting every single one of them in a negative way, but Brouzenvert, Berventy, Pattery and Perventia most of all – because deep down they knew that it was only a matter of time before they started losing their children one by one. By an ancient witch's hand.

The rest of the families' members present got that and didn't try to comfort Brouzenvert any further – better to let him take out his anger now before Feever started attacking them for real. The nine of them waited for a half-hour more, but by that time it was already painfully clear that nobody else was coming.

The two families climbed onto their respective pickup trucks and resumed traveling down the empty cement road, not knowing where they were headed, or what the future held.

Chapter 8

The beginning of the witch trials

General Scrouch was the mayor of a small town by the name of Salem during the year 1692. Salem's citizens had chosen him specifically because he had promised to look after them and to strive to make their small community prosper in the best way imaginable. General Scrouch certainly had a plethora of ideas for Salem, realizing them one by one. In the eyes of the citizens, this man was good and caring, nigh on the perfect mayor of Salem. But the reality was the total opposite. This man was interested only in sex, money and power – not necessarily in that order. He did not care for the town, or its citizens one bit. He cared about money. And that was his primary aim when he ran for mayor – so he could rob the poor, innocent citizens, filling his pockets in the process.

The ideas he was making happen were tiny, but he was realizing them strategically – in a way to keep the illusionist veil draped in front of the citizens' eyes. That's why he had created a reputation for himself as the best mayor of Salem so far. Scrouch had fooled the townsfolk for quite some time – the unsuspecting people had elected him in the year 1688, four years after the previous General had perished due to the Black Plague. And now the year was 1692, four full years into General Scrouch's reign. Four years of creating a web of lies and empty promises so masterfully that no one had suspected him of foul play yet.

For a year, he had also been cheating on his wife Ahronia with one of the local prostitutes – Eris. General Scrouch and Ahronia had been together for ten years and at some point, he had become bored of fucking the same woman, moving on to Eris's services. Eris didn't mind at all – General Scrouch was paying well for her services, and she didn't have much of a conscience to regret sleeping with a partnered man. The two of them had met on the cobbled street in front of the town hall, deciding to spend the night together. Afterward, they had come to an arrangement – Eris was to come to his office four times a week, receiving her payment after she had provided her services.

Now, Eris emerged at the entrance to his office once again, her décolletage wide open, an eager smile spread across her face. When General Scrouch noticed her from behind his oak desk, he got hard instantly.

"Close the door," he motioned and she obeyed.

Scrouch inched closer to her, like a predator, his hand finding its way under her long skirt, feeling the moisture. Scrouch became even harder, wondering if he would just come by fingering Eris. The prostitute was moaning hard while the General was sliding his long index finger in and out. After he was done playing, he whispered in her ear firmly, "Give me a blowjob, sweetheart."

She nodded affirmatively and kneeled, Scrouch reveling at the sight. Then, Eris unbuttoned his dark cowboy pants eagerly, shoving his penis down her throat, massaging it with her right hand. He groaned in pleasure, Eris tracing the rest of his cowboy attire with her free hand. They stayed like that for a few more minutes, before the General moved his obedient hussy to the oak desk. He removed her corset and skirt completely and penetrated her again, beginning to fuck her wildly, while she moaned loudly. The General was always fucking Eris wildly, not sparing one breath, his mind firmly set on the view that he wasn't obliged to treat prostitutes with respect. He knew Eris didn't mind that a tad, used to being treated like garbage.

~~~~~~~~~~

Three more weeks went by in the town of Salem, Massachusetts. The local life proceeded as usual – the townsfolk continued living their ordinary lives, Scrouch continued fucking Eris. Until one day, when Eris arrived in General Scrouch's office for another 'session', bearing unsettling news.

"Close the door," the General commanded, feeling excitement in his pants, after Eris closed the door, usually indicating that after this action she was all his for the taking. General Scrouch stood from his chair behind his desk and walked around it, shoving a hand up Eris's skirt upon reaching her. Eris pushed his hand away.

"What is it?" the General asked angrily – he didn't like to be kept waiting. "I am paying you, remember? What's the problem then?"

Eris started walking back and forth in the General's office, her hands shaking and her forehead drenched in sweat. "I need to tell you something, General Scrouch."

"Do it faster, please," General Scrouch ordered again, shoving his right hand in his undergarments, starting to stroke his member.

"Look," she started, her voice trembling. "My period, it…" Eris paused, "…well, it's late. By three weeks!"

The excitement in Scrouch's dark pants died and he took his hand out. "What?" His voice cut through the air as he began slowly stepping toward her.

"Well, yeah," Eris continued. "My period is late, and I worry I might be…"

41

"Pregnant?" the General finished for her, his voice devoid of any emotion or sympathy.

Eris nodded. "I went to visit a friend," she said, "who has a gift of sensing these sorts of things well, and she told me there's a high possibility that I might be pregnant!"

Scrouch continued looking at her, expressionless. "Your friend, Eris?" the General asked. The next moment he felt his whole being filling with rage, raising his hand and slapping Eris. He'd clearly taken her by surprise, but she kept her balance. "She must be some random disgusting slut like you, am I right?" He gripped her shoulders tightly, baring his teeth. Eris started crying and Scrouch inched so close to her that his elevated breath was now millimeters away from her face. "YOU ARE NOT TO TELL ANYONE ABOUT THIS, DO I MAKE MYSELF CLEAR?" he shouted. "I won't let you ruin my reputation in this town. If you open your mangy mouth, I am going to kill you, understand?"

Eris nodded; her face stained with more tears.

"I will cut you into little pieces if I find out you've told someone!"

Eris nodded again, fear creeping into her facial features. General Scrouch continued shouting and after several minutes he threw her forcefully to the floor of his office. Eris landed with a thud, the General upon her within mere seconds, holding in his hand a long, sharp knife he'd taken from the desk drawer. Her eyes widened in terror. With the knife, Scrouch ripped her clothes open, Eris crying even louder now. She had no idea what she'd gotten herself into.

General Scrouch slapped Eris, making her shut up, forcefully flipping her on her stomach. Wiping his sweaty forehead, pushing his dark brown fringe out of his eyes, Scrouch shoved his penis up Eris's ass, while she was crying and begging him to stop. Scrouch raped Eris without giving a fuck about her emotions or pleas. He came on her back, pulled his dark pants back on, and kicked her upward on the floor in disgust.

"OUT!" he shouted, showing her the door with a hand as if she didn't already know where it was. He refused to pay her for today's *'session'*.

Eris regained her balance, stood on her feet, and weeping, left General Scrouch's office.

The General turned around, looking at Salem in the cold night, through the two vast sets of wooden blinds, resembling windows, located a few inches behind the desk in his office. He was Salem's mayor – *HE!* Scrouch had to do something, hadn't he? Eris was going to whine her mangy mouth about her pregnancy all over town – he couldn't trust a prostitute to keep her mouth shut. Even though what he had just done, the General was the one who had to shut her mouth – permanently. And fast.

General Scrouch was aiming to avoid news of his affair becoming common knowledge – he knew some of the townsfolk had probably already been aware, but he had a reputation to uphold. He didn't want his wife Ahronia to find out because she could have divorced him. And if that indeed happened, the citizens of Salem would begin to question his leadership and his place in their society. The General couldn't afford to lose that, because this position, as mayor of Salem, was providing him with privileges and luxurious items. Scrouch loved this high-end life.

He was determined to do something about the Eris's problem – even if he had to sacrifice Salem itself to achieve it. General Scrouch could see the citizens on the main street out front beginning to retreat to their houses, the only lighting coming from burning candles within the small buildings and torches of fire, spread here and there along the corners of the street. General Scrouch had to do the same.

The General headed for the door to his office, closing it behind him. He exited the building through the staircase, leading down to the first floor, that he wasn't usually using for anything except storage, and started walking home, expecting to see his wife Ahronia, staying up late once again, waiting for him.

~~~~~~~~~~

General Scrouch entered his home, finding his red-haired wife Ahronia reading a book on the sofa, next to the vast fireplace, as expected. The two of them barely said 'hello' to one another, Scrouch not being in the mood and Ahronia too immersed in her book. They hadn't gotten along for years and that meant no sex – that's why General Scrouch turned to the prostitutes of Salem. He had even stopped viewing Ahronia as his wife, but rather as *something*, an item, giving him status in the small community of Salem.

"The dinner is on the kitchen table." Ahronia let him know, without turning her eyes away from the book she was holding, leafing through it steadily.

Scrouch nodded and started for the kitchen, located a few inches away from the living room where Ahronia was sitting when her book suddenly caught his attention. "What are you reading?" he asked her.

Ahronia looked at him with disdain, evident in her eyes. *"The history of witches through the centuries."*

"Is it any good?" he inquired, but he really didn't care because Ahronia had just given him a fantastic idea. A way to take care of Eris and her unborn child.

"More interesting than a lot of things in this house," she muttered under her nose, the General hearing her loud and clear. He knew that she was talking about him and intended to say something but eventually gave up, deciding he didn't have the might to deal with this shit. He left Ahronia to her book and made for the kitchen.

~~~~~~~~~~

Two more weeks passed, during which General Scrouch continued fucking Eris even though she didn't want to lay with him anymore. He had even stopped paying her. The elapsed time also gave General Scrouch an opportunity to spread rumors all over Salem about a coven of witches, taking residency in their small community, their numbers growing by the second.

Due to him being mayor and added with the fact that the townsfolk believed him, the rumors caught on like fire, and soon all of Salem knew that witches existed. A lot of the citizens were dead-scared, asking the General on a daily basis how he was going to handle the matter.

But was already on it – he had given direct orders to a bunch of his guards to build a rectangular wooden platform, littering the surface with wooden logs and stakes, erecting wooden poles. It was Crouch's personal responsibility to prepare burning torches. At precisely 2100 hours tonight, he was going to issue Salem with a statement that would have gone down in history.

The General had just finished one of his numerous *'sessions'* with Eris – this time he had penetrated her so hard, she bled. "Dress yourself," he said with disgust, while buckling his mocha belt. "You are going to be present at my statement, whether you like it or not!"

"You're right, I would rather not attend at all!" Eris hissed angrily after she had dressed, spitting in Scrouch's face, turning to run. The general quickly caught up to her, grasping her head with his sizeable hand, slamming her against the corridor's wall, outside of his office. Eris crumbled down on the ground, her tears overflowing.

"Your tears just make me more excited!" he said and put a hand on his crotch demonstratively, squeezing it lightly. "But we don't have time for another go because I would be late for my statement!" He made Eris stand up forcefully, and walking down the staircase, threw her out the back door of the first floor – his office and main headquarters were on the second. But not before ensuring she would be indeed present at his statement, by threatening to slit her throat otherwise.

~~~~~~~~~~

The entirety of Salem had gathered in front of and around the vast wooden platform, most of them eagerly anticipating General Scrouch's statement. His statements had always been of great importance, and attendance nothing short of mandatory. Among the public, there was also a citizen by the name of Feever, who lived with her family just a couple of streets away from the town center, where all of them had now gathered. Feever was glad not to live at the exact center of the town due to all the commotion usually taking place there. Her family had been practicing witchcraft for centuries but had kept it a secret, expecting the worst from Salem's scared, paranoid, enslaved crowd. Eris and the friend that had told her about her almost certain pregnancy, were also amongst the crowd, leaning against each other for moral support.

~~~~~~~~~~

General Scrouch climbed the small set of stairs on the left side, leading right up to the wooden platform, and positioned himself right in front of the two towering wooden stakes and dry wood logs below, so all of Salem could lay eyes on him.

"Dear citizens of Salem," he started, plastering a huge, fake smile, inspecting the thousands of faces, staring back at him. Occasionally, he'd gotten the urge to just annihilate them all, because every single one of them irritated him in some way – even Ahronia. "I called for you, at this late hour, to discuss a pressing and dangerous matter I observed looming over our heads for the past two weeks."

Most of Salem's citizens were all ears, clearly not wanting to miss a word.

"This matter is in the form of a specific *activity* that's shaping up to be quite disturbing for Salem and us – its citizens!" he announced, reveling in the silence, all eyes on him. "Do any of you know the meaning of the word *'witch'*?"

~~~~~~~~~~

Whispers started passing through the crowd, most of them not able to come up with an intelligible answer. Feever, who knew what the term meant better than anyone in the town's center, kept her mouth shut as if someone's life depended on it. Her ears sharpened to what General Scrouch had to say.

~~~~~~~~~~

"A *witch* is someone who practices dark magic and satanic rituals!" he informed the crowd, remembering the ten or so lines he had memorized from Ahronia's book. "Often, these *'acts'* or *'rituals'* are being made solely for the purposes of harming non-witch people. In some cases, they could even lead to death!"

The crowd erupted into startled and terrified gasps.

"In the past two weeks, as much as it pains me to say it, I've noticed members of our small society, *here*, in Salem, practicing those exact aforementioned rituals," the General said, conveying such deep emotion as if he genuinely cared about his admiring following.

~~~~~~~~~~

Feever looked at him, startled – there was no way he'd found out *she* was a witch, was there? There simply couldn't have been a possible way – she and her family had hidden that part of their lives from Salem so well. And her family wasn't the only family in Salem with witchcraft roots – Feever knew of many other members of their community, practicing magic, that hid just as well as her family. *Who could have been so stupid as to expose themselves? As to* let someone catch them in the act?

~~~~~~~~~~

"Understand, my dear citizens," he continued, despite the commotion, integrating a feigned sense of worry within his voice. "The people practicing witchcraft are dangerous. They are dangerous to *me*, to *you*, to *all* of Salem! Throughout history, witches have been associated with evil prophecies and the devil itself!" That wasn't entirely true because there were good and bad witches. But General Scrouch had skipped the part in Ahronia's book about the good kind of witches, interested only in the information feeding his agenda. "I want you to know, my dear citizens, that I am deeply determined to eradicate this danger that looms over us!" Scrouch said so proudly, sensing the crowd beginning to eat up his words like a hungry orphan, of whom Salem had so many. "I am committed to protecting all of you, to protecting Salem!" The General made a pause, flexing the fingers of his right hand inward, making a sign to his guards, standing in the first row of the crowd, to fetch Eris and her friend. "And today, I will start doing it!" He then raised the same hand high in the air, as if he had just won a trophy. Most of Salem's citizens also raised hands, applauding him, the General drinking in their praise like a never-ending wine.

"Let me go!" Eris shrieked as one of the guards was dragging her onto the platform.

"These two women," Scrouch pointed at Eris and her friend, turning toward them on the platform, "have been engaging in witchcraft activity for the past two weeks. Who knows how long they've been doing it for? I found out for sure just a few hours ago, confirming my observations!" His eyes fixated on Eris, the General feeling the corners of his mouth twisting into a huge smile, knowing that he would soon make Eris shut her trap, once and for all.

The residents continued murmuring amongst one another.

"What?" Eris inquired, her eyes widening. "A *witch*? I don't even know what this term means, how could *I* be one?"

"Neither do I!" her friend added.

~~~~~~~~~~

Feever mulled that statement over for a moment. There was no way in hell that those two were witches – one of them was the town's most famous men and women-pleaser, and the other one was her friend, rumored to be a psychic.

~~~~~~~~~~

"You are a danger to our community!" Scrouch said, still pointing at the two women where they now stood in front of the wooden poles, their wrists restricted by the two guards with ropes, tied around the poles' surface. "Salem must be protected at all costs, right, citizens?" The General turned to the audience, who began cheering, raising their fists high in the air once again.

"WITCHES!" some shouted.

"BURN THEM AT THE STAKE!" others shouted.

"THEY MUST SUFFER!" the third group of enthusiasts shouted.

General Scrouch cracked a devious smile – he had successfully fooled the whole town.

"Wait, wait a minute," a man by the name of Sarvit joined the commotion of voices – a witch and the ancestor of the Fehrenberg family. "If you really think these two women are witches and deserve to be punished, don't you think it's only fair for you to listen to what they have to say first – and *then* serve the verdict? You all can't just point fingers at someone, claim they are a witch, and then burn them at the stake! You *need* to give this person the right to defend themselves, and afterward, if you still think they are guilty, maybe then you could burn them at the stake!"

General Scrouch pierced him with his eyes – everything had been going so well, and some low-life Salem mouse just *had* to step up and cease the exciting activities ahead.

"*I* find Eris guilty!" Scrouch claimed. "*I* find both of them guilty, so what more do you need? *I* am Salem's mayor; it is *my* duty to protect this town, and *my* judgment is clear when I say that these two women need to be punished for witchcraft crimes against the community of Salem! If *you* don't agree with me, you could just keep your opinion to yourself or maybe join them, because *I am* the *leader* of this town and I know what's best for it!"

"I never meant to offend you," Sarvit apologized. "I was just expressing an opinion – that is still allowed around here, isn't it?"

General Scrouch gave him an even viler look, not at all pleased with his authority being challenged by Sarvit. He had defied him, and the citizens had seen that, some of them giggling.

"Of course, it is still allowed!" the General screeched through clenched teeth, containing his rage, but not the hatred, waging in his eyes. "But the verdict is clear – these two women are to be burned at the stake, being a threat to our small community!"

The two male bodyguards must have tied Eris and her friend to the wooden poles extremely tight because Scrouch could hear their cries of pain. *Good,* he thought. *The tighter, the better!*

Then they handed their emperor the two torches he had brought to the platform earlier in the evening. He raised them in front of all of Salem's eyes as if the torches were crowns.

"People of Salem – today we annihilate an immense threat to our community. After these two witches are gone, Salem will be better off!"

Almost everyone from the audience, except for Feever and Sarvit, cheered him on. That was music to his ears. The General drank the view in for a few moments, before turning over to Eris's stake, slithering closer to her like a viper. He gave her a pitiful look, leaning close to her ear, so his breath could be one of the last things Eris felt. "I'm going to miss your ass."

"Go to hell!" she spat out, tears streaming down her cheeks, the realization sinking in that her life was ending. General Scrouch smiled broadly in response as if she had just told him something sexually invigorating.

General Scrouch stepped away from his former pleaser and drew one of the torches near the firewood below Eris's legs, witnessing orange-crimson flames starting to flicker. Then he put the same torch against the back of the firewood, so all the pieces could be covered. The flames began gradually engulfing Eris's body, her echoes of pain and the smell of her sizzling skin wafting through the night air. Mixed with her crying and shouting, a creepy, agonizing sound sealed the night. The General then moved his attention to Eris's friend, who was begging him to stop. But Scrouch did the same to the rumored psychic, the flames not sparing her convulsing body. The two women were being burned alive, crying and shouting, while the crowd was cheering, happy to witness all the torture. Scrouch happiest of them all.

~~~~~~~~~~

Feever stepped away from the crowd, inexorably repulsed by what she had just witnessed. Sarvit followed her example shortly after. Both of them were disturbed by the General's impulsive actions but also worried because both of them *were* witches, as well as their families –

and General Scrouch had just exposed the witches' world to the naïve citizens of Salem. They didn't know how he knew about the existence of witches, but he must have done – even though he had just burned two non-witch residents at the stake.

That meant only one thing – from that moment on, Sarvit and Feever had to be extra careful practicing magic, because if they were caught, they would probably be also burned at the stake. Feever wasn't all that worried about herself than she was for her family – she was the only immortal witch in their heritage so far.

~~~~~~~~~~

The Salem witch trials had begun. And General Scrouch didn't intend on stopping now. He had gotten rid of Eris and her baby, but soon he was going to realize that this *'witch mania'* was going to bring him even more money and power than before – and the General would have never turned down those two assets. But the *'witch mania'* had only just begun, the consequences of which would prove disastrous to the town of Salem, Massachusetts.

Chapter 9

Pacifika, Marisii, and Kayla

The oldest Fehrenberg sibling Pacifika had been living far, far away from her family. She had moved out of the family house a few years ago, after finding out about *The Curse*. The oldest sister just couldn't wrap her mind around the fact that *some* witch was going to come for her and her family, intent on eliminating them all. That's why she had made the difficult decision to part with her relatives for as long as possible. But the time for the fear to settle in had come – her parents Pattery and Perventia had called her, bearing the news that Feever had awoken from her slumber, probably soon coming for them.

For Pacifika that meant only one thing – she had to pack her luggage and reunite with her family, as soon as possible. Pacifika knew that for her other sisters, Kayla and Klacifia, that news bore the same meaning. Pacifika managed to pack all her luggage in a single duffel bag, leaving her rented one-room apartment, reaching the bus stop in a timely manner. When the bus arrived, she bought a ticket for the ride from the driver and located a seat at the far end of the vehicle. Making herself comfortable, Pacifika put her headphones on and when the bus set off, she dozed off.

~~~~~~~~~~

The night soon made itself noticeable by the silence and the pitch-black darkness. The bus was surprisingly empty, with only a few more seats occupied. The driver yawned continuously, probably sleep-deprived, judging by the dark circles around his eyes. None of the passengers noticed him falling asleep at the steering wheel, leaving the moving vehicle without an active driver.

On the road ahead, covered in shadows, a tall female figure stood, unmoving, as if a vehicle approaching her was the most normal occurrence in the world. The figure raised her head high, shifting her new raven cloak to a comfortable position. The bus was rapidly approaching, almost upon her, when the woman raised her hand in the air. The vehicle stopped immediately in front of her as if hitting an invisible wall, lifting from the cement within seconds and flying above the figure's head. The bus rolled over on the road a couple of times before coming to an abrupt stop upside down.

~~~~~~~~~~

Pacifika Fehrenberg was trying to emerge from the now catching fire vehicle, passing the deceased passengers and driver. She eventually succeeded, kicking open one of the front windows, crawling from underneath it. The blond-haired woman stood shakingly on her legs, only to notice the dark figure in front of her. The mysterious woman flashed her a grinning smile.

"Pacifika Fehrenberg," the figure addressed her, chuckling. "It's such an honor to finally meet you!" Her smile vanished, just as fast as it had come, the woman outstretching her hand toward Pacifika, making her fly backward. Pacifika landed with a loud thud a few meters away from the engulfed in flames vehicle. She raised her head shakily, the woman approaching with a steady step. "My name is Feever." Pacifika's eyes widened in horror.

Feever inspected her bleeding, frail form, slumped on the asphalt, in disgust. "Yes, the same Feever you're probably thinking about," the onyx black and Prussian blue-dressed witch assured her, upon seeing the shock, settling on her facial features. "The *same* Feever, who cursed your family, and the same Feever, the face of who would be the last thing that you ever see!" Feever was just raising a hand toward Pacifika again – probably to torture her more, when she felt two cold, titanium objects, spiking her hand. Feever scanned her hand, observing the wine-red blood disappearing and the wound closing momentarily after. She supposed those two sharp objects that had just come right through her hand, were the same objects the guards at the museum had fired at her. The same objects she fired at the Fehrenberg family in their own home – if she wasn't mistaken, they were called bullets? A continuous, wicked laugh erupted from her mouth.

"Who dares interrupt my revenge?" Feever inquired, turning toward a tall, chocolate-haired boy that stood behind her, gripping a pistol in his hands, now pointing it at Feever's head.

"The name is Marisii," he announced with a confident edge to his voice. "Marisii Klauzer!"

"Splendid!" Feever almost clapped her hands. "We've got one Fehrenberg and one Klauzer – today can't get any better than this!"

Marisii cracked a cheeky smile. "There's always room for surprises!" Marisii began stepping closer to Feever, simultaneously shooting bullets at her, until the magazine emptied out.

With her right hand, Feever motioned all the bullets away from her, the silver objects flying past her and landing on the asphalt behind. "You think your stupid bullets can hurt me?" The powerful witch laughed. "Well, they can't really hurt *me*," she raised both her hands in the air, moving them slowly toward Marisii. Now all the bullets Marisii had fruitlessly used on Feever hung in the air, next to her. "But they can hurt *you!*" Within a second, she angrily thrust her hands toward him, the bullets following her command, their endpoint Marisii. Seeming to expect such a move, he swiftly stepped away, avoiding all bullets – except for one. The culprit buried itself deep into Marisii's right shoulder, the young man groaning in pain.

Feever turned her attention back to Pacifika, only to find her gone – the place on the asphalt she had lain helplessly on was empty. The witch turned to Marisii, but he had vanished as well. The witch started looking around in the night, lit only by the burning vehicle behind her, and she noticed both of them limping toward a crumbling factory near the main road, through tall, thick bushes, supporting each other's weight.

"You want to play, eh?" she commented, and throwing back her raven, silk cloak, Feever headed for the bushes with long, purposeful steps.

~~~~~~~~~~

Pacifika and Marisii entered the factory through its non-existent door, climbing up to the second floor – maybe that wasn't the best idea, the factory's stairwell creaking and the walls chipped all over, but it was the best option they had. *This factory must have been abandoned for years*, Pacifika thought, judging by all the rusty equipment on the first floor; she mulled over that fact while positioning Marisii on a dirty, torn mattress they had found in one of the compartments.

"Are you okay?" she asked him worriedly, motioning to the wound in Marisii's shoulder.

"It's just an injury," he claimed. "I'll be fine!"

Pacifika eyed him unsurely. "Why did you risk your life for me?" Pacifika and Marisii barely knew each other, both of them leaving their families a few years ago. Her scalp had stopped bleeding, but Pacifika was still hurting all over.

"You and me, your family and my family – we're all in this together!" Marisii said. "The Curse looms over both our families; if we don't work together, if we don't help one another, we will all be doomed!"

"Thank you for what you did back there by the way," Pacifika said with a warm smile. "You got injured because of me!"

"Don't mention it," Marisii shrugged. "When I heard that Feever has risen, I immediately set off to collect my brothers Morven and Brouzun. But I had to take another direction to reach them faster. And it's a good thing I did – otherwise, Feever would have killed *you* already!"

Pacifika and Marisii heard the eerie, disturbing low thud from shoes, coming from somewhere in the distance – somehow there wasn't any doubt in Pacifika's mind that *that* sound belonged to Feever's intricate, 17th century black shoes. Pacifika placed her index finger to her lips in silence, rising from the torn, old mattress, her feet moving soundlessly across the cracked floor. Pacifika noticed and picked up a rusty shovel from the opposite end of the space she and Marisii were in. She hid behind the door that was barely hanging onto its edges, deliberately leaving Marisii out in the open, waiting for her chance to strike.

"What are you doing?" Marisii whispered.

Pacifika was glad to see that the bleeding from his shoulder was receding.

"Trust me," Pacifika whispered back. "Stay exactly where you are – *I'm* going to take care of *her!*"

Pacifika heard the sounds of creaking stairs and the footsteps, steadily approaching.

As if to make herself known, Feever declared, "Oh, children, where are you? I *promise,* I won't hurt you!"

"Yeah, right," Pacifika muttered under her nose, gripping the shovel's handle, like holding onto a lifeboat.

"I just want to skin the both of you alive slowly, so you can feel as much pain as possible!" the witch said angrily, but also with a certain calmness to her tone. "Because of you, I lost *everything* dear to me!" she added longingly, throwing both Marisii and Pacifika into a state of confusion. "You *all* need to pay for your mistakes! I *will not* rest until you've paid!"

Pacifika could see, through a tiny crack in the door, Feever finally reaching the entrance of the compartment, her eyes flashing fiercely upon noticing Marisii, lying defenseless on the torn mattress. She stepped inside, slowly and steadily.

"Where's Pacifika?" Feever inquired. "Did she leave you *that* quickly?"

Marisii threw her a hate-filled stare, and Pacifika grabbed the opportunity, attacking Feever and hitting her on the head with the shovel.

"Naïve girl," Feever hissed as if Pacifika was simply a nuisance. Feever grasped her by the neck, with her long, but at the same time delicate fingers, and threw her from the second floor against the stairwell, connecting the floors.

"NO!" Marisii screeched.

Pacifika landed on a dusty, old table, with a crash, her mind drifting into unconsciousness.

~~~~~~~~~~

"I'll come back for her later," Feever said, turning her attention back to Marisii. The witch raised her right hand high in the air, simultaneously lifting him from the mattress, making him choke, desperate for a whiff of breath. "*You* are going to be my first *victim!*" she said victoriously. "*Your* blood will be the first *spilled*! *You* are going to be the first step to exacting *my revenge*! And you, my dear *boy*, will be the first *death*, many of which will soon follow!"

Feever clenched her fist and Marisii's throat started closing in on itself. She couldn't believe this was actually happening – after all those years of slumber, Feever was finally going to start punishing the two families, finally going to start killing, finally going to start drawing and feeling the blood of those two horrendous families.

"Hey, Feever," a distant, enraged voice addressed her, none other than Kayla Fehrenberg's – the second-born Fehrenberg sibling. "Feel this!" Everything after happened so fast that Feever didn't even have time to react.

Kayla Fehrenberg threw a vial, infused with a dark blue liquid, probably a potion. The vial shattered against Feever's lean body, rendering her motionless as if someone had just cemented her body. As a result, her hold on Marisii eased, him falling back to the mattress. Kayla Fehrenberg ran to Feever from her place on the creaking stairwell – she had literally appeared out of nowhere – and punched her in the face, Feever falling to the dusty floor, still not able to move even a finger.

~~~~~~~~~~

"Come on, let's get out of here!" Kayla prompted Marisii, helping him stand up, supporting the weight of his injured shoulder with her own. "We need to hurry!" Kayla said as she and Marisii were leaving the compartment. "The potion is going to contain her for only a few minutes. I've got a car parked out front – let's get Pacifika and bolt!"

"How did you find us?" Marisii asked surprisedly.

"I was luckily passing by and heard screeching voices!" Kayla said. "I had to check it out and it's a good thing that I did, otherwise Feever would have already had two fresh corpses by her hands!"

Marisii chuckled for a moment – that was almost the exact same thing *he* had told Pacifika when he had saved her from Feever's earlier attack by the burning bus on the road.

When they reached Pacifika, lying in an ocean of dusty debris, Kayla let Marisii go, picking up her older unconscious sister in her arms. "Do you think you can help me take her to the car?"

Marisii nodded affirmatively, and the two of them, combining their efforts, took Pacifika to the car, parked on the road a few dozen meters away from the still burning bus – it was a whole miracle it hadn't exploded yet. They placed Pacifika on one of the back seats carefully, taking the two front seats themselves. Kayla lit the ignition fiercely.

"I was concocting this potion for months!" Kayla said while the car drifted away from the factory. "And it is only going to slow her down for a mere few minutes!"

~~~~~~~~~~

Feever began flexing her fingers, the effect of the dark blue potion wearing off. Feever's mind had fully recovered from the potion, and a few minutes later, her body did too. She rose on her feet, letting out an inhumane, almost animal growl. For a second time, the witches she despised more than anything, had outsmarted her. And she knew that *she* was supposed to be the superior individual.

~~~~~~~~~~

"What does this mean?" Marisi asked Kayla, the factory now far in the distance.

~~~~~~~~~~

Feever emerged from the factory's entrance, catching a faint glimpse of the car's indistinct form, down the road. The witch started screaming at Kayla and her accomplices, unconsciously setting the factory on fire. Within mere seconds, the factory had caught so much fire, it blew up, debris flying all around Feever, but not even scratching her, as if she was controlling their direction. The massive explosion soothed her nerves to an extent, her screaming ceasing. She had to capture them all, capture, torture and kill them slowly, and make them pay for what their family line had done to her all those years ago. Feever had lost so much because of them.

The witch moved away from the explosion with a steady, confident stride, planning her next move. Feever was a powerful witch, who possessed many gifts and magical abilities, which were yet to manifest. She was a special witch – unlike others of her kind, she couldn't be killed with a weapon of any kind, and whenever someone tried to draw blood off of her, the wound closed back up in a matter of seconds, just like it had when Marisii had fired at her. Those man-made kinds of weapons, Kayla's weak potions, could have only slowed her down for a few moments.

Feever smiled; a smile because deep down she supposed that she was going to emerge victorious from this battle, rendering every single member of the Klauzer and Fehrenberg families dead. She anticipated the taste of all their warm, red, pulsating blood. Feever was confident she was going to rise, her reign accompanied by death, blood and destruction. She imagined a river of blood, flowing all around her, the corpses of her enemies floating at the surface.

~~~~~~~~~~

"It means that we're up against an almost impossible to defeat opponent!" Kayla grimly uttered in the car, plunging both her and Marisii into deep silence. The only sound that could be heard for the remainder of the journey in the night was the noise coming from the car's engine.

Chapter 10

"She's going to be okay."

Teela, her sister Tiffany, and her boyfriend Kasteron were flipping through The Book's pages with the hope of finding *something* to help them defeat Feever, or at least slow her down. The two families had stopped their pickup trucks further down the almost abandoned road, a small meadow located a few meters away. Teela, Tiffany and Kasteron had settled on the luggage compartment of one of the trucks. Berventy and Pattery were located close to the vehicle, watching over their children, and Kastilius, Klacifia, Perventia and Brouzenvert were seated on the meadow, amongst all the emerald grass.

"The Book is describing how in time we will gain our respective magical abilities," Teela said, who was holding the valuable item. "But we need *those* powers now – the fight against Feever has already begun!"

"Darling, the time *will* come," her father Pattery softly said. "But there's nothing we can do about it now."

Berventy suddenly chuckled.

"What?" Pattery asked her.

"Can I have The Book for a second?" Berventy asked Teela.

"Of course." Teela nodded and passed The Book over to Berventy carefully.

Berventy flipped through the pages herself, stopping at a specific one. "I've scanned through this book many times, and one thing has always held my attention! Read the first paragraph on page 79," Berventy instructed Teela, passing her back The Book.

Teela grasped its metallic covers, her mouth opening: *"The descendants of the Klauzer and Fehrenberg families will receive their individual powers later on in the battle against Feever. But until then, in order to protect themselves against that wicked witch, they would be able to create specific potions to slow down her reign of terror. Those potions are hopefully going to keep all the descendants safe until they start finding their powers. They are, however, extremely difficult to devise, and even harder to find the ingredients for, but the descendants MUST create those potions because their temporary survival depends entirely on it."* Teela read, her eyes dropping down to the bottom of the page. *"Written by Sarvit Fehrenberg."*

Without any warning, Tiffany took The Book from Teela's hands, and flipped through to the next page, revealing dozens of hand-drawn and colored images, in front of Berventy's eyes, portraying the potions, all the ingredients listed below the images. *"A potion for stopping the enemy for five minutes,"* Tiffany read. *"A potion for temporary time cease, a potion for smoke, a potion for invisibility, a potion for temporary shackling the enemy in chains."* The potions were numerous, and of various kinds.

"That means we won't be so defenseless against Feever, after all," Kasteron declared, sounding genuinely happy, pointing at the potions. "That, right here, is our most valuable weapon against her for the time being!"

"Yes, that's right." Berventy smiled, immensely gladdened by the fact that they had found a temporary delay of their uncertain futures. All five of the families' members in or gathered around the truck smiled. Tiffany, Teela, and Kasteron resumed inspecting The Book's various contents, while Pattery drew Berventy to the side, away from their children.

"This is amazing!" he exclaimed. "I've scanned through The Book dozens of times, but I never even considered the possibility that *those* potions could prove helpful in any way. I've always thought they wouldn't prove useful to the children!"

"The potions are mighty, Pattery," Berventy reassured him. "They were designed by Sarvit Fehrenberg himself, probably with the help of Mour Klauzer. They are going to aid our children until they gain their powers – our task until then is to do everything in our power to protect them!"

"I know," Pattery nodded. "But I worry though – a handful of days are left until Feever shows up again, to claim her first victim. And none of the children has received their power yet!"

"Obtaining the power comes at a very specific time, Pattery," Berventy started explaining, recalling all the knowledge she had drunk during the years, leading up to The Curse. "Their powers will make themselves known when our children experience a specific emotion – for example, grief, fear, or happiness. They need to experience *that* emotion so deeply in their hearts, that they scream. Then, they will feel the abilities surging through their veins – and that's when they will become more powerful than ever before!"

"But The Book says that at least one descendant should have received their individual power by now!" Pattery said. "Berventy, I'm worried – what if none of them finds their power, and Feever just kills them all? Without a real fighting chance?"

"I choose to believe that soon they will start receiving the abilities, one by one," Berventy said, turning over to look at Teela, Tiffany, Kasteron at the back of the truck, and Klacifia and Kastilius in the distance. "Look at them," Pattery turned toward them. "They smile and laugh because they just found out that their burden is not as big as it seemed, all of them able to fight, in a way. It's remarkable – we all dumped this vast volume of information on them just a couple of days ago, but look at them. Their moods aren't darkened by The Curse. And do you know why that is?"

"Why?"

"Because they know that as long as they have each other, everything will be fine!" Berventy said. "They know that they're better together, stronger side by side. They *will* obtain their individual abilities, I'm sure of it, but their *true* power comes from deep within them, and from within each other! They *will* get through this, I know it – our children are fighters and powerful witches, who are yet to unlock their vast potential. I believe in them. Do *you*?"

Pattery's gaze flickered for a second from Berventy to Teela, Tiffany, Kasteron, Klacifia and Kastilius, and then back to Berventy.

"I believe in them too." He smiled. But suddenly, something made that smile vanish, his facial features distorting as if he'd just realized something horrible. "What about The Order?"

"What about it?"

"When is it going to appear?"

"Today, at 00:00, sharp."

"So, you're basically saying that at midnight tonight we will find out who is likely going to be Feever's first victim?"

Berventy nodded reluctantly. She, Brouzenvert, Pattery and Perventia had lied to their children about whether there'd been a way to tell who was going to be the next victim. The four of them just didn't want to load them with more information, seeing as they had had enough already. The Order, and everything about it, was written at the back of The Book, amongst the very last pages. And Berventy, Brouzenvert, Perventia and Pattery had read all about it. When Feever's visit every three weeks approached, the name of her next likely victim was going to appear at the back of the voluminous object. There was a small column, and in it, the name of the victim would magically appear.

Berventy and Pattery remained in silence shortly after, just watching their children, when a car pulled up right next to them. The front doors swung open, revealing the mildly injured Kayla Fehrenberg, and the much more injured Marisii Klauzer. Upon noticing them, everyone else ran toward them. Berventy hugged her son Marisii.

"What the hell happened to you?" Berventy asked him with a screech, noticing his gaping, bleeding wound on the right shoulder, probably caused by a bullet.

Brouzenvert reached his son as well moments later, giving him a hug. "My boy, are you okay?"

~~~~~~~~~~

Pattery and Perventia had their daughter Kayla wrapped in an affectionate embrace. Through the curtain of arms, Kayla saw her sister Tiffany eying Kayla's vehicle, and noticing her oldest sister Pacifika, lying unconscious on the back seat.

Tiffany pointed at the back seat, her voice shaking: "Is she dead?"

Teela stepped closer to Tiffany, her face darkening as well.

Kayla was able to escape her parents' hugs. "She is not dead, but unconscious!"

"What happened?" Perventia inquired.

"We were attacked by Feever," Marisii answered instead. "I saved Pacifika, and Kayla saved me – we all saved each other! But while doing that, Feever managed to change the trajectory of one of the bullets I shot at her, and later threw Pacifika from the second floor of this abandoned factory."

"Oh, my god, are you alright?" Berventy asked, her hands frantically inspecting her son's face, clearly looking for more wounds. "How did you manage to escape?"

"I made this potion; it took me several weeks, but it was able to literally freeze Feever for a few precious seconds," Kayla Fehrenberg said with a pleased smile. "You should have seen the look on her face when we slipped out from under her nose!"

"The important thing is that you're all alive!" Pattery said while Perventia went to check up on Pacifika.

Kayla looked awkwardly at her younger sisters Tiffany and Teela, whom she hadn't seen for *years*. Klacifia was observing the exchange from the side.

"I'm back!" Kayla tried to soften the awkward situation without much luck. Teela inched closer to Kayla, looking her right in the eyes.

"Thank God you're alright." Teela's voice almost broke, and then she pulled her older sister into a tight embrace. Then Tiffany, and momentarily after, Klacifia, also joined the affectionate gesture.

~~~~~~~~~~

After Berventy and Brouzenvert had finished raining down on Marisii with love, the chocolate-haired man turned over to his present brothers – Kasteron and Kastilius. Suddenly, he giggled. "We haven't seen each other in a while."

"You think?" Kasteron chuckled, hugging his older brother by a few years, tightly. Oddly, Kastilius didn't join in the hug. He had always been more *particular* than the rest of his brothers – he didn't take pleasure in family gatherings or whenever someone from his *own* family hugged him. Kastilius had never had the urge to communicate wholesomely with any member of his family – he didn't know why that was. He supposed he just didn't enjoy all those family activities and gestures.

~~~~~~~~~~

Two of the Klauzer family's members were still missing – the oldest siblings Morven and Brouzun. All the members of the Fehrenberg family had now arrived. Pattery couldn't help but notice the look Brouzenvert gave him, knowing perfectly well the reason; because he and Perventia had all their kids now with them, and Brouzenvert was still missing two. Pattery didn't know where exactly Brouzenvert's frustration stemmed from, but he hoped Brouzenvert didn't think Pattery's family was in any way privileged. Because there was *nothing* privileged in wanting for all of your family to be safe and sound.

~~~~~~~~~~

Perventia helped her daughter Pacifika, who was now conscious, to emerge out of the car. For a person who had been thrown from the second floor against a table, she was doing surprisingly well, able to walk almost without limping, only a few scratches obscuring her face.

"She's going to be okay," Perventia announced to the others with a wide smile, after inspecting Pacifika's condition; she was no doctor, but Pacifika knew her mother had some basic knowledge. "Pacifika is *really* going to be okay!"

Pacifika's body hurt all over, but she didn't feel any misplaced or broken bones, and her skin was mostly intact. Although with one hell of an effort, she headed to her father and sisters, to hug them. Pacifika Fehrenberg didn't know how or why, but she just *knew* she was going to be okay.

Chapter 11

00:00

"You know we *must* do this, right?" Brouzenvert asked his son Marisii. "Otherwise, you could die!"

"I know," Marisii said.

"Just do it!" Berventy said and closed her eyes while pressing one of Pattery's shirts to Marisii's shoulder, trying to tackle the bleeding that had thankfully subsided in the last few hours.

Brouzenvert touched the long, scorching piece of metal to Marisii's shoulder, followed by a howl of pain. The night had arrived and Brouzenvert had decided to close his son's wound the best way he possibly could at this time, considering that all of them were in the middle of a highway, the closest hospital probably miles, even days, away. Brouzenvert hated seeing Marisii in pain, but there was no other way. Thankfully, the bullet had come straight through, making sealing the wound with the scorching piece of metal, easier.

A few moments later, Brouzenvert finished closing Marisii's injury with his makeshift equipment. "Easy now; it's over. It's all over," he said soothingly.

Marisii, however, continued to howl in pain, the echoes invading the night. Brouzenvert hugged Marisii tightly, careful not to hurt him, and Berventy took his right hand in hers.

"It's all over," Berventy said as well, caressing Marisii's head, his screams beginning to decrease gradually, his body clearly beginning to relax.

~~~~~~~~~~

The time for The Order had come. The clocks in both trucks were indicating 23:56. The children from both families had gone to sleep in the trucks, or near them. Berventy, Brouzenvert, Perventia and Pattery were standing on the grass in the meadow, having flipped open The Book on one of the last pages, all waiting for a name to appear in the designated column. The four parents had gathered to find out which of their children they were going to lose first. Which of their children was going to die the soonest.

23:57 – Brouzenvert didn't think he would be able to take it if one of his kids' names appeared in the column; he simply couldn't. Deep down within himself, a scary part was hoping against hope that one of the Fehrenberg family's children was going to take the fall. Brouzenvert knew he wasn't supposed to think like that, but he just wanted to protect the family he had created and raised with Berventy.

~~~~~~~~~~

Pattery grasped Perventia's hand, hoping that none of the children's names would end up in the column. But at the same time, he knew that was never going to happen. The Order was accurate – whoever appeared in the designated space in The Book, was likely to perish at the hands of Feever first. But there *was* a sort of a loophole – if, say, someone decided to sacrifice themselves for the person whose name appeared

70

in the column, it was possible. The rules were endless and there *was* a way around them, even though in the end someone *was* going to die.

~~~~~~~~~~

23:58 – Perventia had a feeling of dread. Dread that one of *her* children would draw the short straw. The mother didn't know how she had that feeling, or why; she couldn't explain it. But she simply *knew* that one of Pacifika, Kayla, Klacifia, Teela, and Tiffany, was going to be the chosen one.

23:59 – The Book started shaking violently on the emerald grass, where it was carefully placed, indicating that the time to show who was to be Feever's first victim had almost arrived.

00:00 – The Book stopped shaking, The Order's column magically stained with ink. Perventia, Berventy, Pattery and Brouzenvert all knew that the revelation had come. Neither of them wanted to look at the page; they were fearful to do so. But *knew* that they *must.*

Berventy Klauzer picked up The Book from the grass and let out an inhumane sound – something tinged with relief but mixed with grief.

"What?" Perventia asked. "What is it? Whose name is written on there?"

Brouzenvert drew closer to his wife, cracking a small smile, planting a kiss on her forehead.

Perventia, her patience waning, snatched The Book away from Berventy's hands, her eyes scanning the column and the terrifying, news-bringing ink. Upon seeing *the name* on the page, Perventia dropped The Book and sank down to her knees on the grass, her eyes watering violently. Perventia had known that the name on the page was going to belong to one of her daughters, she was sure of it – and now, it was confirmed. Perventia burst into tears now, ceasing Brouzenvert and Berventy's positive moods.

~~~~~~~~~~

Pattery, confused by the whole situation, picked up the sizeable book in his hands, his eyes darting across the page. With The Book in his hands, the bronze-haired man sank down on the grass, crying out loudly, next to his wife. A part of him absolutely *refused* to accept the harsh reality of what he had just read. Perventia clung to him, seeking comfort in his arms. Pattery held her as tight as he could, both of them crying. He dumped The Book back on the greenery all around him, devoting all his attention to Perventia.

The Order had spoken; on one of the very last pages of The Book, the name *'Teela Fehrenberg'* was inked in delicate, eerily-looking block letters. Or, also known as the youngest sibling of the Fehrenberg family.

Chapter 12

Efforts and doubts

The two families were still on the road. The two pick-up trucks had been traveling along the highway for about a day, their passengers not having even the faintest idea of where to head next. The families knew they had to keep moving, and that's why they couldn't allow themselves to stay in a hotel, for now. They had parked on another secluded part of the highway, settling themselves on another meadow. Dinner was almost ready – nothing special, just a couple of sandwiches with drinks and small dessert bars. The two families had to get used to this kind of life – being on the run, eating simple food. Pulling up to go to a fancy restaurant was out of the question.

Tiffany Fehrenberg was sitting on the grass, The Book flipped open in her hands, trying to find something, *anything* useful to help both families in the fight against Feever. And her eyes located something that made Tiffany frown and sadden, at the same time.

"Have you found anything useful, dear?" Perventia Fehrenberg, who was sitting next to Tiffany, asked.

The others also weren't that far away from the second-youngest member of the Fehrenberg family, sitting on the grass and sharing the sandwiches.

"You know what, Mum?" Tiffany answered, turning to her mother. "I feel like *I* need to do something, to help our family and the Klauzer family in *some way*. I can't just sit around, doing nothing, watching Feever killing us all one by one, you know? We just got Kayla, Pacifika and Klacifia back! We hadn't seen them for *years*, and now we're all here, *together*! And I just can't fathom the thought that very soon one of us could *die*."

Perventia was silent for a moment as if concealing something from Tiffany.

"Do you understand, I just have to do something about it!" Tiffany continued determinedly, breaking Perventia's reverie. "I was hoping that this *book* would help, but do you know what I actually found instead?"

"What?"

Tiffany Fehrenberg tightened her grip on *The Book*'s metallic covers, narrating: "'*With every victim, with every life Feever claims, belonging to either the Fehrenberg or the Klauzer family, she would grow stronger. The more members of the two families she kills, the greater her powers would become. Written by Mour Klauzer.*' Feever is plenty powerful now, let alone when she *actually* starts killing us! We can barely fend her off *now*, what leaves when she gathers more power? The witch bitch, as you called her, would probably eliminate us with a bare flick of the finger. *I have to do something!*" Then, Tiffany started flicking through The Book, with furious speed. "I have to do something – I have to unlock my power, or summon a spell, or create a potion…"

Perventia inched closer to her on the grass, silently stopping her with a hand. She looked at her. "You *will* unlock your power, I assure you – but only when the time comes! And until then, *all* of us are going to fight with every ounce of strength we possess!

You don't have to do anything, or feel obliged to do anything! The only thing that is required of you, my daughter, right now, is to just simply be with your family. And, maybe to help your sister Kayla, to make some potions tomorrow morning."

Tiffany's eyes flashed like bright thunder; after all, that *was* a way to help both families.

"Kayla said that she's got some ingredients, stashed at the back of her car, so we'll be able to concoct a potion or two," Perventia smiled at her daughter. Tiffany returned it, and Perventia pulled her into an affectionate embrace.

~~~~~~~~~~

And tight – because a part of her knew that Tiffany wasn't going to be the first victim and because Perventia knew that she would get to spend more time with her, than with Teela. "Come on, let's go grab some dinner." Perventia nudged Tiffany closer towards the others with a hand. Tiffany sat next to her father Pattery, and Perventia went to sit next to her daughter Teela, who was enveloped in her boyfriend Kasteron's arms. Perventia looked at her, almost longingly, one hand caressing Teela's head. The mother bear was soon going to lose one of her pups, and she had a feeling her whole world was going to collapse at the seams when that happened.

~~~~~~~~~~

The two families were huddled together in almost a secret circle. Marisii noticed that one of his younger brothers, Kastilius, had moved away from the rest of them, sitting at another patch of the meadow, fiddling with the emerald grass in his hands.

"Excuse me," Marisii said to the others. "I'm just going to go talk to Kastilius."

Berventy directed him an affirmative nod, and Marisii made his way toward his brother. He had been having this odd nagging feeling that something wasn't right with Kastilius – ever since he hadn't reacted in any way upon seeing Marisii returning from a battle with Feever herself. They hadn't seen each other for years, and Kastilius had barely given him a glance when he saw him yesterday. Marisii reached Kastilius, and once again the older brother wasn't graced with even a look.

"Hey," Marisii said, his voice slightly firmer than usual.

"What?" Kastilius almost screamed, throwing some grass in the air he had just ripped out.

"What's up with you?" Marisii cut straight to the chase. "Yesterday, when you saw me you looked like you wanted to be as far away as possible, and now you don't *even* want to dine with your *own* family? What is it?"

"Nothing," Kastilius simply answered, still not turning even to the side, to look at his older brother.

"What's the problem?" Marisii insisted. "I know that this whole deal with The Curse is difficult and all…"

"I don't give a toss about the stupid curse, okay?" the angered Kastilius stated. "I just don't care; do you understand me? Ever since I was little, I felt like I just didn't belong in the Klauzer family; I felt like an outsider – like someone, who couldn't find their place in the environment they were put in. I didn't want to take part in family dinners or gatherings then – and I surely don't want to do it *now*! I'm not interested in whether Feever or Peeper is going to kill us all, okay, I *just* don't care! I have never felt like a true part of this family, and I have no desire of sharing even *one* meal with you all, got it?"

"Look, I know that the situation is burdensome, but you shouldn't behave this way!" Marisii was getting angry and upset with his younger brother at the same time. He wanted to tell Kastilius that he, better than *anyone*, knew how Kastilius felt. But he couldn't – he just couldn't.

"Don't you get it?" The tension in Kastilius's voice rose. "Get this through your *dumb* head! I don't give a fuck whether we will all be murdered or executed by anyone, or not. I don't give a fuck about The Curse and I…" Kastilius paused, as if in doubt. He finally looked at Marisii, who was standing above him. "And I don't *care* about any of you!"

The last sentence punched Marisii in the gut as if someone had just hit him with a bunch of rocks. It was possible for Kastilius to be angry and upset, the pressure of The Curse might have proven to be too much for him, but to say that he didn't care about his family?

"You know what?" Marisii said, still upset, his voice almost stammering. "Just stay that way, *alone*, for a while – I think you need the time to think. Think about the things you said, and think if you indeed meant them! Because if you meant them, then you don't belong with the Klauzer family."

"As if I would lose anything if I don't belong with any of you!" Kastilius let out an eerie, almost wicked laugh.

Marisii said no more and walked away from Kastilius. He just couldn't fathom why his younger brother was behaving this way – what *made* him behave this way. Marisii, even if he was incredibly angry, wouldn't have ever said such a drastic thing. A part of him hoped that the vile things Kastilius had said were going to prove to be just a rebellious-teenage phase and that soon he would be himself again. That was the precise reason why he decided not to disturb the others with this information – for the time being. Marisii Klauzer returned to the others, acting as if there hadn't been *any* problem with Kastilius at all. While he'd been gone, they had started a small fire, to warm themselves in the freezing night that was threatening to consume them.

~~~~~~~~~~

Kastilius's gaze averted to the fire and all the families' members dining, gathered around it, and his throat gagged, threatening to spill the last thing he ate; whatever that was. Kastilius began feeling a strong animosity toward the two families – he didn't know why that was. The only thing Kastilius *knew* was that with each passing day spent with each one of them, the harder it was for him to stand being around, or even *look* at them.

Chapter 13

Potion making

Kayla Fehrenberg had gotten a move on making potions, and now she was in her element. All the others helped in her endeavors, except for Kastilius Klauzer; once again, he wanted no part in any even remotely family-related activity.

"I'm so glad I got the opportunity to aid you in making these potions, Kayla," Tiffany said cheerfully. "I really feel like I'm doing something important!"

"You really are, Tiff," Kayla smiled in response. "So, we've got a potion for temporarily enveloping the enemy in chains and an invisibility potion. Which is next?"

Tiffany looked at The Book, open wide in front of them, placed on the back compartment of one of the trucks. *"A potion for temporarily stopping the enemy,"* Tiffany read.

Kayla put a dark purple plant inside a long, glass vial, the object letting out a slight puff of smoke. Then, she added something else, this time a dark green herb, and the bright red liquid now turned bright green. The rest of the members of the two families were watching Kayla in her element, gathered around the pick-up truck. Then, the young woman put the third, and then the fourth ingredient, and the potion turned a vivid blue-orange color.

"This one is done!" Kayla announced triumphantly, sealing the glass vial with a small cork, replacing it inside her black bag, where the other two ready-to-be-used potions, lay. "Next?"

"A flying potion!" Pacifika exclaimed incredulously at their eldest sister.

"Done!" Kayla announced after about ten minutes.

"Mist potion," Klacifia added.

"Done!" Kayla answered after about five minutes, this time.

"A potion for summoning a shield," Perventia continued.

"Done!"

"A potion for a small-scale, temporary explosion," Marisii said.

"Done!"

"A potion for summoning a bow and arrows," Kasteron continued, frowning. "A potion for a bow and arrows? We can always buy it from somewhere, why would we need a potion for *that*?"

"Every single potion we make is going to come in handy at some point," Kayla let him know. "You may be laughing now, but I assure you that the more, the merrier!"

Kasteron nodded understandingly, and Kayla plunged back into her area of expertise. After another 20 minutes, this potion was produced as well. The two families continued making potions, able to concoct ten further ones before the ingredients ran out. In the end, they had just a few potions shy of 20 – but, as Kayla had said, every single one of them would come in handy in some way. Kayla placed the last, warm to the touch, potion in her black bag, sealing it immediately after. She whipped her head around to her helpers, announcing: "Now we have something to fight with when Feever comes. However small and not effective for a long period of time!"

"Are you kidding me? It's fantastic!" Tiffany exclaimed in excitement. "We will be able to defend ourselves – that's what's important!"

"That's right, Tiff," Kayla smiled at her sister Tiffany.

~~~~~~~~~~

The younger sister had a good feeling about their first battle with Feever. Tiffany didn't know where it was coming from, but she somehow *knew* that *she* could take on Feever. That *feeling* reassured her that she *could* help her family and that together they *could* start trying to defeat her.

Chapter 14

The library

After Kayla Fehrenberg had concocted all the potions with the help of her family and the Klauzer family, with the exception of Kastilius who had earned himself a scornful look from his brother Marisii, the two families had come up with a sort of plan. It consisted of the Fehrenberg family and the Klauzer family going in search of other ingredients, and then heading to a library, where they could peacefully discuss possible other potions. There was just something about the confines of a library that made it feel safe to the two families. They wanted to explore other potions, possibly more powerful ones. After picking up some magical ingredients at a Wicca shop, the two families stepped out of the two pick-up trucks, a vast and ancient-looking library towering above them. A large sign at the top stated with words engraved in gold: Straightvur library. They started for the entrance, when suddenly Perventia stopped Teela, grazing her shoulder lightly with her hand.

"What is it?" Teela asked her mother.

Perventia Fehrenberg didn't have the strength to tell Teela that she was going to be Feever's first victim – the mother just couldn't bear to see the expression on her daughter's face when she found out the ugly truth. At the same time, Perventia wanted to give Teela some sort of a fighting chance but couldn't help it and fake a smile. "Be careful, yeah? *Promise* me to be careful!"

"Of course, Mum," Teela chuckled slightly, as if not knowing why her mother was telling her that. Perventia knew Teela had *always* been careful; there wasn't any need to remind her. But Perventia did it anyway; just in case.

~~~~~~~~~~

Marisii Klauzer had the honor of sliding open the two huge wooden doors of the library. They were a vivid pecan color, proving to be heavy for Marisii, who had to put an extra bit of strength into the action. At last, he opened them fully, revealing a vast space, lined with huge six-meter shelves, stacked with books. Along the sides of the shelves, dozens of wooden tables with chairs could be observed by the two families. The place had distinct smells of old and new books, the two of them mingling in the air. Countless windows lined the two floors, and at certain places there were glass displays, concealing important documents, ancient scrolls, or precious artifacts that could only be looked at, not touched. The library was so huge, it would have been pretty easy to get lost.

Marisii headed for the reception to let whoever worked there know that he and the rest of the two families were going to spend a fair amount of time in the building, 'reading' books. In truth, they were going to create new potions, not read books; but he had to bamboozle the receptionist somehow, didn't he? Upon arriving, though, Marisii noticed there wasn't *anybody* at the reception. Instead, the young man spotted the circular, silver library bell, and pressed it, ringing it slightly. Marisii looked around and something caught his attention – a tall, black-haired young man, probably older than Marisii by just a year or two, trying to balance a dozen books in his hands, and failing. Most of the volumes thumped to the floor, the man emerging from what Marisii supposed was the storage room. Marisii chuckled at the library man's clumsiness, witnessing him approach. A pair of black-framed glasses rested on his nose.

"How can I help you?" the man asked Marisii, seemingly breathless. Maybe from carrying all those books around.

"Hello," Marisii greeted him politely, a small smile spreading across his face. "My family and I are constantly traveling around the globe and we rarely get the chance to stop and enjoy a library as beautiful as this one! The opportunity suddenly knocked on the door, and we want to spend as much time as possible in this place of superb knowledge."

The library man raised his glasses with a finger, smiling at Marisii's attempt at a speech. "Of course," he answered. "That's what the libraries are for, aren't they? Knowledge and some enjoyment along the way!"

"I agree," Marisii winked at the library man, giving him an almost suggestive smile.

"You have a pretty big family," the library man said, his eyes averting to all the people waiting in the library hall, near the entrance.

"Actually, my family and I are accompanied by another family; we've been friends ever since I can remember!" the chocolate-haired man clarified. The two of them seemed to be at approximately the same height, maybe an inch or two difference.

"Splendid!" the library man cheerfully replied, directing a smile at Marisii, it being returned.

Marisii's eyes set on the name tag, pinned to the black T-shirt the library man was wearing, another smile grazing his facial features: "Thank you for the help, *Makio.*"

~~~~~~~~~~

Kayla took out the bought potion ingredients from the Wicca shop and set them on the wooden table in front of her and the remaining members of the two families, looking at the potions already placed on the table. Amidst all the pressure, Perventia Fehrenberg had taken The Book with them, setting it on the table as well.

"These potions might be weak," she observed with a frown. "They won't be able to hold Feever for long!"

"Relax, honey." Teela saw Perventia, who was positioned next to her older sister, trying to comfort her by placing a hand on her shoulder. "We still *need* them to defend ourselves against her! Better weak than nothing!"

Kayla began concocting some extra potions in more small glass vials; everyone observed her doing it, except for Kastilius, Kasteron and Teela. Kastilius moved away from them, heading somewhere in the library, his face scrunched up in anger as usual. Teela told Perventia that she was going to take a look around the library with Kasteron by her side.

"Okay," Perventia agreed with a nod. "But don't take long."

Teela returned the nod and then started dragging Kasteron between all the bookshelves, out of sight. She pushed him against a rack and pressed her lips against his, as if they were a life-saving substance. Then, Teela got to work on unbuttoning his shirt.

"Here?" Kasteron uttered a laugh of surprise.

"Here!" Teela confirmed, working on the buttons quickly, so she could see Kasteron's exposed flesh.

~~~~~~~~~~

In the meantime, Kastilius Klauzer wandered around all the bookcases and shelves, inspecting them with absent-minded interest. Once again, he hadn't desired to help either of the two families, opting to wander around the library instead, thinking it would be better for everyone that way.

~~~~~~~~~~

Kayla Fehrenberg worked fiercely on the potions, with the rest of the two families' members aiding her loyally.

~~~~~~~~~~

The librarian Makio continued to overwhelm himself with dozens of books, trying to carry them from one spot to another in the storage room. He had to organize them all by genre, and then by name. Makio had the feeling that he would never be able to keep up – new titles kept appearing, making him more and more confused.

~~~~~~~~~~

Kayla and company were making potions; Kasteron and Teela were making out, getting ready to engage in other, more specific activities; Kastilius was walking further and further into the vast library; and Makio continued trying to sort out various titles. *And* that's when the two towering wooden doors of the building slid open. They did so slowly, with an eerie, creaking sound that somehow killed every other commotion inside the library – even the motions of lips interlocking and books clattering.

Kayla stopped talking with the others, Kastilius stopped walking about, Kasteron and Teela stopped kissing and running their hands all over each other, and Makio stopped organizing the volumes, all their ears sharpened to the loud sound coming from the entrance. Another sound echoed throughout the library – the sound of approaching hard, confident footsteps.

~~~~~~~~~~

Makio raised his glasses with his index finger, appearing out from the storage room. The young librarian witnessed a woman with incredibly dark hair, covered in a dress mixing shades of onyx black and Prussian blue, her feet encased in old-fashioned low-heeled shoes, the same color as her dress. She also had a long, dark silk cloak, draped across her shoulders, almost like a shawl but not quite.

"Hello," Makio greeted her, the initial shock of her not quite old-fashioned but not quite modern clothes either, fading. The woman looked at him questioningly. "Welcome to the Straightvur library. How can I be of help?"

"By shutting up!" The woman raised her voice a level, thrusting her hand up in the air, forcing Makio to fly out of the reception, landing on top of one of the glass displays nearby, shattering it. Glass shards littered the floor, the silence interrupted, the echo intensified. Makio quickly lost consciousness afterward.

~~~~~~~~~~

Feever put her hand down, smiling, a part of her *knowing* that her enemies had heard the sounds loud and clear. "I've come to play!" Feever shouted through the library, her voice reverberating against the walls. And as if to make her presence even more known, she raised both her hands in the air, causing *all* the library windows to shatter into a million pieces, reducing them to debris, showering the space.

Feever started inching closer to the heart of the library, her footsteps sure and unwavering, when her eyes caught the figure of Marisii Klauzer.

~~~~~~~~~~

Kayla and others ditched the potions they were making – and in their panic, they even ditched most of the already finished potions, on the table. All of them started looking for a way out of the building, careful not to make even the tiniest sound. In their hurry, they even forgot to take the book of shadows with them, which was lying wide open on the table next to the potions, up for grabs.

Chapter 15

Hide and seek

"Look who we have here." A wide smile formed on Feever's face as her eyes set on Marisii Klauzer.

Marisii had separated from the others unintentionally, getting lost in the process, his misfortune in the embodiment of Feever. Fortunately for him, he had managed to snatch away a single potion from Kayla's stash, keeping it safely in his pocket, in case the need to use it arose.

~~~~~~~~~~

"Marisii Klauzer." Feever said his name with precision while stepping closer to him. "We meet again." She looked like she was *on* something, smiling happily and expectantly. "I couldn't finish you off the first time we met – or one of your little lady friends, for that matter! But now it seems like I will get a second chance?" Feever's nefarious laughter echoed off the library's walls; she knew the question was rhetorical. *Of course,* she anticipated the chance to shred Marisii to pieces. Although, her primary aim today was none other than Teela Fehrenberg. The reason she had chosen Teela precisely was that she was the youngest daughter of the Fehrenberg family – and by killing her, Feever would cause great emotional damage to the whole family. But realistically, what was stopping her from ending Marisii, as well? That way, she would have ruined the Klauzer family, too.

"What have you done to Makio?" Marisii suddenly hissed at her.

"Knocked him out – nothing special!" the witch stated, a slight disinterest creeping into her voice for a moment. "I don't need *him*; he's useless to me! I came here for you, witches, *and* only you! You should feel special, don't you think?"

~~~~~~~~~~

"Ohhh, I feel special alright," Marisii spat out in anger, reflected in his eyes. His fingers found the potion in his jeans pocket.

"I'm going to enjoy this so much," Feever said, an extra layer of orange-crimson color adding to her face, as a huge fireball formed in her right hand.

Marisii had no time to lose; he flashed out the glass vial, containing the purple potion, and threw it in Feever's direction. At the same time, she threw the fireball through the air, the two entities connecting. Upon touching each other, they formed a small explosion, causing Marisii to step back. But Feever didn't even blink.

Feever charged another ball into her palm, getting ready to throw it when Kastilius emerged from a nearby corner, shielding Marisii's body with his own, arms protectively thrust out in the air. "If you want him, you will have to go through me first!"

Something peculiar occurred – Marisii witnessed Feever getting distracted, immediately snuffing out the fireball upon seeing Kastilius.

"What are you doing?" the incredulous Marisii asked Kastilius. *"Now* you decide to start caring about your family?"

"Better late than never, don't you think?" Kastilius chuckled as if this whole thing were merely a joke to him.

Feever's eyes lingered on Marisii and Kastilius a few seconds longer, then swung her hand outward. Marisii and Kastilius flew through the library, their backs connecting with a firm chipped wall, their bodies slumping down on the ground, unmoving but still breathing.

Marisii was barely conscious when he heard Feever speaking. Was she indeed speaking? Or were the words just a product of his insufficient state of mind right now?

"I would *never* hurt *you,* Kastilius," Feever tenderly said, her footsteps fading far away.

~~~~~~~~~~

Feever was walking deeper into the library when her ears picked up on an odd sound, and she immediately whipped her head around. An enormous rack of books was falling down toward her, the volumes already assaulting her. The witch appeared unimpressed, snapping the fingers of her right hand, immediately teleporting herself away from the falling rack. It crashed to the polished floor with a loud and continuous thud. Feever raised her head, seeing the mothers of the two families standing opposite her – Perventia Fehrenberg and Berventy Klauzer.

"If you think we will let you harm our children, you're wrong!" Berventy bared her teeth like a wolf, throwing a light blue potion in Feever's direction, who easily deflected it with her hand, the potion dying in a liquid pool on the floor behind her.

"Oh, I don't need your permission!" Feever stated, deflecting Perventia's wine-red potion. "I've come for Teela, but I have no reservations about harming the two of you as well!"

Feever's face twisted into a dark frown and she lifted both of her hands high in the air, causing both women to lift from the floor simultaneously. As always, the witch knew their throats had begun to close in on themselves, suffocating them. "How I will revel in the fact that I have killed the two bitch ancestors of Sarvit and Mour!" *Feever* bared her teeth this time, noticing that Berventy's face had begun reddening to dangerously intense levels, Perventia holding on to dear life.

"Hey, Feever!" a voice behind her shouted.

Feever started turning around to see whom it belonged to, but not softening her grip on the two mothers.

"Try this on for size!" Kayla Fehrenberg hissed.

Everything happened so fast – Feever had almost turned to Kayla, but not entirely, leaving her back vulnerable, while still holding the two women high up in the air. Kayla released a potion, Feever feeling the glass vial breaking against the dark satin-cotton material of her dress, rendering her almost useless, chains engulfing her feet, arms and body. Unwillingly, Feever dropped Berventy and Perventia back to the floor, her grip on their throats utterly gone.

"KAYLA, RUN!" Perventia screamed at her daughter. The young girl followed her advice and disappeared from Feever's sight within seconds.

Feever felt the anger boiling in her veins and let out an unearthly growl, managing to free herself of the chains by breaking them with the strength of her witch heritage and skills. Even more angered than before, her eyes set on Berventy and Perventia again, who were still recovering on the floor from her earlier attack.

"Try your own medicine!" Feever hissed like a snake, willing books from all around the shelves to start falling on top of Berventy and Perventia. This time, it simply took her one flex of the fingers to make all the books surrounding them assault the two women, who were trying to protect themselves with hands, raised in front of their faces. "And for the grand finale!" Feever exclaimed, making a whole *rack* of books fall and bury them. Feever didn't even know if she had killed them, their bodies barely distinguishable amidst all the books and the broken brown wood. She wondered aloud: "Just in case!" With a flick of the wrist, she made the opposite six-meter book rack fall on top of the already crumbled one.

~~~~~~~~~~

Pattery Fehrenberg , who was hiding behind a bookshelf with his daughter Pacifika, saw what happened. His fist tightened in anger, the other one holding a potion. "She's gonna pay for this!"

"No, Dad!" Pacifika stopped him from emerging out and throwing the potion. "Let's first find the others, and then *act*! Strength in numbers!"

"Pacifika, *your* mother could be dead and you're telling me to *wait*?"

"Don't say *that*!" Pacifika almost slapped him on the shoulder. "I'm sure she will be alive and well, with only a few scratches!"

"Surpriseeee!" Feever almost screamed in amusement when she showed up behind the shelf, startling Pattery and Pacifika out of their hiding place. She must have been eavesdropping on them for the last 20 seconds or so.

"Shit!" Pattery swore. He and Pacifika started running frantically away from Feever, but the longer-time witch sideswiped their legs with a magical notion of her hand.

"I believe we weren't able to finish our first meeting, too! Seriously, we gotta stop meeting like *this*!" Feever stepped closer to Pattery and Pacifika, the two Fehrenbergs trying to get up from the floor. But their efforts proved fruitless as Feever pushed them back. In a sense, Feever had totally spied on Pattery and Pacifika, whooping them. "A shame, don't you think?"

Pacifika eventually succeeded in getting up and began frantically running away, clearly trying to escape Feever's looming and approaching grip. But the older witch didn't permit that to happen, smashing the long blond-haired Fehrenberg against a book rack, with a flick of the wrist. Pacifika crumbled down to the floor, rendered unconscious.

"Don't you dare touch my daughter!" Pattery shrieked from the ground.

Feever inched closer to him from above, lightly caressing his face. "I first want to touch her *daddy!*" The raven-haired witch kneeled and frowned, all fake genuineness gone, squeezing Pattery's right cheek.

Pattery screamed, feeling his face growing hotter by the second. He guessed the older witch's primary aim was to accelerate his body temperature, effectively killing him in the process.

~~~~~~~~~~

Feever smiled broadly; she could feel *his* pain surging through *her* veins, and that made her giddy with happiness.

"Stop right there!" Kayla said, emerging from a nearby corner yet again, holding another potion between her fingers.

"You again?" Feever almost sighed. "Can't a person get rid of you?" Without her grip on Pattery's cheek faltering even one bit, Feever forced Kayla to fly up to the second floor of the library with her other hand. Her body found a few racks, following her older sister's fate. But better safe than sorry – and *that's* why Feever sent a fireball flying upward, lighting up the numerous volumes on the second floor.

Pattery's right cheek was badly burnt, as was most of his neck. If someone didn't do *something* soon, the father would have died. As if on cue, Brouzenvert appeared out of another corner with a gun in hand, directing bullets at Feever. She looked at him in boredom, the bullets not fazing her even one bit. They went straight through her skin and the wounds closed momentarily after. She formed a gun in her free hand herself, shooting Brouzenvert in the shoulder and then making him meet with the wall behind – those simple man-made weapons couldn't have hurt *her*, but they did a spectacular job on *him*. Still kneeling in front of Pattery, one hand firmly pressed to his cheek, burning it, the ancient witch heard another person approaching.

Klacifia Fehrenberg was running towards Feever with a victorious battle cry, knife raised in hand. Upon reaching the target, she was apprehended by the more experienced witch, the knife plunging into Klacifia's leg. Then Feever forced her to kiss the same wall, Klacifia crumbling down next to Brouzenvert.

Feever's attention returned to Pattery now that she had temporarily eliminated most of the two families' members. She touched his other cheek with her free hand, scorching Pattery even further.

Suddenly, her ears picked up on an odd sound, and she whipped her head around towards the library's wooden double doors, only to witness them fly off their hinges, two young men driving into the library on two black motorcycles. They drove towards Feever determinedly and in synchronicity kicked her square in the face, making her fly backward and free Pattery.

"We need to take him to a hospital, Morven!" the first man said upon seeing Pattery laying on the ground, shaking in pain, his skin sizzling.

"Right away, Brouzun!" The other boy confirmed, helping the convulsing Pattery climb up onto his motorcycle. The two young men were the last remaining members of the Klauzer family. Morven lit up the engine and made for the now completely destroyed entrance.

Feever knew he intended to head for the nearest hospital available. And she couldn't *allow* that. The witch stood up from her spot on the floor, eyes ablazing.

"I hope you do know that you will pay dearly for this!" Feever warned him, her voice sharp as a razor blade, a knife forming in her hands out of the blue.

She headed for him, intending to slice and dice, but at the last moment, Morven ducked swiftly, killed the motorcycle's engine and kicked her in the back. Feever staggered only for a second, her head turning around, looking for its prey. Morven climbed onto a surprisingly still-standing book rack and managed to jump from it and punch Feever with a fist, while she was distracted. The raven-haired witch looked at him, eyes inspecting his every move – he had taken away her chance of killing Pattery Fehrenberg.

Feever stood up even straighter now, regaining her steady posture. Her eyes were boring into Morven, her inner being feeling nothing but contempt for this individual. Then, her eyes averted to the other two family members, lying on the floor nearby; Pattery was unconscious and Feever had no idea what Brouzun was doing. He was just kneeling on the floor, next to his father, trying to resuscitate him maybe? She looked back at Morven, still thinking about how yet again a chance for doing something – *anything* – had been taken away. And from a Klauzer. Feever was fed up; she had come here to execute her first victim as a part of her beautiful curse, and all she was getting so far were childish tricks and strong words. She was sick of it.

"ENOUGH!" Her voice cut the air. She raised her hands high above her, causing the *whole* library roof to crumble and fall into pieces all around them. The bookshelves and racks which were still standing fell on top of one another. All the stone pillars, holding the library in place, crumbled down to pieces, except for one, which was barely supporting the weight of the enormous building. "YOU WANT ME TO BE BAD?" Her eyes were flashing with rage as she shouted. "FINE! I'LL BE *BAD*!" The mighty Salem witch thrust her hands once more in the air, vigorously, putting all the force she possessed into the motion, causing Morven to fly across the air towards a wall. But Morven didn't *actually* hit the wall – that would have been a blessing. He went *through* the wall, destroying it with his body, landing on the front yard outside, blood oozing out from his scalp and nose.

The library had become, simply, a ruin – almost everything had been toppled down or destroyed. The second floor was burning brightly; all of the book racks and shelves had fallen down, most of them reduced to pieces; the roof annihilated; a big gaping hole in the wall Morven had exited through.

From under one of the toppled-down book racks, a young girl with dark brown hair was removing books from all around and on top of her, eventually emerging out. That immediately attracted Feever's attention. Feever remembered the girl's name as Teela Fehrenberg, who had unsurprisingly been almost buried to death. The Salem witch started making her way towards the Fehrenberg witch, knowing deep down that she was going to *get* what she originally came here for.

Chapter 16

A fallen family member – Part 1

Feever sprinted down to Teela Fehrenberg and pushed her with both her hands, making her fly backwards and meet the cold floor.

Feever directed a laugh at her. "Teela, Teela," Feever said. "You will get the honor of being my first victim, darling!"

Perventia and Berventy were trying, with enormous efforts, to emerge out from under all the books and the book rack burying them. Kastilius and Marisii had begun to regain consciousness, so had Brouzenvert, Pacifika, and Klacifia. Kayla was stumbling shakingly, trying to get to the first floor from the second. Morven was slowly fading, and all the rest were so injured that they could barely move.

Teela was convulsing on the floor painfully, fully aware of the approaching figure. Kasteron and Tiffany were missing. Kasteron and Teela had been separated when the bookshelves and book racks had begun to fall all around them, Teela distinctly hearing her mother and Berventy's screams. One rack had fallen right between them, with all the books serving as a barrier. Teela supposed her sister Tiffany had likely hidden somewhere, waiting for a suitable moment to appear.

All of the two families' members, who were conscious, were now trying their best to get to Teela. She saw them putting all their strength left into the actions, but they could barely move due to their injuries.

~~~~~~~~~~

Feever suddenly looked at all the crawling figures, situated all around her at the heart of the library, the ruined bookshelves and racks a few meters away, and cracked an almost victorious laugh. "Look at how pathetic *you* are!" she sneered. "I'm about to murder your daughter, your friend – and you can't even do anything about it! Don't you feel powerless? Weak? Pitiful? Because that's what you all are! I will first kill your daughter, and then I might as well kill the rest of you! Should I even bother with The Curse now, seeing as you're not even formidable opponents? Easy targets right now – that's what you two families are! I can easily execute you – *one by one!*" Feever paused, and smiled again, witnessing all the pain she had inflicted – and all the pain she was *yet* to inflict. "But I won't do that, I won't make it so easy on you! After all, I want it to be fun; killing you all at once is no fun! NOT AT ALL!"

Feever stood rooted to her spot, mere centimeters from Teela Fehrenberg now, witnessing the shaking, crawling members of the two families. After a moment, the Salem witch decided that The Curse's first victim needs to be claimed *now*. Feever turned her head around, facing Teela, when she felt someone attacking her from behind. Out of the corner of her eye, she caught a glimpse of her attacker as Kasteron Klauzer – Teela's boyfriend. He looked vastly injured, but somehow, he *still* had the will to defy her.

"KASTERON!" Teela shrieked, the grief so painfully evident in her voice.

Feever was still trying to get him off her back – literally. After a few more moments, Feever was able to get a clear shot and wave a hand, making Kasteron meet up with the last remaining pillar, barely holding the building's structure together. He remained conscious but had been rendered useless to fight.

"Teela!" he uttered, the same amount of grief filling his voice.

"Don't do it!" Perventia said, who, alongside Berventy, was slowly inching closer to the Salem witch. Feever turned around to face her. "Leave us alone!"

"*Leave you alone?*" Feever asked incredulously. "After what your ancestors Sarvit and Mour did? They deserved to suffer – and so do *you*!"

Kayla finally reached the first floor, and Feever directed her gaze at her, witnessing the young woman crumbling down to her knees.

"Let my sister be!" Kayla said weakly.

"Just look at you all!" Feever said. "Begging, defenseless! You *disgust* me!" Feever managed to shake those feelings away, knowing that she had more important matters to attend to. "It's time!"

"NO!" Perventia said.

"YES!" Feever smiled, and hungrily approached Teela, reaching her at last.

"Leave her alone!" Kayla said.

"Get away from us!" Pacifika joined the pleas from the first floor, not far from where Teela and Feever were situated.

"No!" Klacifia just almost whispered from the end of the first floor, almost out of sight, but not quite. There was such total silence for a few moments afterward.

Feever smiled at Teela broadly, almost genuinely. Then, the three-hundred-years-old-and-counting-witch closed her eyes shut, plunging her right hand deep inside Teela's chest, where her heart was. Feever heard a shrill cry and various screams, but not even an octave from Teela. How was that possible?

Feever fluttered her eyes open, witnessing her right hand plunged deep inside someone *else's* chest.

Her hand was holding someone else's *heart.*

Chapter 17

A fallen family member – Part 2

Feever pointed her right hand towards Teela Fehrenberg 's chest, while everyone else in the mess of a library was screaming and begging her not to do it. From a nearby corner Tiffany Fehrenberg popped out – she was completely intact, neither injured nor bruised by all that had happened in the past hour or so. Tiffany saw everyone else from her family and the Klauzer family in a worrisome state on the ground, shrieks erupting out of most of them. She turned her head in the direction they were all looking and saw the ghastly picture – the witch Feever, her hand inching threateningly closer to Teela's chest. Too close for comfort. Tiffany didn't have time to think – she only had time to react. And that, she did.

Tiffany started running towards Feever, who closed her eyes, smiling. And just as Feever was about to plunge her right hand deep into Teela's chest, Tiffany pushed her younger sister out of the way, taking her place, feeling Feever's cold fingers inside her chest.

"TIFFANY!" Teela screamed, the shock taking control of her voice.

"NOOOOO!" Perventia shrieked loudly, tears overflowing all at once.

Pacifika, Klacifia, and Kayla's eyes were filled with tears too, but the sounds they made were indistinct, grief and shock preventing coherent speech. Pattery was unconscious, unbeknownst to what was occurring around him.

~~~~~~~~~~

Feever's eyes remained shut only for a second more, opening to witness the sight of her hand in Tiffany's chest, instead of Teela's. She could feel her heart, pulsating in her unrelenting grip. The Salem witch would be lying if she didn't say she was slightly surprised – Feever had come to the Straightvur library for Teela Fehrenberg. But at the end of the day, a victim was a victim, and Tiffany would have done just as well.

~~~~~~~~~~

After all, The Order clearly stated that if someone sacrificed themselves, it wouldn't be entirely necessary, or possible, for the person whose name was in the column at the end of The Book, to die. If someone sacrificed themselves, The Order *could* be changed – as it was happening right now.

Violent drops of crimson blood started dripping on Tiffany's clothes, turning them into a vibrant wine-red color. Her mouth was painted in the liquid as well. The floor was stained with blood, Feever's hand was stained with blood. Tiffany looked at Feever directly, her vision starting to blur indefinitely, feeling her heart slowing down in the witch's hand. Then, the young woman looked at Feever's unrelenting hand, as if to make sure she wasn't imagining it.

Feever looked at her, gracing her with one of her signature wicked smiles. "Thank you, Tiffany."

Tiffany Fehrenberg *was* still alive. Her vision was steadily blurring, and her consciousness began proving faulty, but she was *still* alive. She was entirely aware of the screams surrounding her, and all the crying, the sounds of pain – Tiffany could *feel* the grief, borne by the fact that she was dying. Tiffany was proud that she had sacrificed herself for her little sister Teela. Tiffany wanted to help her family in a meaningful way, to protect them somehow – and now, she had succeeded. She had protected a member of her family, refusing to give Feever the satisfaction of taking away *this* specific life. Tiffany Fehrenberg raised her head toward the ceiling, which was barely existent now. Through the gaps, she looked at the vibrant blue sky and for a moment, it seemed so beautiful. Tiffany saw her entire life on tape – from the first moment when she was brought into this world, to the present time when her time on this earth was ending. Her eyes fluttered shut, not by her volition. Suddenly, she wasn't able to hear the screams and shouts of the two families anymore.

So, I am the first, she thought to herself.

~~~~~~~~~~

And that's when Feever ripped her heart out, Tiffany's lifeless body crumbling down to the floor, all life snuffed out. The screams and cries intensified by octaves afterward. Perventia cried and screamed so loud, she could have been dying out of grief. Kayla, Pacifika and Klacifia started screaming at Feever, who had just taken their sister away from them. Teela sobbed quietly, without saying anything. Even Tiffany's bright long brown hair with gold highlights was stained with blood now, and for some reason, that added to the whole feeling of desperation of Teela. *Why did you do that, Tiffany?* she thought to herself.

The whole picture was grotesque and grief-stricken.

~~~~~~~~~~

Feever was now stepping amidst Tiffany's freshly-drawn blood, fresh heart in her hand. Feever examined the organ closely; it was still throbbing, blood still dripping from it. Then, a smile found its way onto her lips. The Salem witch had just killed her first victim and was feeling unearthly happy. She looked at the heart once again, then closed her eyes and instantly drew the organ close to her lips and nostrils. Feever started gradually inhaling the odd scent through her mouth and nose. And then *something* happened.

Several dark waves, resembling sabers, started extorting out from the heart, infusing directly into Feever through her mouth and nose. Feever was slowly extracting the undeveloped magical power of Tiffany Fehrenberg. Feever's eyeballs turned onyx, much like a part of her dress, the heart turning a similar color, rock-solid. Even more dark waves started infusing into Feever, and she could distinctly feel their immense power filling her, in a sense partly completing her. The organ's surface turned even harder, despite Feever's doubt that it was possible.

In a few moments, the numerous dark waves ceased erupting out from the vital organ – Tiffany Fehrenberg 's whole life energy and magical power were effectively transmitted to Feever. Feever had claimed not only the young witch's life but also her power. Feever's eyes returned to their normal emerald-hazel color, all onyx drained. Feever's delicate fingers felt the heart once again, wanting to remember the sensation. But that didn't stop the mighty witch from doing what she intended to do. She closed her fingers around it, crushing the organ. Unclenching her fist a few seconds later, Feever let dozens of tiny onyx-colored rock-solid pieces fall on the stained floor in front of her. The witch could see Tiffany Fehrenberg 's loved ones becoming witnesses to all that, clearly not knowing if they were devastated, or already dead.

Feever clapped her hands once as if cleaning them from any heart residue and then looked at every single family member present and conscious, most of them still shaking. "Now you feel *my* pain!"

Feever waved a hand triumphantly and solemnly, dark waves, similar to those that had emerged out from the heart just seconds ago, wrapping her body, making her disappear and leaving the two families to experience the full extent of their grief rather than killing them all now. That would have been the merciful option. And she couldn't allow herself such weakness.

~~~~~~~~~~

After Feever disappeared the screams and shouts decreased drastically – but the sobs could still be clearly heard. They gradually intensified, soon becoming the only sounds in the demolished space.

Chapter 18

Unlocking the power

Teela approached her sister's body on the floor slowly. She wrapped her arms around Tiffany, seeing the still distinctive shock drawn across her face. In the place where her heart used to be, there was a vast gaping hole, the blood almost ceased. Tiffany wasn't breathing.

"My big sister." Teela started caressing Tiffany's face. "Why did you do it?" Her tears had been evident for quite some time, but now they burst out violently. "*I was supposed to die, not you. Why did you do it?*"

The grotesque and grief-stricken scene affected the other members of the two families as well, their cries just as hard and just as loud as Teela's. Tiffany had been the fourth child of the Fehrenberg family, with Teela being the fifth and last.

"*I should have been in your place!*" Teela said, now stroking Tiffany's bright brown hair with gold highlights. "I should have gone away from this world – not *you!*" The tears started choking her, making their way inside her throat and nostrils. Teela hugged her sister's body tightly, and for a moment, just for a blissful fraction of a second, Teela thought Tiffany was going to wake up. But that *thought*, that *feeling* was nothing more than cruelty, a fraud. Teela eased her grip on Tiffany, looked at her sister's face one more time, and reluctantly closed her eyelids.

Silence.

Each one of them had stopped wailing painfully, looking around miserably and sobbing quietly instead. Teela felt anger – such anger that she'd never felt before. The finality of her closing Tiffany's eyes made her realize that her sister wasn't *ever* coming back – the intense anger because of it was growing. Teela was *angry* that her sister Tiffany was dead, was *angry* that that terrible curse was looming over them all, *angry* that she and her family had to pay for mistakes their ancestors had made, but most of all – *enraged* at Feever, because she was the *one* who had taken Tiffany away from her. She was the *witch* who had ripped out Tiffany's heart mercilessly and consumed its undeveloped power, crushing it into dozens upon dozens of tiny onyx bits, sprinkling it all over the now-dusty floor, in front of all the *people* Tiffany had ever loved.

The intense anger grew even further. Teela Fehrenberg gripped her sister's body even tighter than before, letting an immense cry out of her throat, as if she was on the battlefield, having just lost her entire squad. *That* cry was unnatural – something mixed between a growl, a wail, and a shriek, Teela letting it out for at least a dozen seconds. After that time, she continued to emit the sound, but much quieter.

A small orb of intense white light appeared through one of the shattered window frames of the library, heading toward Teela. The dark brown-haired girl looked at it curiously, with a tinge of incomprehension. All the others saw it too.

The orb of white light reached Teela after a few seconds. Silence had engulfed the ruined library, all who were conscious observing the peculiar scene. The orb looked like it was staring at Teela for quite some time, having positioned itself right in front of the young witch's face. Then, the orb headed straight for her forehead, disappearing inside, infusing her whole body and being.

Teela Fehrenberg felt immense power in her veins – she had never felt something like this before. But she *knew*. Knew because she felt ten times more powerful than before. Knew why she felt that way. Knew what that little orb of white light meant.

With that anger she experienced, that unearthly cry she had let out, both caused by Tiffany Fehrenberg's death, Teela had unlocked her witch power. The anger that she felt before signified that intense emotion, required of a Klauzer or a Fehrenberg family member to experience, in order to unlock their hidden within individual power. Teela Fehrenberg was yet to learn what her power *exactly* was, but she knew that from now on she wouldn't be so helpless against the mighty Feever, as before.

From now on she would be able to fight Feever and – most importantly – avenge Tiffany's untimely death. Teela had unlocked her witch power, her heritage.

And that made her tremendously powerful.

Chapter 19

A rescue mission

Brouzun Klauzer was running toward the library, after initially disappearing from the battle against Feever to look for medical help for Pattery. He stepped into the ruined space determinedly, several doctors and paramedics following him. An ambulance was parked out front, waiting to take the next patients – it had already taken Pattery Fehrenberg to the nearest hospital, who was of the highest priority right now. Everyone that had participated in the battle was in shock, not registering anything as they were being taken away from the crumbling building and loaded into the ambulance by the doctors and paramedics. They took extra care to load everyone – including the librarian Makio, and Tiffany Fehrenberg 's corpse, the huge gaping hole in her chest still evident. The paramedics and doctors closed the vast ambulance's doors and within minutes, were driving away from the library. Brouzun dared to take a look through the two square windows at the back of the ambulance, witnessing the library collapsing in on itself.

~~~~~~~~~~

The doctors and paramedics escorted all the patients to the hospital's foyer, with the swift help of Brouzun Klauzer.

"What are we dealing with?" A beautiful nurse turned around from behind the reception counter. She had long, flowing around her, orange-crimson hair, the shades mingling pleasantly, giving accent to her light brown skin tone. The nurse was wearing a small blue lanyard with a name tag, stating: *'Medical nurse Annora'*.

"Two women with multiple injuries and bruises," Brouzun stated, forestalling the medical staff that came with him. Brouzun meant his mother Berventy, and their friend Perventia. They were barely standing, Berventy at moments seeming as if she were about to pass out. "An unconscious man with multiple bruises," talking about Makio. "Two boys with faint bruises," meaning Marisii and Kastilius. "An unconscious girl with slight burns and smoke inhalation," Kayla. "An unconscious man in critical condition," meaning his brother Morven. "A girl with a puncture wound in the leg," Klacifia. "A girl with slight bruises," Pacifika. "A man with a puncture wound in the shoulder," meaning his father Brouzenvert. "A girl and a boy with multiple bruises!" Brouzun finally finished, out of breath, meaning Teela and his brother Kasteron.

"Take the two women, the girl and the man with the puncture wounds, the girl with the burns and the boy in critical condition, to the intensive care unit!" Annora commanded the medical team that had brought the patients – it was clear who oversaw the hospital. "Take the rest to the minor injuries ward at once!"

The team, aided by several medical nurses, took the patients to the two hospital units, beginning to do everything in their power to save them.

Chapter 20

A hospital visit

The hospital staff had taken the bullet out of Brouzenvert's shoulder, bandaging it carefully. They also took care of Berventy and Perventia in a timely manner. As a whole, all of the families' members were recovering in their assigned hospital rooms, except for Morven, who was still in a life-threatening condition. Makio had also regained consciousness, recovering just as fast as the others. Marisii and Kastilius recovered almost immediately after receiving some medical care, especially Marisii, whose bullet wound had to be checked again by medical professionals. They took some much-needed rest, simply because out of all the families' members, with the exception of Brouzun, the two of them were the only ones who had gotten off lightly. Feever had spared them. And Marisii couldn't explain to himself why – the only thing he knew was that when she took one look at Kastilius, she had hesitated in killing them.

Kayla was recovering relatively fast as well, but her burns would mark her for life. Pattery was undergoing operations all week. Both he and Morven were on the brink of life and death.

Pacifika recovered effortlessly, and Klacifia had been bandaged thoroughly, her puncture wound slowly but painfully healing. Teela and Kasteron were also healing. The hospital staff had taken great care of the two families, including Makio, trying to save Morven and Pattery for an entire week now.

Pattery had such a high percentage of burns, mainly on his face and neck, that it would have been a holy miracle if the hospital staff had been able to save him. And if they did save him, his face would have been marked from scars for life – much worse than Kayla's case, whose burns were mainly situated on her body.

Ever since arriving at the hospital, Morven hadn't even come-to once. The surgeons had been able to locate multiple broken ribs with a CT scan, and internal bleeding. His major operation was about to take place in a few days, the surgeons deciding to do several minor ones in the meantime. They had waited long enough – if they didn't do the major operation soon, Morven would have been gone.

Feever had wanted to inflict a major blow to the two families and had succeeded – she had wounded almost all of them, brought two to the brink of death, and eliminated one – Tiffany Fehrenberg. Feever had ripped her heart out, devouring her undeveloped power right in front of her friends and family's eyes. Her corpse was now in the hospital's morgue, awaiting a decision on the Fehrenberg family's side, as to what to do with it – whether they were going to bury her or donate her still functional organs to other patients who were in desperate need of them.

~~~~~~~~~~

Perventia Fehrenberg was worried. Just a *week* ago Feever had murdered her daughter Tiffany in cold blood, managing to inflict multiple injuries on Perventia's own family, and the Klauzers. One week had already passed – and Feever was scheduled to visit them once every *three* weeks. Right now, both families were in a ghastly state, not knowing whether they would be able to fight again so soon.

"I want to see my husband; his name is Pattery Fehrenberg!" Perventia demanded of the head nurse Annora.

"Mrs, I don't think that's wise at the moment," Annora, who was standing next to Perventia and Berventy's beds, the two mothers sharing a room, informed her. "Right now, Mr Fehrenberg is recovering from yet another operation. And he's still unconscious. You can see him after tomorrow's operation, after which we will determine how well he would fare with all the injuries and procedures."

"I want to see my husband now!" Perventia raised her voice an octave.

"Perventia, the nurse said it would be better if you waited…" Berventy said but was unceremoniously interrupted by Perventia.

"Stay out of this, Berventy!" Perventia directed her a steely gaze. "Look," Perventia looked Annora straight in the eyes – there was something oddly familiar about the head nurse's appearance. Maybe she had seen her picture somewhere? Perventia couldn't quite place it. "My family and I went through *literal* hell! You have no idea and you will *never* have an idea what we went through before coming to this hospital! I *lost* a member of my family, one of my daughters – and listen to me when I tell you that I *won't* lose my husband too! I would trade my life for his if it came to it! So please, I am asking you to let me see my husband!"

Annora eyed the blond woman for a second, but then, much to Perventia's surprise, nodded affirmatively. Perventia almost jumped out of the bed in enthusiasm, slipped on her slippers, and together with Annora, headed for Pattery's room.

Upon seeing him Perventia almost croaked out in pain, but quickly recomposed herself, knowing she wasn't alone with him quite yet. "Can I have a few minutes alone with my husband?"

"Are you sure that's the best thing for you…"

"Yes, I'm *sure* that's the best thing for me right now!" Perventia raised her voice for a second time today, glad to find out it still had an effect – seconds later, Annora had gone.

Perventia shut the door and then pulled the blinds down, so as not to be seen. She went to Pattery, lying in the bed, and looked at him – both his cheeks and whole neck were covered in bandages. The systems were making that tiny beeping sound, making Perventia nervous. But at the same time, that sound was calming to Perventia, indicating that Pattery still had a pulse. He was unconscious and Perventia grasped his hand in hers, tears tumbling down her face. She wasn't sure if he was going to recover – she wasn't sure if *any* of them were going to recover after all that had happened. Perventia Fehrenberg wasn't sure of herself, or anything anymore.

"I'm sorry!" Perventia sobbed, crouching next to Pattery, her gaze locked on him and his dreadful state. "I should have done something! Feever was scorching you and I couldn't do anything, because I was unconscious! You suffered and I, who am supposed to be your anchor in everything, couldn't do anything!" Perventia tightened her grasp on her husband's hand. There was space on the bed next to Pattery, and Perventia, feeling like her knees might give out from grief, sat next to her husband, not letting go of his hand for one second.

"I should have been in your place! I should have been the injured one! I should have…" Perventia paused, letting her sobs cloud her speech for a few moments. "I would *trade* my life for yours, and if I could do it, I would – right now! If I could die in exchange for your life, for your recovery, *I would*! I would die for you thousands and thousands of times, again and again! I knew my life was completed ever since the moment you walked in it! And that's why it is yours." She caressed his hand, feeling his rough skin with her thumb. "I am yours – and I always will be! Feever is going to come again in two weeks, but I will *not* let her harm any of our other children! I'm going to stand in front of her – she can stab and punch and attack me all she wants, but I will not let her harm them!" Perventia was confident she could do that – but a part of her knew that she wasn't as powerful a witch as Feever, and coming up against her at this close proximity and with such intentions, would probably bring about her own death.

"When you awake you will have a reason to cheer *and* a reason to grieve! Teela, whom we thought we're going to lose, is alive!" Perventia began crying, this time from happiness. "She's *alive*, Pattery! She even received her power! Do you understand, one of our *kids* received their power?" But then her face darkened upon remembering the reason to grieve, adding another shade to the already dimly lit hospital room. "But you will sag when you find out that one of our other daughters Tiffany died. She died in the most terrifying and despicable way at the hands of Feever! Now Feever possesses the undeveloped power of a Fehrenberg family member, and is mightier than before! But you know what? Tiffany is a hero; our daughter is a *hero*! She sacrificed herself for Teela by blocking Feever's path! Tiffany saved Teela, Pattery! We've been trying all our lives to encourage *all* our daughters to get along, and Tiffany sacrificed her own life to preserve Teela's! Do you understand that we've raised five beautiful women, who support one another? Tiffany left this world a hero and her sacrifice won't be in vain – we *will* avenge her death!"

Perventia kissed Pattery's forehead, which had a single small bandage on it, probably due to a scratch. "I love you, Pattery," she said. "I love you more than myself!" Perventia snuggled up next to Pattery, careful not to let too much of her body weight onto the bed, still holding his hand. Suddenly, she perceived a flicker of movement at his hand, grazing hers. And at that moment, she *knew*.

That was a sign that Pattery had understood her – he had heard her, had comprehended all she had said. A smile, born entirely out of joy, found its way onto her face, and Perventia snuggled up even closer to her husband.

Chapter 21

"Stay."

Marisii was lying in his hospital bed, next to that of his brother Kastilius, his mind occupied by thoughts of the librarian Makio – and more specifically, whether he was doing okay. Marisii wanted to check up on him and see how he was – but was that appropriate? After all, they had met one moment and in the next Makio was flung through the library, without knowing why, or what was happening. The librarian was bound to have many questions.

Marisii noticed Kastilius burrowed deep in thought as well and decided to initiate a conversation. "What are you thinking about?" Marisii asked him.

"Nothing," Kastilius answered sharply. "I'm just mulling over what happened, that's all."

"Maybe you're thinking about the heroic deed that you did?" Marisii smiled.

"Oh, that?" Kastilius cracked a suspicious laugh. "I don't even know why I did it, so don't get too excited!"

"I think I know why you did it!" Marisii said.

"Is that so?"

"Because you finally realized that you are a part of this family and you belong with us!" Marisii stated matter-of-factly. "You almost sacrificed yourself for me – that's something only a hero would do. And in the process, you stood up not only for me but also for our entire family!"

~~~~~~~~~~

But from all that Marisii had said, only one portion caught Kastilius's attention – the words *'you belong with us'*. Those words echoed in his mind and made him think. Did he *really* belong with *them*? And if that was even remotely true, why had he always felt like he was meant to be someplace else? *With* someone else?

The truth was, he was thinking about what Feever had done. Why was she so bent on killing Marisii but the second she saw Kastilius, she'd lowered her guard? Why hadn't she harmed them? She was chasing them all in order to kill them gradually, wasn't she?

~~~~~~~~~~

"I'm going to go check up on Makio!" Marisii said enthusiastically, almost jumping out of the hospital bed.

"Makio?" Kastilius asked, a tinge of confusion present in his voice.

"The librarian," Marisii clarified. "I want to make sure he's okay after everything that happened."

"As you wish," Kastilius said.

Marisii cracked an excited smile, exiting the hospital room. He noticed the head medical nurse Annora, who just happened to be passing by.

"Excuse me," Marisii stopped her. "Where can I find Makio's room? He was with my family and I when we came here – tall, black hair, wearing glasses?"

"Room ⊠918 – just at the end of this hallway," Annora said.

Marisii thanked her, and the two of them set off to opposite ends of the hospital. Marisii quickly located Room ⊠918 and entered. Upon seeing him, Makio smiled widely, from where he was sitting upright on the hospital bed.

"If it isn't the man from the reception," Makio chuckled, making space for Marisii on the bed. But he chose to remain standing. "I thought you were dead. That woman who invaded the library showed me who's boss!"

Marisii chose to refrain from commenting on this topic, preventing Makio from asking too many questions in the process and involving him in his family drama.

"Who was that dame?" Makio asked, still chuckling. "I gotta admit, she looked terrifying!"

"I haven't the faintest idea," Marisii lied with a smile.

"Enough about her!" Makio said, leaving his half-eaten yogurt on the side table – Marisii didn't know how he hadn't noticed that Makio was eating. He guessed his mind was occupied by other things. "Anyway, I'm glad you aren't dead!" Makio laughed lightly, causing Marisii to do the same. "I'm also glad to be seeing you!"

Marisii smiled – Makio was very kind.

"It would have been a shame for such a handsome man to die!" Makio smiled again, but clearly with a sense of purpose behind it this time.

"You think I'm handsome?" Marisii couldn't help blushing.

"Believe me, you are," Makio said. "I've seen my fair share of men, and they can't hold a candle to you!"

"Thank you."

"You're welcome," Makio answered warmly, and then the two of them remained silent for a few moments.

"I wanted to check whether you were okay," Marisii tore the silence. "That's why I came."

"I'm fine, thank you for coming and checking." Then another smile appeared on Makio's face, the sense of purpose brighter than ever. "And what's the handsome gentleman's name? I never heard him say it."

"Me?" Marisii blushed even more.

Makio nodded.

"Marisii Klauzer," at last he introduced himself.

"You know," Makio echoed a laugh. "Your name sounds oddly exciting. Especially your surname – it adds a layer to your whole name that sounds interestingly charming!"

"Thank you, I guess?" Marisii answered, all signs of blushing going away. Why was Makio paying him so many compliments? What was the purpose behind them?

"Can I ask you something?" Makio said carefully.

"Shoot."

"Are you gay or straight? Cause I'm sensing something hetero, but also gay about you."

Marisii's body shifted uncomfortably, tensing; he didn't think it was appropriate or right for Makio to be asking him such privacy-invading questions. And so directly too. Makio was quick to apologize after apparently noticing Marisii's reaction.

"No, no, I didn't mean it as a bad thing!" Makio said. "I'm sorry if I made you feel uncomfortable. I just have this odd feeling, with which I can sense people's sexual orientation. But yours is hard to figure out – I think you might be playing for both teams!"

"Yeah, you're right," Marisii said, still alarmed, "I *did* feel uncomfortable, and I don't think it's really polite to be asking me such questions. For your information, even though I'm almost 20 years old, I've never had a significant other – a boyfriend *or* a girlfriend. And I've never felt a particular attraction to either of the genders, so I can't really answer your inappropriate question!"

"So, you're asexual?"

"For now," Marisii said. "I think I'm still in this phase where you're figuring out your sexuality, trying to discover what you like and what you don't. None of the genders have attracted me with anything, so I guess for now I identify as asexual, as you guessed."

"Right," Makio said. "I'm really *sorry* if I made you feel in any way uncomfortable. I'm just more direct with people, you know. I just say what I think when I think it, without thinking twice. I'm sorry."

"Don't worry about it," Marisii assured him. "It's a good quality in some respects."

"It's not always good." Makio shook his head.

Marisii had inched closer to the bed and Makio, now only half a meter separating them. Marisii looked at him curiously. "What about you?"

"What *about* me?"

"What's your orientation?" Marisii asked him his *own* question.

"I'm gay," Makio answered bluntly. "I've always been gay. I've never felt anything more than friendship towards a member of the female gender. You're not a homophobe, are you?" Makio's voice suddenly tensed at the last question.

"Of course I'm not!" Marisii responded, almost straight away. "For me, homophobes are people who are afraid of the different, people who *refuse* to accept the different, and that's why they harass anyone who dares to identify themselves as something outside of their toxic views. Their behavior is stupid and not needed!"

"I'm really glad you think that way," Makio smiled genuinely. "Once again, I'm sorry."

Marisii had already forgiven him because Makio seemed like a nice, genuine guy, and Marisii appreciated meeting such people.

"Don't worry, it's all good," Marisii assured him once more, causing himself *and* Makio to smile. "I should better get back to my room – I did what I came here to do," Marisii said, running his right hand through his impressive-looking chocolate hair.

"No, stay," Makio said, stopping Marisii in his tracks, who had already headed for the door. Makio's own black hair looked messy, yet oddly charming. His black-framed glasses were cracked, but still resting steadily on his nose and above his ears. "I'm all alone in this room and you're really nice company. Why don't you stay to chat a little bit longer? I enjoy communicating with you because it's clear that you're a broad-minded, respectful individual, with a humane understanding of things."

"You're the same. I guess that's why we understand each other?" Marisii nodded warmly, trying not to smile for the hundredth time today. He pulled a small, soft armchair out of the small side table nearby, and took his seat next to Makio's bed, facing him directly. "I will *stay*."

Chapter 22

A peculiar meeting

Kastilius was standing next to his hospital room's window, observing the commotion on the street out front. The cars and people were moving about with, Kastilius guessed, the same pace, bored in their mundaneness. The room's door was propped wide open, the commotion in the corridor outside of it quite evident. But his ears picked up on someone's footsteps approaching – the person closed the door shortly after entering. Kastilius turned around, his eyes finding a woman with deep raven hair, wearing a long dress mixing shades of onyx black and Prussian blue, low-heeled shoes and a long dark silk cloak enveloping her shoulders, and dragging on the floor behind her as she walked.

"Please, do not be scared!" Feever's voice was almost a worried whisper. "I mean no harm."

"First," Kastilius said, observing her carefully, "I'm not scared of you even one bit. And second, I've got nothing to lose, so give me your best shot!"

Kastilius had never felt like a true part of his family, thinking there must have been something wrong with him. He didn't consider himself depressed, but he just thought his life served no point. Feever looked at him compassionately. Kastilius couldn't comprehend why she was behaving in such a way ever since her attack on the Straightvur library. Why was she looking at him *that* way? Why didn't she want to tear him apart from limb to limb like she had the others? Why had she stopped her attack on Marisii and *him*?

"Can we talk?" Feever asked, inviting him to sit on one of the two beds in the hospital room with a gentle wave of her hand. But he shook his head.

"I think you can talk just as well from where you're standing," Kastilius said, not wanting to be too close to the mighty Salem witch.

"Okay," Feever agreed, continuing to observe Kastilius with that compassionate, almost empathetic look. "Kastilius, can I ask you something?"

"Go ahead."

"Have you ever had a feeling that you don't belong with your family?" Feever said. "An intrusive feeling that burns you from the inside? A feeling that just *tells* you that you belong somewhere else?"

Kastilius regarded her with an expressionless gaze. "Why are you asking such questions?" His voice rose an octave.

"Please, just answer my question," Feever said.

"Why do you need *this* answer?" The volume of his voice decreased, the young man moving away from the window and inching closer to Feever, ignoring his previous reservations. "You can kill me right here and right now, so what are you waiting for?" He bared his teeth. "I thought you wanted to kill us all, right? Why don't you start with me? Why are you asking me such questions – you need some sort of information, is that it? Is that why you chose not to attack me in the library?"

Kastilius had been angry all his life, not just from this moment, and of Feever's questions.

"I will provide you with answers to every single one of your questions," Feever assured him in a calm, soothing tone, "but first, I will need the answers to *my* questions!"

Kastilius found himself calming down gradually. He scratched his forehead lightly and looked at Feever again, his voice's tone returning to his usual one: "I've felt like an outsider in my family all my life if that's what you want to know. I've never…" He paused for a moment, remembering the past 16 years. "I've never felt like a part of them, or anything else. So yeah – to answer your question yeah, I've never felt like I belonged with them! Tell me now, why do you need this answer?"

Feever let out a sigh of relief. She was watching Kastilius and suddenly, tears formed in her eyes, overflowing almost instantly after.

Kastilius was taken by surprise – Feever gave the impression of a woman who wasn't moved that easily by anything. Kastilius had been left with the impression that the woman standing before him wasn't capable of emotions. And yet there she was, crying, seeming more vulnerable than ever. And if he were any of the other members of the two families, he would have tried to take her on right here and right now. But Kastilius didn't want that. More importantly, he didn't think he would be able to outsmart or defeat her, even in her moment of supposed distraction. But for whatever reason, inconceivable to him, after seeing her so vulnerable, he wanted to hear what she had to say. Kastilius didn't want to try to fight Feever – just hear her story.

"I found you!" Feever said, her voice slightly nasal. "I finally found you after all those horrible years I spent encased in that coffin!"

"What are you talking about?" Kastilius inquired with a frown on his face. While talking to her he didn't feel any fear or worry, simply because he was neither afraid of, nor worried by, the Salem witch. "What coffin? Why are you crying? You found *me*? When have you even looked for me? And why?"

"Give me your hand," she said, outstretching her own.

Kastilius drew away precariously.

"Trust me," Feever said pleadingly. *Her eyes*, Kastilius thought, *are sincere. "Please."*

Kastilius stepped a bit closer, watching Feever's outstretched hand. He shrugged his shoulders – as he'd said earlier, he had nothing to lose, so why the hell not? Kastilius intertwined his hand with Feever's. A vast lilac-white light started erupting out of the place where their two palms were linked together. Kastilius closed his eyes involuntarily shortly after, the torrent of light too bright for him to handle. He soon realized that even with his eyes closed a picture started playing out in front of him.

Chapter 23

Kastilius's birth – Part I

Feever slammed the wooden door after herself, her round belly aching.

"Mother?" she asked, panic in her voice. "Mother, are you here?"

Feever's mother – Henrietta – emerged out of the kitchen, which was linked to the living room. Feever, from her place on the doorstep, hadn't initially noticed her at all. But Henrietta's sharp look in her eyes immediately told her that *she* had noticed that Feever's waters had broken.

"It's time, Mother!" Feever said, and then she felt a firm kick in her stomach and let out a shrill cry.

Henrietta helped Feever walk to one of the bedrooms on the first floor, positioning her carefully on the mattress. Feever screamed out in pain again.

"Harietta, come here at once, whatever you're doing!" Henrietta shouted.

Harietta – Henrietta's sister and Feever's aunt – reached the bedroom within mere seconds. Feever looked at her and knew that she didn't need any further explanation.

"Bring warm wet towels from the kitchen immediately!" Harietta instructed Henrietta in panic, and she disappeared from the room. Harietta stepped closer to her niece, getting down to her knees, taking Feever's hand in hers for support. "Relax, darling," Harietta said. "Everything's going to be okay!"

Feever gripped Harietta's hand tightly and screamed again. "I wish Sinistery and Kervantii were here."

"I know," Harietta said, her voice darkened. "Me too, my darling."

Henrietta came back from the kitchen with the warm wet towels and also a bucket of warm water, which she set on the floor, next to the bed. There was a certain pattern to this family's appearance – they were all relatively tall with extremely dark, and long hair, with Harietta being the exception who had light chestnut. Their cheekbones were prominent, their faces radiating with a trace of a certain light, which had clearly been snuffed out by something.

"Keep one on her forehead," Harietta instructed Henrietta, and she listened. Then Harietta focused all her attention on her niece. "Okay, now I want you to push. You will feel terrible pain and for a moment you might feel as though you're dying, but I promise you it will all be worth it at the end!" It was clear Harietta had assisted women in labor before – the way she held herself, the way she chose her words carefully, but at the same time bluntly. "Are you ready?"

Feever nodded.

"Push!" Harietta said and Feever started pushing, still holding on to her aunt's hand, her screams of pain resuming with a new level of intensity. The wet towel almost fell off.

"You can do it, honey!" Henrietta encouraged, taking hold of her other hand, Feever's grip immediately tightening.

"Again!" Harietta said.

Feever felt the baby's head emerging out slowly. Feever pushed again. And then again. And again.

"It's almost over," Henrietta said, almost in relief, tears forming in her eyes. "Just one more push, honey!"

Feever took a deep breath and pushed, putting all the strength left in her body into the motion. Harietta let out a relatively high-pitched sound of happiness, Feever felt immense relief and pushed the towel away from her forehead, and Henrietta smiled broadly. Harietta cut the umbilical cord with a small knife she had in her pocket, carefully took the little crying baby in her arms, and almost immediately passed it on to its mother.

"It's a boy," Harietta announced.

Feever smiled at *her* baby, marveling at the sight of this little creature, caressing his little head and hands.

"What are you going to call him?" Henrietta asked her daughter.

Feever looked up at her mother and smiled genuinely, her whole body warm with a feeling she hadn't experienced in a long time – *happiness*. Harietta had been right – it *was* worth it.

"Kastilius," Feever said, "his name is going to be Kastilius!"

Chapter 24

Kastilius's birth – Part 2

While admiring Kastilius the three women suddenly became distracted by a loud sound, sounding like dozens upon dozens of approaching footsteps.

"What's going on?" Feever asked Henrietta and Harietta, worry darkening her voice.

"Stay here!" Henrietta instructed and then she headed carefully for the front door, leaving Feever and Harietta by themselves in the bedroom. Feever's mother opened the door to see what all the commotion was about. In return, she got a vast crowd of angry townsmen, holding flaming torches in their hands. The night had fallen, and the torches were lighting the citizens' already red faces.

"What do you want?"

"We heard Feever had the baby," one of the citizens said, a middle-aged man, leading the crowd. "General Scrouch sent us to kill the baby because when they grow up, they might prove to be a threat to our community! We *need* to protect Salem; at all costs!"

"Excuse me?" Henrietta asked in immense disbelief. "You've come here to kill a baby? A defenseless, innocent baby?"

"That's right!" the leader of the crowd confirmed.

"Haven't you taken enough away from us already?" Henrietta said, a lingering, profound sense of sadness in her vocal cords. "You and your *general*? What's the matter with you folk? Why are you listening to that prick Scrouch? It's clear the only things he's interested in are money and prostitutes – he doesn't care about you, *or* Salem. And despite all that, you continue to serve him!"

"We need to protect Salem!" the man said.

"You think by killing a *baby* you're going to somehow keep Salem safe? Safe from what – overpopulation?"

"Salem is mighty, and it always will be – we'll make sure of that!" the man said and Henrietta could clearly see that his brain had already been brainwashed beyond repair by Scrouch. "Now please, step aside so we can do our job!" The man started entering but his path was instantly blocked by Henrietta.

"No!" she said firmly. "You have no right to enter my home!"

"We are working under direct orders from General Scrouch," he almost hissed at her. "If you interfere, we will have to eliminate you too!" Then he tried entering again but he was once again blocked by her.

"Do you remember the moment when you took everything away from my family and I, because you and your mighty general thought we were witches, but you didn't have any proof?"

The man nodded in response.

"Well," a huge, devious smile spread out over Henrietta's face, "now you do!" Henrietta waved her right hand high above her and the man suddenly lifted from the ground, stuck in the air. Henrietta was obviously controlling that state, with the rest of the townsfolk letting out terrified gasps and wails. "We're witches!" Henrietta said, eyes bulging out like a madman's. "Dangerous witches that are not afraid to use their powers!" Henrietta turned to the rest of Scrouch's followers. "A small example of what may happen to you too!" Henrietta waved her left hand in the air, and out of the blue, a five-meter-long wooden pole appeared directly below the man. Now both the pole and the man were lingering in the air, their fates entirely in Henrietta's hands. She then lowered her right hand, and the man fell spine first on the pole, impaling himself, blood splattering his fellow citizens and the ground around them. They all gasped in disgust, fright, and surprise at the same time.

"Anyone else willing to try me?" Henrietta cracked a wicked smile, noticing immediately after how two of the citizens started running in her direction, each with a torch in hand. The impaled man fell on the ground loudly, because Henrietta's hands were now focusing entirely on the two approaching figures – the witch now outstretched her hands in their direction, causing the torches to fly out of their hands and fall on their heads and bodies, setting them on blazing fire. The two men started frantically running around, screaming and trying to escape the approaching fiery death.

"BURN THE WITCH!" One of the dozens of women in the crowd screamed. Henrietta closed the door shut, locking it immediately after, feeling the citizens' loud banging on the wood surface. Henrietta returned to Harietta and Feever in the bedroom within seconds, her feet skittering on the floor.

"You need to run – *now!*" Henrietta told her daughter Feever.

"Why, what's happening?" Feever asked, clearly confused by Henrietta's words and all the shouting and banging outside their house.

"General Scrouch has sent an angry mob to kill Kastilius! They see Kastilius as a threat to Salem's future and think that by killing him they will somehow protect Salem!"

"That's madness!" Harietta declared.

"I know," Henrietta said, "but I'm hardly surprised. Scrouch would do anything to *'protect Salem'.*" Then she turned to her daughter, a proud look in Henrietta's eyes. "That is why you need to run, honey! They want Kastilius but we won't let them have him! We won't let them take him away from us too! Harietta and I will buy you as much time as we're capable of – you take Kastilius and run far, as far away as you can manage from this pathetic excuse of a town!"

"But I can't leave you," Feever said, looking as if she had almost forgotten about the newborn baby in her hands, amidst all the panic. "You're the only family I have left!"

Henrietta leaned in close to Feever and Kastilius, gently caressing Kastilius's bright pink forehead with her palm. "From now on Kastilius is going to be your family! Protect him, dear, protect him and don't let anyone ever hurt him!"

Harietta and Henrietta helped Feever stand up from the bed, with the now crying Kastilius in her hands. In the next moment, a male citizen broke in through one of the two wooden windows in the living room, holding a long flaming torch in his right hand.

"BURN THE WITCHES!" he was shouting while threateningly approaching the three witches at a steady pace.

"Are you nuts? This is our home, get out of here!" Harietta commanded, thrusting a hand in the air and making him fly out the window he had come through.

"BURN THE WITCHES!" The three women heard a fanatic-sounding woman shrieking from outside. Then they heard glass in the kitchen breaking, Henrietta's nostrils invaded by the sudden smell of smoke fumes. *Fire* – an entity that was sure to hurt two out of the three witches.

"Honey, you need to go!" Henrietta said and then together with Harietta, they aided Feever in reaching the back door down the hallway of the first floor of the two-story house.

"Will I ever see you again?" Feever asked them. As she looked at them, tears formed in her eyes.

"I sincerely hope so, my dear." Harietta smiled warmly in response.

"Go!" Henrietta almost commanded and a second later Feever was gone.

The front door gave in and crumbled loudly to the floor, both sisters noticing the dozens of footsteps approaching, searching. They smiled at one another and stepped out of the bedroom, locking gazes with the dozens of citizens walking about in their house.

"Are you ready to smash some witchphobes?" Henrietta asked her sister.

"Oh, yeah," Harietta smiled deviously. Then, the sister witches outstretched their hands up in the air in synchronicity, making two female citizens situated at the front of the crowd, bump against one another, their skulls cracking sharply.

~~~~~~~~~~

Feever was running away from her *own* home when a citizen jumped out in front of her, effectively blocking her path.

"MOVE!" Feever shrieked, holding the crying Kastilius in her arms, her knees drained of strength.

"Wait, wait." The citizen stopped Feever from killing him, who was just about to wave her hand. "I need to tell you something important!"

"And why would I listen to anything *you* have to say?"

"General Scrouch indeed gave the order to kill your baby. *But* he got the intel and the suggestion for the kill from…"

"Let me guess – Sarvit and Mour?" She smiled – but this time that smile was infused with indescribable anger.

"How do you know that?"

"It just makes perfect sense!" Feever clarified and waved her hand towards the citizen lightly, making him fly out of her way.

Suddenly, the Salem witch heard an explosion and immediately turned back in the direction the sound was coming from. Her house had just blown up in pieces. She looked around carefully but there was no one left alive, except for her and the citizen whose life she had decided to spare, who was now retreating to Salem. Two more people Feever loved more than anything else in the world had been taken away from her. Where would it end?

Feever stared at her ruin of her house for a few more seconds, then looked at her son Kastilius who was still crying. Pressing him against her chest, the witch resumed running, not daring to turn back again.

Chapter 25

A smart exchange

Several centuries later the medical nurse Annora was standing behind the reception in the hospital. She had recently graduated from the medical university in Kasterfainz and had started working at the hospital, initially as a paid intern. But within several months Annora had been given more and more responsibilities and she was steadfastly on her way to becoming head nurse. She was now called in to assist in delivering a baby. Annora started running to the designated room – ⊠402, reaching it within a minute. She entered the room almost immediately, registering the woman who was about to deliver the baby and her husband holding and squeezing her hand in his supportively. Annora quickly realized that she hadn't been called in for any assistance – *she* was supposed to deliver the baby. Annora could hardly believe it, even though she had passed her specialty training with flying colors. But still, the more expert medical team must have really trusted her.

"Hello," she introduced herself, "my name is Annora and I…"

"Brouzenvert, and this is my wife Berventy!" the man interrupted her in a hurry. "I don't think we have time for chitchat, do you? *Help her!*"

Annora stepped closer to Berventy, who was laying on the bed in pain, and took her free hand: "Everything's going to be alright!"

Berventy squeezed Annora's hand rather hard, and then the medical nurse let go of it and got down to business.

~~~~~~~~~~

The baby was born in a timely manner, safe and well. Huge smiles appeared on Berventy and Brouzenvert's faces when they saw the little guy out into the world. The parents explained to Annora that this baby boy was their fifth son – but they had no clue as to what to call him.

"I just need to take him for some additional tests. They shouldn't take long, and it will give you time to think of a name." Annora smiled genuinely at Berventy and Brouzenvert, who passed the baby boy on to the nurse. Annora left the hospital room, gently holding the newborn in her arms.

Annora made her way to the postnatal ward and upon reaching it she took her staff card out of her pocket, flashed it in front of the scanner and after the beep and the green light, she gained access to the ward. Annora stepped inside and placed the baby in a hospital bassinet carefully. She watched him for a few seconds, admiring the little twitching form in front of her.

"You are one healthy little babe, you know that?" Annora said with a smile. That was her first delivery and she was immensely happy that it had proceeded successfully.

Annora suddenly heard the sound of the door opening and turned to see who it was. It must have been someone from the hospital staff – no one else had access to the postnatal ward or any other ward of the hospital for that matter. Not without their staff card. To her surprise, Annora saw a tall woman with dark hair, wearing a long dress mixing shades of black and blue and old-fashioned low-heeled shoes of similar colors, carefully holding a baby in her arms.

"Hello," Annora said and stepped closer to the woman that had appeared out of literally nowhere. "I don't mean to be rude but how did you get in here? Only the hospital staff has access to this ward."

The woman freed one of her hands, putting all the weight of the baby on the other, and lifted it in Annora's direction, her voice cutting like a razor: "Hypnosis!"

Suddenly, Annora forgot all about her duties as a staff member of the hospital, forgot all she ever knew about her life – the only thing she was *certain* of now was her obedience to this odd woman; her wish – Annora's command.

"My name is Feever and you are under *my* control!" the woman said.

"I am under your control!" Annora repeated essentially, her voice sounding like a robot's, who had just been ordered to do something and its master expecting it to be done without a second thought.

~~~~~~~~~~

"Listen to what I want you to do," Feever began, her right hand still poised in the air towards Annora. "I want you to take this baby I'm holding in my hands and give it to Berventy and Brouzenvert Klauzer! Because they clearly have no idea what to name him, suggest the name Kastilius. If they refuse, be insistent! This baby *won't* carry any other name, only Kastilius. Do you understand?"

"His name will be Kastilius!" Annora confirmed, hypnotized.

"Good," Feever said gladly. "Give their baby up for adoption; or throw it in the trash, I couldn't care less! But you need to exchange the babies no matter what – even at the cost of your own life!"

"Even at the cost of my own life!" Annora repeated mechanically.

Feever, still keeping her hand in the air, stepped closer to Annora and passed her by. Her eyes set on Berventy and Brouzenvert's baby – the name Klauzer was printed on a sheet of paper and glued to his hospital bassinet. Feever carefully placed Kastilius next to the bassinet, freeing her left hand, her right still controlling Annora. She directed her left hand toward the Klauzers' baby, whereupon he lifted and hovered in the air. The baby started crying.

"Shut up!" Feever commanded, and the baby ceased. Feever looked around all the other bassinets, noticing a section of the postnatal ward, further down the vast space, labeled 'For adoption'. Feever placed the baby in one of the free bassinets in the section and lightly squeezed her own hand, making the baby sink into slumber. Then she turned to her son – Kastilius. Feever gently took him in her now free left hand and placed him inside the Klauzer bassinet. She planted a firm kiss on his tiny forehead, the baby smiling at her.

"I love you, Kastilius," she said while watching him, unconditional love in her eyes. "One day in the distant future we will terrorize the Klauzer and the Fehrenberg families together. You will fight by my side, and together we will avenge our loved ones! You will grow up in Berventy and Brouzenvert's care, but when the time comes you will join me and, together, we will rule the world! The two of us are going to make the people who hurt us pay dearly!" Feever took a small blue bracelet out of her single dress pocket and tied it around Kastilius's tiny wrist. "Keep this bracelet. With the help of it, you're going to recognize who the foe and who the friend is, one day when we meet again."

Feever sensed movement in Annora's limbs and turned her head to see the nurse's right hand twitching lightly. Her consciousness must be trying to shake off the trance. Feever had to hurry.

"I love you, Kastilius," the witch said again. "We *will* be together again one day, I promise!"

Feever drifted away from her only son, but without much desire to, and headed in Annora's direction one last time, all the while still keeping her right hand poised in the air. "Make Berventy and Brouzenvert accept the bracelet around the baby's wrist as a gift from this hospital or something! Convince them that the bracelet is a lucky charm, bringing happiness and health or some bullshit, and that Kastilius *must* wear it all the time. You got that?"

"I got it," Annora answered mechanically.

"Good," Feever nodded, pleased. Then, she squeezed her right hand tightly and Annora collapsed to the floor, her eyes closing. Afterward, Feever flicked both her hands in front of herself and disappeared into a puff of blue and purple smoke.

~~~~~~~~~~

Annora returned to room ☒402, smiling widely at Berventy and Brouzenvert. "You will be happy to know that your baby is in excellent condition!"

"Thank *you*," Berventy said sincerely, "you really helped us!"

"There's no need," Annora continued to smile, "that's my job." The nurse left the checklists she was holding, on the table next to Berventy's bed and Brouzenvert's chair and drew nearer to the two parents. "You know what, I think I might have a solution to your 'baby name' problem. It's more of a suggestion really."

"Is that so?" Brouzenvert said, Annora sensing a tinge of surprise in his voice.

"Yes." Annora nodded confidently. "What do you think of the name 'Kastilius'?"

Brouzenvert and Berventy discussed it for a few moments, visibly excited by this unusual suggestion.

"We named our previous son Kasteron," Berventy said to Annora, her eyes shifting from her husband to the nurse. "So, I think the name Kastilius would fit the baby perfectly – it has a certain ring to it!"

"How did you come up with such a name?" Brouzenvert also looked at Annora, with a smile. "It's not a name you meet every day."

Annora mulled his question over for a couple of seconds, trying to remember how she had *indeed* come up with such an unusual name. Yet her mind didn't offer any intel. "It just appeared in my mind, I guess. You like the suggestion then?"

"It's perfect!" Brouzenvert exclaimed happily.

"I'm glad you like it." Annora smiled yet again. "Oh, another thing – I took the liberty of tying a tiny blue bracelet around your baby's wrist, as a gift and a 'thank you' that you put your trust in us for this very special event. We do that with all the newborns – it's proven to bring luck and good fortune. I hope you don't mind?"

"We don't," Berventy said. "In fact, that's really kind of you, thank you for that."

"The pleasure is all mine," Annora said with a smile, not having even the faintest clue what had happened, when had she put the bracelet around the baby's wrist, and why had she suggested the name 'Kastilius'.

Chapter 26

"Soon."

The torrent of vast lilac-white light, consuming Feever and Kastilius's entwined palms, disappeared, their hands ceasing contact. Feever's eyelids snapped open – Kastilius had moved to his hospital room's window, a bit dazed, but fully conscious at least.

"Kastilius?" Feever said. "Are you okay?"

It all made sense for Kastilius now. He now knew why he never felt like he belonged with the Klauzer family, why he could never feel the love of his mother Berventy, his father Brouzenvert, or all his brothers, toward him. Ever since he could remember he had been wearing that bright blue bracelet the medical staff had gifted him on the day he was born. *That* bracelet was the one thing he could always count on – the one thing in his life that was real. Precisely why he had been wearing it ever since that day, oddly still fitting his wrist after all these years. Even now, the blue bracelet was tied around his right wrist – and Feever noticed that.

"I see you're still wearing the bracelet," Feever said softly.

Kastilius just averted his eyes toward the bracelet, holding onto it like a lifeboat, not saying anything in response.

"I know all I've just shown you is incredibly hard to believe," Feever started. "But it's the *truth*! I gave you up to the Klauzer family because I wanted you to be safe. And to grow up so when the time came you could fight shoulder to shoulder alongside me. So together we could get revenge on the people who hurt us! I wanted you to watch my enemies, so when you joined me, you could tell me what you've learned. But most importantly, I wanted you to be safe and grow up in a hassle-free environment."

Kastilius sniffed – his 'real' mother Berventy had never said anything even remotely close to that.

"*But* now I see that maybe it was a mistake," Feever continued. "You've felt rejected for so many years all because of what *I* did!"

"What?" Kastilius said, a certain edge to his voice.

"I gave you to *them*, and they…" Feever paused. "They couldn't even provide you with a drop of love. For 16 years you've lived in a family you felt rejected and misunderstood in! And it's because of me – *I* gave you to *them*, I made that choice!"

"NO!" Kastilius screamed suddenly, making the formidable Salem witch Feever jump. He stepped closer to her. "Yes, *you* made that choice, *you* gave me to them, but *they* are the ones at fault for how I felt! For most of the years I was growing up I kept hearing the same – how Brouzun got accepted into a high-end college, how Morven found a prestigious job, how Marisii turned out to be such a kind and reliable individual, how Kasteron had such great luck with girls! My so-called 'mother' Berventy was telling me all that and then looked at me with an uncertain gaze that screamed: '*What are* you *going to turn out to be?*'. When I turned to my father Brouzenvert he just shrugged me off with a hand, stating that it was too early for me to worry about such matters."

Feever looked at him, tears pooling in her eyes. Kastilius felt his own tears threatening to become evident.

"And you're right," Kastilius said suddenly, after a momentary pause. "I want to get revenge for what they did to me, and you. I also want to know the full story of what their ancestors did to you back in Salem, and how exactly they hurt you. The events you showed me seemed like only a fraction of the story!"

"Of course," Feever said, her tears doubling, finally overflowing.

"And I need to know one more thing," Kastilius said, keeping his in check for now.

"Yes?"

"Do you love me?" Kastilius asked her unsurely, his voice quivering.

"*Kastilius,*" Feever said, stepping even closer to her son. "You're the most precious person in the world to me – of course *I love you!*"

Kastilius smiled broadly – he couldn't remember the last time someone from the Klauzer family told him they loved him. Or more specifically, he couldn't remember the last time he could feel such genuine affection – if there ever really was any. He started walking toward Feever with a confident stride, pulling her into a tight embrace. Feever wrapped her arms around Kastilius's waist because he was at least ten centimeters taller than her. The two of them stayed like that for a few seconds – mother and son, in each other's arms – before breaking apart. Kastilius suddenly heard footsteps, approaching from the hallway outside – he recognized them as Marisii's by the excited force with which he was usually striding.

"I have to go," Feever said, even though Kastilius could sense she didn't want to.

"What?" Kastilius's voice gave away his sudden fright of separation. "But you just came!"

"I'm going to be back!" Feever assured him. "Very soon, I will return to you and *then* we'll be ready to unleash our revenge on the two families! In order to make them suffer to the greatest extent possible we've got to wait for the right moment, do you understand?"

Kastilius nodded. "Promise me that you'll be back!"

"Of course I will be back, my love. Soon, very soon, we *will* be together again!" Feever smiled warmly once again.

Kastilius returned the smile with an even broader one and dried his tears with the long sleeve of his T-shirt. He believed her. He *believed* her with his whole heart and soul. Feever raised her right hand in the air and disappeared into a cloud of black smoke. It dissipated fairly soon after she left.

Kastilius saw Marisii coming into the hospital bedroom with his gaze set on the polished tiles. Kastilius supposed the clueless Marisii hadn't suspected anything out of the ordinary.

"Kastilius, are you okay?" Marisii asked, his eyes inspecting Kastilius's. "Have you been crying?"

Kastilius, who knew he must have looked unusually happy, quickly plastered his usual frown, infilled with anger, back on his face. "When haven't I been okay, you fool?"

And those three short lines of speech were the last things they said to one another for quite some time. Marisii started for his bed, lying down. And Kastilius continued to stare out through the window, just as before, but this time buried deep in thought about his mother Feever.

Chapter 27

Perventia and Pattery

Pattery had regained consciousness a few hours earlier. He felt his right cheek obscured by a huge bandage. With one hell of an effort, he rose from the bed and went to the square mirror, situated at the opposite end of the hospital room, hanging on the green wall. Pattery examined his reflection in the mirror – a 5'11 handsome man, with stubborn stubble and bronze hair. His face reflected his pain from what had been happening to him and his family lately. He peeled the bandage off of his face slowly, a thought at the back of his mind that if he did it faster it would have hurt, and looked at himself in the mirror once again. His whole right cheek and a part of his neck were obscured by Feever's handprint. He had tried to protect his family when she had used her powers on him. When Feever had placed her hand on Pattery's cheek she marked him for life and in that moment took away his every chance of protecting his daughters. And then, he remembered – his daughters!

Teela, he thought. According to The Book, Feever's first victim would have been Teela.

"Pattery?" He heard a familiar voice behind him – Perventia had entered the room.

Pattery turned his burned face toward his wife and when she saw the still continuing aftermath of the attack in the library, she covered her mouth with a hand, tears forming in her eyes.

"She..." Perventia stuttered, obviously meaning Feever. "What has she done to you?" Perventia crossed the small distance separating them and started caressing Pattery's face. "She ruined you."

"Honey," he said, grabbing her hands tighter than usual. Perventia must have gotten the hint because she stopped caressing his bruised face. "That doesn't matter now. I'm not in pain."

Perventia sniffed.

"But you need to tell me," he continued, his tone firm. "Is everyone okay? Teela, is she..." He couldn't allow himself to finish the sentence – to say what he knew to be true out loud.

Perventia's voice came out shakingly. Pattery saw her shivering just by saying it. "You and Morven had it worse," the blond woman started as if initially evading the nagging revelation. "All the rest of us are healing relatively fast thanks to all the hospital staff." Perventia paused. And Pattery knew it was coming. "Teela and Tiffany..."

Pattery let out a sound that was a mixture between a croak and a growl. "Did they both fall victims to Feever?"

"No, no, no, no," Perventia said. Now both Pattery and Perventia's eyes were obscured by tears. "After you lost consciousness the rest of us continued to fight Feever – but she was too strong! She cornered Teela and none of us could help her – we could barely move after Feever's attack..."

"And?" Pattery asked, even though a small part of him didn't want to find out.

"Feever outstretched her hand," Perventia started explaining, "heading straight towards Teela's heart, when..."

147

Pattery knew that the answer that was about to follow would have crushed him.

"...when our brave Tiffany blocked Feever's path, positioning herself in front of her sister."

Pattery let out another mixed sound, more intense and louder than the previous one.

"Tiffany sacrificed herself for Teela!" Perventia said, making it clear as if it wasn't before. "Feever ripped out Tiffany's heart and consumed her undeveloped power. Our little, kind, brave Tiffany's heart."

In the next moment, Pattery erupted into tears, not able to hold back the bubbling up emotion any longer. He made his way to his bed just barely, feeling his knees giving out, threatening to bring him down to the cold floor forever. Perventia sat on the bed next to him, hugging him, both of them grieving over the loss of their second youngest daughter Tiffany Fehrenberg. After about 20 minutes of loud sobs, Pattery felt himself slipping into a panic attack. Perventia noticed that right away. She took his face in her hands and looked him right in the eyes.

"I LOVE YOU!" Her voice raised an octave. "You know that, right? We *will* get through this and everything else that that witch bitch serves us. Do you understand? Like I said when we were explaining The Curse and our family's heritage to Tiffany and Teela, we will push back triple as much! We will make her *suffer* in the precise way she made us!"

Pattery nodded affirmatively, feeling his whole body and mind relax. Perventia had been able to prevent the panic attack from fully occurring. She pulled him closer and kissed him protractedly. With that kiss, Pattery felt as if she somehow quietly confirmed all she had just said.

Chapter 28

Teela's discovery

Teela was standing in her assigned hospital room – she had been put with her boyfriend Kasteron but right now she was by herself. Kasteron had gone over to his parents' room to discuss Morven's upcoming operation today.

Teela was thinking about her older sister Tiffany. She remembered how Tiffany had sacrificed herself for her – the gruesome picture played out in front of her eyes numerous times. Teela *hated* herself. Hated herself for letting Tiffany die – she had just been crawling there, rendered useless to do anything because Feever had overpowered every single member of the two families. How would they defeat her even? Not only was Feever a powerful witch, but also she had taken Tiffany's undiscovered power, which would most probably make her even mightier than before.

We stand no chance against her, Teela was thinking, while heading toward the small bathroom on the opposite end of her room, her limbs finally crying out for any sort of movement. Teela crossed over the bathroom's threshold and walked to the mirror, above the sink. She looked at herself in it. And in there she found a girl who had just lost her sister, expecting to lose another dear to her person, at the hands of Feever. Teela had unlocked her power, but she had not yet found what it exactly was – what was the point of that power then?

She needed it in order to protect her family and herself. She couldn't allow herself to just sit around, waiting for her power to make itself known whenever it felt like it. Teela couldn't take it. She remembered the rage that had surged through her veins at the sight of her sister Tiffany crumbling down to the ground, lifeless, her crimson heart in Feever's hand. Now *that* same rage was overtaking her – stronger than ever.

As Teela was standing in front of the sink, she raised both hands high in the air and then brought them down against the sink's solid white surface. The sink crumbled to her feet into dozens of pieces. Teela jumped, not comprehending what was happening, and involuntarily raised a hand toward the mirror. It blew up into a million pieces, flying in all directions like wild rain. Teela covered her head with her hands, ducking, acutely aware of some of the glass shards flying in her direction.

After the terrible rain had stopped, the dark brown-haired girl turned her head toward the destroyed sink and mirror, standing back up. She opened her eyes, a sight never seen before unraveling in front of them – it looked like a nature element had swooped through the bathroom.

What had she just *done*? She had just waved her hands and… Her eyes averted to the toilet seat – it was raised. With fear in her eyes and unsteady, shaking right hand, Teela waved toward the seat. Next thing she knew, it tore from its base violently, crashing into the bathroom wall. Teela jumped back, her heart racing in her chest. A slightly scared smile found its way across her face.

Perventia Fehrenberg appeared at the bathroom's entrance, only to witness the destruction Teela had caused, sweat glistening on her forehead – she must have heard the crash and come running.

"What happened?" she inquired, worry creeping into her voice. "Are you okay? Who did this?"

"*I* did," Teela said, smiling broader than before.

"*You?*" Perventia struck Teela as surprised. "Does that mean…"

Teela's gaze darted from the fresh destruction in the bathroom to her hands, her smile growing wider and wider.

"I think I discovered my power," Teela said, her eyes not wavering from her hands for even a second, which now felt profoundly infused with power.

Chapter 29

Morven's operation

Marisii Klauzer was preparing himself for his brother Morven's operation. Up until that moment, the hospital staff had been trying to steady him, unsure whether or not Morven's system would be able to sustain the operation. But it had become imperative now – Morven remained in a coma and his condition was getting progressively worse and worse. Odds were fifty-fifty whether he would live after the operation or not – but it was better than nothing. Attending the operation was of vital importance to the Klauzer family and almost all of its members would attend.

"Come on, start getting ready," Marisii prompted his brother Kastilius. "I won't be late to Morven's operation because of you."

Kastilius looked at Marisii. "You know, Marisii," he stood up from his bed, "I don't want to attend the operation!"

Marisii looked at his brother in shock, from his place next to his own bed. He couldn't believe the words that had just escaped from Kastilius's mouth. *"What?"*

"You heard me," Kastilius said with an incredibly cold voice. "The chances of him surviving after that operation are minimal, at best. I don't want to waste my time waiting for him to die!"

Marisii thought he might faint from shock – he knew Kastilius was insensitive, but his words now shook him deep to the core, as they never had before.

"DO YOU HEAR YOURSELF?" Marisii shouted in frustration. "He is your *brother*! What waste of time? You *must* attend – you're a part of *this* family!"

Kastilius squeaked with his mouth. "I've never felt like this! And I never would! I *don't* want to attend Morven's stupid operation and wait for him to drop dead!"

Marisii looked as if at any moment now he would grab Kastilius by the throat and strangle him.

"And would it be such a bad thing if he did die?" Kastilius said. "Feever would kill us all anyway!"

Marisii was staring at Kastilius, unable to recognize him. "I don't know you," the older brother suddenly said. "From now on you are no longer a part of this family, do you understand? GET OUT!"

Kastilius gazed at him, looking as if he were about to burst into laughter.

"GET OUT!" Marisii repeated, unable to keep his rage in check.

Kastilius began gathering his stuff from his and Marisii's hospital room. There wasn't that much, and he was able to grab them in less than five minutes. Then he headed for the door. But not before stepping close to Marisii, only a few inches separating them, whispering in his ear. "I want you to hear me well, *brother*. Very soon, *your* whole family is gonna regret all they've done. Remember this!"

Marisii, unable to control his impulses anymore, raised a fist above Kastilius. But his little brother reacted faster and brought down his *own* fist on Marisii's face.

~~~~~~~~~~

Then Kastilius disappeared out of the room, looking for the hospital's exit. He knew exactly what he would do now – Kastilius was going to find his *real* mother Feever, intending to give her something that would make both of them immensely powerful – The Book. Kastilius knew it lay buried somewhere underneath the library's debris. And then he smiled at the thought that with all that had been happening lately, neither of the two families had thought to look for the one item that could destroy them all if it fell into the wrong hands.

~~~~~~~~~~

Marisii reached the entrance of the surgical ward of the hospital to find his mother Berventy, his father Brouzenvert, and his brothers Brouzun and Kasteron, already standing there in anticipation. It looked to Marisii that all of them were recovering from their wounds relatively fast.

"Where's Kastilius?" Berventy asked, her voice wavering. Marisii saw his mother practically shaking all over.

Through the clear see-through partition glass in front of them, they could all see the surgeons getting ready for the operation in the specifically designed room opposite the Klauzer family. Morven was lying on an operating table, unconscious, several breathing tubes attached to his nostrils and a breathing mask placed over his mouth. The family were painfully aware of Morven's condition, now on the brink of life and death.

"He's not coming," Marisii said bluntly.

"What do you mean *he's not coming*?" Marisii could sense the confusion in his mother's voice. "He's not gonna come for his *brother's* operation? What's wrong with this boy?" Her limbs seemed like they were also shaking. Marisii thought they were more like itching to kick someone.

"I will explain everything later," Marisii said. "What are the surgeons saying about Morven?"

"I don't know, but they are just about to begin the operation," his father Brouzenvert said, his voice wavering, just like his wife's.

"Well, what are we waiting for? Let's go in!" Berventy started for the door next to the vast partition glass, but Marisii stopped her by placing a hand on her right shoulder.

"Mom," Marisii said with a careful, soothing tone. "You know that we're not allowed to go in there!"

"But…" Berventy said, "…Morven needs me! He can't get through this operation without his mother – *I have to* be there for him!"

"Honey," Brouzenvert said, "let the surgeons do their jobs – they know best!"

"No, NO! THEY KNOW NOTHING!" Berventy started shouting. "They don't know what scares Morven, nor what he likes! They know nothing about his allergies! Do they even know his blood type?"

"Mom," Brouzun joined the conversation as well, "we're all worried but we have no other choice. We need to let the surgeons do their jobs; there's nothing else for us to do right now."

"But what if Morven isn't able to handle or live through the operation?" Berventy asked the question that had been preying on everyone's minds, her eyes going back and forth from her husband to her sons. "What if Feever took one of our children and brothers, without us even realizing it?"

Tears pooled in her eyes. Brouzenvert pulled her into a tight hug.

"I can't lose him!" Berventy was crying when she escaped the hug after a few seconds. Again, she looked first at her husband, then at her sons. "I can't lose any of you! And Kastilius…" she made a slight pause, "…he just… it has always been hard for him to feel like a part of this family. But despite him not being here to support his brother when he needs it the most, Kastilius *is* still a part of this family!"

Marisii mulled that over for several moments. His mother was right – Kastilius was *indeed* one of them, even though he outright refused to accept it. And Marisii had told him all those vile things just a couple of minutes ago, and now God knew where Kastilius was. A part of him hated himself for attacking Kastilius in such a direct way, but another part thought it had been needed for quite some time now.

The surgeons in the surgical ward opposite the Klauzer family commenced the operation. Berventy almost adhered herself to the partition glass to observe closely, Brouzenvert, Brouzun, Kasteron, and Marisii standing right next to her. The surgeons began taking the needed surgical instruments to make the first incision into Morven's chest. Marisii stood on Berventy's right side and took her hand in his. She then took Brouzenvert's hand in her left hand, and he took Kasteron's hand. Then Kasteron took Brouzun's hand.

The operation was shaping up to be a long one for the Klauzer family – they had no way of knowing whether Morven was going to wake up after it. But the Klauzer family knew one thing better than anything else – as long as they were together, they were *stronger.*

Chapter 30

Several days later

Marisii was hanging out with Makio in his hospital bedroom, engrossed in a conversation. For the last couple of days, the two of them had been spending a lot of time together, chatting on various topics.

"You know," Marisii said, "I'm really glad you're here. I feel like I can talk with you about anything."

Makio smiled broadly. He, too, had been enjoying Marisii's company. But during the last few days, he had been gathering the courage to ask Marisii something. And he felt like now was the moment. "Marisii?"

"Yeah?"

"The last couple of days have been really nice – and you're absolutely right, we can talk about anything because we understand each other," Makio started, his voice a slight tremble. "But I want to ask you something. It might sound a bit weird to you, and you might even refuse, but I want to ask you about it nevertheless."

"Go ahead." Marisii smiled.

"Do you want…" Makio started but then suddenly stopped.

"Do I want...?" Marisii said.

"To go out on a date with me tonight?" He finally spat it out, and anxiety that Marisii was going to refuse right away or even get angry at him, instantly engulfed him. Makio was gay but he had never had much luck with guys – he had had a single relationship, which had ended badly for him because his boyfriend at the time was jealous of a friend of Makio's, growing toxic over time. *Makio* had ended the relationship, so he could keep his mental state in check, but he was still hurting. But at the same time, he wanted to move on with someone else – someone who *understood* him.

~~~~~~~~~~

Marisii mulled over Makio's offer. Marisii genuinely enjoyed spending time with Makio, and he had never been out on a date in his life – if he didn't count the unsuccessful ones with dumb girls who blew him off, deeming him not interesting enough. It didn't matter for Marisii if he was going to go out on a date with a boy, or a girl – he knew the important part was what was inside.

"Sure," Marisii responded with a smile on his face, "it will be fun – we're going to go to a bar, laugh, and who knows? Maybe even dance."

~~~~~~~~~~

Makio smiled broadly – had Marisii seriously just said yes? "So, it's set," Makio said and rose from Marisii's bed, on which the two of them had been sitting. "I will pick you up at 8 o'clock sharp, from your room."

"You know where to find me." Marisii smiled, lifting his hands in the air demonstratively.

Makio returned the smile. Anxiety and excitement were battling one another in his stomach – he was finally going to go out on a date with a boy, with whom he felt like himself.

Marisii was also evidently excited. He rose from his bed and headed towards Morven's room after letting Makio know what he intended to do. With a wave of his hand, Makio sent him on his way. Not long after that he also left Marisii's room.

~~~~~~~~~~

Brouzenvert and Berventy were situated in Morven's room, sitting on two cushioned chairs, with Morven himself sitting up in the hospital bed. Berventy and Brouzenvert were visibly excited to see him – Morven had survived the operation and now, several days later, was recovering swiftly. The three relatives hadn't seen one another properly in a long time – Morven and his older brother Brouzun – the two eldest sons of the Klauzer family – had left their home many years ago. They had had a huge fight with their parents regarding The Curse and then had left their family, wanting to live a normal life for a couple of years at least. Similarly to what the eldest daughters of the Fehrenberg family – Pacifika, Kayla, and Klacifia – had done, Morven knew.

"I love you so much." Berventy hugged Morven, tighter than usual.

"Okay, okay," he said, out of breath, "don't kill me."

The three of them laughed for a moment.

"She can't help it," Brouzenvert said. "We're just so happy you were able to sustain the operation, my boy!"

"Please," Morven chuckled cheekily. "You think I would give Feever the satisfaction that easily?"

"You've always been a tough boy!" Brouzenvert said firmly, although a smile appeared on his face.

~~~~~~~~~~

At this exact moment, Marisii entered the bedroom, his smile so wide it almost reached his ears.

"To what do we owe this smile, son?" Brouzenvert said, Marisii thought with excitement in his voice. Marisii knew his father Brouzenvert had never really seen him *that* happy.

"I've got a date tonight," Marisii announced, feeling his limbs tickling.

Marisii thought his mother Berventy appeared surprised and he supposed it was because he didn't usually go around dating people.

"You go, tiger." Morven smiled encouragingly.

"Who's the lucky girl?" Berventy inquired.

"Yeah, son, tell us about her," Brouzenvert prompted him. "Is she someone from the Fehrenberg family? Just be careful not to steal Teela from Kasteron." Then Brouzenvert laughed and winked at Marisii.

Marisii suddenly felt extreme discomfort in his gut. His *date* was with Makio – why were his parents asking for a girl? Was there something wrong with going out on a date with a *boy*? "Actually," Marisii started, all the previous enthusiasm drained from his voice, "my date is with Makio – the librarian, who was with us when we fought with Feever. Why are you asking for a *girl*?"

"Oh," Berventy said, once again taken aback. Marisii could see that Morven was also surprised. But then he noticed his father Brouzenvert tightening his fists against his legs.

"Well, there's nothing wro…"

"ABSOLUTELY NOT!" Brouzenvert screamed, his rage surprising everyone in the room. He rose from the chair he was sitting on, knocking it over.

"What's the matter?" Marisii's tone betrayed his fear.

"NONE OF MY SONS WILL BE GAY!" Brouzenvert continued shouting uncontrollably.

"Look, Dad," Marisii started, striving to maintain a calm tone, feeling like his father might explode any second now, "I don't even know if I like him. Makio just asked me out, and I want to find out what could happen."

"Brouzenvert, maybe you shouldn't react so sharply," Berventy said.

"*Not react so sharply?*" Brouzenvert asked, making it seem like the apocalypse. Then his eyes shifted to Marisii, scorching with rage. "That's a shame! Horrific!"

Tears formed in Marisii's eyes within seconds – had he done such a vile deed?

"Dad, you *really* need to calm down," Morven said, as if warning him. "Marisii is a grown man, who can make his own decisions!"

Why was it only his father who couldn't support him?

"I WON'T ALLOW SUCH *SODOMY!*" Brouzenvert declared loudly.

After these words, Marisii erupted into tears and ran away from the hospital room. He just couldn't take his *own* father telling him he was an abomination anymore. He couldn't take being shamed because he wanted to go out on a date with a boy, who understood him. Marisii bumped into his brother Kasteron, and Kasteron's girlfriend Teela, on the way out. They gasped when they saw him.

"Marisii, what is it?" Kasteron searched his brother's face frantically.

Marisii didn't answer his question, just kept running, his tears increasing and increasing.

~~~~~~~~~~

Pattery Fehrenberg rose from his bed, groaning quietly. He was feeling much better than before and wanted to put on the clothes he had come into the hospital with – he was sick of wearing the plain hospital gown. Perventia Fehrenberg stood in front of one of the vast windows in the room nearby. "Do you need some help, honey?"

"Thanks, but I think I'll be fine." Pattery's face was still slightly hurting, because of what Feever had done to him back in the Straightvur library. He was sure that there would be a few scars once his face had fully healed. Pattery was also tired from what had happened – he had lost his daughter Tiffany, and he wasn't even conscious to try and prevent it from happening. But at the same time, Pattery was happy that Teela had found her individual power. Now their chances of fighting and trying to defeat Feever were much greater than before.

~~~~~~~~~~

Perventia could see all that and wanted to do something – anything, to comfort her husband. Pattery stripped down his hospital gown, wearing nothing but violet-crimson boxers underneath. Perventia shifted from the window to Pattery, observing him – even with dozens upon dozens of scratches and cuts he still remained the sexiest and the most beautiful man she had ever seen. Perventia always got excited seeing her muscular husband, wearing nothing but his tight-fitting underwear.

Pattery reached for his black shirt on one of the coat racks, next to the mirror that was hanging from the wall, and slowly put it on. He started buttoning it, but then Perventia's tender hand stopped him. She connected her lips with his passionately, her other hand finding its way inside his boxers.

"What are you doing?" Pattery said.

"Sshh," Perventia whispered playfully, her lips still on his, "enjoy the moment."

Then, she moved from his lips to his neck, kissing it slowly, tenderly, careful to apply just the right amount of spit onto the surface of his skin. After that, she started kissing his whole muscular body – his chest, his abs, his biceps. Even after all the years they had spent together, Perventia *adored* her husband and wanted to show it to him on a regular basis. Her lips reached the waistband of his violet-crimson boxers and she made quick work of them with her hands, discarding them on the floor.

"You don't have to do it, honey," he claimed, but his penis thought otherwise.

"That always calms you down," she said confidently. "As I said, *enjoy the moment.*"

Perventia grasped her husband's whole penis in her right hand and confidently put the whole length of it in her mouth, beginning to work her usual tongue play as well. Pattery moaned loudly in excitement.

"YES!" he shouted. Perventia liked the fact that he wasn't able to control himself. She knew oral sex always drove him crazy. "MORE!"

Perventia intensified her tongue play and applied more spit to Pattery's penis shaft.

"MORE, HONEY!" He continued to moan, Perventia determined to make him come. But not before teasing him a little. She felt Pattery's hand on her blond head, instructing her when to go faster and slower. Another loud moan. "MORE!"

Chapter 31

Makio and Marisii's first date

Makio and Marisii were in a men's clothing store, with Marisii trying on several different leather jackets. Marisii had asked Makio to accompany him on the little shopping errand, but during the whole commute to the store, Marisii hadn't said even a single word.

"That one looks really good on you," Makio almost sighed out loud when he saw Marisii in the third leather jacket – he was mesmerized from the sight in front of him. The leather jacket clung to all the right curves and angles of Marisii's physique.

"Yeah, I guess," Marisii responded neutrally while looking at himself in the tall mirror in front of him. After several moments, the chocolate-haired man drew away from the mirror.

Makio couldn't just stand by and watch this any longer – something was clearly bothering Marisii.

"Marisii, what's going on?" Makio asked, his voice insinuating a tinge of concern. "You've been slumped for the past few hours and now, when we're actually on our first date, trying on clothes that look fabulous on both of us, you look like you'd rather be somewhere else. Almost like this whole date is unpleasant for you."

"I..."

"Were you unsure about our date?" Makio didn't let him finish. A sudden fear flooded his system. He hadn't been out on a date in a very long time, let alone get along with someone as much as he did with Marisii, and he was afraid to not mess things up. "Is that why you look so crestfallen?"

"No," Marisii answered right away, within a mere second – almost like he didn't want Makio to get the wrong idea. Marisii stepped closer to Makio and quickly passed him by, sitting on the small red couches at the opposite end of the dressing room. Makio was still standing up on his feet, observing Marisii. The younger man ran a hand through his hair. "Look, I... something happened that..." Marisii stopped as if the words just couldn't escape his mouth.

Makio stepped closer to Marisii and kneeled in front of him, placing his right palm on Marisii's right cheek, their eyes meeting. "You can tell me." Then the older man let his hand fall back to his side.

"You know my father Brouzenvert, right?"

"I remember him, yes."

"I told him, my mother and one of my brothers that I'm going out on a date," Marisii said. "At first, they were all very excited – until my mother asked me who the lucky girl was."

Makio knew this all too well and what was about to follow.

"I told them I'm going out on a date with a boy, and my father freaked out!" Tears began assaulting Marisii's eyes. "My mother and brother were surprised but they accepted it. But my father started shouting obscenities about how when you like a member of the same gender, you're a sodomite, and then he said that he wouldn't allow any of his sons to be gay!" Marisii buried his head in his hands, murmuring: "Those were his exact same words!"

Right now, Makio wanted nothing more than to rip Brouzenvert's larynx out. He was a *classic* example of a typical homophobe, who, for whatever reason, just *couldn't* accept that boys could be attracted to boys and girls to girls.

"Listen to me," Makio said, looking at Marisii, who raised his head and looked at him too, "there's *nothing* wrong with liking a boy when you're a boy. Your father is one of those people, a homophobe – they're afraid of something that's different, and something that they could *not* possibly understand, so that's why they hate it. My parents – both my mother and father *were* homophobes. When I was in high school, they threw me out of my own home for liking a guy in my class. They said I have dishonored the family."

Marisii continued staring at Makio, his tears ever-growing. Makio gently placed his right hand on his.

"For a really long time after I felt like someone who wasn't deserving of happiness – just because I liked my own gender, I thought I didn't deserve love in my life. But some time passed, and I found people – friends, that accepted me for who I was. Friends, who assured me that there was nothing shameful or disgraceful with me liking a boy." Makio squeezed Marisii's hand lightly. "I'm here for you," he said. "And that's the only thing that matters!"

Without any sort of warning, Makio was pulled into a tight hug. Makio clung to Marisii's arms, not being able to let go. They stayed like that – in each other's arms, for a few minutes, before Marisii finally broke free of the hug. His tears had completely ceased.

"Now," Makio said, "can I just note how cool *you* look in that jacket?"

Marisii laughed.

"I'm serious. If you don't buy it for yourself, I will!" Makio claimed with a firm yet playful tone.

"Let's go to the tills then," Marisii smiled.

"Don't you want to try something else on?"

"Makio," Marisii continued smiling, "we can't spend the entirety of our date in a clothes store!"

Makio smiled back at Marisii, almost chuckling, his stomach in a knot – he couldn't believe that a guy such as Marisii could possibly exist.

~~~~~~~~~~

Makio and Marisii went to a bar – Makio ordered onion rings and a random cocktail from the menu, and Marisii got some gin and potato crisps.

"I bet I will beat you at darts!" Makio said suddenly, sitting on a wooden stool at the counter, next to his date.

"I accept the challenge!" Marisii said confidently when he saw the dartboard adhered to the wall, next to the half-empty pool tables.

Then both men rose from the wooden stools. They walked to the pool tables, passing them by, aiming for the dartboard. The loud chatter between customers and bartenders around the two guys didn't bother them in the slightest. Makio picked up the darts missiles from the board and turned back to Marisii.

"You win by throwing a missile into the inner bullseye – basically, the tiny red circle at the center of the board," Makio explained.

"What's going to be the prize for the winner?" Marisii asked, a cheeky, flirty smile, plastered across his attractive face. For the first time ever he felt like himself, free and genuinely having fun.

"We'll see," Makio winked at him and passed him two of the missiles. Then, without even waiting for Marisii to get ready, he shot a missile toward the dartboard, landing right in the green circle outside the red center. "It's your turn."

Marisii took some time to prepare but then he shot his own dart, also landing right in the green circle, centimeters away from the red center.

"You've played before?" Makio asked surprisedly.

"Several times – when I was a kid," Marisii said.

Makio chuckled. "You're good," he said, fiddling with the other dart in his right hand, raising it in the air. Then, he looked at Marisii and winked at him again. "But I'm better!" Makio shot the dart and it landed right in the middle of the tiny red circle at the center of the board. He smiled at the win, letting out a light gasp.

"You beat me!" Marisii laughed whilst talking. "Congrats, you really *are* good at this game!"

"I believe we said the winner has to claim a prize," Makio said, his tone playful as if Marisii was the board and Makio the dart.

"What do you desire?" Marisii said, hoping that Makio wanted the same thing as him at that very moment.

"I want you to kiss me!" Makio said.

Marisii smiled broadly – ding, ding, ding.

"But if you don't want to, that's okay…" Makio made a pause, his brow suddenly sweating. "I'm not forcing you to…if you don't want to, that's okay…"

Marisii stepped confidently and dangerously closer to Makio.

"Come here!" Marisii almost commanded, grabbing Makio by his leather jacket's collar, and placing his lips on his. Marisii had never kissed anyone before, and he was far from being expert in it, but when Makio's lips connected with his, Marisii felt like he'd always known what to do. Marisii wasn't on edge about it, or anxious that he was going to mess something up – he just kissed Makio passionately, not giving a fuck what the people around them, or his homophobic father, would say. He really didn't give a fuck – all he wanted to do, right at that moment, was kiss this guy he was on a date with. Makio's skin scraped against Marisii's a bit, because of the faint stubble present, but somehow that just added more passion to the kiss. They remained like that – kissing, for a few minutes, until they drew away from one another. Contrary to what was going on inside Marisii's head, the people surrounding him and Makio were actually *smiling* at them, as if cheering them on.

"Wow!" Makio just said.

Is this impression I detect? Marisii thought.

"Yes, *wow!*" Marisii almost repeated, surprised at himself for what he'd just done. He had always been shy and had never had much luck with dating people, but when Marisii's lips had been on Makio's just a few seconds ago, he just knew he didn't *need* any luck.

~~~~~~~~~~

On the way back to the hospital, Marisii and Makio barely spoke – they were both evidently still taken aback by what had happened back at the bar. They reached Makio's room at the end of the hallway they were walking down.

"Well," Makio said, "I think that was one very successful date, wouldn't you say?"

"I most definitely would," Marisii answered, his voice exhibiting no doubt.

"I want to ask you something," Makio said.

"Shoot."

"Do you like me?" Makio asked. "Or you went out on this date to see if something could happen?"

Marisii paused momentarily. "Look, I'm still new at this," Marisii started. "I've never been in a relationship before, but to answer your question yes – *yes*, I do like you. And I'm curious to see in what way that is going to develop. We get along pretty well, and today's date was something that made me feel at ease – I felt as if I belonged, for the first time ever. And yeah, I want us to try."

"I'm glad you said that." Makio felt as if a sudden weight had been lifted off his shoulders. "In case it's not clear, I like you too and I, too, want us to try." Makio leaned in for a goodnight kiss, but Marisii suddenly flinched away from him.

"Let's not hurry with the second kiss, okay?" Marisii said. "Let's first go out on a few more dates and take it from there, is that cool?"

Makio understood – Marisii couldn't dive into something that was so new to him that fast. "Deal," Makio nodded with a smile. "Goodnight, Marisii."

"Goodnight, Makio," Marisii said and then set off on the course to his room down the opposite, far end of the hospital hallway.

Makio stayed rooted to his spot, observing Marisii as his form grew smaller and smaller, eventually disappearing from his line of sight. Then, he retreated back to his own hospital room.

Chapter 32

Leaving the hospital

The two families were packing their bags. They were ready to leave the hospital – they had stayed there for about three weeks, in order to recover and regain their strength. But that 'break' from reality they had allowed themselves was going to prove costly because Feever was due to visit again any moment now.

Brouzenvert and his wife Berventy were in their room, gathering their possessions in duffel bags. Brouzenvert couldn't wait to leave that hospital, even though without it he himself would never have recovered; half of his family had nearly died inside of it.

"I really think you should talk to Marisii, Brouzenvert," Berventy said with a bitter tone.

Brouzenvert knew his wife didn't approve of his behavior toward his son dating a member of the same gender. "There's nothing to talk about," Brouzenvert said.

"Yes, there is!" Berventy was insistent. "Brouzenvert, you are a father of five boys – *you* need to be their example! They need to learn from you and know that you support their choices and anything they wish to pursue! I don't want you to lose Marisii because you rejected him because of your own problems…"

"Enough!" Brouzenvert raised his tone. "I said what I wanted to say."

"Are you really prepared to lose Marisii over something that happened to you 20 years ago?"

Brouzenvert shifted his head toward her seriously. "Berventy," he said with a cold voice, "do I need to explain to you again why I act in such a manner? Why I don't want our son to date a *boy*?"

"Yes, I think you do need to," she answered.

"Because I don't want my son to experience the same pain I did 20 years ago!" Brouzenvert started, his tone slightly shaking now. "As you well know I'm bisexual and back then I liked a boy – Kersten was *everything* to me! In the beginning, he liked me too, we went out on dates, we were making out, we even slept together – but he always had second thoughts about dating a guy. His parents weren't approving of our relationship – *they* were the homophobes, not *I*! One day they told him to choose between them and me – to choose between the person who loved him and was ready to give him the entire world, and the people who hated him because he was different from them! And Kersten made his choice – he chose *them*. He then invited me over to his place for dinner for whatever reason – and against my better judgment, I went! When I got there, there wasn't any dinner – just his father, holding a giant belt, which he used to beat me up with! He then said to never even think about doing such abominations ever again with his son, or another member of the same gender! That night I left Kersten's home, bleeding and injured, ending up in a hospital on the exact same night! So that's why I don't want our son to date a boy – I'm just trying to protect him from the pain that I endured myself! Pain that almost ruined my entire life! *Can you* guarantee that Makio wouldn't just mess around with Marisii in some way? *What's* the guarantee that Makio and Marisii would be happy together without the people around them judging them for being different? I'm sorry, Berventy, but I can't risk it – it's better that my own son hates me, thinking I'm an insensitive homophobe, than to let him get hurt!"

Berventy nodded slowly, and the two of them didn't raise the subject again.

~~~~~~~~~~

Marisii and Makio had set off together from their rooms and met the other members of the two families in one of the long, crowded corridors of the hospital. Marisii didn't even look at Brouzenvert.

"You all look mostly healed and judging by the look of your duffel bags, ready to leave the hospital!" The medical nurse Annora flashed them a wide smile when they reached the reception. Three weeks ago, they were at that same reception, barely holding on to dear life.

"Yes, I think it's time for us to go," Berventy confirmed Annora's observations, worrying that Feever may appear out of a random corner any second now.

As Annora was leaving the reception, and with the same wide smile, she suddenly pulled Berventy into a tight hug.

"Thank you for all your help," Berventy said. "Without you, we would never have survived."

"That's our job," the nurse said. "I'm glad we were able to save all of you." Her eyes darted over to Morven amidst the big group in front of her. "How are you feeling?"

"Way better than before, thank you," Morven answered truthfully.

"Just don't put any pressure on yourself with any physical or overly emotional activities during the next couple of days, and you will be as good as new! Be mindful and take care of the wound and everything's going to be perfectly splendid!" Annora advised.

Morven nodded.

"I wish you nothing but the best for the future," Annora said, her eyes returning to Berventy, who looked at her again. "But please, no matter what you've all gone through and what you're yet to encounter, take care of yourselves! You asked me not to publicize your curious case that I still don't know the details of, and I won't do it – but you need to *promise* me that you will stay safe!"

"We will do our best," Perventia added, seeming to Berventy buried deep in thought.

"I've arranged for your vehicles you left back in front of the library we found you in, to be brought over to you here. They're in the front parking lot – you will find it instantly when you go outside!" Annora said.

"Once again, thank you for everything!" Berventy said.

Annora nodded with a smile that seemed to Berventy more than polite. Then, the two families and Makio headed for the front double doors. They slid apart to let them pass and simultaneously show them their vehicles, parked out front. Just as Annora had said they would be.

Suddenly, something dawned on Berventy – something that they had all forgotten amidst all the chaos and destruction Feever had caused. Upon Berventy seeing the two pick-up trucks again, memories of what had happened to her and her family started flooding her mind in a swirl. The Klauzer and the Fehrenberg families had been so busy with trying to survive and get better that they had forgotten the one thing that could prove deadly to them if it fell into the wrong person's hands.

That thing was The Book – the two families never picked it up after the library was reduced to rubble. Berventy thought that maybe it would still be there, under the library's debris, waiting for them. Or maybe Feever had already got to The Book, planning how to use it against the two families. Berventy suddenly forgot about Kastilius's disappearance, forgot about Marisii and Brouzenvert's quarrel, even forgot about Perventia and Pattery's deceased daughter Tiffany for a moment – all she could think about right now was The Book.

"We forgot The Book," Berventy voiced out her anxiety to the others. She could tell, by the looks appearing on their faces, that they had all forgotten about The Book until now – just like her, fear and shock painted on them.

Without uttering another word, the two families and Makio climbed up onto the trucks, starting the engines immediately after. Both trucks' tires screeched back in the direction of the ruined library – where so many bad memories lay.

Chapter 33

Feever's raining rage

The hospital's front double doors slid apart once again. Inside the lobby stepped a woman clad in onyx black and Prussian blue dress, a dark silk cloak draped across her shoulders. She started heading toward the reception of the hospital slowly, but steadily. The medical nurse Annora noticed the approaching figure. "How can I help you?"

The woman pulled her silk hood back, looking the nurse straight in the eyes. "Have you by any chance seen two families lately going by the names of Fehrenberg and Klauzer?"

"Why do you need this information?" Annora asked, her voice slightly tense.

"Just tell me," Feever said calmly.

"Yes, I've seen them – they were patients here and they just left a couple of minutes ago – I could sense something *horrible* had happened to them and they couldn't stay any longer."

"Interesting," Feever said. The witch was speaking as if she were in a game, choosing her words as if they were pieces on a chessboard. Feever realized by what Annora had just told her that this whole hospital had helped her mortal enemies heal from their injuries – on the one hand, she was grateful because her son Kastilius also needed to be tended to with his mild injuries, but on the other hand, she wanted to murder each employee of the hospital, because thanks to them the two families had probably fully healed by now, ready to oppose Feever. Right now, the witch was trying to figure out which side in her was going to prevail, so she could decide her next move.

"What do *you* think?" Feever asked the nurse. "Did they look okay when they left?"

"Considerably," Annora confirmed, "but how is that any of your business?"

"Answer my questions when I ask them!" Feever said with a slightly angered tone – she was still trying to find out which side was going to prevail.

"I'm sorry but if you're not injured or in need of any urgent medical care, I would ask you to wait in the designated seating area in the lobby, or just outright leave!" Annora said, waving toward the front double doors with a hand. "We've got a job to do, and more new people keep coming every hour, *actually* needing medical care!"

Feever looked at her in surprise, her eyes squinting.

"Please, *do not* waste our time!" Annora said sharply.

At that moment Feever finally found out which side was about to prevail. Feever outstretched her hand toward Annora, making the expert medical nurse fly through a glass door several steps behind her. She quickly rose back to her feet afterward, looking at Feever with shock and mild fright. All gazes around the two women were fixed firmly on Feever, who now turned around, examining all of them.

"Listen to me very carefully!" Feever raised her voice a notch, her gaze jumping from one person to the next. "*You* helped the people who hurt me – *the people* who took what was most precious to me! While I'm trying to take my revenge you're just helping and cheering them on! And that's why I don't view you as any less a threat than them!" Feever could see the confusion in the patients' and the staff's eyes, having no idea what she was on about.

"I'm asking you please to leave," Annora said warningly while trying to take little glass particles out of her hair, "or I will be forced to call the police!"

Feever's head whipped around toward Annora, a wicked cackle erupting out of her throat. "Is that supposed to scare me?"

"Security!" Annora screamed. Two tall and lean men appeared out of a nearby corner, heading toward the witch intruder. "Get her out of here!"

The two security guards placed their hands on the guns in their holsters, attached to their belts, simultaneously.

"There's no need for things to get ugly, ma'am," one of them said; "just leave this hospital and all will be forgiven and forgotten!"

Feever smiled upon hearing that threat. "I don't think so," she said. Immediately after, the other security guard took his gun out of the holster, pointed it at Feever, and pulled the trigger. Feever immediately raised her hand in the air, instructing the bullet to go back in the direction it had come from, striking the guard in the eye, instantly ending his life. The other security guard started running toward Feever, but she just squeezed her right hand into a fist, snapping his neck. "Now," she said with a broad, adventurous smile, "who wants to have some fun?"

Many of the people in the lobby and the corridors nearby ran for the front doors. They were automatic and instantly opened. But when the crowd of innocents actually reached the doors, intending to flee, Feever used her telekinetic powers and made the double doors snap shut with incredible speed, slicing most of the people in half.

"You," Feever said, pointing towards Annora, "come with me, NOW!"

"I'm not going anywhere with you!" Annora refused almost immediately.

Feever's face turned boiling red. She then waved her hand once again in Annora's direction and the medical nurse flew from the reception through the now opened, but stained with blood, front doors of the hospital. Feever could see that the nurse had landed in the almost empty parking lot out front, her nose and forehead painted with blood. Afterward, the witch turned around toward the hospital's main corridor nearby, waving both of her hands, crackling lines of fire exploding out of her palms. The fire engulfed the whole corridor, and now the walls were brightly burning, the flames threatening to reach the ceiling.

People all around Feever were running for their lives, trying to get out, but Feever now blocked the only way out on the first floor of the hospital – the two double doors, by making them slam shut with her mind, destroying the movement sensor in the process.

The remaining nurses on the floor reached the reception, trying to ring someone, probably the local authorities, but with no such luck. Feever knew the commotion around was making it hard to hear anything, and the electricity in the whole hospital now began flashing on and off.

Feever formed a vast circular rock in her right hand, with lots of sharp angles, resembling spikes. She willed her mind to activate her X-ray vision and it did, the witch craning her neck up toward the ceiling of the first floor. The witch could see the whole building's construction and where its foundations lay, exposing its weak spot. Feever concentrated for a few seconds and then shot the ball of spiked rock up toward the ceiling. Her weapon annihilated the spot of the ceiling it went through, disappearing out of sight and traveling with the speed of light. Feever could hear the rock's path of destruction, annihilating pillar after pillar, grazing person after person, on the two upper floors of the hospital.

Feever started walking toward the doors calmly, her ears picking up on the sounds of the ceiling and whole floors beginning to crumble and fall down behind her, burying thousands of helpless innocents alive. Feever exited through the double doors that opened for her, and only her, and started making her way in Annora's direction, who still lay on the parking lot out front. Upon reaching the head medical nurse, Feever turned around to the collapsing hospital.

"Don't you love knowing you can annihilate a certain thing in such a short period of time?"

Screams and shouts were audible from inside the collapsing building – people begging for someone to help them, begging for their lives to be spared. A series of explosions initiated from the far end of the hospital, moving steadily throughout its length to the front.

"*That* could have been you!" Feever said to Annora, pointing to the hundreds of dying figures inside.

"Why did you decide to spare me?" Annora asked, still laying on the pavement.

"Because I want the families that you helped, or more specifically one of them, to know that because of *you* their real son is forever lost! I want them to hate *you* the way they hate *me*! The only difference is that I've got powers with which I can defend myself against any attack – *and you don't!*"

Annora looked at her with rage, Feever knew, while the hospital was leveling itself to the ground.

"Now, be a dear and stand up," Feever instructed. "Or I will make you stand up!"

Annora stood up a few seconds later.

"Good," Feever said, "now, follow me!"

~~~~~~~~~~

Annora followed Feever – but not before turning around and stealing one last glimpse of the burning hospital. That was her life, in there she was helping people, and that brought her the greatest joy in life. She had made friendships for life there – and now all of her colleagues were inside the building, being crushed or burned to death.

All of that had disappeared – reduced to just dust and ashes as if it had never existed. So many innocent souls wasted by a crazy angry woman, who, it was clear to Annora, possessed some sort of magical abilities. A woman, who was evidently seeking revenge on the two families for *something*.

Chapter 34

Meeting at the library's ruins – Part 1

The Klauzer and Fehrenberg families reached the library's ruins in a timely manner. Berventy was the first one to emerge out of the pick-up trucks and go to the library's remains – she started digging through them, frantically moving bricks and debris.

"Where is it?" Berventy croaked in frustration. Makio, Brouzenvert, Perventia, Pattery, and their kids were also helping Berventy locate their most precious item.

Berventy Klauzer couldn't see even a mild trace of The Book anywhere. But there was also good news – Feever was also nowhere to be seen and she thought the witch might not have gotten to it just yet.

"How could we forget it?" the eldest daughter of the Fehrenberg family, Pacifika, grabbed her head in frustration.

"We were too busy trying to stay alive, Pacifika!" her younger sister Kayla said.

"Stop bickering and continue searching!" The third child of the Fehrenberg family, Klacifia, said.

"It isn't here!" Perventia almost screamed, her tone betraying her anger. "Where could it be?"

"Looking for this?" A familiar male voice asked from behind them. Berventy was the first one to turn around, finding her son Kastilius standing next to the ruins in front of her, holding The Book in his right hand, smiling for whatever reason.

"Oh, Kastilius," she said and started walking toward her son, intending to give him a huge hug. For the past 20 minutes or so, amidst all the chaos and worry, she had completely forgotten that her son was still missing.

"That distance is close enough!" Kastilius said and Berventy ceased walking within a couple of inches from him.

"Kastilius," Marisii said, "are you okay? After our fight…"

"That is all in the past," Kastilius smiled, his right hand not tearing away from The Book for even a second.

"You've found The Book," Berventy said cheerfully, but her tone betrayed her hidden tenseness. "That's great! Give it to us, we were really worried that we had lost it forever or that it had fallen into Feever's hands."

"The Book stays with me," Kastilius said coldly. "You lost the right to touch it!"

"What?" a confused Berventy asked. "Kastilius, what are you talking about?"

"What he should have said a long time ago!" A deadly familiar female voice spoke. It belonged to Feever, who showed up from the nearby street corner, holding the medical nurse Annora by the right shoulder, forcing her to move forward. Feever then took her place next to Kastilius and he handed her The Book.

Shock and confusion were steadily becoming visible on the two families' faces.

"The Book is now ours!" Feever announced to the two families.

"*Ours?*" Brouzenvert said. "Kastilius, what the hell are you doing? Why did you just give *her* The Book? What's the matter with you?"

"What's happening, 'Father', is that *Feever* had the guts to tell me the truth about who I am!" Kastilius said.

"About who you *are*?" his brother Kasteron asked him, who was positioned next to Teela. "What's going on?"

"What's going on is that my supposed parents, called Berventy and Brouzenvert, have been lying to me all my life!" Kastilius said. "I've never been their son and that's why I could never feel like a part of the *damn* Klauzer family!"

"Not our son?" the horrified Berventy asked. "Kastilius, we raised you – *I* saw you being born, I held you in *my* hands, I remember your first words and steps, I remember everything about you!"

"Memories that were meant for someone else!" Feever corrected. "Kastilius is *my* son, and he always has been – I placed him in your family for almost 16 years, so when I awoke from my slumber I could have a grown-up warrior, next to me, ready to seek revenge alongside me! And for some observation, of course."

"Are you out of your goddamn mind?" Berventy almost shouted at her. "What lies have you been feeding him?" Then, the gingerbread-haired mother turned to Kastilius. "Please, do not listen to her – she brainwashed you! You are our son – *mine and Brouzenvert's*. And you always will be!"

"Feever told me the truth!" Kastilius continued. "When I was a baby, she switched your son with me, so I could grow up in your family! Remember this blue bracelet I've been wearing almost all the time ever since I was an infant?" Kastilius showed his right wrist to Berventy. "My *real* mother Feever gave me this bracelet, before parting with me for 16 years! She showed me a vision from the past, explaining exactly what happened and why she had to leave me."

"She's lying!" Brouzenvert said. "Kastilius, are you really that stupid as to buy her silly lies? You grew up with *us*, we raised you

– how could you think, for even a moment, that this disgusting witch could be your mother?"

"Interesting," Kastilius answered, "this disgusting witch showed me more love for 16 minutes than you all could accomplish for 16 years!"

"Is that why you're behaving this way?" Berventy asked him. "You don't feel loved, is that it? Kastilius, we *do* love you – I love you; your father loves you; your brothers love you! Even if what Feever has said to you is even remotely true, would you *really* go with her? A wicked witch who is hell bent on killing us all?"

"Berventy," Feever's voice came out as a warning, "I would *never* hurt Kastilius! *Never!* He is *my* son and it's time for him to take his rightful place next to me!"

"You're a filthy bitch who's so infilled with hate that it hurts her!" Berventy bared her teeth in a snarl as if she were a vampire who was about to bite into Feever's throat. Just like a predator, Berventy started pawing closer to Feever. "You're so desperate to hurt us that you've come after my son! I hope that one day you will burn in hell and rot for eternity there, you stupid cunt!"

"Mind your language, Berventy!" Feever said, the distance separating her and Berventy's faces mere centimeters now. "I can annihilate your whole family right here and right now!" Feever looked at the Fehrenberg family's members. "Just like the way I ripped your precious Tiffany's heart out and crushed it in front of your very eyes!"

Murmurs and fists tightening began spreading through the Fehrenberg family like a chain reaction.

~~~~~~~~~~

Teela could sense her own anger growing exponentially in her body.

"She seemed pretty terrified to me before I snuffed her life out!" Feever said. "I sincerely hope she suffered!"

"ENOUGH!" A scream erupted out of Teela's throat, and she quickly raised her hand in the air toward Feever and Kastilius, pushing them back with her power of telekinesis. The sudden wave of rage and power that came out of Teela's hand eventually pushed Feever and Kastilius to the ground, the Salem witch dropping The Book.

Then Teela looked at both of her hands – every time she used her newfound power, she felt herself growing mightier and mightier.

Berventy walked to The Book, resting on the litter-infested ground, picked it up, and then went back to Brouzenvert and the others – all the while Kastilius and Feever were getting progressively back up on their feet.

Chapter 35

Meeting at the library's ruins – Part 2

Kastilius and Feever rose from the ground, their faces turning a flaming red color.

"I see someone's found their power," Feever said, looking at Teela. "The emotion causing it to activate was anger, right? Anger for your sister Tiffany dying because of *you*?"

"Tiffany is dead because *you* killed her!" Teela screamed.

"Weird," Feever said, "my original goal was you – Tiffany blocked my path, sacrificing herself for you. *And* that's the only reason she died! The way I see it you should have died, not Tiffany! You, Teela, *are* the one to blame!"

"I will make you sorry you ever said that!" Teela spat out, her eyes locating some metal poles amidst all the debris around all of them. She lifted the items with her right hand, aiming them at Kastilius and Feever. Kastilius stood in front of his mother, deflecting the metal poles with a hand, the objects piercing a billboard on the street in front of them.

"I shared a lot of my knowledge and power with Kastilius – he already had some untapped power, but I helped him find it!" Feever said proudly. "And now he's almost as powerful as me – and much more powerful than *any* of you!"

"So that's what you've been doing for the past couple of days?" Marisii asked Kastilius, Berventy sensing a saturated mixture of disappointment and surprise in her son's voice. "While we worried like crazy about where and how you were, you've been working and conspiring with Feever behind our back?"

"Kastilius, please," Berventy said, still holding on to a shred of hope that she would be able to convince Kastilius that he was still *her* son, "I don't care what Feever says – you are my son, you're your father's son, and you have four brothers who love you – brothers that Feever wants to murder! Are you really going to join her over something that may or may not be true? Are you really going to help her murder the family you grew up with for the past 16 years? The family you've known your entire life?"

"I belong with Feever," Kastilius said. Feever placed a hand on his shoulder. They looked like one now. Kastilius's detachment from the Klauzer family seemed so evident now. "My place is next to her, fighting to avenge for what *your* family line did in Salem all those years ago!"

"We don't even know what you're talking about," Brouzenvert said. "We don't even know what our ancestors did to anger Feever so much as for her to come after us, determined to kill us!"

"Kastilius, please." The oldest sibling of the Klauzer family, Brouzun, joined in the conversation as well. "Stop this nonsense and come back to us! Everything could go back to the way it was – it's not too late!"

"*The way it was?*" Kastilius repeated. "You mean the time when you, Morven and Marisii didn't talk to the rest of us for years, because you were too upset about The Curse? Or when Berventy and Brouzenvert kept going on and on about how their every child was successful at something – *except me*? And while we're at it, why don't we go back to the way all of you were looking at me all these years – as if I was someone whom you accepted into your family reluctantly, as if I wasn't a part of you – an outsider even! I spent only a few days with Feever, but they were enough for me to realize where my true place is, where I belong! And unfortunately," Kastilius said, raising both of his hands in the air, his whole body shaking and shivering – but seeming like it was intentional, "that place is not with you, Klauzer family! '*Serpentina Suvarva*'!" Kastilius screamed.

A second later a wave hit Brouzenvert and Pacifika. Both of them flew back, crumbling to the dust-infested ground, next to the debris, groaning in pain. Black slime appeared out of their lower limbs, spreading over their body and upper limbs, finding its way into their mouths, nostrils, and eyes.

"WHAT DID YOU DO?" Pattery screamed, running toward his uncontrollably writhing daughter.

"I poisoned them!" Kastilius said calmly as if that were the most normal thing in the world. "See, during the past couple of days when Feever and I were in possession of The Book, I had a lot of time to study it! I found this really interesting spell, called '*Serpentina Suvarva*'. That is the oldest-known poison to witches, more effective and deadlier than any other poison in the world! Accept this as my parting gift to you – a gift that will tide you over until the next time we meet. The poison will reach Brouzenvert and Pacifika's hearts within 21 days! But hey, there's also a positive side to it." Kastilius smiled.

"And what might that be?" Marisii screamed.

"There's a medicine on an island called '*The Island of Lost Hopes*' – it's enough to save both of them," Kastilius said.

It was ironic really. The two families' hope was waning and the only way they could save their loved ones was to travel to an island that had the words 'lost hopes' in its name.

"But that antidote hasn't been produced ever since the Salem witch trials ended, so good luck finding it!" Kastilius said.

"How could you do this?" Berventy asked through tears, desperation obscuring her voice. She was now crouched next to Brouzenvert, witnessing the man she loved more than herself in so much pain. And that added to her desperation. "This is your father Brouzenvert, who raised you and loved you for every single day of your life!"

"I think my time with you is over," Kastilius said and turned around to his mother Feever, who removed her hand from his shoulder. "What do you think – is it time for us to go, *Mother*?"

"Not quite yet," Feever said with a smile and raised Annora, who had been standing next to her and Kastilius for quite some time, not uttering a word, high in the air, and threw her in the two families' direction. "That's the medical nurse Annora – the one I hypnotized to swap the babies 16 years ago. If you're looking for someone to blame more than me for this whole situation, blame her!"

No one softened Annora's fall – the two families and Makio even stepped back, letting her land roughly next to all the ruins. The orange-crimson-haired nurse looked at Berventy and the writhing Brouzenvert, seemingly confused.

"See you in three weeks," Feever told them. "I can't wait to see whether Pacifika and Brouzenvert are going to be alive for our next meeting! And Kastilius's move pleasantly surprised me – I'm not going to kill either one of you today, seeing as my son practically killed two of you already. Like mother, like son, eh?"

"See you in three weeks for the next part of The Curse, Klauzer family!" That line signified his official detachment from the Klauzer family, his past being left behind. Kastilius flicked his right hand high in the air, making both himself and his mother disappear into a cloud of violet smoke.

~~~~~~~~~~

The black slime had fully absorbed into Pacifika and Brouzenvert's bodies, now making its way toward their hearts, more than ready to stop them when the time came.

Chapter 36

On the way to The Island of Lost Hopes

"Pacifika," Perventia said, crouching next to her daughter who was writhing in agony and screaming. Brouzenvert was in the same condition as Pacifika, their screams pure torture for their loved ones.

"We can't let them die!" Morven said, looking at his father Brouzenvert. "I don't care what Kastilius poisoned them with, we can't lose them!"

"Do you have any suggestions?" Kayla asked, who was now within inches of her older sister Pacifika, watching her. Kayla had grown up with Pacifika, and even though the two of them hadn't been speaking to each other that much over the last couple of years, they were *still* family. Kayla wasn't about to lose her sister – not another sister, not after she'd lost Tiffany.

~~~~~~~~~~

"Kastilius mentioned something about some island of lost hopes?" Morven asked. "If his words are to be believed, there's a cure there that could save Brouzenvert and Pacifika!"

"Why would he say that if there wasn't a catch?" Klacifia asked. "Maybe he and Feever want exactly that – to make us go to that island, so they can set a trap for us or something!"

"Trap or not," Berventy said, directing her gaze at Brouzenvert, still crouching next to him, "I'll be damned if I let Pacifika and Brouzenvert die because of a stupid witch! Whatever is waiting for us on that island, we will face it the same way we've done so far – as one family!"

That was the first time someone said that the two families equaled one – they were fighting this vile witch together, they grieved together, and tried to survive together. Their fates were intertwined, and they should have counted on each other – now, more than ever.

Berventy stood up from the dusty ground, turning to Perventia, who was only a few meters opposite her, trying to console Pacifika, who was positioned next to Pattery. "Give me The Book," Berventy said and Perventia did as she was told. Berventy couldn't remember when she had given Perventia The Book – probably sometime after Kastilius and Feever decided to directly attack them.

Berventy started flipping through The Book – her right hand passed the pages containing information about The Curse, then the pages describing potions, and finally reached the page with the information it was looking for. "There it is!" Berventy exclaimed, taking a slight breath. "'The Island of Lost Hopes' *is an island that doesn't exist on any map – it is situated in another universe, access to which can be gained only by the combined power of the Klauzer and the Fehrenberg families. The island is a mystery, and it is dangerous – threats lurk from every corner. ATTENTION,*" was scribbled across the page in capital letters, "*traveling to another universe is dangerous and unpredictable – you could meet your doppelgangers. They might be the* same as you, but they might also be totally different. These doppelgangers could ask you to take them with you back to your own universe – DO NOT DO THAT UNDER ANY CIRCUMSTANCES! That could trigger unforeseen consequences for you and your entire universe!"

"Splendid!" Marisii exclaimed sarcastically. "Now we have to protect ourselves from ourselves?"

"Marisii, we've got no other choice!" Berventy said. "Your father and Pacifika are dying – you heard Kastilius yourself, when the poison reaches their hearts they die! I won't allow it! Not while there's something we can do to stop it!"

"Berventy is right," Perventia said.

Berventy looked at her with a smile – she liked Perventia because the two of them were similar in so many ways.

"Feever already took Tiffany away from us – I won't give her the satisfaction of taking Pacifika away too!"

"Since we're all on the same page, let's get to it!" Berventy said, still holding The Book open in her hands. "We don't have time to lose!" And Berventy plunged her mind into the pages, providing instructions of how to get to the island: "If it's absolutely necessary to get to 'The Island of Lost Hopes' here's what you should do: join hands together in a circle. Once the circle is complete and all the families' members are united as one, try channeling your magical energies toward one another. Even if you haven't activated your power yet, you're witches – that's in your blood and it always will be. After you've done that, you should be able to cross over to the other universe. A portal will open up – but keep in mind that those kinds of portals are also unpredictable, and anything can happen! That's why, again, go to the island only if it's absolutely necessary, and after exhausting all other possible options!" Berventy paused for a moment. "The island is famous for 'Ameralda's cure' – it can mend any type of pain or illness within a timely manner. Do be mindful of the fact that the cure is immensely difficult to find and if you do find it, there may be a price to pay in order to acquire it. Ameralda is an ancient goddess, inhabiting the worlds, ever since the very beginning of *time – she is wicked and likes to play games. That is why it is best if you don't have give-and-take with her. We wish you all the best of luck – we believe in you!"* Then, Berventy saw that the bottom of the page was signed with Sarvit and Mour's initials.

"Assemble in a circle!" Berventy instructed and was glad to see the others listened to her. The two families outstretched their hands and started holding their respective partners' hands, forming a circle of bodies above the agonizing Pacifika and Brouzenvert on the ground.

"Now close your eyes and concentrate!" Berventy said. She placed The Book in front of her and joined hands with Marisii on her left side and Perventia on the right. "Free your mind of anything else except *The Island of Lost Hopes* and each other – channel your magical energies toward one another, think of a moment in your lives with your family that made you happy!"

Makio was situated outside of the circle – because he wasn't a part of either of the two families, he was just standing close to them, observing them concentrate.

Tiny sparks started flashing between all the connected palms, growing greater by the second. The portal was opening up and the two families willed themselves to isolate their minds from anything else but each other, and the island. After a few more moments, the portal grew to its maximum six-foot size and the two families' eyelids snapped open, the palms disconnecting. The portal was crackling with an intense, almost electrical energy, painted in deep-sky color.

Perventia and Pattery were the first ones to go through it, Pattery carrying Pacifika in his arms. Kasteron and Teela went through second. Then Kayla and Klacifia. Annora, Berventy, Morven and Brouzun were the next in line, Brouzun supporting Brouzenvert's weight on his shoulders as he went through, and Berventy carrying The Book.

~~~~~~~~~~

"Maybe you should stay here," Marisii turned over to Makio – those two were the only ones who hadn't gone through the portal yet.

"*Marisii*," Makio said, craning his neck a little bit to the side, "your *father* is dying – and I want to do everything in my power to help you stop it!"

"But The Curse is not after you," Marisii answered; "you could just stay here and not get involved in all my family drama!"

"When I turned around toward you at the library's reception, I made the conscious choice *to* get involved in your family drama. Brouzenvert may be a jerk, not approving of you and I dating, but he doesn't deserve to die!"

Marisii smiled broadly – he really wanted to see whether things would work out between him and Makio. Marisii was still insecure about dating and relationships, but he felt like that wouldn't matter when it came to Makio – their communication just seemed to flow in such a natural way. "Are you sure about this?" Marisii asked him again. "That other universe could prove dangerous – do you really want to risk your life for me? I'm not even sure that I…"

"I know you're still not sure about this – about us," Makio interrupted him. "I like you, Marisii, and I'm willing to wait and see if you would want to have something – anything, to do with me! I *want* us to go out on another date and see if this thing between us could develop into something greater. I'm ready to do whatever it takes for that to happen. So, yeah, I'm coming with you to this odd island, whether you like it or not!"

Marisii smiled once again – to a certain extent he maybe felt a sort of guilt that he was enjoying this blooming interaction with Makio right now while his homophobic father was dying. Marisii knew very well what his father thought of him dating boys – but at the same time, Marisii had to think of his own self and what *he* wanted from life, for once. Or more specifically, *who* he wanted in that life. "Let's go then."

The two of them took their place in front of the bright, sky-colored portal. Makio's hand was slightly shaking. Marisii couldn't read Makio's thoughts, but he supposed that was caused by the fact that Makio had only ever known the world of ordinary humans – he had never gone through a portal to another world. But then again, neither had Marisii.

Marisii took Makio's hand in his, wanting to comfort him more than anything else in the world. Marisii noticed Makio's cheeks turning a bright red color and flashed him an encouraging smile. Then, the two men walked through the portal, the device closing immediately behind them.

Chapter 37

Arrival on the island

Kayla and Klacifia Fehrenberg had a rough landing. The two sisters fell into a deep indigo sea, next to The Island of Lost Hopes and had to fight the unrelenting waves to swim to shore.

Kayla emerged from the waves first and pulled Klacifia, who was a little further out in the sea and having difficulties, to the shore.

"Are you okay?" Kayla asked her younger sister Klacifia, the two of them laying on the sand, their chests rising and falling steadily.

"Yeah, yeah, I'm okay," Klacifia assured her and after a few moments, the two of them rose, making their way through the various vines, leaves and trees. "What is this place?"

The Island of Lost Hopes *looks like heaven*, Kayla thought – every flower had blossomed, there was a water fountain not far from where Kayla and Klacifia were walking, a small mountain that looked so peaceful with its vibrant green, and birds, who were chirping all around the island. Everything looked so calm that Kayla thought a person could have easily lost themselves in this place, in this universe.

"It's just so beautiful," Klacifia said, looking around herself, in awe.

"Remember what The Book said," Kayla reminded her. "This place was going to be beautiful and incredibly tempting but is actually deceptive and wicked!"

"Kayla, it's so beautiful," Klacifia said as if she hadn't heard Kayla's words at all. "At least try to enjoy this place! After everything we've been through, I think we deserve five minutes of rest in a *beautiful* place such as this."

"Okay," Kayla agreed, although reluctantly, "but remember – we came here to collect *Ameralda's cure*, so we can extract the poison out of Pacifika and Brouzenvert's bodies!"

"Of course, I wouldn't forget about this!" Klacifia exclaimed.

"Come on," Kayla said, "we need to find the others…"

But Kayla stopped short in her sentence, suddenly noticing that someone had been watching them from the bushes opposite them. Who knew how long that person had been hiding there, spying on them? A split second after Kayla and the person's gazes met, the mysterious individual sprinted deep into the jungle.

"Hey!" Kayla shouted after the person, beginning to run after them. She was vaguely aware of Klacifia's footsteps following her. "Hey, stop!"

Kayla accelerated her pace – when she was little, she had been running a lot in school during gym class, and in her free time. As a result, she was able to reach the mysterious figure within a few minutes. When Kayla had closed the distance between her and the figure to one meter, she made a huge leap, landing right on top of the creep, both of them tumbling to the ground. The figure managed to escape Kayla's grip and resumed running, but Kayla kicked them in the back of their knee a second later. Now, the person's face was buried in the emerald grass, with Kayla hovering above.

"Who are you?" Kayla said, while forcedly turning them over to face her. "What do you want from us?"

Klacifia had just reached Kayla and the mysterious person, late only by a minute.

Kayla saw long caramel hair just like hers, and facial features identical to hers. The person who had been watching Kayla and Klacifia was a young girl, probably in her early twenties. In fact, Kayla knew for sure that the mysterious girl was 23 years old. Kayla suddenly realized why this girl looked so similar to her, there was no denying it – because *she was her.*

An identical twin. A twin, who was dressed in torn clothes that resembled rags, her hair a tangled mess and her face stained from dirt.

But the original Kayla still couldn't believe it – she was essentially looking at *herself.*

Chapter 38

The second Kayla

"Who are you?" Kayla asked her twin, her face moving a few centimeters away from the twin's.

"I'm...I'm Kayla," the girl stuttered.

"No, I'm Kayla!" she screamed angrily. "What are you trying to do? We won't take you back to our universe, The Book warned us about impostors like you!"

"Ex...excuse me?" the girl claiming to also be Kayla said. "What universe are you talking about?"

"Tell me your name one more time!" Kayla raised her voice considerably. "And this time the real one! I won't ask again!"

"My *name* is Kayla," the girl said again. "I don't know why we look so alike; I've never met you before in my life!"

Kayla now fully removed herself from the girl, standing up simultaneously as her double.

Klacifia could notice the still significant fear, drawn across the girl's face.

"Klacifia?" the girl asked when she saw her. "Klacifia, is that really you?"

"Do we know each other?" Klacifia asked the girl unsurely. She had begun to dislike this new universe she and her sister had arrived in. Klacifia had been mesmerized by this island's beauty just a few minutes ago, but maybe Kayla had been right – this beauty was fraudulent, just a mask, underneath which was hiding something insidious.

"I'm your sister Kayla," the girl told Klacifia.

"I told you – I'M KAYLA!" Kayla said, her voice high-pitched.

A second later, the girl that looked identical to Kayla, jumped back, trembling. "I'm sorry," tears rolled down her cheeks, "I really don't know what's going on. I'm the last survivor of my family and…"

"What?" Kayla asked.

The girl sniffed. "Years ago, the witch Feever started coming to claim her victims – The Curse activated and within a month she had managed to kill the whole Klauzer family and most of mine."

Klacifia Fehrenberg started realizing that in this alternative universe the events, regarding The Curse, had played out differently than back in hers. Maybe this girl really was Kayla – just from this universe? And not some creature, trying to deceive them?

"My mother Perventia and my father Pattery fought hard – but Feever still managed to kill them both. Feever murdered Tiffany first, then Teela, then Klacifia, then Pattery, then Pacifika, and at the end my mother Perventia! She was too powerful, and we couldn't stop her! But before my mother died, she placed me under this protection spell that hid me from Feever. I'm positive Feever is still looking for me to this day, but I disappeared from the radar altogether!"

"If what you're saying is true," Kayla said, "would you be able to tell us what could happen if Feever is successful in killing all members of the two families, taking away their powers?"

"If that ever happened, Feever would be able to place every human being or magical creature under her control," the twin blurted out almost immediately. "She would become the most powerful witch in all of history, able to completely wipe out all mankind if she wishes so! If Feever ever succeeds in killing me too, she would be able to crown herself queen of the entire world and do whatever she wants with it! She would be *unstoppable!*"

Klacifia didn't know about Kayla, but she herself had never thought about that. And now, after Kayla's question had been answered, Klacifia wished she and her sister never *got* the answer. Klacifia never even supposed The Curse could be *that* mighty – she didn't even know why Feever had cast it in the first place. But she supposed the witch must have been pretty angry to cast such a destructive spell. But could this doppelganger's word even be trusted?

"Please, take me with you," the girl suddenly said. "I'm the sole survivor of the two families and I can't let Feever find me! *Please.*" The tears intensified, her whole face damp now.

"Do you remember what The Book said about the doppelgangers?" Klacifia asked Kayla, her voice initially a whisper. "They would do anything to convince us to take them back with us to our universe! This is obviously a mere trick to make us sympathize with this girl! And how would she know what would happen if Feever killed all of us, huh?"

"Enough, Klacifia," Kayla said calmly, as if not even hearing Klacifia. "The girl is clearly scared and confused. The least we could do is allow her to accompany us on the quest of finding Ameralda's cure. She lost all her family and clearly, in this universe, Feever has almost won! Let's not give her the satisfaction of *actually* succeeding. There's no harm if we let this girl come with us."

Klacifia looked at Kayla's doppelganger, her eyes inspecting her from head to feet. "I still don't trust her."

"You don't have to," Kayla said. "Let's stop thinking about murder and survival for once, and help a person in need, shall we? Survival, book, and curse are three words that we have been hearing over and over for the past couple of weeks – is it so bad if we forget them for a moment and focus our attention elsewhere?"

Klacifia nodded reluctantly. She wondered why Kayla had suddenly warmed up to this *stranger*. But no matter what Kayla thought, Klacifia was going to keep an eye on this 'new' Kayla. It was just majorly convenient for her to show up out of nowhere, meeting specifically *them*, and tell a sob story to make them help her.

"Tell us more about this universe and this island," Kayla said, stepping closer to the doppelganger.

Klacifia observed from the side, not uttering a word more.

Chapter 39

Makio and Marisii

The portal opened and spat out Makio and Marisii in the middle of the jungle, closing immediately after. They rose from the ground and Marisii could notice the indescribable beauty of this island but didn't allow himself to be overly mesmerized by it. Marisii knew that he couldn't give in to the beauty because he had come here to do only one thing – find the cure for his father Brouzenvert, and his friend Pacifika. Makio and Marisii started walking through the vast jungle, pushing through leaves and overgrown bushes, when Marisii felt his forehead drenched in sweat.

"It's so hot here, wouldn't you say?" Marisii asked Makio and grabbed his indigo shirt in his right hand, starting to wave it back and forth.

"It's boiling indeed," Makio said, a sudden smile forming on his lips. "But if you can't take the heat, you can always remove your shirt. Just saying."

Marisii looked at him in surprise. "Are you flirting with me?" Marisii asked, not sure how to feel about that.

"Maybe," Makio responded. "I'm sorry, I would stop if it makes you feel uncomfortable?"

Marisii could sense the tension in Makio's voice. He gave him a shy smile. "A little," the younger man said. He liked Makio flirting with him, he just wasn't used to it.

"If you wish I can turn around while you change. I'm not sure you brought any spare clothes with you though," Makio offered.

Marisii smiled and then nodded. A second later Makio's back was turned to Marisii.

Marisii began unbuttoning his indigo shirt, stripping it completely off his body. He then tied it around his waist. A few moments passed and Makio had been right – he didn't have any spare clothes. Marisii intended to put his shirt back on, his hand reaching to untie it from his waist, but then he stopped. What was he doing? Makio had just flirted with him and Marisii had made him turn around while he changed? Because he was too anxious about Makio seeing him half-naked? Or maybe he was anxious that his body didn't look toned enough for Makio? What if Makio didn't like it?

"I'm ready," Marisii announced, his hand completely withdrawing from his shirt.

Makio turned around to face Marisii, witnessing him half-naked.

Marisii noticed his eyes lingering on his body and Makio's own body unable to move. If Marisii wasn't mistaken, he would have thought Makio looked mesmerized? The sun was shining brightly above them, lighting Marisii's frame and making it stand out even more.

"Do you work out?" Makio asked him suddenly.

"A little," Marisii admitted. "From time to time."

He chose not to acknowledge his right shoulder scar, caused by Feever when The Curse had first started. And he was glad that Makio didn't ask any questions about it.

"I thought you were going to change?" Makio asked, biting his lip.

"As I said, it's hot," Marisii said. "I'm thinking of staying like that for a while." Marisii had begun gaining confidence whenever he was around Makio, and he liked that. Never before had he felt so secure in himself.

"I don't mind that one bit," Makio smiled cheekily. "In fact, I was hoping that you wouldn't put your shirt back on."

"Were you now?" Marisii laughed. His eyes picked up on something in the bushes nearby Makio. The tall, chocolate-haired man cut the distance between them and started fumbling through the bushes, looking for the thing he'd seen. A few dozen seconds passed, with Marisii fighting the overgrown emerald bushes and Makio standing on the side, when Marisii finally gripped the handle of the item he had been looking for. He regained his full posture again, turned to Makio and smiled victoriously. "Machete!"

"Wow!" Makio said. "What do you intend to do with that?"

"We need to find Ameralda's cure as soon as possible," Marisii said, carefully inspecting the machete's sharp metallic blade with his index finger, "and we're surrounded by overgrown leaves, vines and bushes – I'm going to use that to cut them down!"

Marisii commenced his intended activity, swatting through the greenery, showing no mercy, his muscles protruding from the effort. Eventually, he turned to Makio and realized he had been watching him concentratedly, just as before.

"Do *you* want to cut them down?" Marisii asked the boy with the glasses. Marisii noticed the frame was now cracked in the middle, the glasses barely holding on to Makio's face. It was a whole miracle he hadn't lost them in the battle in the library.

"You found the machete – I think therefore you should do the honors! Besides, *I'm* enjoying the view from here."

"Alright then," Marisii nodded and then turned around, slicing through the last three huge leaves, blocking their path. "Let's go!"

~~~~~~~~~~

Marisii continued cutting through leaves and bushes further down the jungle and Makio was following him, observing with enjoyment. Marisii sliced three more leaves with his machete. Then he raised it again, but Makio saw that there was nothing left to cut. Instead, there was a huge bridge in front of them, supported by crumbling ropes and wooden boards creaking in the wind.

"Let's just find another path," Makio suggested. "This bridge looks dangerous – who knows how old it is!"

"I don't think we have time to do that, Makio," Marisii said. "We need to find Ameralda's cure as soon as possible – we can't let Feever kill another member of the Fehrenberg family or mine! If that happens, we would grow weaker and she – stronger. She will never stop pursuing her dumb revenge, but we mustn't let her succeed!" Marisii paused momentary. "Whoever he is, whatever he's done, Brouzenvert is *still* my father, and I can't give up on him that easily!"

"Okay," Makio said, not pressing the matter any further. Makio understood that family was important to Marisii and that because Marisii was a good person he was willing to forgive his father for the vile deed.

Makio intended to step on the bridge first, but he was stopped by Marisii.

"Let *me* go first," Marisii said. "Just to make sure the wooden boards are enough to sustain even one person."

"Are you sure?" Makio inquired. "This bridge doesn't look stable; I don't want you to hurt yourself."

"And I don't want *you* to hurt yourself," Marisii answered with a smile. "So, let *me* try out the bridge first, okay?"

Makio nodded. Another specific quality he admired in Marisii – Makio knew Marisii didn't know whether their attraction would become something more than a casual flirt, but he didn't want

Makio to hurt himself, nevertheless.

Marisii placed his right foot on the first wooden board slowly. Makio was watching him, trembling.

The wooden board creaked under Marisii's weight but didn't give out. Then, Marisii placed his left foot on the second board, which also let out a worrying sound, but remained steady.

Makio watched Marisii testing out the other boards as well, but this time with ease. None of them gave out under his weight, and he was already halfway over the bridge.

Marisii motioned with his hand for Makio to follow him.

And he did. Makio stepped on the first wooden board, willing himself not to look down. But his curiosity got the better of him and he saw a long river at the bottom of the clearing, surrounded by plenty of rocks. The drop must have been at least 30 feet. Makio began moving along the boards, not liking the sound they sang. The wind was growing stronger.

"Are you doing alright?" Marisii asked him when Makio had almost reached him.

"I'm fine." Makio took a deep breath.

When Makio reached the seventh and eighth bridge board, the wood under his feet gave out and he let out a terrified scream. Makio could feel his body dropping from the bridge, but then he felt Marisii's hand on his. Groaning, the younger man pulled him back up onto the bridge. The faint crash of the two detached wooden boards at the bottom of the clearing reached Makio's ears.

"I got you," Marisii said when Makio was fully back up on his feet, his hands gripping the ropes. The machete was gone now. "I got you."

"I don't doubt it," Makio said with a smile, feeling his heart beginning to relax.

Marisii resumed leading the way on the bridge with Makio following him.

And that's when the very first wooden boards at the opposite end of the bridge, the end from which Makio and Marisii had started, began detaching from the bridge one by one. A split second later, the ropes of the bridge started tearing slowly, one by one. Emanating a ghastly sound. The wooden boards were giving out and falling at the speed of light. And Makio and Marisii had just a few wooden boards left to cross over to safety on the other side.

"Go, go, go!" Marisii prompted Makio and pushed him to the front. "Faster!"

Makio ran as fast as he could while the ropes were tearing and the wooden boards were falling into oblivion. In just a few seconds, Makio reached the last wooden board and jumped to safety on the ground on the other side, escaping the crumbling bridge. Makio turned around, expecting to see Marisii behind him, also having reached safe ground.

But Makio witnessed the last few wooden boards detaching from the bridge and the whole thing breaking, the ropes or the very few wooden boards left not able to support Marisii's weight alone.

The bridge was falling – so was Marisii Klauzer.

A split second later, Marisii disappeared from Makio's sight, the ropes and wooden boards having evaporated.

"NO!" Makio screamed, his pupils dilating. He started frantically searching for Marisii, but there was nothing left of the bridge *or* him.

Fear engulfed Makio's body like a viper, trying to suffocate him. A fear he'd never felt before – it was so cold and numbing. Had Marisii really pushed Makio in front of him – to save him? Was that really the end of Marisii Klauzer – taken down by an old bridge?

"It can't end like this!" Makio croaked painfully, crumbling down to his knees, hitting the ground with a fist. He just couldn't lose the boy with whom Makio could talk for hours on end, the boy who understood him, the boy who, somehow, for such a short period of time had made him believe in love and relationships again.

Makio was just about to erupt into tears, when he saw Marisii over the cliff's edge, climbing on what was possibly the last remaining rope that stretched along the cliff's length.

Makio inched closer to the cliff's edge, outstretching his right hand as much as he possibly could, toward Marisii. "I got you," Makio said; the same thing Marisii had said to him a couple of minutes ago. "I got you and I won't let go!"

Makio felt Marisii's hand grabbing his tightly. Then, Makio pulled Marisii up over the cliff's edge, groaning with the pain. Marisii and Makio both fell on safe ground, Makio on top of Marisii.

Marisii suddenly started laughing.

"You think this is funny?" Makio asked him incredulously. "You almost died!"

"Admit it, it *was* kinda funny!" Marisii kept laughing like a maniac. "That bridge was clearly unstable, but I still insisted on going through it like a complete idiot!"

"You really *are* a complete idiot!" Makio said. "Stop putting your life at risk! I refuse to lose you, idiot, I *won't* lose you!"

"Believe me, you won't get rid of me that easily," Marisii said and then stopped laughing, a smile appearing on his face.

The two of them rose to a sitting position, their legs and hands unintendedly intertwined.

"I'm like glue – I stick," Marisii said.

"I didn't say I minded," Makio also said with a smile, feeling his body beginning to relax.

In the spur of the moment, without giving it a second thought, he placed a hand on Marisii's head and pulled him in for a passionate kiss. Makio could tell he had taken Marisii by surprise, but Makio himself was surprised by the fact that Marisii relished that kiss, leaning in, thirsty for more.

Marisii took hold of Makio's stained leather jacket's collar and pulled him in even closer.

Their kiss continued for a few more enjoyable seconds until they pulled away from one another, looking in each other's eyes.

None of them said anything – they just kept looking and smiling at each other, as if confirming something without saying it out loud.

Chapter 40

Berventy, Brouzenvert, Brouzun, Morven, and Annora

The deep sky portal opened up and threw out Brouzenvert and Berventy first. Brouzenvert landed on the emerald grass, surrounded by leaves, groaning and shaking from the pain his own son's spell had caused him. Berventy had a rough landing next to her husband, almost dropping The Book. Not long after that Morven, Brouzun, and Annora also appeared flying out of the portal.

"Brouzenvert," Berventy said, drawing even nearer to him.

"It hurts!" Brouzenvert screamed.

Berventy cracked The Book open, beginning to flip through its pages. She couldn't stand the sight of her husband in such excruciating pain. Berventy knew that if she and her sons didn't find Ameralda's cure soon, the poison would have reached Brouzenvert's heart. "Just hold on, Brouzenvert! We're already on the island, just hold on a little longer!"

"We don't even know where to start!" Morven said, situated a few meters away from Berventy, next to his brother Brouzun, and the medical nurse Annora.

Berventy didn't grace her son with an answer, continuing to flip through the pages instead. Until she reached the section about The Island of Lost Hopes. *"'Ameralda's cure' can be found in the 'Cave of the Lost', situated in one of the six mountains on the island."* Berventy started reading. *"At the entrance you may be greeted by Ameralda herself, asking what purpose you've come to her island with – she may or may not require a price, for you to gain entry to the cave. Sincerely yours, Sarvit and Mour."* Berventy finished reading, her gaze sweeping over the pages and landing on her sons. "That's our answer – we need to find the correct mountain, containing the cure!"

"But what is this price we may have to pay to gain entry?" Brouzun asked. "What if she wants to claim one of our lives in exchange for the cure?"

Berventy looked at her son Brouzun, her forehead creased in concentration. "I won't allow this!" she said. "Brouzenvert is not going to die, neither will any of my sons – not on my watch! I'm done cowering and I won't let anything bad happen to our family, okay?"

Brouzun and Morven both nodded simultaneously.

"All this," Annora joined the conversation, seemingly out of it, "is it worth it?"

"*What did you say?*" Berventy said with a cold, harsh tone.

"If this witch, called Feever, that's chasing you all, is so powerful as I've seen first-hand," Annora began, "and if this Ameralda really requires life for life, is all the effort to save this man worth it?" Annora finished, pointing to Brouzenvert, writhing in pain next to Berventy.

"You can't talk about my family that way!" Berventy rose up from the ground, leaving Brouzenvert with the The Book, making her way to Annora within seconds, now hovering above the nurse. She looked her in the eyes as if searching for something. "Because of you two of my sons are lost forever – Kastilius, who thinks that

Feever is his real mom and my other son, who *literally* got lost because of *your* stupidity!"

"Oh, I'm sorry, Berventy," Annora said with a certain irony in her tone, "but Feever is clearly a mighty witch, who can do whatever she wants with whomever she wants! If she can overpower you – the *witches* she claims you are – then what's left for me – the mortal girl, who got swept up into this because I just happened to be in the wrong place at the wrong time? I didn't ask to be involved in *your* family drama, Berventy!" Annora rose steadily to her feet, now facing Berventy. "I liked my normal life – but now, because of you and your whole family, I need to look over my shoulder and check whether there's someone standing there like Feever, who wants to eliminate me! And all that just because I was doing my job as a nurse and I helped *your* family!" At the mention of the last 'your', Annora pushed Berventy's right shoulder with her index finger.

"Don't play the victim when you're clearly not!" Berventy bared her teeth like a predator, appalled by the audacity of Annora. "Do I need to remind you that *you* were the one who gave into her hypnosis? And because of that, I lost two sons! And very soon I might lose my husband too, because my own son Kastilius poisoned his father, leaving him for dead! Don't you *dare* play the victim card in a situation, where you're most definitely the culprit!"

"Mom, maybe we have to..." Morven placed a hand on his mother's shoulder, now up on his feet, as well as his brother Brouzun, but Berventy shrugged away from his touch.

"You have no idea what I'm going through!" Berventy continued as if there was no interruption. "Do you see my two sons here – Brouzun and Morven? They're counting on *me* – their mother – to save their father! They're counting on me to protect them from that vile witch Feever, who wants to annihilate us all for something our ancestor Mour and the Fehrenberg's family ancestor Sarvit, have done! We're the ones being punished for someone else's mistakes!

And you're just standing here, thinking you're a victim! But *I* also have to fix *your* mistakes!"

Annora stepped away from Berventy and looked at her. "Look, I get that you're angry and that you need someone to blame! But that someone isn't me – and if you were in your right mind right now, you would have seen that!"

Berventy wanted to say something else, but it dawned on her that she and her family were running out of time to save Brouzenvert. She averted her head toward her sons, leaving Annora alone. "Let's hurry up, shall we? Every second counts," Berventy said and walked back to The Book and picked it from the grass, holding it tenderly like a baby.

Brouzun and Morven helped their father to his feet, and then the five of them started walking through the jungle. Berventy didn't register the island's beauty – she was too angry.

The five of them had only walked about ten steps when they came across Makio and Marisii.

~~~~~~~~~~

Marisii and Makio had stopped to rest in the middle of the jungle, engrossed in a conversation. Marisii chuckled when Makio paid him another compliment about his muscular body, while Marisii was putting his indigo shirt back on and buttoning it. A second later, Berventy, Brouzenvert, Brouzun, Morven, and Annora appeared, and Marisii was so happy to see three out of five of them. Marisii wanted to hug his mother and brothers, grateful that he'd found them, but then he stopped himself when he saw Brouzenvert's eyes inspecting him and Makio.

"I see you've had fun," Brouzenvert commented, his weight supported by Morven and Brouzun, smiling a bit.

Marisii didn't know how to interpret this. Marisii was glad that his mother and brothers had found him – but for some reason, he wished Brouzenvert wasn't with them. Marisii obviously didn't want his father to die – on the contrary, he wanted him to live for years to come. But right now, Marisii just couldn't stand *even* the sight of him. After all, Brouzenvert was the one who had made him doubt himself and the boy he had grown attached to for such a short time. The nerdy librarian-boy he *liked*. "Not that it's any of your business," Marisii said in his defense. "But we didn't do anything."

"Yeah, right." Brouzenvert cracked the same smile as before. "What, can't you get it up? Even with a man?"

"What the hell is your problem?" Makio asked Brouzenvert. "I'm not just gonna stand here and listen to you belittling and verbally abusing your own son!"

"Makio, there's no need to…" Marisii began, but he was interrupted by Brouzenvert.

"That's between me and Marisii," Brouzenvert almost hissed. "Not you and me! You're not entitled to an opinion about this matter, so it would be better if you shut that mouth of yours!"

Marisii intended to say something but he was once again cut short. This time by Berventy: "Let's discuss this later. Right now, we have to find Ameralda's cure. And fast!"

"Fine," Marisii said, his eyes moving away from Brouzenvert's.

"Fine," Brouzenvert said, his eyes moving away from Marisii's.

Chapter 41

The signal

Makio, Marisii, Brouzun, Morven, Berventy, Brouzenvert, and Annora were walking through the jungle toward the closest mountain they could locate. They had halved the journey when Berventy suddenly stopped them by raising a hand. Morven and Brouzun carefully set Brouzenvert on the leaf-infested ground.

"Almost all the members of our family are here, except for Kasteron," Berventy began, "and it doesn't look like the Fehrenberg family are gonna emerge from anywhere soon. We need to send some sort of signal to locate them and prompt them to come to us – we need to get together!"

"Have you got something in mind?" Marisii asked her.

Berventy cracked open The Book, searching across its pages – she was getting really good at using and orienting with it now. Her eyes located the section, labeled '*Combined Power*'. "*In an instance where you ever lose each other and need a signal to find one another, two members of one of the families need to channel their power toward a third member, who in turn would shoot that power out into the sky. Even if not all of you have unlocked your powers, this method would* still *work, as long as at least three family members are present."* Berventy read and then shut The Book closed. "Marisii, Morven – come closer, please."

Berventy noticed her two sons approaching, with Marisii letting go of Makio's hand, which up until that moment Berventy thought he had been holding. Brouzun stood next to Makio, supervising Brouzenvert.

"Good luck," Makio said after Marisii, who turned and gave him a smile.

"Focus!" Berventy told Marisii, glad to see his eyes on her momentarily after. "Join hands."

Morven took Marisii's hand in his and then outstretched his other hand toward Berventy.

Berventy and Morven's palms joined together. A few seconds later, Berventy could see a navy beam of light crackling with energy, painting Marisii's frame first. Then the beam moved to Morven. A few more seconds passed before Berventy felt the surge of power in her veins, transmitted through Morven's wrist, connected with hers. Berventy knew that kind of magic was complicated and couldn't be done by a single person. The mother felt the magic going through her whole body – infesting every limb, invading every sense. She involuntarily closed her eyes and pointed her free right hand toward the bright sky above.

Berventy felt the power threatening to break out and opened her eyes in time to see another beam of light, this time scarlet-colored, painting the sky, much like a flare. Berventy had to squint with her eyes for a second. She only hoped the brightness of the beam was strong enough for Kasteron and the Fehrenberg family to see.

~~~~~~~~~~

Perventia and Pattery, who was carrying Pacifika in his hands, noticed the now scarlet sky. Pattery was glad to see this as Pacifika was worsening by the second. He didn't want to think what might happen if he and his wife didn't hurry up.

"That must be the others!" Perventia said, pointing to the sky. "I think they're trying to give us a signal!"

"Let's get a move on," Pattery said, "we haven't got much time left!" Pattery then looked at Pacifika, who had her hands wrapped around his neck, wailing and sobbing at the same time. Pattery didn't know what Pacifika felt exactly, but by the sweat on her forehead and her intensified screams, he could tell the poison was spreading. Quicker than before.

~~~~~~~~~

"Look!" Kayla pointed to the sky, making her sister Klacifia and the second Kayla look up. The flare had just shot into the sky. "That must be our mother, giving us a signal of her location!"

"Let's get going then," Klacifia said.

The second Kayla nodded after looking at them with what Klacifia deemed as suspicion.

She still thought there was something eerie about this 'new' Kayla from another universe. Her speech pattern, her body language just screamed 'fishy' to her. Her sister Kayla, even though suspicious as well at first, had quickly accepted her doppelganger. But Klacifia had always been *the one* who'd insisted on double-checking people and their intentions, before deciding whether she could trust them or not.

Klacifia followed her sister, who led the path, catching a glimpse of the way the doppelganger was looking at her. Was that malice in her eyes? Or envy?

The three girls quickened their pace, but for whatever reason Klacifia decided to turn around and steal one more look. *That's* when the doppelganger smiled at her. But that smile seemed too forced, almost like an act to Klacifia.

There was something eerie about this 'new' Kayla – and Klacifia was going to find out exactly what.

Chapter 42

An unusual meeting

The portal spat Kasteron and Teela out on an emerald lawn in a random section of the island. The two of them rose to their feet, observing their surroundings. If The Book hadn't warned the young couple that The Island of Lost Hopes is a devilish place, Teela would have thought that it was actually a piece of true heaven.

"So, you finally found your power." Kasteron turned around to Teela, his eyes now focused entirely on her. He was so proud of Teela and his smile showcased that.

"I did indeed," Teela said, extracting herself from the beauty of the island and focusing on Kasteron. "I will now have a way to protect myself from Feever, protect all of us!"

Kasteron smiled again – that smile drove her crazy every time she saw it.

"Come on, we need to find the others," Kasteron prompted, starting to walk. Teela stopped him by placing her hand on his. A second later, her lips were on his, the kiss initiated by Teela. "Not that I'm complaining," Kasteron laughed after a few long seconds.

"But we really need to find our families! Brouzenvert and Pacifika are probably running out of time as we speak!"

"I know," Teela said, "and I won't allow anything in the world to make me lose another sister!" Teela looked at Kasteron, her hand resting against the fabric on his shirt where his chest was. "But can't we set aside just five minutes for ourselves? Ever since we left our homes, running from Feever, I've barely had any time alone with you – I miss you, Kasteron! In every possible way. The whole ordeal with The Curse and Feever took up all our time together – I just need a few minutes *alone* with you."

Kasteron smiled again and kissed Teela. "What are you suggesting?"

Teela chuckled against Kasteron's lips, her hand starting to unzip Kasteron's jeans. "You know pretty well what I'm suggesting." Her hand slid deep inside Kasteron's boxers, massaging his penis.

Kasteron moaned softly. He gathered Teela up in his arms and pressed her against the trunk of the nearest tree they could find. He placed his lips on hers again and got rid of his shirt, almost ripping the buttons in excitement. Then he proceeded to work on Teela's blouse and jeans and then made quick work of her bra.

Teela removed his jeans and boxers, the hunger burning ever so brightly, marveling at the sight of her naked boyfriend. He was even more beautiful that way – bare and completely exposed to her sight. After he removed her panties, she pushed him to the grass and climbed on top of him, the desire to take control fairly new to her.

Teela traced his neck, then his chest, eventually reaching that special place, with her lips. Out of the corner of her eye, Teela noticed him looking for something. After he found his discarded jeans a few meters away, he reached for them, flinching pleasurably at Teela's touch. Teela heard something ripping and was glad to see that Kasteron had opened up the condom she knew he'd stolen from the hospital. He and Teela were both teenagers and it's not like society made it easy for them to access precautions.

Kasteron pulled Teela back up on top of him and kissed her while placing the condom on his penis. Once that was done, he carefully inserted himself inside Teela, who was already plenty wet.

The couple moaned loudly, the scorching sun above them adding to their already acquired sweat.

Teela thought that maybe it was egoistic to make time for her boyfriend and not her family at such an intense, worrying time, but she couldn't help it. She missed Kasteron so much – she missed the feeling of him inside her, his delicate, yet sinful touch, the softness of his lips. Teela Fehrenberg wanted only a couple of minutes alone with Kasteron, wanted to feel close to him for just a little bit longer, and she promised herself that after, the two of them would find their families and resume the search for Ameralda's cure.

Some time passed and Teela could feel herself getting really close to coming. And judging by Kasteron's increased thrusts, she knew they were definitely in the same boat.

That's when Teela noticed someone and screamed, removing herself from her position on top of Kasteron.

Kasteron craned his neck – his expression turning to one of utter speechlessness.

Tiffany Fehrenberg stood proudly before them, in the flesh, waving with a hand. Tiffany, whom Feever had killed so brutally, Tiffany who had sacrificed herself to save Teela.

"Teela." Tiffany smiled at her sister, her eyes glassy from tears. "I missed you so much!"

Chapter 43

Tiffany

Teela realized Kasteron and she were naked, and she started putting her clothes back on, next to Kasteron, who was doing the same.

"Tiffany?" Teela asked, rising from the emerald grass simultaneously as she was putting her blouse back on, not able to believe her eyes. "How is that possible? Are you really here?"

The person standing in front of Teela looked like Tiffany, spoke like Tiffany. But was that person really Tiffany? Teela's brain rocked around inside her skull, trying to find a plausible answer. But Tiffany had died saving her. Feever had killed her and taken her power. Teela had seen that with her very eyes.

Kasteron stepped closer to Teela, almost protectively.

Teela inched closer to Tiffany, her eyes inspecting her up and down as if looking for some sort of flaw in the code that was her body.

"Yeah, it's me, little sister." Tiffany smiled at Teela.

A second later Teela wrapped her arms around Tiffany, tears of happiness overflowing – Teela didn't know how Tiffany was here, didn't know whether her sister was indeed alive or The Island of Lost Hopes was just playing a cruel trick on her. The only thing she did know was the fact that her sister was here, in the flesh, and Teela could see and hug her one more time. An opportunity that Feever had snatched away up until this moment.

"I missed you so much," Teela said.

"I missed you too, Teela," Tiffany said, the sisters' embrace ending. "It was so horrible. Feever ripped my heart out and drank my undeveloped power..." Tears gathered in her eyes. "And it was so, so dark. I remember you all screaming while Feever was killing me, knowing there was nothing you could have done to save me! Those screams are chasing me every night in my sleep; I can't seem to ever run away from them!"

"The important thing is that you're *here* now," Teela said and cupped Tiffany's face in both her palms. "You're safe! The screams are over. And *I* won't let anyone, and I mean *anyone*, ever hurt you again!"

"Teela," Kasteron said from behind Teela and Tiffany, "don't you think this is all a little bit suspicious?"

"She's alive, Kasteron." At that Teela turned over to her boyfriend, shrugging her shoulders. "What else could possibly matter?"

"The Book warned us that this island is gonna try to deceive us in some way!" Kasteron began, his voice firm. "What if *that* is its way?" His eyes darted over to Tiffany. "Showing the face of the person you want to see most right now? The person, whom you miss the most!"

"Kasteron," Teela almost hissed, "my sister is alive. And here. I don't care about the details!"

"Just try to think," Kasteron said, his palms interlinked. "Is it even remotely possible for Tiffany to still be alive when you and me *both* saw her dying at the hands of Feever?"

Teela shifted her head toward Tiffany. "Maybe this person is just this universe's version of Tiffany," Teela said, wanting to believe her own words more than anything else in the world. "Do you remember that The Book stated that each one of us has a doppelganger in this universe?"

"I'm not a doppelganger," Tiffany said, seemingly offended. "I'm your sister, Teela! Don't you believe me?"

Teela's face softened. "Of course I believe you." Teela wrapped her arms around Tiffany one more time, but not before directing a vicious look at Kasteron.

"Thank you." Tiffany smiled, the tears in her eyes receding. "So, how's the new power?"

"What did you just say?" Teela almost screamed, instantly removing herself from Tiffany.

"I asked how's the new power?" Tiffany said, but then Teela noticed something in her facial expression shifting. Was that worry?

"How do you know I found my power?" Teela asked, the suspicion in her voice evident. Maybe Kasteron was right – maybe *this* Teela was just an illusion, some deceit.

"I don't…"

"That happened *days* after you perished!" Teela said sharply. "There's no way you can know that!"

Tiffany didn't say anything.

"You're not my sister!" Teela was suddenly hit with the realization.

"It's *me*, Teela," Tiffany said, her voice a plea. "I *am* your sister – the one who used to stay up with you all night long to binge watch TV shows, the one who you walked through the school corridors and sat at lunch with, the *one*, who you felt like you can share anything with, because you, out of all your sisters, were closest with her!"

Tears formed in Teela's eyes for a second time today. "I want to believe you," Teela said. "Believe me, I want to believe you more

227

than anything in the world right now! I want you again next to me, so we can fight Feever side by side. I want to binge-watch TV shows and talk all night with you again." Her tears erupted, rolling down her cheeks. "But I can't." Teela collapsed to her knees on the ground, aware of Kasteron's presence next to her a second later. "I fucking miss you, Tiffany!" Teela looked up at the figure, standing a few inches away from her. "But you're not her! You're not my Tiffany!"

"Very well," the girl said and raised her hand demonstratively in the air. Tiffany's face vanished and, in its place, appeared one of a mature middle-aged woman, with long emerald-raven hair. The woman was clad in a long black dress that reached her feet and spilled slightly on the grass around them. At certain places bright green leaves were pinned to the dress, making it stand out. The woman looked at Teela and Kasteron, smiling as if the two teenagers had just proven something to her.

~~~~~~~~~~

"Who are you?" Kasteron asked the odd woman, holding the sobbing Teela in his arms.

"My name is Ameralda," the woman introduced herself, "and I'm the Empress of this island! I heard you've come here to look for Ameralda's cure, or famously known as the *cure*, which only *I* can provide!"

"Then why was all that theatre needed?" Kasteron hissed.

"Mind your language!" Ameralda hissed back. "Because I can choose not to provide you with the cure and leave your father Brouzenvert and Teela's other sister Pacifika, to die."

"How do you know their names?" Teela asked Ameralda, Kasteron watching her slightly withdrawing from his arms, to face Ameralda. "How do you *even* know any of this?"

"Oh, honey, please." Ameralda chuckled and waved a hand in the air. "I know everything that's happening on my island – there's no way for a person to come to this island, or do anything on it, without me finding out! The Island of Lost Hopes is my creation – I named it as such because only desperate people with lost hopes ever come here, looking for answers to their predicaments. When it all started, I decided to test each individual who set foot on my island, to see if they were worthy enough of my cure!"

"And are we worthy?" Kasteron said.

"So far none have been," Ameralda said. "Hundreds upon hundreds of people have come here, looking for the cure, but they never obtained it from me – they were just not *worthy*. But I see something in Teela that I didn't see in the others – determination and bravery!"

Kasteron and Teela looked at her uncomprehendingly.

"I temporarily took the form of your sister to see how you were going to react when you saw her having risen from the dead." Ameralda's attention shifted from Kasteron to Teela, Kasteron observed. "Your reaction showed me that you possess the determination and bravery to fight for your family. You proved that you deserve Ameralda's cure," Ameralda said. "You will find it in the *Cave of the Lost*, situated in one of the six mountains on the island, where I will be, waiting to give it to you. You, Teela Fehrenberg, will be able to give the cure to your sister Pacifika and prevent her from dying!"

"Thank you," Teela smiled through tears.

Kasteron was so happy to know that his girlfriend wasn't going to lose another sister.

"Regarding you–" Ameralda's gaze shifted to Kasteron. "I'm sure you've also got determination and bravery in you, but I haven't seen that yet! You better prove it soon, otherwise, there will be no cure for your father."

"Wait, what?" Kasteron asked, the bafflement evident in his voice.

"I will be waiting for you all in the cave," Ameralda said and thrust her hands up in the air, disappearing from her spot.

"How can I prove it to you, damn it!" Kasteron hit the greenery below with a fist.

~~~~~~~~~~

Teela smiled – she wasn't able to save Tiffany, but she was going to save Pacifika. The feeling of guilt that she had neglected her family for 15 minutes, disappeared.

A red flare suddenly shot out into the sky, painting it in deep scarlet, Teela and Kasteron raising their heads. Teela instantly knew the red flare was a sign from her and Kasteron's families, showing them in which direction they needed to head.

Chapter 44

The Cave of the Lost

Berventy was stood in front of three caves she and her family had located with the help of The Book, situated in one of the island's mountains, holding the item in question wide open in her hands. She was trying to figure out a way to tell which cave was the correct one.

Perventia, Pattery, and Pacifika had already joined Berventy, Brouzenvert, Morven, Brouzun, Marisii, Makio, and Annora. Out of the corner of her eye, Berventy noticed Teela and Kasteron approaching. Teela was smiling about something and went to give her parents a hug. Shortly after, Berventy turned around and saw Klacifia, Kayla and another Kayla heading toward them.

All their mouths gaped wide open with surprise upon seeing the two Kaylas. And while they looked identical in terms of facial features and body structure, one of them was clean and the other dirty.

Berventy noticed the dirty Kayla starting to cry upon seeing the Fehrenberg family.

Pattery pulled the clean Kayla aside and Berventy was confident he could tell who his daughter was. "Kayla, what's going on? The Book warned us there may be doppelgangers in this universe who would try to fool us!"

"I know," Kayla said, "but she's lost her entire family – Feever killed them all, and she's the sole survivor! I thought that if I allowed her to come with us and see *a* version of her family again, even for a little while, she would feel better. Just look at her, Dad – who knows what exactly she's gone through?"

Kayla's hair was a tangled mess, her clothes were streaked with dirt all over, her eyes and shaking hand betraying her fear.

"Okay," Pattery said, "but we can't take her back with us in our universe!"

Berventy saw the doppelganger Kayla trying not to eavesdrop on Kayla and Pattery's conversation, but failing.

"It's too dangerous and in doing so we may disrupt the natural order of things in both universes!" Pattery said and with that, he and his daughter finished their conversation.

Berventy's eyes stayed rooted for just one more second to the doppelganger Kayla, seeing her squinting her eyes for a second, before turning around to the three wide caves again and starting to read a passage from The Book. "*'Serventi kore tuva korven'.*" At those words a wide and bright beam of light shot out of The Book, heading straight for the three caves. This was the recognition spell and Berventy knew she was powerful enough to cast it. She was getting more and more acquainted with The Book and chanting basic spells was becoming second nature.

In the long years when Berventy and Brouzenvert had been raising their boys, she hadn't forgotten witchcraft completely – she was practicing it on a weekly, sometimes monthly basis, with the desire to absorb and master as many spells as she could. So when the time to fight Feever came, she and her family would stand a chance. Berventy was yet to unlock her individual power, but that didn't stop her from casting small spells such as this one.

The three caves lit up furiously – the first one, on Berventy's left, colored in blue, the second one, opposite Berventy, painted in red, and the third one, on Berventy's right, shot out a bright green torrent of light.

Berventy checked The Book again. "It says here that the one which is painted in green is the correct cave." Then, she closed the voluminous object shut.

They all stepped inside The Cave of the Lost, accelerating the pace – time was even shorter now for Pacifika and Brouzenvert, and the two families had to work quickly.

~~~~~~~~~~

Ameralda was patiently awaiting them at the heart of the cave. She was glad to hear them approaching in the brightly lit space. Ameralda turned around to face her island's visitors, a smile planted on her lips. Her long emerald-raven hair was flowing freely in all directions as she moved, and her black dress with leaves pinned along its fabric material, looked more elegant than ever. The torches along the walls seemed to burn brighter now, coloring the cave in crimson-orange light. "I'm glad you could finally make it," Ameralda continued smiling, raising her hands around her demonstratively. "Welcome to 'The Cave of the Lost'!"

"I'm sorry, who are you?" Perventia asked.

"Oh, I'm the *one* who should be sorry," Ameralda said, her hands lowering. "I haven't introduced myself to all of you properly." Ameralda's posture straightened, her chest rising steadily up and lowering down. "My name is Ameralda and I'm the Empress of this island. I've been ruling it for over a thousand years. In fact, I was the one who created it, and I know everything that takes place on it. There's no way for you to do something without me finding out about it. I already tested Teela and she earned the cure for her sister Pacifika. But so far, none of the Klauzers' family members has proved themselves as deserving of the cure!"

"So, you're *the* Ameralda?" Marisii asked her. "As in Ameralda, from whom we need to take Ameralda's cure?"

"For a pretty boy, you're quite slow. And *take* is a really unfitting word," Ameralda said. "You need to earn it!" Two more torches lit up on the wall near Ameralda's face, revealing two wide purple curtains behind her, hanging from the roof of the cave. She patted them with a hand. "Behind these curtains," she said, "stands the cure you can cease Pacifika and Brouzenvert's suffering with." She started pulling them open slowly, as if savoring the moment. "Teela Fehrenberg is going to receive my cure right now. But I want Marisii Klauzer to undergo a specific process to show me he's worthy of the cure for his father!"

Kasteron stepped up, closer to Ameralda. "I thought you wanted *me* to be the tested one?"

"That I did," Ameralda said, pulling open the two curtains slightly more, "but I also appreciate the honesty of this island and what it signified over the years, and there's something that's been left unsaid between Marisii and Brouzenvert Klauzer." She saw Marisii looking at her uncomprehendingly, but she knew Brouzenvert knew *exactly* what she was talking about. "Only then can I give the cure for Brouzenvert as well." Ameralda pulled open the two purple curtains entirely, and turned her back on the two families and their companions. A second later, her smile faltered and then completely vanished.

As always, Ameralda found the small vial, containing the lilac liquid, resting on top of a tall marble pillar. She had left the cure atop the pillar a few hours ago – and it was still there, waiting to be drunk by Pacifika and Brouzenvert.

But there was one vial.

Ameralda had left two. One for Pacifika and one for Brouzenvert – and now her brain was racking around in her skull, trying to come to terms with the harsh reality of only one cure, enough for Pacifika, *or* Brouzenvert.

Ameralda screamed with all the power she had in her body, realizing she had been tricked by her sworn enemy – the infamous witch Feever.

Chapter 45

Ameralda's cure

"That bitch," Ameralda screamed, angered. She turned back to the two families. "Feever must have taken one of the cures!"

"What do you mean *taken?*" Berventy asked, her voice betraying her panic. "I thought you monitored everything happening on this island? How could you let this slip past you?"

"I don't know how she did it," Ameralda said and the shivering Brouzenvert could see the anger bubbling up inside of her. "Maybe she used some sort of masking the presence spell, but… I'm afraid the cure is now only one. And it's going to be enough for only one person."

Brouzenvert could sense the pain in her voice – she must have really wanted to help both him and Pacifika, but she had been tricked, and now her hands were tied. Brouzenvert's body began betraying him, sensing his organs threatening to shut off.

But how could any of them choose between Pacifika and Brouzenvert? How could they even begin to think about who deserved the life-saving substance more?

Pattery was helping Pacifika stay on her feet. But now Brouzenvert saw the blond woman crumbling down to her knees on the rocks, unable to hold on.

"Darling?" Perventia said, her husband and she kneeling next to their daughter. "Pacifika?"

Pacifika let out a pain-infested scream and Brouzenvert could see her fingers beginning to turn an onyx color, one by one.

"It's started," Ameralda said upon seeing what Brouzenvert had observed just a moment ago. "The poison has begun making its way toward her heart."

Immediately after Ameralda's words, Brouzenvert felt a sharp pain in his chest, his knees giving out completely. His body met the hard rock ground, his fingers also beginning to dye in onyx.

"Dad?" Marisii said, clearly worried, and knelt next to his father on the cave's floor.

"You need to decide quickly," Ameralda said. "They don't have much time left."

"Marisii, listen to me," Brouzenvert said with extreme effort. If those were going to be his last minutes on this earth, he was going to make them count. He had to tell his son the reason behind his actions.

Marisii listened intently, Makio close to him. The rest of the families' members and Annora were watching the scene close by. Berventy, Kasteron, Morven, and Brouzun were in the closest proximity.

"Marisii, I'm so sorry for behaving in such a way," Brouzenvert said, and Marisii looked surprised to hear it. "I don't mind for you to date a boy." Brouzenvert noticed even Makio's surprise.

"But you said…" Marisii's voice disappeared for a second. "You said you wouldn't allow any of your sons to be gay, you said it."

"I know what I said." Brouzenvert assured him. "But I said that and reacted in such an ugly way because I was afraid – afraid of you getting hurt! The same way I got hurt all those years ago!"

"What are you talking about?" Confusion took charge of Marisii's voice.

"I'm bisexual, Marisii," Brouzenvert said and knew that would be hard to believe for Marisii, even Makio. "I always have been." Brouzenvert managed a smile before a scream erupted out of his throat – his legs had the same onyx color now. "Many years ago, even before I met your mother, I was dating a boy – I was such head over heels for him. I loved him deeply, and all my firsts were with him. But he wasn't comfortable with his own sexuality and never wanted word to get out that he was gay. His parents were *the* homophobes, constantly brainwashing him with beliefs that if he was dating a guy, he committed a sin. His name was Kersten and I loved him with all my heart!"

Tears slid past Marisii's eyes, his cheeks damp now. He took his father's hand in his. Makio's eyes were watering as well.

"They knew about him and I dating, and one day they told him to choose – them or me."

Marisii started crying as if sensing where this already gruesome story was heading.

"A couple of days later Kersten invited me over to his place for dinner," Brouzenvert said.

Brouzun, Morven, Kasteron, and Berventy were now crying as well. The Fehrenberg family soon followed.

"I entered the house and within seconds I was thrown down to the floor by Kersten's father. He bared his teeth at me and undid his belt, sliding it away from his jeans. Kersten's mother and Kersten *himself* were watching on the side, saying nothing as his belt came down on me again and again. I tried to escape," Brouzenvert said, his eyes overcome by tears, "but there was no way out! Kersten's father continued hitting me with his belt, shouting that I must never touch his precious son again, or do any sort of abominations with any member of the same gender. I could feel myself bleeding from three different places and I really thought Kersten's father was going to murder me right there on the spot." Brouzenvert smiled through physical pain – but his emotional pain was now greater. "But he didn't do it. He continued beating me with the belt until he decided I'd learned my lesson. Then he kicked me out of his home. I was lying in a hospital for weeks after that!" Brouzenvert touched his face and arms – there were light marks there. "Do you see these scars?"

Marisii nodded. "When I asked you about them you told me they were caused by something sharp when you were a kid," Marisii said. It was evident what exactly they were caused by now. Kersten's father's blows with the belt were so hard, they'd left marks.

"I'm not saying that to make you feel sorry for me," Brouzenvert said. "There's really no excuse for what I said to you back in the hospital – it was rude and repulsive, and I realized that in my quest to protect you, *I* was the one who actually hurt you. When you ran out of Morven's hospital room, tears staining your eyes, I realized that I'm not any better than Kersten's father – an insensitive, brutal homophobe!"

"No, Dad," Marisii said, squeezing his hand as if he were afraid it would evaporate. "You're not even remotely like that jerk! You were just trying to protect me – you never hated me for liking a boy!"

"How can I hate you?" Brouzenvert smiled, this time from happiness, and the tears doubled in his eyes. He made a hand gesture to Makio to come closer, moving his fingers toward himself. Makio knelt next to Marisii. They were both resting their legs on the hard rock ground now. "I saw your smile when you said you were going out on a date with Makio – I'd never seen you smile so genuinely by anyone or anything. You spent years racking your brain around why you didn't like girls or go on any dates. You couldn't like anyone." Brouzenvert's eyesight shifted to Makio. "And then suddenly Makio came along. You hadn't gone out on even one date and he was already making you smile just by talking about him." His eyes returned to his son. "Marisii, don't you understand? Everything I said or did was because I was trying to protect you from the same burning pain I experienced. But now I can see that you're *happy* – I see your body tingling and a smile appearing on your face every time Makio comes around. That's all I ever wanted for you, my dear son – someone who makes you happy, someone who causes butterflies to form in your stomach, someone you feel you can share anything with! I don't care if you're dating a boy or a girl – all I care about is for you to be happy!" Brouzenvert caressed Marisii's face with his hand.

Marisii sighed at the gentle touch and clung to his father's hand. Brouzenvert could sense that Marisii didn't want to lose him now that everything had finally gotten out in the open. "I forgive you," Marisii said. "I would forgive you a hundred times, I love you, Dad!" Marisii pulled his father into an embrace, careful not to cause him any more pain.

"I love you too, son," Brouzenvert said, feeling his voice growing weak. But no. Just no. He was going to say what he was going to say – he wouldn't let Kastilius's poison take that away from him.

Berventy, Morven, Kasteron, and Brouzun knelt all around Brouzenvert, their faces stained with fresh tears. None of them wanted to lose Brouzenvert – to have their family inexplicably shattered.

"Make my kid happy, Makio," Brouzenvert said when Marisii pulled out of the hug, but not his hand. "Don't let anyone hurt him the same way I was!"

Marisii's other hand connected to Makio's hand. Now both of his hands were held by two people who were so important to him, Brouzenvert knew. Makio looked directly at him, with adoration.

"I would never let that happen," Makio said.

Brouzenvert's neck craned to Ameralda painfully, noticing even *her* crying.

"I'm sorry," Ameralda said and all eyes turned to her. "Both you and Pacifika deserve to receive the cure. You told your son all that, you essentially told him the *truth*, and that's a quality I admire most of all. I'm really sorry – the cure is only one and you need to decide who's going to drink it."

There was a pause – the crimson-orange flames painted everyone's faces in their glow, the only sound in the cave now the crackling of the flames from the torches. Because of that, the tears on everyone's faces looked as if composed of blood. A liquid so vital, yet possessing the ability to be so fatal.

"Give it to Pacifika," Brouzenvert said firmly.

Pattery and Perventia looked at him, the dying father catching a glimpse of surprise in their eyes.

"My time has ended," Brouzenvert said. "And Pacifika's time is just beginning – please, give the cure to her, she deserves it!"

"But Brouzenvert, you don't deserve to die!" Berventy's voice cracked.

Brouzenvert felt Berventy placing her head against his chest. He wanted to soothe her more than anything. "The Curse doesn't care who deserves to die and whom to live – it's intended to claim the members of our families, one by one, until Feever fulfills her stupid revenge."

"But…" Morven said. "There has to be another way! Things can't just end like this!"

"There isn't," Brouzenvert said and for the first time, he felt like his whole family realized that was the total truth. "Please, give the cure to Pacifika – don't let my sacrifice be in vain!"

Ameralda walked to the tall marble pillar and acquired the small vial with the lilac liquid with a wave of a hand.

Brouzenvert saw her approaching and was ready for her question: "Are you sure about this?"

"The only thing I've been surer about in my entire life is the love I have for my family!"

Berventy smiled through tears.

Ameralda went to Perventia and Pattery and handed them the cure. Brouzenvert saw them taking it slowly and very carefully, their gaze landing on him. "Thank you, Brouzenvert," Perventia said through tears.

"Your sacrifice will not be forgotten!" Pattery removed the cork top from the small glass vial, containing Ameralda's cure.

Brouzenvert could vaguely hear thirsty gulps, coming from Pacifika's direction. He was glad, he had done a good thing. But that positivity didn't last much longer – his neck was quickly blackening. And his heart was steadily slowing down its beat.

"I love all of you," he told his family. "My beautiful Berventy, you were the greatest life companion. I want you to find love again – even if that's not with me." He looked at her, trying to capture the image of his wife, who was so evidently heartbroken. He caressed her face, his fingers against her skin a wonderful feeling. "My brave Marisii." Brouzenvert's eyes shifted to Marisii and Makio. Marisii's hand was still gripping Brouzenvert's. "Fight for each other and don't let anything prise you apart!" His eyes then traveled to Kasteron. "Somehow, I know that you, Kasteron, will keep getting into trouble!" Brouzenvert laughed, so did Kasteron. "Be happy with Teela, you deserve her." And at last, his eyes found his two sons left. "Morven, Brouzun, I know our paths split up all those years ago and I know we hadn't been on the same page for many things, even before I left. But I need you to know that I've never stopped loving you!"

"We know, Dad," Brouzun and Morven said simultaneously, "we know."

"You're all the light in my life." His face was growing darker and darker now. *I love you!*"

His whole face turned onyx. He looked at his beloved one last time, and then his eyelids fluttered closed. His heart stopped. His hands and whole body relaxed lifelessly. His last breath escaped past his lips and Brouzenvert Klauzer died, sacrificing himself so a young girl could keep on living, telling his family how much he loved them one last time. And deep down, knowing that they were always going to carry him with them in their memory.

Wherever they went.

Chapter 46

"The most beautiful girl I have ever seen."

A long time ago – even before Brouzun, Morven, Marisii, and Kasteron were born and before the Klauzer family was at all formed – Brouzenvert had just walked out of the hospital his ex-boyfriend's parents had put him in. And more specifically Kersten's father, who had hit Brouzenvert with his belt over and over again, until every place on Brouzenvert's face ached beyond recognition.

The sunlight shone brightly in Brouzenvert's eyes, as he stood in front of the hospital's entrance/exit. He shielded his eyes with a hand, grateful to have spent a few days in the hospital, completely cut off from the outside world. Brouzenvert had changed from his hospital gown back into his usual, now torn-up clothes. He felt his wallet and keys in his front pockets, grateful he hadn't lost them in that devastating night. Brouzenvert descended the single flight of stairs in front of the hospital, walking intently in a certain direction.

Upon reaching his house, he took the keys out of his right front pocket, dropping them a second later. He bent to pick them up and when he did, Brouzenvert noticed the bright indigo spots lining his hands. He straightened up and looked at himself in one of the two-story house's windows – dozens of scratches were obscuring his face, the plasters there now soaking with fresh blood. His fingers touched his face and he screamed – his face burned up in pain just by their tips.

Brouzenvert realized that a different person was looking at him in the reflection – that person wasn't the same Brouzenvert Klauzer, who gave his heart away so easily just because he loved the person he was with so madly.

That person had disappeared – now standing there was another Brouzenvert Klauzer, who was covered in injuries and bruises, not wanting to find love ever again.

"Come to *'The Gathering'*," a voice sounded close to him.

Brouzenvert's reverie was shattered and he now noticed a boy, aged no more than around 16 or 17, handing out flyers down the street. The boy reached Brouzenvert and thrust a flyer in his hand, the title *'The Gathering'* printed at the top in red block letters. Under it, there were the words: *'for anyone who loves dancing, pleasant music, good food and quality wine'.*

"The Gathering will be held on Friday in the town square, in case you're interested," the boy said, his eyes skittering over Brouzenvert's face. "I think that may make you forget about whatever happened to you for a few moments."

Brouzenvert looked at the flyer again, and then back up at the boy, smiling tiredly. "I doubt that."

"Just give it a try," the boy said, "you never know what could happen."

The boy continued walking excitedly down the street, Brouzenvert watching him almost chasing a woman with a dog, shouting that The Gathering was of great importance, stating the time and place. She started purposefully avoiding the boy, but he eventually caught up with her.

Brouzenvert looked at the flyer for the third time – in the background was a picture of random people, dancing, looking like they were genuinely having fun. Brouzenvert folded the flyer in two and put it in his almost torn-up pocket. Then he walked up to the door of his house and almost forgetting he was holding the keys in his other hand, unlocked it. He closed the door behind him, raced up the stairs to the second floor and collapsed on the small single bed in the house's single bedroom, too exhausted to strip out of his dirty, tattered clothes.

Even sleep couldn't provide him with the escape of reality he so desperately needed. Nightmares, involving Kersten, his father, and huge leather belts began taking shape in Brouzenvert's head, chasing him like a pack of predators.

~~~~~~~~~~

The Gathering was due to commence at eight o'clock sharp. Brouzenvert had almost forgotten to check the time of the event, but thankfully it was clearly stated on the back of the flyer. The time was seven now and Brouzenvert was brushing his teeth in the bathroom while putting on a violet shirt at the same time. Before allowing the soft material of the shirt to envelope his shoulders he looked at himself, shirtless, in the bathroom mirror. But he quickly tore his gaze away as he remembered how much Kersten had admired his body the first time they had slept together.

Not allowing the bad memories to take the better of him, he slid the shirt on his shoulders and fastened the buttons, spitting the toothpaste and rinsing his mouth. He combed his dark chestnut hair as much as he was able, put on black jeans and matching shoes. Brouzenvert then put on his favorite black leather jacket and sprayed just a speck of cologne on himself.

Brouzenvert wasn't looking for another relationship at this gathering – he just wanted to forget about Kersten for a moment and do something other than sitting around in his house, *alone*, all day, thinking about how the person, whom he once felt he could share anything with, had betrayed him in such a brutal way.

Brouzenvert picked up his wallet and keys from the nightstand in his room. He never went anywhere without them. Then he walked up to the bathroom mirror to look at his reflection one last time, before heading out of the house.

The time was seven-forty and Brouzenvert headed for the town square with a steady stride. It took him just about 20 minutes to get to the square and when he did, The Gathering had already begun. Another reminder of his suffering – whether he was there or not, life kept on going.

A big crowd of people had turned up, most of them invading the vast table at the center of the square, offering a variety of meals, light snacks, and wine. Brouzenvert seemed to recall from the flyer that the catering of the event was free. He saw a single designated person behind the table, taking orders and trying to serve as many customers as he could at once. Around the table, people were talking amongst themselves. Most of them seemed to be having a good time, laughing and even dancing, all the while consuming the free food and wine. There was also a tall stage, not far from the table and the crowd of people, a pop band of three members playing a catchy song on it. The spectators seemed to enjoy that song. All except for one.

A tiny ball of anxiety started forming in Brouzenvert's stomach – there were too many people surrounding him and he was beginning to think that coming to The Gathering wasn't such a grand idea.

Trying to make his anxiety disappear, he walked up to the table and told the boy working there to pour him white wine and give him something – *anything* – to eat. The boy nodded as an answer and a few seconds later, gave him the glass of white wine and a paper plate with all kinds of delicious-looking crackers and muffins.

Brouzenvert picked up one of the muffins and started shoving it in his mouth as if somebody were chasing him.

"Hey," he said to the boy who had served him, tiny pieces of dark muffin flying everywhere. "Weren't you the one handing out the flyers?"

"Yes, that's me." The boy nodded with a smile. "The Gathering is a way for me to make some money. Don't tell anyone but I'm saving up to buy the new line of *Power Rangers* funko pop figurines."

"Pop figurines?" Brouzenvert raised a brow questioningly.

"They are these small, incredibly cute figurines of different pop culture characters," the boy explained, his tone excited. "Do you want to see my collection sometime?"

"Ahh, there's no need," Brouzenvert politely declined the offer, thinking this boy was slightly weird.

A woman came up to the table next to Brouzenvert and flung her plate, full of spaghetti Bolognese at the boy on the other side. She bared her teeth. "I don't like that!"

Brouzenvert saw the boy starting to try and clean his now reddened white shirt. "I'm sorry to inform you," the boy said, "but the world doesn't revolve around *you* and your needs!"

The woman's mouth dropped open.

"Goodbye!" the boy said to the woman, waved with a hand dismissively and then moved to another part of the table, customers already lining up there.

Brouzenvert couldn't hold back his smile and noticed the woman giving him a cold glare, before walking away from the table.

He continued smiling and even laughing until his eyes suddenly landed on something in the crowd – or more like *someone*, who caught his attention. This girl in the crowd near the stage, dancing freely and excitedly, her long gingerbread hair flying in all directions as she moved. She was clad in an ebony dress with a cleft at the end where fabric met bare thigh skin, and raven high heels.

This girl was strikingly attractive – but the thing that captured Brouzenvert's attention wasn't the dress or the heels.

It was the huge, gratified smile, plastered across her face. Her beauty also showed in how natural it was. She hadn't put on too much make-up and had let her hair flow free on her back and shoulders, rather than restricting it in the confines of a bun or a hairband. She was graceful, finesse in its truest form.

"Oh, my God," Brouzenvert said, still looking at the girl, now snacking on crackers, which, seemingly like the muffins, were flying out of his mouth. A couple of girls had the misfortune of passing by Brouzenvert at this exact same moment. They said something, seemingly outraged, just like the woman who had assaulted the boy with the spaghetti, but Brouzenvert's whole attention was already elsewhere.

Suddenly, Brouzenvert saw the girl approaching, seemingly leaving all of her admirers, or friends for a moment. He dropped the paper plate with the crackers and muffins, sweat furrowing his brow. Had she noticed him watching her? Was she now headed toward him to give him a *lesson*? Just like Kersten's father had given him one.

To his great relief, she passed him by, picking up some biscuits and sliced cheddar on a paper plate. For a moment he thought the girl might just pass him by for real, and forget about him altogether, like one other person he used to know, but she didn't. She looked at him instead. Brouzenvert was well aware of how his face looked – bruised and tattered, littered with plasters. He had changed them yesterday, but they were probably turning bloody once again.

"What happened to you?" the girl said, the excitement that Brouzenvert saw in her in front of the stage vanishing.

"It's a long story," Brouzenvert said, attempting a smile. "It's not something I'd like to talk about – it's something I'd rather forget."

But the girl continued looking at him. Was he that repulsive? "Well, isn't that what The Gathering is exactly for?" She smiled, picking up some more biscuits and cheddar, but this time different types. "Escaping reality for a night."

Brouzenvert saw her starting to walk away, but then she suddenly stopped. Why, he didn't know. He realized he was on edge only when he felt both of his palms drenched in sweat.

"Relax," she said with another smile, "I don't bite."

"You promise?" Brouzenvert attempted a slight smile again.

"So," she handed him a biscuit off her paper plate, and then set the plate on the table next to her, "are you having fun?"

"Not really," Brouzenvert picked up the biscuit, bringing it to his lips. "There's too many people!" At that, he spat several biscuit pieces on the girl unintentionally. "Oh, I'm so deeply sorry!"

The girl laughed. "I told you, I don't bite." Still laughing. "There's no need for you to shoot me with biscuits!"

"But I didn't want to..." Brouzenvert intended to apologize but after a few seconds he, too, burst into laughter – something he hadn't done ever since Kersten. "You can never be sure, you know. It is my solemn duty to find out if you don't bite and that's why I'm shooting you with biscuits!"

The girl raised her hand, touching her pointer finger to her thumb. "Splendid."

Both of them burst out laughing again.

"You know," Brouzenvert said and looked into her eyes – they seemed so innocent and pure. "That's not a flirt attempt or something but..." He suddenly became serious, his playful tone disappearing without a trace.

"Are you okay?" she asked him, the worry evident in her voice. "Did I say something to offend you?"

"No, no..." Brouzenvert felt a smile finding its way across his lips. "Just..."

The girl looked at him, a question in the silence.

"You're beautiful," he said, earning himself a wide smile from her. "Maybe the most beautiful girl I have ever seen."

Her smile didn't waver. "Not attempting to flirt at all, I see," the girl said and both of them laughed once again.

The woman with the spaghetti made a comeback, holding another paper plate of spaghetti, heading toward the boy behind the table.

"Ma'am, I told you." The boy sighed. "The world doesn't revolve around you."

The woman threw the plate toward him, the dish landing on his now white-red shirt. "How do you like that, huh?"

The boy started removing the paper plate, which had stuck stubbornly to his shirt.

Brouzenvert and the girl he had recently met were observing the scene on the sidelines.

The boy, working behind the table, took a huge black plastic spoon out of a vast bowl, containing a red liquid, most likely tomato sauce, Brouzenvert assumed. After the spoon had richly absorbed the liquid, the boy flung it at the woman, her bright-colored outfit turning crimson. "And how do *you* like *that*, huh?"

Someone shouted at the top of their lungs: "FOOD FIGHTTTT!"

The whole crowd headed for the table, grabbing handfuls of food, commencing the fight.

Brouzenvert and the girl erupted into greater laughter than before, as the food was bouncing off of them, slamming into their faces, staining their stylish clothes. But they didn't seem to care, obviously having fun.

"Come at me!" The spaghetti woman hissed, throwing a spoonful of green olives in the boy's direction.

"You want some of this, don't you?" Some kind of pie flew through the air, splashing into the woman's face, a few pieces hitting Brouzenvert and the girl.

"What's your name?" Brouzenvert asked her.

"WHAT?" she shouted back amidst all the commotion.

Brouzenvert saw even the pop band, who was playing just minutes ago, climbing off of the stage, enthusiastically joining the food fight. *"WHAT'S YOUR NAME?"*

*"*BERVENTY!*"* Her voice was still raised, the smile still on her face. *"AND YOURS?"*

*"*BROUZENVERT!*"*

Her smile was contagious, and he couldn't resist himself.

"It's very nice to meet you," she said, this time without shouting it out.

"WHAT?"

"I SAID *IT'S VERY NICE TO MEET YOU!*"

"CHAMPAGNE FOR EVERYONE!" Brouzenvert heard one of the band members say, recognizing his voice from the band's catchy song earlier. He saw a volcano of champagne erupting near him, showering the event's guests.

Brouzenvert looked at Berventy, his smile unwavering. And she looked back at him in the same way.

At this event, these two souls bonded and at first, they were hanging out together as just friends. They became really close with one another and as time passed, they found out there was something more underneath the surface of their friendship.

Because they weren't *just* friends.

Brouzenvert and Berventy Klauzer were soulmates.

Chapter 47

"The fault for that is yours."

Berventy was still holding Brouzenvert's hand tightly in hers. Marisii, Morven, Brouzun, Kasteron and Makio were standing on the side, next to his body, as if half-expecting him to wake up any time soon. As if expecting all that had happened to be a bad dream. But it wasn't a dream – that was the reality.

Pacifika had gulped down Ameralda's cure, her limbs, which had been turning a dark color, cleared. Perventia and Pattery were sitting on the cave's hard floor, huddled close to Pacifika, Kayla, Klacifia and Teela positioned next to them.

The medical nurse Annora was standing close by, a silent observer and the island's empress Ameralda was walking back and forth, seemingly buried in thought.

Moments later, purple smoke started fizzing inside the cave. Not long after a wide cloud formed out of the smoke, revealing the witches Feever and her son Kastilius.

Berventy turned around toward them, gaze cold.

"Hello," Kastilius said, waving to all of them with a hand. "Did you miss me?"

Berventy let go of Brouzenvert's hand, letting it fall on the hard floor. The cave was still brightly lit by the torches stuck along the walls and the emotion, written on Berventy's face could be evidently seen, reflected in them – contempt. She stepped forward, closer to them, her eyes fixed on Kastilius. "Do you have *any* idea what you've done?"

"I think that was quite obvious," Kastilius said, looking to Feever for a moment, who nodded. "I poisoned Brouzenvert and Pacifika. We said there's a cure for the poison..." Kastilius laughed giddily, like a child.

"Which was enough for only one of them," Feever finished with a smile. "And the way I see it, Pacifika's the winner!"

"The cure was distributed into *two* vials!" Ameralda, who had been standing by the tall marble pillar behind Feever, said.

Feever turned around and uttered a surprised laugh when she saw Ameralda. "Oh, Ameralda," she said, "long time no see."

"Save your pleasantries, Feever." Ameralda hissed. "The cure was distributed into two vials – one for Pacifika and one for Brouzenvert. I wanted to test them and see if they were both deserving of the cure. But you took that opportunity away from me!"

"You and your talk about honesty." Feever rolled her eyes. "Don't you get tired listening to yourself sometimes?"

"You tricked me!" Ameralda's tone raised an octave. "And now I'm realizing Brouzenvert too was deserving of the cure, but you stole one of the vials somehow! You took his life!"

"We've known each other for so many years," Feever said. "You know that's nothing new for me."

"But they *both* deserved the cure!" Ameralda insisted. "You meddled in *my* affairs and you know pretty well I don't allow *or* tolerate that!"

"And what are you gonna do?" Feever said, Berventy sensing a laugh bubbling up. "You will drown me in flowers? Or shoot me with a rainbow?"

Berventy saw Feever inspecting Ameralda from head to toe – from her emerald-raven hair to her unique dress with leaves pinned to the fabric and bare feet.

"Look at you, you're pathetic! You're not even a particle as powerful as me!" Feever said. Kastilius was still beside her, facing the rest of the families' members. "You might have been on this planet much longer than me, but you and I both know that in a battle between the two of us, *I* would be the one emerging out alive!"

Ameralda didn't say anything back.

Berventy was aware of Feever's words and their possible truthfulness. She didn't know either of the two women well, but she had seen Feever's power and how much havoc and grief it could wreak. She knew Feever had gone to the trouble of casting a powerful curse and laying down to sleep for more than 300 years, just to get revenge. She *knew* painfully well Feever had woken up during her slumber for a brief moment, just to swap her son with Berventy's, in order to hurt Berventy's whole family even more.

"You two killed Brouzenvert!" Berventy said and watched as Feever turned her attention back to her. "Kastilius, how could you? He was your father!"

"I've never had a father," Kastilius said. "Only a mother who fought for me every waking moment of her life!"

"He took care of you!" Berventy raised her voice once again. "*We* raised you, Kastilius, not that vile woman!"

"DON'T TALK ABOUT MY MOTHER THAT WAY!" Kastilius shouted, his voice reverberating through the cave. Then he threw a spell toward Berventy, its distinctive black color similar to the one he had used on Brouzenvert and Pacifika.

Berventy couldn't react fast enough, but thankfully for her, Teela, who had already found her power, did. Berventy saw the deadly spell ricocheting to one of the torches in the wall next to her, exploding. She looked at Teela and said a silent *'thank you'*.

"Impressive," as if Feever almost congratulated her. "But that's nothing compared to what I can do!" Feever waved her right hand in Teela's direction, making her fly through the cave and bump against one of its walls. "That's how you use telekinesis, hun!" Feever said and then stepped closer to Brouzenvert.

"What do you think you're doing?" Berventy stepped closer to Feever, blocking her path. Their faces were now just an inch away from one another.

"Brouzenvert is dead. I'm going to take his power!" Feever smiled at Berventy, her voice thinning. "Just like I did with Tiffany Fehrenberg!"

Out of the corner of her eye, Berventy saw Pattery stir. Not taking her eyes off Feever's, she squinted at her. "You will have to go through me to take Brouzenvert's power!" Berventy erased the last inch of distance, Feever's face and hers only a centimeter apart now. "Do not touch my family." The coldness in Berventy's voice was saturating. "'Cause I *will* make you regret it."

"I need to see it to believe it!" Feever waved with a hand, pushing Berventy out of the way.

Berventy felt herself flying through the cave, landing on the hard floor next to Teela, who was just getting back up on her feet, but without meeting the stone wall. Berventy quickly averted her eyes in Feever's direction, seeing her doing another wave, causing Marisii, Makio, Brouzun, Morven, and Kasteron to fly in different directions of the cave, clearing the path to Brouzenvert.

"'*Sekere tu kere!*'" Berventy said a spell, hoping it would reach Brouzenvert. Teela and Berventy were still both slumped on the floor. "I need you to distract Feever!"

"What are you planning?"

"Just do it!" Berventy said and was glad to see Teela rising from the floor and using her power on Feever, making her fall on the ground herself momentarily.

Kastilius ran toward Teela but was intercepted by Marisii, who pushed him away.

"You're nothing," Marisii said. "You always have been!"

Berventy ran toward Brouzenvert, taking a small knife out of the pocket of her denim jacket.

"Right now, I'm more than *you* ever were!" Kastilius thrust a hand toward Marisii.

On her way to Brouzenvert, Berventy saw her son Marisii flying through the air above her. But she had no time to lose. She reached Brouzenvert a second later, dropping to her knees above him. Then she touched the blade of the knife to the inside part of her palm, tearing through flesh. A few seconds passed and Berventy discarded the knife somewhere next to her. She raised her cut palm above Brouzenvert's face and neck, tightening her fist. The crimson blood started dripping from her palm to Brouzenvert, coloring his face and neck.

"Is she doing…" Feever said as she was getting back up on her feet, her eyes widening. "She's doing the *'Blood Magic'*! Kastilius, stop her!"

Berventy saw her once-son approaching but Teela nailed him to the wall, both of her hands raised in front of her. "*'Sekere tu kere!'*" Berventy started chanting frantically, her voice shaky. "*'Sekere tu kere!'*" Below her, Brouzenvert's body started to light up. Berventy saw Feever thrusting her hand toward Teela, making her collide with the wall behind her. By the way she collapsed to the ground afterward, Berventy supposed she had lost consciousness. "*SEKERE TU KERE!*" Berventy shouted, propelled by Brouzenvert's body lighting up more and more. Someone took Berventy by her bleeding hand and she knew perfectly well who that *someone* was.

"You shouldn't have done the Blood Magic!" Feever said.

"I already did!"

Feever frowned and without batting an eye, she twisted Berventy's right shoulder. A scream erupted out of Berventy's throat, and she was shoved to the ground a second later by Feever, far away from Brouzenvert.

~~~~~~~~~~

Feever knelt next to Brouzenvert, pulling up one of the long see-through sleeves of her cotton-satin dress. She plunged her hand deep into Brouzenvert's chest, where his heart was – just as she had done with Tiffany Fehrenberg not so long ago. But something odd happened and Feever frowned. She expected her hand to reach for Brouzenvert's heart and close around it, but that did not happen – her hand just bounced back at her instead. The witch tried again but every time she tried a bright light erupted from Brouzenvert's chest, burning her hand in a way she had never experienced before. Feever kept trying a few more times, but the pain was too much and even *she* couldn't handle it. Her limb was forced to flinch away.

The Blood Magic had been done…

~~~~~~~~~~

…Berventy had had just enough time in the past couple of weeks spent in the hospital to read voluminous sections of The Book about different spells and types of magic. She had stumbled upon some very interesting words in a spell, called the 'Blood Magic', memorizing them. The spell consisted of a family member saying the words *'Sekere tu kere'* over a fellow, but fallen family member, dripping their own blood on them and in the process protecting them from anyone stealing their undeveloped power. The spell also gave immunity from The Curse to all the members of that family for a certain period of time. There wasn't any information in The Book about how long the

Blood Magic was going to protect Berventy and her children, but she supposed it would have been enough for at least one or two of her children to unlock their power until then. But Berventy knew the Blood Magic was limited for each family, able to be used only once. And Berventy had just done that.

Someone's laugh took Berventy out of her reverie and she saw Ameralda laughing at Feever.

"You say you're so powerful," Ameralda said, "you say you can defeat me without much effort, but just now a witch, who hasn't even discovered her power, tricked you! You couldn't predict that, could you?" Ameralda's laugh turned into a high-pitched giggle. "How is it getting a taste of your own medicine?"

Berventy rose from her spot on the cave's floor, a few meters away from Feever and Brouzenvert, and looked at Kastilius, disappointment burning in her eyes. "Your father wanted to believe in you," she said, observing Kastilius releasing himself from Teela's grip and stepping closer from his spot near the wall. "*I* wanted to believe in you!"

Kastilius raised his eyebrows.

"But there's no point." Tears now pooled in Berventy's eyes. "You're not the boy Brouzenvert and I raised! You're just his twin! You're not our son! Not anymore!"

"I've never been *your* son," Kastilius said. "And yes, you're right, I'm not that angry boy who didn't know where he belonged anymore!" He walked over to Feever and placed a hand on her shoulder. "Now I'm something better! A boy who knows who his true friends and enemies are! A boy who knows which his true family is, and which is not!"

"Do you know that person over there?" Berventy pointed to Brouzenvert's corpse, now left alone by Feever who had risen back to her feet, next to Kastilius. "He was your father! He was the person whom you *poisoned* and left for dead!" Berventy looked at Kastilius, as if measuring the person who stood before her eyes.

"The fault for that is yours, Kastilius!" She expected her words to trigger some sort of reaction – *any* reaction, in Kastilius, but they didn't even faze him. She saw his eyes finding hers.

"Until next time," Kastilius said, "Berventy!" Then he waved his right hand in front of his face, disappearing in a cloud of violet smoke.

Berventy's shoulder was killing her, but she managed to find the strength to keep herself on her feet and look at Feever. "Stay away from my family!" Berventy said. "Stay away from both our families! I don't care about your stupid curse – if you so much as lay a finger on another one of us, I *will* come for you. And *kill* you." Berventy could feel her blood boiling deep inside her.

"I guess we'll see who kills who," Feever said, Berventy sensing the challenge in her voice. "See you in three weeks when I will come to claim my next victim!" Feever also waved her right hand in front of her face, disappearing in a cloud of identical violet smoke.

Chapter 48

The funeral

Pattery had insisted on digging Brouzenvert Klauzer's grave all by himself. "It's the least I can do," he had said to Berventy, still thinking about the selfless act Brouzenvert had done – he had given up his life in order to preserve Pacifika's. He had been digging the grave amidst the island's jungle, with a shovel Ameralda had provided. Pattery wiped his brow clean of sweat with the outside part of his palm, looking to his daughter Pacifika, who stood a few inches away from him.

"I would never be able to repay for what Brouzenvert did," Pacifika said, touching Berventy's shoulder. "But if you need anything – anything at all, I'm here for you. We all are."

Pattery saw Berventy nodding without uttering a single word in response. A few more moments passed and Pattery, having finished the grave, motioned with a hand for Morven to assist him. The two men carefully placed Brouzenvert's body into the gaping hole in the ground.

~~~~~~~~~~

Ameralda stood near all the two families' members, observing the scene. She didn't want to admit it, but she was worried that if the two families buried Brouzenvert on the island they could have affected the timelines in both universes negatively. But Ameralda didn't have the heart to tell them no – Feever had tricked them all, and she just couldn't deny them that right, especially the Klauzer family. And even though she was worried, Ameralda didn't think there would be such a drastic change in the two universes if Brouzenvert's body was laid to rest here.

~~~~~~~~~

The medical nurse Annora also stood close by, but much like Ameralda she also didn't say anything. She hadn't asked for it, but she was inevitably being pulled into these two families' drama. Annora had no clue what her next move would be, but decided to wait until the Klauzer family buried their fallen member.

~~~~~~~~~

Makio was standing next to Marisii and he carefully laced his fingers with Marisii's. But then he felt them hastily drawing away.

"Not now!" Marisii said.

Makio understood that right now the best thing he could have done for Marisii was to let him grieve for his father. He shifted his head in another direction, witnessing Pattery and Morven emerging out of the grave, with the help of Brouzun and Kasteron.

~~~~~~~~~

Teela wanted to say something to her boyfriend. Anything really, but she considered the fact that his attention was completely occupied by his father's funeral.

~~~~~~~~~~

Pattery walked to the pile of earth he had just dug out and picked up the shovel where he had left it next to the pile. He handed it to Kasteron and stepped aside to let him take a handful of earth with it and let it rain all over Brouzenvert.

The shovel was then passed to Morven, who did the same. Silence had descended upon them, the only sounds coming from the island all around them. Brouzun and Marisii were next in line, breaking the silence only for a moment when the earth plunged deep into the grave.

No one wished to say anything – they only wanted a moment of peace in which to bury Brouzenvert and momentarily forget all about The Curse and the vile witch Feever.

~~~~~~~~~~

Brouzenvert's sons had had their turn and now it was time for his wife Berventy. She was passed the shovel by Marisii and picked up a handful of earth, her hands shaking. She threw the earth into the grave and unable to tear herself away she looked down, seeing Brouzenvert's corpse laying so motionlessly in the hole amidst all the dirt, eyes closed.

Tears started rolling down both her cheeks. Berventy dropped the shovel in front of her legs and started running for the island's beach, allowing her tears to freely overflow and not allowing for her sons to see her in such a state. Before she left, she heard a mature woman's voice saying, *"I got this"*, vaguely aware of that same woman following on her heels.

She possessed no sense of time at a place like this, but she reached the island's beach after what she thought were simply minutes. Berventy's face was warmed in orange light and her eyes found the mesmerizing sunset across from her, behind the sea. It was so bright and beautiful.

Just like Brouzenvert when Berventy had first met him at The Gathering all those years ago. He had been all bruised back then and Berventy remembered not being able to comprehend why someone would do such a vile thing to a charming and smart man such as him.

"He deserved more, you know," Berventy said to Perventia, whose footsteps she heard reaching her from the jungle behind her. "Brouzenvert has always deserved more!" Berventy's back was turned on Perventia, the gingerbread-haired woman still watching the bright sunset. All the years she got to spend with Brouzenvert.

"As my daughter said, neither she, nor me, nor anyone else from my family will ever be able to repay for what Brouzenvert did!" Perventia said.

Berventy smiled. "That's my Brouzenvert," she said, the pain evident in her voice. "Always so noble and generous."

A second later, Berventy felt Perventia's hand on her left intact shoulder. She turned around to her blond friend. "My boys," she said. "They shouldn't see me like this! They shouldn't see their mother weak!"

"What are you talking about?" Perventia said. "You just *lost* your husband. You are allowed time to grieve."

"But they will expect *me* to be strong for them," Berventy said, Perventia's hand still on her shoulder. "There's no one else they can count on – now I'm the one who needs to protect them! If they see me weak, they will..."

"Hey," Perventia said, "they would *never* see you weak! You defied Feever by doing the Blood Magic, protecting your sons from her the next time she comes!" Perventia smiled. "Not many people can praise themselves on defying the witch Feever and *actually* living to tell the tale!"

Berventy smiled again.

"You're strong, Berventy Klauzer," Perventia said. "Stronger than I would ever be! Your boys believe in you…" A pause and a smile. "*I* believe in you!"

"But I'm alone," Berventy's eyes started wetting with tears again. "I lost Brouzenvert and it's up to me to protect them!"

"Don't you see?" Perventia said. "You're not alone! You've got your sons, and you've got Pattery, my daughters and me! We will fight Feever and protect each other *together*! *You are not alone!*" Perventia repeated. "You will grieve for Brouzenvert, but I strongly believe that that loss will make you stronger. You will learn from it and next time you will be able to look that wicked witch in the eyes and make her pay for what she and her son did to your husband."

Berventy smiled even wider now. "Thank you, Perventia."

"Always." Perventia smiled and a second later the two women hugged.

~~~~~~~~~~

The two women standing on the sand near the sea enveloped into an embrace were two women willing to do whatever it took to protect their families. Perventia Fehrenberg and Berventy Klauzer had something Feever didn't – each other.

Two beams of white light formed around Perventia and Berventy and they ended the hug to see what was going on. A moment later, the beams of light transformed into a single white orb of light, directed toward Perventia. Then the orb stopped in front of Perventia for a few seconds. It was as if it were considering something, before plunging itself into her forehead.

Perventia Fehrenberg felt immense power growing from her head, traveling to her limbs and body. The power completely overtook her, and she could see her hands and feet shining with bright white light, supposing the rest of her body also shined in a similar manner. A few seconds passed and she looked at her hands again, disappointed to find they weren't shining anymore.

But Perventia was now smiling.

Berventy looked confused.

Perventia had supported Berventy in a moment when she needed it most. By assuring her friend she was not alone and telling her they were going to get through what awaited them together, Perventia Fehrenberg had earned her individual power.

Berventy was silent for a moment as if thinking about something. "I'm so happy for you, Perventia," Berventy said out loud.

"Thank you," Perventia said and smiled at her friend. "But there's no need for you to say it twice."

"But I didn't," Berventy said; "first I thought about it and then I said it."

"Is that so?" Perventia asked, dumbfounded. "Well, that can mean only one thing..." Suddenly the picture of Berventy, standing on the sand in front of her disappeared. Her eyes were clouded by a flashy picture of Pattery instead, running through the jungle toward the beach. The picture was gone a few seconds later. "And now Pattery is going to come and ask us where we've been."

Two seconds later, Pattery appeared out of the jungle next to Perventia and Berventy, gasping for air. "Where have you been, you two?"

Berventy turned to Perventia. "You can see the future?"

"I think so," Perventia flashed a wide smile at both Berventy and Pattery. "As well as reading minds!"

"So..." Pattery croaked.

Perventia nodded in excitement. "I found my power!" Perventia crossed the distance between herself and Pattery, taking his face in her hands, connecting her lips with his.

~~~~~~~~~~

I'm happy for you but you don't have to shove it in my face, Berventy thought, not bothered whether Perventia heard her this time. But she was evidently busy with other activities anyway.

Berventy then turned back to the sunset, the sun almost gone now behind the sea's vast horizon. She started coming to terms with her loss. He was never going to kiss or touch her again. Never going to even look at her one more time. The finality of him not being able to return to his family ever again was soul-crushing to her. And she had to accept it in order to try and find a way to protect her children from the Salem witch. Her right shoulder was killing her, and she had to find someone to pop it back into place, but in her grief, she had completely forgotten about it and the pain it emanated.

Just a few more seconds at peace and I will get it fixed, Berventy thought with the faintest of smiles, continuing to look at the vanishing sunset.

Chapter 49

Farewell

Berventy, Pattery and Perventia returned to the others.
"Mom," Morven said when he saw his mother, hugging her. "Are you okay?"

Berventy nodded. "I just needed some time alone." Then the mother saw Ameralda looking in their direction.

"You two are very brave families," she said. "I admire your courage and I'm terribly sorry Feever tricked you."

"Feever tricked all of us," Perventia said. "But I think I speak for everyone when I say how grateful we are for all you did for us – you provided us with your cure and thanks to that my daughter Pacifika lives to see another day."

Pacifika smiled at Perventia.

"After Tiffany, I just can't handle the thought of losing another one of my daughters," Perventia continued after a pause. "So that's why I thank you, Ameralda, from the bottom of my heart!"

"Both Brouzenvert and Pacifika deserved to receive the cure," Ameralda said, her gaze directed at Berventy, who was acutely aware of Ameralda's compassion. "I assure you, Berventy Klauzer,

Feever is going to get what she deserves! No *one* crosses my path and lives to tell the tale!"

Berventy just nodded.

"I'm really sorry for what happened," Ameralda said, "but I think it's time for you all to leave The Island of Lost Hopes. It would be beneficial for both universes if our paths don't cross ever again."

Perventia looked at her with what Berventy deemed as estrangement.

"Don't get me wrong," Ameralda added. "But I've got an island to rule and a witch to get revenge on. You got what you came here for – Ameralda's cure. But now it's time for you to go so both of the universes can proceed to operate as usual."

"You're right," Pattery said. "It won't be better for anyone if we extend our stay," then he looked at the two families. "It's time for us to continue our journey in our universe just like it's time for Ameralda to continue hers."

Ameralda nodded and snapped her fingers, opening a wide, tall, and crackling with energy bright emerald portal next to Pattery. "That's going to take you home at the place you set off from," Ameralda almost announced. Then the empress snapped her fingers a second time, making The Book appear in Berventy's hands. "You forgot that in the cave. From what I observed this book is of great importance to you and, more importantly, it helps you fight against Feever and her son." Then Ameralda turned to Berventy, Pattery, and Perventia. "A piece of advice – protect it with the same precision you protect your children!"

The three of them nodded, aware that whatever happened they needed to protect The Book at all costs – they didn't know what could happen if it ever fell into Feever and Kastilius's hands again, but they thought it wouldn't be something good. They had forgotten the item once in the ruins of the library and now once more in the cave. Berventy, Pattery, and Perventia realized that couldn't happen again.

"I wish you all the best in your future endeavors," Ameralda said, looking at every single one of them. "I'm confident each of you possesses the qualities to defeat Feever. Use those qualities wisely and one day you might emerge victorious."

"Thank you," Teela said, "for everything!"

Ameralda nodded with a smile.

Teela was the first one to go through the portal.

Berventy looked at Brouzenvert's newly dug grave and headed toward it while the rest of the Fehrenberg family members and Annora were stepping through the portal. She placed her free hand on the dust and a single tear shed from her right eye. "I love you," a sigh. "I will always love you, Brouzenvert." Then she walked to the portal, clutching The Book tightly in her right hand, and she jumped inside of it.

~~~~~~~~~~

Brouzun, Morven, and Kasteron were the next ones to jump inside the emerald portal. Only Marisii, Makio, and the two Kaylas were left. Makio stepped closer to the portal, but Marisii placed his hand on his, pulling him toward him. Marisii just now noticed that Makio had lost his glasses. Probably when the bridge crumbled from beneath their feet, almost killing them both. But that didn't faze Marisii – glasses or not, Makio was the same insanely attractive guy.

"Hey," Marisii said, looking into Makio's eyes, "I'm sorry for the way I acted."

Makio smiled. "You just lost your *father*, Marisii," Makio said, his right hand now on Marisii's neck. "It's alright to be angry."

Marisii cut the distance between them even further, placing his lips on Makio's, a new hunger blazing inside of him. Their kisses went on for a couple of minutes and when they pulled away from one another, they were both grinning. Marisii intertwined his fingers with Makio's and the two men headed toward the portal when Ameralda stopped them.

"I remember something your father said, Marisii," Ameralda said, turning to the chocolate-haired man. *"Fight for your love,* I think he said. I support him in that statement. I became a witness of your love for only a few short moments, but I can confidently say that you two deserve it!"

"Thank you," Marisii said, squeezing Makio's hand tightly.

"This island changed all of us for the better," Makio said, smiling at the emerald-raven-haired empress. "We won't ever forget what you did for us!"

"I won't forget you too," Ameralda said, also with a smile, and then Marisii and Makio, their hands still in each other's, stepped through the portal.

~~~~~~~~~~

Kayla saw Ameralda looking at her and her doppelganger. "Each one of you needs to go back to their universe," Ameralda informed them. "Farewell," she said and waved her right hand in the air, disappearing altogether in a mist of emerald smoke.

"Well," Kayla said, turning to her doppelganger. "I guess that's it then. It was really nice to meet you, *Kayla,*" she said. "And I really hope you find solace somewhere, in someone, about what Feever from this universe did to your family."

"I really hope so too," Kayla said, hugging the other Kayla. A single tear rolled down her cheek. "And I'm sorry."

The original Kayla felt something sharp assaulting her stomach. She stepped back from her twin and saw a huge knife plunged deep into the right side of her stomach. Her mouth dropped open in blood-dripping shock and she saw the doppelganger's right arm covered in her own crimson blood.

"I need my family next to me again," the twin said, tears in her eyes. "And I want to get revenge for what Feever did to all of them." Then she stepped closer to Kayla, pushing the knife deeper into her stomach. "I'm sorry," she said again and pushed the original Kayla to the ground.

Kayla looked at her twin from the emerald grass, tears now pooling in her eyes as well. "Why are you doing this? I was so nice to you, *why* would you do such a thing?" The sharp pain in her stomach was intensifying by the second.

"This is the only way," the other Kayla said, stepping closer to the still opened portal. "*Persto me mesto!*" Immediately after saying that, the doppelganger's streaked with tears and mud face, cleaned up, and her dirty, torn clothes were replaced by shiny new ones. "Now *I* will be Kayla Fehrenberg!"

"I will find you," the original Kayla Fehrenberg croaked out. "You won't get away with this!"

"Oh, I think I already have." The other Kayla cracked the faintest of smiles. The other Kayla saw her looking at her with pity. "Farewell, Kayla! Thank you for the golden opportunity you provided me with!"

A second later the twin-Kayla jumped inside the emerald portal and it immediately closed behind her. The original Kayla saw that and wanted to say something – do something – but all she could manage was lose consciousness, her motionless head hitting the grass.

Chapter 50

General Scrouch and Ahronia

E vening in Salem. Women were closing their wooden blinds and windows. The men were finishing chopping wood for the fireplace, joining their wives and children around the table for dinner. It had been two weeks since Eris and her friend had been burned at the stake without any signs that Salem's townsfolk were *actually* practicing witchcraft. The town was fairly quiet this evening, with General Scrouch looking at the main street of Salem through the wide-opened wooden blinds of his office.

"You're mine," he said. "You're all mine, this town belongs to me." There was a knock on the door and the General groaned in frustration. He sighed. "Come in."

The door opened and when he turned to face his visitor, his flaming red-haired wife Ahronia was standing there. He looked at her in boredom, adjusting his brunette sheriff hat, contributing to his overall sheriff attire. "Why are you here?" he asked her. "What do you want?"

"I want to talk to you, Scrouch," Ahronia said, pointing to the empty wooden chair in front of his desk. "May I?"

"Do I have a choice?" General Scrouch sighed, motioning to the chair with a nod. He sat in his high leather chair on the opposite end of the desk himself, freeing his dark brown hair out of the sheriff's hat, placing it on the wooden desk. He saw Ahronia adjusting her long ruby dress. "What is it?"

"Two weeks ago," she started, her voice slightly shaking, "you accused two young girls of practicing witchcraft and burned both of them at the stake!"

"One of them was a filthy slut," Scrouch said, thinking of his toy – the prostitute Eris. By killing her he had fixed a problem – her pregnancy. "But I gotta admit, she was giving fantastic head!"

~~~~~~~~~~

Ahronia's eyes widened. Not because of her husband's affair – she knew about that all along – but because that was the first time he had outrightly said anything about it. And he had confessed in front of her – *her*, the woman he had been married to for so many years. Ahronia could hardly remember what he had been like before becoming such a tyrant, at all. A tyrant, interested in nothing but money, power, and easy sex. Why had she married him? What exactly had attracted her to this vile person? These questions she had been asking herself every single day, the answers to which she couldn't find. But at least Ahronia knew that she had been feeling nothing but contempt for Scrouch for a long time. And she suspected the feeling was mutual.

"I'm not interested in hearing about your infidelities," Ahronia said, trying to erase what she had just heard and envisioned from her mind. "I came here to ask you if you even realize what you're doing."

"What's that supposed to mean?" the General said, seemingly taken by surprise.

"Well, you burned two young women at the stake for a crime they didn't ever commit. You accused them of witchcraft without any real proof! You just said you've been noticing witch activity and turned the whole town against them!" Ahronia said. "Scrouch, don't you realize that what you started could destroy Salem for good? You commenced a witch hunt and convinced our whole community that they're vile creatures, their only purpose being killing people! That *will* have consequences for Salem, Scrouch – do you know what I've been hearing for the past two weeks, since the public execution in the town square?"

"Please," he said, leaning back into the leather chair, "enlighten me."

"The other day, while taking a stroll I heard two men talking about how they've noticed their two female neighbors communicating in a strange language and because of that they were suspecting them of being witches, casting spells to curse and cripple them. Then, the two men said they were preparing wooden stakes to strike the witches with and end their sinful practice once and for all!"

"What of that seems wrong to you?" Scrouch said, his voice betraying his confusion. "There's a *real* threat roaming the streets of Salem, Ahronia. *Witches!*" He said the last word as if it were poisonous to his tongue.

"And just yesterday, while walking home I heard a woman telling her friends that her neighbor was fucking her husband. And because she believed her husband wouldn't be so stupid as to cheat on her, that neighbor had put her devious seducing spell on him!" Ahronia carefully placed her hand on top of her husband's, wanting to put some sense into him, but he immediately withdrew his hand, as if not wanting even the slightest physical contact with Ahronia. "Scrouch, these rumors are a poison that will gradually infect the whole town and destroy it in the process!" She raised her tone an octave with this sentence, tired of playing nice. "The citizens are turning against one another, and everyone suspects everyone of witchcraft – some of them are even threatening to kill each other! And all of that because of something *you* started the night you executed those women!" Ahronia laughed ironically. "You even said something about a demonic power looming over Salem, and now everyone is turning paranoid and panicked about people they've known their whole lives!"

"You really need to be careful how you talk to me!" Scrouch shouted, rising out of his chair, the item in question clattering with a loud thud to the floor. "Last time I checked *I* was the mayor of this town and I know what's best for *my* town! If I suspected someone of witchcraft, I would execute them on the spot, protecting Salem in the process!"

Ahronia's fists tightened and she also rose from her chair, looking straight into Scrouch's deep black eyes – the devil's eyes. "I've endured all kinds of shit from you!" she said. "Unending affairs with prostitutes, years during which you looked at me with nothing but contempt and boredom, not saying two words to me, hurrying to get to your latest whore as if you didn't have a wife to go home to! A wife that waited for *you* during all those long cold nights!" Her face was now mere centimeters from the General's, a single tear shedding and rolling down her right cheek. "A wife that waited for you to kiss her, to touch her, to tell and show her that you loved her!"

"Is that your argument?" Scrouch chuckled. "I hadn't fucked you enough?"

"But I looked past it," Ahronia said, ignoring his remark. "I looked past that and everything else you did to me, and keep doing. Maybe it was because of the stress that you had the whole town looking up to you, or because you just had a lot to deal with. But I ignored all that and left you alone, too scared that if I said anything, you would have said something dismissive or even hit me."

"You're so right about the last part!" He raised his massive hand and swung.

But Ahronia caught his hand just in time and looked him even deeper in the eyes. "That stops now!" she said and pushed his hand away from hers with a violent shake. "Salem is my town too and I will protect it!" A pause. "Even if I have to kill you to do it!"

General Scrouch raised his eyebrows as if not believing what he'd just heard. "You?" He laughed. "The nice, cute Ahronia? Or should I say the not fucked enough Ahronia?"

"From now on you will treat me with respect!" Ahronia said, more confident than ever, wishing to remove the wooden desk separating her and her ghastly husband, and just do something, *anything*, to assert her position. "And if you don't stop with your witch mania, I will dethrone you as a mayor of Salem, whatever it may cost me!" Ahronia headed for the door of the office but then she turned around, facing Scrouch again. She shrugged her shoulders. "You lost me, Scrouch," she said. "If you don't want to lose the town too, along with your life, you should cease your witch mania and tell the citizens of Salem that the witches amongst our community have died with Eris and her friend!"

Ahronia resumed walking to the door, but then the General's voice stopped her.

"What if I don't do it? What if I don't listen to you and continue with my *witch hunt*, as you called it? What are you going to do then?"

The red-haired beauty bent to the floor, as if to retrieve something, and took a long, seemingly sharp knife, out of one of her see-through lace stockings. Within seconds, she rose back to her full height and threw the knife toward Scrouch. One more second later, the knife missed the General's face by millimeters, piercing one of the wooden blinds behind him instead.

Little did he know, Ahronia had missed on purpose. She wanted to show him that she was serious about protecting Salem and possibly scare him into submission. "Did I make myself clear enough for you?" But without waiting for an answer, she stormed out of General Scrouch's office.

~~~~~~~~~~

"She…" he mumbled but then his face turned flaming red, an identical shade to Ahronia's hair, and he banged both his fists on the desk, a few items falling loudly to the floor. But as much as he wanted to hit his wife and beat her to a pulp, he knew he couldn't kill her – if something bad were to happen to her, the whole town would know it was all his fault. When he was elected as mayor of Salem in 1688, the citizens saw their union as the perfect, dream marriage, the perfect, dream family. And while most of the citizens knew of Scrouch's infidelities and his contempt toward Ahronia, they chose to see the bright side of things – the side it was the most convenient for them to see. And that was precisely the reason why he was still tolerating and living with her, essentially still married – so Salem's citizens could see the good, kind side of General Scrouch.

Someone burst in through the now opened door and Scrouch raised his head to see a man by the name of Mour Klauzer in his office, without having knocked or being invited. "What do you think you're doing, Mour?" he said, appalled. Scrouch had seen this man a few times around Salem. "You can't just barge into my office and…"

"Apologies, General Scrouch," Mour said, his chest heaving. "But there's been a development in Salem!"

"A development?" Scrouch asked in confusion, the knife Ahronia had thrown at him still protruding out of one of the wooden blinds, located inches away from him.

"A witch development," Mour said. "Dozens of citizens are reporting witchcraft being practiced near their homes!"

General Scrouch picked up his sheriff hat from the desk, his cowboy boots clicking on the wooden floor, and placed it on top of his head. The golden star with his name on it, etched into the hat's fabric, glinted in the fading light of the office, streaming in through the opened wooden blinds. Then he picked up his sleeveless beige coat from the chair on the ground and slid his arms into it, not remembering when he had taken it off. "Show me!"

Chapter 51

The witch trials in Salem – Part I

Sarvit Fehrenberg finished up with his dinner and stood from his chair, next to the neatly set dinner table. He kissed his wife Striisar, as well as his daughters Tiffany and Alexandra"I've got a task I need to attend to," he said and then headed for the door.

"This late?" Striisar said with a frown on her face. "You always have a task to attend to – you've hardly been home lately."

"Come on, honey, you know it's important," Sarvit said. "I will come home as soon as I'm finished." At that Sarvit left the house, walking through the mostly empty night streets of Salem, heading to meet his dear friend Mour Klauzer.

~~~~~~~~~~

Mour Klauzer took General Scrouch to two brightly lit houses, several voices coming out from inside. Following tightly behind were a dozen of Scrouch's men, the General having called them to assist with the finding the witches matter.

"In this house," Mour said, pointing to the first house, closer to him, "lives a man by the name of Kervantee – tens of citizens have noticed his husband engaging in and practicing black magic and satanic rituals." Then Mour averted his finger in the direction of the second house. "And in there lives a woman named Sinistery – there's a rumor going around town that her husband is a participant in several occult circles who practice the use of magic and sacrifice animals."

General Scrouch looked through the window of the first house – there was Kervantee, sitting around the table with his family and husband. Scrouch remembered seeing them around town ages ago, but never fully acknowledging their presence. Now, Kervantee was bringing a glass of what seemed like wine, to his mouth, and his husband laughed at what seemed to be a joke told by Kervantee.

"Get them out of there!" General Scrouch ordered and the dozen men barged into the two houses. They brought Sinistery and Kervantee out by force, but left their husbands and kids inside.

"Kervantee?" Sinistery asked the man. "Brother, what's going on?"

"I don't know," he said and then looked General Scrouch in the eyes. "What do you think you're doing? You have no right to come barging into our homes in the middle of the night and kicking us out of there like a pack of wild animals!"

General Scrouch smiled a bitter smile. He had had enough insubordination for one day. And he was done tolerating it. He quickly walked to Kervantee and punched him in the face with a fist.

Sinistery jumped, Mour looked away, as did the husbands and kids, watching the scene unraveling from the doorsteps of the two houses.

"I am Salem's mayor," General Scrouch said and Kervantee raised his head to look at him, blood coming out of his nose. "I can do whatever the hell I please!"

"Excuse me…" Kervantee's husband – Thomas, said, and General Scrouch turned his attention over to him. "But what's this all about?"

"These two have been accused of witchcraft!" Scrouch made clear, looking at Kervantee and Sinistery.

"What in the world?" Thomas asked uncomprehendingly, but his forehead breaking out in a sweat betrayed his lie.

"Those are simply rumors!" Kervantee said. "You don't have any proof!"

"At least a couple dozen of Salem's citizens claim that they saw you two practicing magic," Scrouch said, incredibly convinced of his own words. "And this Mr. here," Scrouch pointed to Mour by his side. "He knows what's best for Salem and as a good, conscientious citizen informed me of your devil practices!"

Kervantee and Sinistery looked at him at the same time. "Mour?" they said, again in unison, seeming to know him.

But Mour didn't provide them with an answer – he just looked away from them as if they were complete strangers.

"Rumour or not," General Scrouch continued, "I have to ensure the safety of Salem and those living in it by eradicating all evil out of the town!" He looked at his guard men and nodded. They walked to the barn nearby and when they came back, they had tens of lit torches in their hands. One of them walked over to Sinistery's husband and two kids and pushed them back inside their house, closing the door behind him. "You are *that* evil!" He then nodded at another one of the men. "And you need to be eradicated!" The man threw the first torch inside Sinistery's house, flames immediately beginning to form like a wild, hungry beast.

~~~~~~~~~~

"NOOOOO!" she screamed, unable to escape the tight grip of one of the guard men. Inside the burning house were her kids, her husband,

282

her family. And now she was hearing the high-pitched screams of her two little girls, and through the window, she witnessed her husband, trying to protect them from all the flames with *his* body. "WHAT THE HELL ARE YOU DOING?"

Another one of the men pushed Thomas and his kids inside their house forcefully, closing and chaining the door, so they couldn't escape.

"Scrouch, that wasn't what we agreed on..." Mour said, but Scrouch interrupted him.

"What did we agree on *exactly?*" Scrouch asked him. "You came to me, claiming that you had information about witches! Well, now that we've identified the perpetrators, I'm going to eliminate the threat!"

Sinistery fell to the ground, tears rolling down both of her cheeks, her bright lilac hair a tangled mess, her nails dug deep into the earth beneath her. Soon her face also met the earth. She felt the man's grip disappearing, probably because she posed no threat anymore.

The screams coming out of her house soon quickly subsided, when three men threw their lit torches through what remained of the large, beautifully crafted window. The flames soon engulfed the whole house, from all sides.

Sinistery wanted to go rushing inside her house, to do something, to save them from the devil flames, but she knew she couldn't – it was simply too late for them. Sinistery had just lost a significant part of her family and could now only watch helplessly and wait to meet her own fate.

~~~~~~~~~~

"DON'T YOU DARE!" Kervantee screamed at one of the other guardsmen, who was getting ready to throw a torch inside Kervantee's house. Kervantee turned around suddenly, his pecan hair also a tangled mess, and in that way was able to escape the steady grip of the man holding him. He ran toward his house, his husband, his kids. Kervantee saw them through the window, huddled close together underneath the dining table, which still had food served on it. For a moment, he thought he would be able to save them. Tears of joy started erupting out of his eyes because he had almost reached the front door.

And that's when three brightly lit torches flew past Kervantee, one after the other, and came crashing through the window into the kitchen, right where Thomas and the kids were hiding underneath the table. Kervantee had almost reached the door handle, chains all around it. But then he saw his family. And heard their screams. They echoed deep within his ears. He saw the merciless flames engulfing his kids and husband. "NOOOOOOO!" Kervantee croaked out, hysterical, pulling desperately on the handle. He wanted to go inside the house and save his family, but he felt a sharp pain from a bullet in his right shoulder and he fell to the ground, turning around and seeing that General Scrouch had shot him with his gun. Mere seconds later he was brought up to his feet by two of Scrouch's men, brought and shoved to the cold, now muddy ground, next to his sister Sinistery.

"Throw in another two, just for good measure!" Scrouch ordered and the men threw another two torches per house.

The screams and shouts had awoken the whole of Salem, and now curious citizens were coming out from around streets and turns.

Kervantee placed his hand on top of Sinistery's and she squeezed it as if it were a lifeboat – last salvation. They were both crying, having lost their families, not knowing what would happen to them from that moment on.

~~~~~~~~~~

Pretty soon the two burning houses were encircled by the townsfolk of Salem, all of them whispering between each other, sounding like ghosts in the black night. A few of them were even pointing fingers at Kervantee and Sinistery, crying out the word 'witch'. Sarvit Fehrenberg soon appeared on the scene and walked over to his dear friend Mour Klauzer.

"We did the right thing," he said encouragingly and squeezed Mour's shoulder.

"Did we actually?" Mour asked unsurely and backed away from Sarvit's hand. "Look at them," he pointed to Kervantee and Sinistery, sobbing down in the mud. "They lost everyone they love – and all because of us! Was it really worth it, considering the grief we've brought them?"

Sarvit wished not to answer, fully realizing the vile magnitude of his and Mour's actions and the consequences that were probably going to follow.

"We were protecting our families," he said after mulling it over. "And that's all that matters!"

~~~~~~~~~~

General Scrouch's wife Ahronia also appeared at the scene shortly after Sarvit had arrived, wearing the same long ruby dress and lace see-through stockings that she had threatened her husband earlier with. She had vowed to dethrone him from his post as a mayor of Salem if he didn't stop the witch mania – and Ahronia was now suspecting that he was up to his old tricks again. She looked at him questioningly, but he obviously didn't want to look at her, turning away and focusing his attention on the citizens.

"Dear citizens," he started with the same ceremonial tone which he had used to announce the existence of witches in Salem just two weeks prior. "The last two weeks proved silent and peaceful for our small town."

The crowd was all listening to him like good, hypnotized sheep, interested in what their good mayor had to say.

"But, alas, the witchcraft deeds didn't end when we executed the two initial demons."

Ahronia laughed slightly – he was full of bullshit and he knew it. "Yeah, *we* executed them!"

Scrouch paid no attention to her and opened his mouth to continue.

~~~~~~~~~~

A woman with dark, almost raven hair was making her way through the crowd, toward Kervantee and Sinistery, laying in the mud.

General Scrouch paused for a second, distracted, then continued: "The witches in Salem are real," he said. "And they continue practicing their black magic despite all our efforts to thwart them!" He raised the volume of his tone, wanting every single one of his subordinates to hear him loud and clear. "THEY DON'T CARE ABOUT THE CONSEQUENCES OF THEIR BLACK MAGIC! THEY DON'T GIVE A DAMN THAT THEY WILL DESTROY SALEM WITH THEIR BLACK MAGIC!" And then he went back to his usual volume. "I'm your mayor." He saw the woman finally able to get through the crowd, shock and bewilderment drawing on her face upon seeing Kervantee and Sinistery in the mud. "And I'm inclined to protect our town and you at all costs!" And then Scrouch raised his hand high in the air triumphantly. Almost all of the citizens did the exact same and started chanting and shouting his name in unison, praising him.

He loved people praising him – Scrouch wanted them all to know that he owned them, every single last one of them.

~~~~~~~~~~

Feever knelt on the muddy ground, next to Kervantee and Sinistery, hugging them. Then she glanced over to their houses, realizing that General Scrouch had killed both their families cold-bloodedly. "What the hell is going on?" She let the tears fall with no limit, not being able to comprehend why somebody would do that to her brother and sister. The three siblings never practiced magic, not in large quantities at least. They were always careful when *actually* engaging in magic, and so far, no one had been able to catch them in the act.

Henrietta – Feever, Kervantee and Sinistery's mother – and Harietta – their aunt, managed to also reach the epicenter of the scene and see what was going on. They all knew General Scrouch well, as he did them.

"Your children," he said, pointing disgustedly at Kervantee and Sinistery.

Feever had now pulled them both in for a tighter embrace, wanting to somehow save them from Scrouch's observing, merciless gaze.

"Tens of citizens claim that they saw them practicing black magic and satanic rituals!"

"Do you have any proof?" Henrietta asked, next to her sister Harietta in the mud. "You can't just accuse a young man and a young woman of witchcraft without having any plausible proof!"

"All the proof I need is the statement of this man," the General said, waving over with a hand to Mour Klauzer.

Henrietta, Harietta, and Feever looked at him. "Mour?" they said at the same time. Then, they looked at his shorter friend next to him. "Sarvit?"

"This good man came to me and informed me of their witch activity!" Scrouch said, evidently proud of Mour and his deed. "At least a dozen citizens came to him, worried and shaking for their lives, informing him of what your kids had been up to! This man was just good and conscientious enough to come to me and relay that important information about these evil witches!"

"What witches?" Harietta said sharply. "Is that your proof? A statement of a random man who just happened to hear some vile random rumor about our children?"

Scrouch looked at her, his face expressionless. "That's enough for me to decide their verdict."

The townsfolk started rejoicing at their mayor's words, shouting out loud that they wanted Kervantee and Sinistery's deaths as soon as possible.

"NO!" Ahronia shouted and stepped up from her place amongst the townsfolk, now all gazes pointed in her direction, an eerie silence hovering between them. She looked at the citizens. "Aren't you tired of accusing someone of witchcraft without any substantial proof, condemning them to certain death?"

The citizens started whispering amongst one another once again.

"It's not right," Ahronia said, sounding like she was trying to convince them to change their stubborn minds. "You can't just send someone to the stake for something that no one is sure that they *actually* did!"

"We need a trial!" Henrietta said and all gazes shifted over to her. "A fair trial in Salem's courtroom to decide whether Kervantee and Sinistery indeed practiced witchcraft!"

Ahronia nodded. "In that way, we will find out for sure whether they're guilty!"

But the crowd didn't seem entirely convinced just yet.

Feever realized that Henrietta, Harietta and Scrouch's wife Ahronia were trying to get Kervantee and Sinistery out of certain death, trying to allocate some sort of justice in this corrupted, chaotic, and unruly town. "Look!" Feever rose from the mud, leaving her brother Kervantee and her sister Sinistery in the comfort of their mother and aunt, her Prussian blue and onyx black dress now stained. "Look at these two houses!" Her finger pointed at the orange-red flames. "Your General *did* this. *He* burned these houses, taking away my brother and sister's families!"

The citizens started muttering disapprovingly, obviously in the dark about that aspect.

The General's face was flaming red by what Feever had said.

"General Scrouch did this!" she repeated, the reality of it fully sinking into her mind. "He killed four small children and two men, without giving them the right to defend themselves! Without giving them the right of having a fair trial!" Then her eyes averted to Sarvit and Mour. "And those two helped that happen, accusing my family of witchcraft, without having seen them practicing it directly!" And right then, at that moment, Feever looked at them with rage, burning brightly in her heart, dead set on getting revenge on them for what they had done to her family. "Sarvit, Mour, and General Scrouch *butchered–*" she said that last word intentionally to get some sort of reaction out of the crowd and make them stir– "FOUR SMALL CHILDREN AND TWO MEN!" And then Feever decided to take it down a notch, realizing they were gone, and that she would never see them again. "The least you could do for them is giving their loved ones–" she pointed to Kervantee and Sinistery once again to emphasize her point, as if it weren't already painfully clear– "a fair trial in the courtroom, where it can be decided whether they're witches indeed, as you all so surely claim!"

~~~~~~~~~~

The crowd changed their opinion after Feever's speech and started trying to convince General Scrouch to amend his initial decision to kill Kervantee and Sinistery instantly, without any trial. The mayor found himself in quite a predicament – if he refused to accept Feever's suggestion, the citizens would begin hating him and could even rebel against him and end his reign, because he, with the help of Sarvit and Mour, had *indeed* butchered four small children and two men, without any proof whatsoever. But if he chose to accept the suggestion and did assemble such a trial for Kervantee and Sinistery, he could have turned the odds in his favor. To somehow prove that Kervantee and Sinistery were witches, to prove that around here his word stayed, to show that the murders of these six innocent souls would serve purely and honestly for Salem's protection, and – most importantly – to give Salem's population a chance to see him as more majestic and more authoritative than ever, strengthening their faith in him in the process.

"Take those two to the dungeons!" Scrouch ordered and his men forcefully brought Kervantee and Sinistery up to their feet, pushing Henrietta and Harietta away. "The trial will be held tomorrow, at twelve o'clock noon sharp, in Salem's courtroom!"

His security started dragging Kervantee and Sinistery in the direction of the town's dungeons. The crowd once again started rejoicing with audible shouts and hands raised high in the cold night air. General Scrouch cracked a wicked smile, washing in the glory and knowing that that was his town and those were his people, ready to back him up on whatever he set his mind to.

Shortly after, the citizens started heading to their homes, exciting chatter now polluting the air about the upcoming witch trial for Kervantee and Sinistery tomorrow.

Ahronia looked at Scrouch. "I warned you," she said and also left the scene, the houses still burning, but way less than before.

Scrouch sent her off with a contemptuous look and not long afterward, he, too, decided to flee the scene, needing to blow off some steam from all the pressure with some hussy.

~~~~~~~~~~

Feever turned to Sarvit and Mour. "Just tell me one thing," she said. "Why?"

"We were just protecting our families," Mour answered.

"By destroying *mine?*" she said in disbelief. "Destroying theirs?" she croaked, meaning Kervantee and Sinistery's. "My family and yours hardly know one another," Feever said. "What did we ever do to you to make you want to ruin us completely?"

"It's nothing personal," Sarvit said. "We did it for the people we love."

Only Henrietta, Harietta, Feever, Sarvit and Mour were left in front of the two still burning houses – everyone else had gone home for the night.

Henrietta now looked at Sarvit. "You know," she started, "you're true villains."

"You think you've done the right thing because you were protecting your families," Harietta added, "but you *murdered* four kids at their mere start in life, and two men, tearing out their loved ones' hearts!"

"You ruined our family," Feever finished. "And now, I'm going to ruin yours!" Feever threatened, and together with her mother and aunt, they drifted away from Sarvit and Mour into the night, leaving them all alone in the now present quietness.

~~~~~~~~~~

"We've been over this hundreds of times," Sarvit told Mour, who still wasn't sure of the decision the two of them had taken together. They had met at the town center, a few meters away from the wooden platform, on which Eris and her friend had been burned at the stake two weeks ago, before Mour had gone to General Scrouch's office to alert him of Kervantee and Sinistery practicing witchcraft. "This is the only way, Mour! Our families and Feever's are the only witch families in Salem – the witch hunt has commenced and it's only a matter of time before someone exposes us or them!"

"And you're saying that by accusing Feever's family we would somehow be saving ours?" Mour asked, still unsure of Sarvit's words.

"That's exactly what I'm saying," Sarvit responded. "I know what we're about to do is horrendous and vile, Mour, I don't want to do it any more than you do! But it has to be done! Sometimes in life, you need to do something horrible in order for something good to continue existing and even bloom – and that *good* thing is our families!"

"But who knows what's going to happen to Feever and her family?" Mour said. "You know Scrouch, you know how unscrupulous he is. He will kill them without the bat of an eye!"

"That is why we would only accuse Kervantee and Sinistery of witchcraft and leave Feever, Henrietta, and Harietta out of the equation."

"But they also have families," Mour said. "Kervantee and Sinistery have families just like we do! What makes you think it would be right to destroy theirs, but keep ours intact?"

Sarvit sighed continuously, seemingly exhausted. "Look," he said and took his friend's right hand in his. "I know you don't want to do it; I know that if we *do* do it, we would be no better than the devil itself! But that's not a matter of choice – it's eat or be eaten, us or them!" And then Sarvit looked Mour in the eyes, which slowly, gradually, started accepting the fact that that had to be done. "Our families or theirs!"

Mour stepped closer to Sarvit and pulled him into a short embrace that ended a few seconds after it started. "Okay," he said, agreeing with Sarvit at last. "Tell me what to do."

Chapter 52

Dungeons of Salem

The town's dungeons were located below the ground, right next to Salem's courtroom. General Scrouch's men, dragging Kervantee and Sinistery by the shoulders, opened the two quadratic wooden doors, which looked as if they were meant to protect from a tornado, and began descending down the stone stairs into the darkness. Kervantee and Sinistery offered no resistance, not wishing to – the two of them had lost their kids and husbands, what else did they have left to fight for?

Not long after, the four figures reached the holding cells, meant for prisoners in Salem. Each of the men took a rusty key out of their pocket. The guy holding Kervantee pushed him down to the floor and then went to unlock the first cell – there were a total of five. The rusty door, composed of metallic bars, opened with a loud squeak. Then, the man forced Kervantee back onto his feet, only to rudely push him inside the cell, bringing him back to the dusty, mud-stained floor. Kervantee landed with a loud thud inside his cell.

"Hey!" Sinistery said. "Just because we're prisoners doesn't mean you should treat us that way!"

The second guardsman, who was holding Sinistery, slapped her across the face. Then he left her for a second to open her cell, next to Kervantee's. "We can treat you however we want!" he noted, before hauling her inside the cell. Sinistery hit the cell's wall hard and crumbled down to the ground.

Then the two men locked the cells.

"Enjoy your last night!" the man, who had thrown Sinistery inside her cell, said. "Tomorrow you will burn at the stake, filthy witches!" Scrouch's men lingered for a few more minutes, evidently enjoying Sinistery and Kervantee's suffering, and then they left, locking the two wooden doors at the top of the stone stairs.

"Sinistery?" Kervantee said, who was still on the floor but had managed to lift himself up a little bit, going to the front part of the metallic bars. He outstretched his hand through them.

His sister had a hard time lifting herself up from the floor – everything hurt from the impact with the wall, but she managed to move toward the front part of the cell, finding her brother's hand with hers. "I'm so sorry for Thomas, Kervantee," she said, for the first time mentioning the name of Kervantee's husband since the fire that had killed both of their families. "I'm sorry for all of them." Sinistery's tears could not be kept in check, and they spilled.

"They shouldn't have paid for the fact that we're witches," Kervantee said, tears forming in his own eyes. "They knew we were witches, knew how dangerous that was in a town such as Salem, and despite all that they didn't care – they just wanted *us*, no matter whether we were witches or not!"

"I love you, Kervantee," Sinistery said, squeezing her brother's hand. "I want you to know that just in case tomorrow is our last day on this earth!"

"I love you too, Sinistery," he said. "I really do hope that Salem's citizens will somehow realize just how much of a tyrant Scrouch is and that he is the real enemy here."

"I doubt that," Sinistery said. "Scrouch has been this town's mayor for at least four years already – he's placed the entire town under his boot!"

~~~~~~~~~~

A cloud of lilac smoke, just like Sinistery's hair color, appeared in front of Sinistery and Kervantee. Out of the cloud stepped Feever, the smoke dissipating behind her.

"Feever?" Kervantee said, seemingly startled. "What are you doing here?"

The raven-haired witch stepped closer to them and fell to her knees, taking their intertwined hands in her own. "I had to see you at least one more time before the trial tomorrow," she smiled at her brother and sister, tears rolling down her cheeks. "I know it was dangerous for me to use magic and come here but…" Feever paused, letting the tears drop freely to the floor. "I'm so sorry for your kids and husbands!" she said, her voice filled with pain. "They deserved so much better!"

"But what exactly happened, sister?" Sinistery said. "One moment we were sat in our houses, eating dinner, and enjoying the peaceful night, and the next thing we knew we were being hauled out from our own homes, Scrouch and his men igniting them. They killed so many innocents!"

"Did we expose ourselves somehow?" Kervantee asked. "Both me and Sinistery avoided using magic unless absolutely necessary – how was it even possible for them to catch us in the act then?"

"No one *caught* you!" Feever said, rage beginning to seep into her face when she remembered Sarvit and Mour. "The three of us, along with our mother and aunt have hardly been practicing any magic ever since Scrouch got elected as mayor in 1688! It's just not possible for anyone to have caught us engaging in witchcraft!"

"Then what is it?" Sinistery said. "Why did Scrouch have to kill four little children and two adult men? What does he even gain from killing innocent people and blaming it all on us for using magic?"

"The truth is Sarvit and Mour went to Scrouch to let him know of their information about dozens of citizens seeing you practicing magic and 'satanic rituals', as Scrouch labels them."

"What?" Kervantee's voice was almost a shout in the darkness of the dungeons. "We hardly know Sarvit and Mour – we don't even say hi to them when we see them walking about in town. What could we ever have done to prompt them into doing such a vile deed?"

"We haven't done anything," Feever said, squeezing their hands. "After Scrouch's security dragged you to the dungeons, Scrouch himself and the whole town abandoned the scene. Then, it was only me, our mother, our aunt, and Sarvit and Mour standing in front of the burning houses. I asked them why, why would they go to this tyrant, feeding him lies about us, accusing us of a deed we haven't practiced in *years*! They said they did it to protect their families," Feever added. "Sarvit and Mour also engage in witchcraft from time to time, and they said something along the lines of 'better you than us when Scrouch begins hunting the real witches'!"

"Do they have any idea how ugly this is?" Kervantee said, evidently appalled. "What right is there in killing so many innocent people to protect your family, when in truth you're the devils they *really* need protection from?"

"I assure you, my siblings, they will pay dearly for their actions," Feever said. "I've got some ideas about how to make their families suffer for generations to come!" Feever squeezed Sinistery and Kervantee's hands even tighter, not wanting to let go, not at such a time like this one. "But now the priority is you two! It's crucial that we find a way to convince Salem's population that you're innocent of all charges tomorrow."

"But how?" Sinistery said. "Almost the whole town will agree that whatever Scrouch says is the truth – Sarvit and Mour would undoubtedly also back him up, in a bid to save their own asses. There's only three of us – how is it expected of us to convince Salem that Kervantee and I are innocent?"

"Wrong," Feever smiled. "There's five of us, including our mother Henrietta and our aunt Harietta – they will also be present at the trial!" Feever heard the two quadratic wooden doors opening and two pairs of footsteps descending.

"I thought I heard voices coming from down there," said one of the men.

"Do you think someone is trying to bail them out?" the other asked.

"I need to go." Feever kissed Kervantee's hand first, and then Sinistery's. "I love you both unconditionally!" Then, she had to let go of her siblings' hands, even though that was the last thing she wanted to do. Feever started raising her hand in front of her, but she was suddenly stopped by Sinistery.

"Feever?"

"Yes, Sinistery?"

"We love you too," Sinistery said and both prisoners erupted into tears.

Tears formed in Feever's eyes too. The young witch looked at them one last time before going – they didn't deserve all of that, their kids and husbands didn't deserve what had befallen them, Feever, Henrietta and Harietta didn't deserve having to watch their loved ones being burned at the stake for something they didn't commit. "We will see each other tomorrow," Feever said and flicked her hand in the air, disappearing in the same cloud of lilac smoke, which she'd come from.

~~~~~~~~~~

Two seconds later the two guardsmen reached Sinistery and Kervantee's cells, only to see them talking to one another.

"You're an idiot!" one of the men said to the other. "Didn't it occur to you that they might be talking to each other? Why do I even listen to you? Someone was trying to bail them out," he said the last part in mocking laughter.

"I'm sorry for trying to ensure that everything will be intact for the trial tomorrow!" the other man said, seemingly irritated.

Shortly after, Kervantee and Sinistery were left only in each other's company to reside in the dark as night prison cells, dreading the day tomorrow that could prove to be their last.

Chapter 53

The witch trials in Salem – Part 2

The sunrise had come. The official court trial against Kervantee and Sinistery was to be held at 12 o'clock sharp, at noon, in the town's courtroom, located at the center of Salem. The citizens began waking up and opening their windows, greeting the beginning of the new day, anticipating the upcoming trial with passion.

General Scrouch had slept with two prostitutes last night to blow off some steam as he had wanted, and he was now waking up naked next to them, on the floor of his office. He started looking for his briefs and upon finding them he put them on, along with the rest of his uniform laying around his office, ready to condemn some witches.

The two women also woke up shortly after and started putting their dresses back on.

"You two were simply amazing last night," Scrouch smiled at them while buttoning his beige coat and pants.

"We're always ready to fulfill our civic duties." The taller woman smiled and walked to the mayor, planting a huge, thirsty kiss on his lips. "If you need more, just say the word – you know where to find us!" She then winked and together with her colleague they left Scrouch's office, leaving him to finish putting on his cowboy boots with a small metal star at the back of them, and his brunette sheriff hat on top of his head, the star with his name shining in the sunlight streaming through the opened wooden blinds in his office.

General Scrouch walked to the wooden blinds and looked down at the town's square, observing the citizens starting to stir. Such a beautiful town. And it was all his.

~~~~~~~~~~

Not far from General Scrouch's office, Kervantee and Sinistery hadn't slept at all in Salem's dungeons. They didn't have the desire to sleep or eat – or anything else for that matter, anticipating the process that would essentially decide their fate.

"Sinistery?" Kervantee called out from his cell.

"Yes, Kervantee?" Sinistery responded from hers.

"Just know that no matter what happens today, I will always be by your side!"

Even though Kervantee couldn't see it, Sinistery smiled a wide smile. "I've always known that."

After that, a few hours passed, during which none of them said a word. Not until the wooden doors to the dungeons opened and down the steps appeared General Scrouch and three of his guardsmen.

"Did you sleep well?" General Scrouch said.

Kervantee and Sinistery didn't even look at him.

"Despite all, I *do* sincerely hope you've both enjoyed your last night on this planet!" Then he nodded and two of his subordinates unlocked the siblings' cells.

Kervantee and Sinistery were forced to their feet by the two men, their wrists being restricted with sturdy handcuffs. They supposed the purpose of that was so that they wouldn't show resistance any more than they already had. But contrary to even them, Kervantee and Sinistery wished to show no resistance.

"You're evil," Sinistery said as one of the men pushed her out of her cell.

Kervantee was also brought out shortly after Sinistery. The four of them started ascending the stone steps, back into civilization, followed by the third guard and the General himself.

"Tell me something new," Scrouch said.

~~~~~~~~~~

The two towering wooden doors of the courtroom opened. The people shouting their lungs outvoiced the space of the room, while Kervantee, Sinistery, General Scrouch, and his people were entering. The courtroom was not only gigantic but also elegant in being so tidy and spacious, constructed on two floors. The courtroom bleachers on both floors were filled with people to their maximum capacity.

"Kill them!" most of the people were shouting, enraged.

"Burn them at the stake!" the rest of the population was shouting, cheers being voiced out at their suggestion.

Right at the very center of the first floor of the courtroom, wooden cells with bars were specifically constructed for Kervantee and Sinistery, a single chair inside each of them, metallic padlocks mounted to the gate of each of them. Behind each of the cells, two lines of seats were designed for the relatives and friends of the accused individuals.

Scrouch noticed his own wife Ahronia amongst the first lines of those seats, probably here to protect the accused and defy him once again. He was seriously getting tired of this insolent behavior.

Scrouch's security escorted the accused to their respective cells, while the General himself headed toward the elevated from the ground central space of the courtroom, specifically designed for the trial leader, located strictly opposite the accused's temporary holding cells. The mayor sank deep into the seat, resembling a luxurious, bejeweled, throne, marveling at all the food and drinks placed on the wooden counter surrounding the throne. *A fitting treatment for a king of the highest honor,* he thought.

Before saying anything, he let his body relax and momentarily closed his eyes, bathing in the cheers of the crowd, who were shouting his name excitedly now. He was their king and they – his subjects.

Upon opening his eyes back up, he let them drift away to the prisoners' cells, gladly seeing his men pushing them rudely inside and locking the padlocks. He also saw their sister Feever, their mother Henrietta and their aunt Harietta, sitting in the front row behind the cells, worried expressions possessing their faces. He knew damn well they'd come to prove their relatives' innocence and protect them in the process.

General Scrouch stopped enjoying the crowd's praises and hit the small wooden hammer against a circular wooden surface, to bring order to the hall. With his other hand, he brushed the metallic surface of his revolver, safely stored in its holster, attached to Scrouch's belt, having brought the gun in case he needed it.

Silence engulfed the courtroom. Several of the citizens threw tomatoes toward the siblings' cells and a selected few of them found their faces, splattering them with tomato juice and insides, painting them in red.

Scrouch couldn't help but smile – he was glad his job was going to be so easy. Salem's population already hated Sinistery and Kervantee's guts. All that Scrouch had left to do was go over the formalities of the court trial and give the citizens the spectacle and entertainment they expected.

"Dear citizens," Scrouch commenced the trial with his deep entrancing voice, leaving the wooden hammer back against the wooden circle. "We've gathered here today for an official court trial against Sinistery and Kervantee, who had been accused of practicing witchcraft and satanic rituals in our small town of Salem."

Hushed whispers started spreading amongst the crowd, gazes drifting from Kervantee and Sinistery to the General, and vice versa.

"The trial will proceed in the following way," he continued, standing up from his spot on the throne and clearing his voice and intensifying its volume, so all could hear loud and clear. "First, I will present what kind of charges there are against the individuals. Then, the citizens of Salem will have the opportunity to present what they've seen, and why they're accusing the defendants of witchcraft. And at the end, the defendants themselves will have the chance to say something in their defense. And when we get to this stage, if there is someone supporting the defendants, they will also have a chance to join and say something in their defense. Without further ado, let the trial begin!" he announced and the crowd burst into shouts and cheers, even louder than before.

They continued throwing tomatoes toward Sinistery and Kervantee, stopping only when the mayor took his gigantic seat back.

The General paused for a few moments and then coughed intently, clearing his throat.

At that Sarvit Fehrenberg and Mour Klauzer looked at him from the first row of seats behind the wooden holding cells. General Scrouch had placed them there on purpose, even though they definitely weren't friends of Sinistery and Kervantee and their relatives. After all, they were his right-hand men now and he wanted them close by to provide statements and such.

"A few days ago," Salem's mayor spoke again, "those good people," he pointed in the direction of Sarvit and Mour, "notified me that dozens of worried citizens had come personally to them, terrified of what they'd witnessed. Namely satanic magic, being cast by the defendants Sinistery and Kervantee. They claim they'd seen the defendants not only practicing magic – but even worse, also magic directed at them, its sole purpose to harm or *even* kill them!" The whole crowd exclaimed in shock and the corners of his mouth twitched into a slight smile – he didn't have time to waste and he felt like he had dived straight into the essence of the problem. "But why am I speaking?" Scrouch said. "Let's give Sarvit and Mour a chance to tell us what they'd personally seen. What do you all think, my dear citizens?"

The whole room erupted into cheers of agreement.

General Scrouch lifted his hand in the air, and he was glad to see that this time he didn't have to use the wooden hammer to quieten the crowd down. His hand had simply done the job. "Sarvit." He turned to Sarvit, planting his gaze on him. "Mour." He then looked at Mour next to him. "Please, stand up and tell us exactly what you've seen."

~~~~~~~~~~

Sarvit and Mour stood from their seats and looked at the crowd, observing them. Mour wished to not speak – he thought what he and Sarvit had done had spun out of control, hence why he wanted to let Sarvit do the talking.

"Dear citizens," Sarvit said, sounding like Scrouch himself, "with terrible anguish in my heart I can say that my dear friend Mour and I indeed received complaints from citizens, genuinely worried about the safety of their families and their own. The examples are endless, oh, it's so dire."

Mour noticed Sarvit placing a hand on his forehead as if he were genuinely sad and worried about what had transpired. He knew Sarvit was just making it up, putting on an act for the audience and Scrouch. And he was scarily good at it.

"Please continue," Scrouch said. "I know it's hard, but we need to expose these witches and prove their guilt."

"I…" Sarvit stuttered. "I love this town just as much as every single one of you, and as much as it pains me to say it – Sinistery and Kervantee are guilty of practicing witchcraft! A woman came to me, saying she'd heard Sinistery whispering satanic things, addressing her."

Mour noticed his lies, however, weren't that well thought through, but the townsfolk believed Sarvit's words regardless.

"Later, she felt unwell and became feverish! What does that say to you? A man then came to me, claiming he'd seen, with his own eyes, Kervantee producing some potions in a big black cauldron. Who knows what he was going to use them for? Maybe to hurt one of our beloved, fellow citizens?"

~~~~~~~~~~

"That's just rumors," Feever jumped out of her seat, unable to listen to those lies anymore. "Your whole evidence, Sarvit, is a series of rumors!" Then she turned to the thousands of eyes staring at her from the bleachers. "Are you seriously going to believe him?"

"SILENCE IN THE COURTROOM!" Scrouch screamed, banging the small wooden hammer against the wooden circle. "You will have time to showcase your point of view, Feever, but your turn hasn't yet come!"

"Dear," Henrietta said from the seat next to hers. "Sit. Soon we will have the chance to say what we think."

Feever directed a gaze, filled with hate, at Sarvit, and sat back. Then, Feever caught a glimpse of her sister Sinistery, looking at her, her eyes full of tears.

"Thank you," the lilac-haired witch whispered.

"I want to say something," a random man said from the section of seats on the first floor, on the far-right side of the hall.

"Please, do say," Scrouch said, interconnecting the fingers of both his hands, pressing them to his lips.

"Supporting the statement of this good fellow citizen," the man pointed at Sarvit, who was still up on his feet, while Mour wasn't. The man bit his upper lip. "I became a witness to a satanic deed by one of the defendants – Kervantee–" he pointed at Feever's brother accusingly. "You, evil man, killed my sheep!"

Feever looked at Kervantee in his cell, who almost burst out laughing.

"What? I've killed your sheep?"

"That's right," the man said. "You cast some sort of spell, and then a week later my sweet little sheep started dying one by one!"

"Is that how it happened indeed?" Kervantee was still laughing.

Feever saw even Sinistery chuckling. And she knew what both of her siblings were thinking, why that accusation was so ridiculous – those townsmen were pathetic, looking for a scandal and the latest gossip, so they could have something interesting and exciting in their ordinary lives.

"You, satanic demon," the man said, waving an accusatory finger at Kervantee, "you *knew* that those sheep were feeding my whole family and killed them nevertheless!"

There was a woman, sitting next to him, drinking whiskey out of a large glass bottle, and Feever saw the man prompting her to stand up with a hand. The woman did as he wanted, seemingly startled, dropping her bottle of whiskey on the floor. "But of course," she said, quite evidently hammered, "Agnus was my favorite sheep and you *killed* it!"

"Death for the sheep killers!" another random citizen screamed, and the rest followed.

"Do we even need any more statements at this point?" Scrouch asked the screaming off its lungs crowd. "I think the verdict is quite clear!"

"NO, IT'S NOT CLEAR!" Feever screamed, jumping out of her seat for a second time. "You, *"dear citizen"*," she said ironically, "are an idiot! I'm passing by your house every single day on the way back to my house, and I could see your nasty sheep – still alive and kicking! But even if they did *die*, the fault for that wouldn't be either my brother's or my sister's – it would be totally *yours* because you would rather fuck your drunk wife several times a day than actually feed your animals!"

The crowd exclaimed in offense.

"How can you talk to us like that?" the sheepman said.

"You all are one collective piece of trash!" Henrietta stood up from her seat, along with Henrietta. "I won't let my kids die just because you're bored, and you wonder what kind of lies to make up!"

"That's right!" Harietta said. "So far what I've heard is that you're accusing my nephew and niece of satanic rituals involving dead sheep, who are still alive, and curses, which made someone catch a fever!"

The townsfolk started talking amongst each other and sentences such as *"They've got a point,"* became audible gradually throughout the courtroom.

Feever saw Scrouch disconnecting one hand from the other, starting to shake, beads of sweat rolling down his forehead.

Ahronia also stood and looked at Scrouch. "You're Salem's mayor," she said, "and my husband." She shivered at those three words. "But you can't condemn this young man and woman and write their death sentence without having any solid proof, and not just random rumors, which may or may not be true!"

Feever saw Scrouch looking at Ahronia, and she could read his enraged expression that his own wife was betraying him.

"Citizens," Ahronia said, a few meters away from where Feever herself stood on her feet, turning over to the crowd. "If you deplore Kervantee and Sinistery without any plausible proof, you wouldn't be any better than the demons and witches you claim they are!"

Dead silence in the hall.

"Whoever you are," Feever said, even though she knew well who Ahronia was, "thank you."

"I'm always ready to fight against injustice!" Ahronia smiled at Feever and then turned back to Salem's population, gathered in the rows of seats on the two floors of the courtroom. "*You* supported General Scrouch in the murder of four innocent children, one man, and one woman. You all just stood there, watching as his men were igniting their houses, burning them alive! You're already tainted," she said. Then she pointed at Kervantee and Sinistery, sitting in their chairs in the wooden cells. "If you send these two innocent souls at the stake, you will forever stain your *own* souls and eternally burn in hell for your sins!"

Grave silence. Feever sensed even Scrouch not knowing what to say after Ahronia's determined speech.

"Well," Feever said. "If that is all, I think that your, our mayor, can proclaim my brother and sister as innocent so we can all go home and forget that everything ever happened!" Feever was smiling, knowing the tables had turned in her family's favor. She could hardly believe her siblings would get out of this safe and, most importantly, alive.

In the next moment, someone burst through the tall wooden doors, into the courtroom. Feever supposed it was one of Scrouch's guardsmen, judging by his red-black uniform. But what was most startling, he was carrying a young girl in his hands that couldn't have been more than eleven-years-old, her face, body, and dress streaked with splatters of bright crimson blood. She was evidently dead and gone from this world. The man walked to the center of the courtroom and dropped her lifeless body to the shiny wood floor. Feever could now see her bright crimson hair, coinciding with the color of the blood.

The crowd erupted into shouts of bewilderment and chaos.

"What the hell is that supposed to mean?" Feever asked.

"*That*, dear citizens," the man said, "is a little girl I found on the street, on the way coming here. She was just lying there, blood staining her every feature! She was dying and I hurried to ask her who did this to her." And then, the guardsman turned around, straight toward Sinistery and Kervantee, pointing a finger at them, his tone deep, dead-serious. "Sinistery and Kervantee!"

The crowd exclaimed in horror and started chanting in anger.

Feever momentarily closed her eyes, sighing desperately. If there had been any fluctuation concerning Sinistery and Kervantee's fates on the crowd's side, it had utterly evaporated.

Shouts could be heard: "SLAUGHTER THEM! BURN THEM AT THE STAKE! DIRTY WITCHES, KILLING A LITTLE GIRL!"

Scrouch smiled. *"I think the verdict is quite clear."*

"WAIT!" Feever screamed in a last bid to save her siblings. To her surprise, the crowd quieted down. "You're all so outraged about this little girl's death and you're blaming my brother and sister for this, but did you think for a second in the same way when Scrouch and his helpers killed my siblings' children? Did you think about the moment when they burned alive in agony and died cruelly, just as that little girl?"

"THEY WERE CHILDREN OF WITCHES!" the sheepman screamed. "THEY DESERVED TO DIE!"

The crowd supported him with more shouts.

"And that little girl," Scrouch pointed at her, "is just an innocent victim of your relatives' witchcraft!"

"But…" Feever started, but she was interrupted by the mayor.

"I wonder," he smiled wickedly. "You're defending them so bravely, so unhesitatingly. Are you doing it because maybe you're also one of them? Another nasty witch?"

"NO!" Sinistery and Kervantee screamed in unison.

Feever was on the verge of tears. She knew her siblings wouldn't let her be dragged into this.

"Don't touch our sister!" Kervantee said. "You want someone, take me! Burn me at the stake, dismember me if you'd like! But do *not* touch our sister!"

"That's not such a bad idea when you think about it," Scrouch said.

"If you feel the need to kill somebody, kill me!" Sinistery said. "Leave Kervantee and Feever alone! If you're looking for someone to blame, blame me! Yes, I did it! I killed that little girl!"

Feever gasped. She knew Sinistery had lied to try to save her and Kervantee.

But the crowd didn't know that. And hence why it erupted once again into shouts of horror at her confession, and this time, pure disgust.

"If me dying would mean saving my family, then so be it!" Sinistery whispered, barely audible.

"ORDER IN THE HALL!" General Scrouch began banging the wooden hammer again, and everyone was silenced. "Ladies and gentlemen, we just got a confession out of Sinistery!"

"You shouldn't have done this!" Feever almost hissed at her sister.

"There was no way I would let you also be killed!" Tears formed in the eyes of both sisters, the remaining members of their family joining them soon after.

"She confessed to murdering that poor child and that's why she is sentenced to the death, to be burned at the stake in the town square!" Scrouch announced Sinistery's fate and the courtroom began filling with claps of approval and content. "As for you, Kervantee," Scrouch turned his head to the other prisoner in the cage next to Sinistery's, "you may not have killed anyone, but who knows what kind of other satanic deeds you've committed, helping your sister Sinistery!"

Feever began sobbing audibly, knowing what the General was about to say, and she herself was about to crumble down to her knees if it wasn't for her mother and aunt catching her last minute.

"For the possible complicity of the murder of that poor little girl and for the practice of black magic I also sentence you to death, to be burned at the stake, right next to your dear sister!"

The crowd screamed so loud when it heard that, it seemed as if it were about to collapse of excitement.

"Please," Feever was brought to the low point of begging Sarvit, Mour and most notably, Scrouch, for mercy. "Amend the verdict. Do not take Sinistery and Kervantee away from me! I can't lose them!"

"*This* is the final verdict; this is the law!" General Scrouch raised a fist in the air triumphantly. "From now on everyone who intends on defaming Salem in any way will be sent to burn at the stake for their crimes!" he announced. "Together as one, we will eradicate the witches from this town, once and for all!"

The citizens jumped out of their seats, clapping, and smiling at Salem's ruler.

"Please," Henrietta said, turning to Sarvit and Mour a few seats away, "do not take away my children! You also have kids, how would you two feel if somebody were to kill them in such a cold-blooded way?"

Sarvit and Mour didn't respond.

Feever hoped with all her heart that they would remember this question. And that this question would haunt them for eternity, wherever they went and whatever they did.

"Sinistery and Kervantee are going to be burned at the stake in the town square at precisely four o'clock today, afternoon time, for their deeds against Salem and its citizens! You're all invited to watch." Scrouch smiled. "May Salem live long and fruitfully!"

"May General Scrouch live long and fruitfully!" The townsmen were screaming in applause.

Feever saw General Scrouch standing up from his throne and starting to wave at the crowd, bathing in their ovation.

"The trial is now officially closed, my dear citizens," Scrouch proclaimed. "Go home, eat, get some rest, and at four o'clock sharp I will be expecting you at the town square, so we can all become witness to the eradication of a vicious poison that has been holding Salem in its grip for far too long! Remember this day, dear citizens, because on this day we begin writing the *true* history of Salem!"

The crowd continued clapping and shouting for another few minutes and then started leaving the courtroom in large groups.

Scrouch's guardsmen unlocked the wooden cells and dragged Sinistery and Kervantee out of there. Feever had to be held back by Henrietta and Harietta, so as not to do something stupid and expose her magic to the world. The raven-haired woman supposed they were being brought back to the dungeons, to await their execution in only a couple of hours.

"How could you?" Ahronia asked General Scrouch, and Feever looked at the two of them. "You condemned two innocent civilians for something they didn't do!"

Feever saw Scrouch on the first floor below her family and Ahronia, grinning wickedly. "I did what I thought was in Salem's best interest!"

"Is that what's in Salem's best interest?" Ahronia pointed to the sobbing Feever, Henrietta, and Harietta, next to her. "You think you would protect Salem by destroying a *whole* family? Wasn't it enough that you already destroyed two others?"

"Ahronia…"

"NO!"

Feever witnessed Ahronia raising her hand at that, walking down the steps to the first floor, facing Scrouch at the center, where the footpath was, between all the rows of seats on the left and right sides.

"You're a tyrant!" Ahronia said, spit almost coming out of her mouth. "One insensitive animal! I don't want to ever see you again!"

"That's too bad because we live together," he laughed, "sweet cheeks!"

"No!" Ahronia said and Feever noticed the determined look in the flaming red-haired woman's eyes. "I'm leaving you, Scrouch! I desire not to communicate or live with you anymore in any capacity!"

"You can't do that!" Scrouch exclaimed, the worry in his voice building. "You would be dishonored, and such an act would loosen Salem's trust in me!"

Feever witnessed Ahronia cracking a smile. "Just watch me!" And then she disappeared out of the courtroom.

The little girl's corpse was taken out of the building and was planned to be burned behind the dumpsters nearby, if Feever heard correctly from the guardsman who had brought her informing the General. Feever supposed the child was just one of the dozens of orphans roaming the streets of Salem, and had been killed by Scrouch's men, simply to prove a point. But there was nothing Feever could do about it now. She felt helpless.

Shortly after, Sarvit and Mour also walked out the two towering wooden doors, which the crowd had opened before them and Ahronia. Feever then saw the General himself looking at her and what was left of her family. Looking at their sorrow, their tears. Their hopelessness. Didn't that man have any compassion in him?

"The witches must be eliminated!" he simply said and adjusted the sheriff hat, resting atop his head.

Feever watched him also depart the courtroom with a steady, confident step, hating that excuse of a human being for his victory. He had sealed her relatives' fates and *there was nothing Feever could do about it.*

She could only huddle closer to Henrietta and Harietta on the seats, and cry alongside them.

Chapter 54

Execution

Four o'clock came. Salem's population had gathered all around the wooden platform in the town square, where only a couple of weeks ago two women had been burnt to death. Sinistery and Kervantee were now being dragged through the city's gravel, past faces looking at them with hate. Sinistery first noticed General Scrouch standing atop the tall wooden platform with the two giant wooden poles and circles of wooden logs awaiting her and her brother. He was positioned between the two stakes and the afternoon sunlight was glinting off his sheriff hat's star. Then Sinistery turned her head to find Ahronia, Sarvit, and Mour also present a little bit further into the crowd at her left side. And at her right side, a little bit further in front of her, directly next to the wooden platform, the bright lilac-haired woman saw her family – Feever, Henrietta, and Harietta. She could sense their bewilderment with the whole situation, but Sinistery had confessed and there was no turning back now.

"Burn the witches!" a familiar voice said, and Sinistery turned around to witness the man with the sheep taking a large red-black tomato out of his wife's leather bag. Then he hurled it at her brother Kervantee, who was only a few centimeters away from her, also being escorted by Scrouch's men. The tomato exploded in her brother's face, staining it with a very dark red, bordering on black, liquid.

"Protect Salem!" a female voice said.

And the next thing she knew, Sinistery was being assaulted with two tomatoes, probably hurled by that same woman. She didn't expect the collision and lost her balance, her knees giving out, bringing her to the mud-stained gravel. Only for a moment.

But that was enough for the citizens to attack her with fists and kicks. Through the curtain of limbs, Sinistery was able to see Kervantee, trying to help her, but he also got dragged along the current of unexpected violence.

"STOP!" Henrietta screamed, panic in her voice. "You're gonna kill them!"

"They're already dead, woman," the sheep man exclaimed and kicked Kervantee determinedly.

Sinistery saw her brother let out a high-pierced screech and heard a crack. Now, through his see-through white, but mud-stained shirt, she could see his ribs beginning to turn a dark violet color. The sheepman must have broken at least one rib.

A few minutes passed before Sinistery saw and heard General Scrouch finally intervening – he'd probably already gotten his fill of violence.

"Dear citizens, please," he said, smiling a tad, "these witches *will* burn at the stake, that's the most suitable punishment for them!"

Sinistery saw the citizens' limbs retracting upon hearing the voice of their mayor.

"Don't get me wrong, I appreciate your enthusiasm," Scrouch said, a hand placed on his chest where his 'heart' was supposed to be, "but these witches *need* to burn at the stake for their crimes!"

315

Scrouch's men lifted Sinistery off of the ground, whose face was now stained with tomatoes and mud, both eyes black and bruised, and her brother Kervantee, who was in an even worse condition than her.

Kervantee and Sinistery reached Feever, tortured, exhausted gazes in their eyes.

"Can I please have one last moment with my brother and sister?" Feever asked General Scrouch.

"I prefer to get on with the execution," he said coldly.

"Please, General Scrouch," Harietta said, looking up to where Scrouch was positioned at the center of the wooden platform. "Allow us to say goodbye to our loved ones!"

Sinistery saw the General looking at all of them, mulling it over. "You've got two minutes."

~~~~~~~~~~

Kervantee threw himself into the arms of his mother Henrietta, and Sinistery into those of her sister Feever's.

"I love you, my boy," Henrietta said.

Kervantee had to duck slightly to get on the same level as Henrietta, being half a head taller than her.

Henrietta looked him in the eyes. "Look at you," she said, "look at the handsome man you've become!"

Kervantee smiled slightly.

"I'm so sorry about Thomas," she said.

"Look on the bright side," Kervantee said, tears gathering in his eyes. Tears of sadness, but also, tears of happiness. "After I die, I will see him again!"

Henrietta smiled a bitter smile and then hugged him once more.

Then, Kervantee bid his farewell to his aunt Harietta. "Auntie." The next moment, he was being squeezed in her embrace, neither one of them wanting to let go.

"Know that no matter what happens today, we will always be a family!" she said, looking into his eyes. "I want you to go out there on that damn wooden platform, and show them that we are still a family and that we are still fighting for one another! I want you to go out there with dignity and head raised high!"

Kervantee nodded.

"One minute," Scrouch's malicious reminder beckoned from the platform like a dark shadow.

Kervantee then walked over to Sinistery and Feever and pulled his beautiful sisters into a tight hug. Who would have thought that after fleeing their native Bulgaria years ago, Sinistery and Kervantee would end up here? Getting ready to be burnt at the stake.

"I want you to know that I will avenge you!" Feever whispered in their ears. "You both deserved so much more than this! I will find a way for us to meet again! I will search to the end of the world if I must!"

"Thank you," Kervantee and Sinistery said at the same time, smiling.

All three siblings had tears in their eyes.

"Thirty seconds," Scrouch said.

~~~~~~~~~~

Sinistery went to hug Harietta and Henrietta. "You really *were* the best mother and aunt a girl could hope for!" she said and then backed away from their embrace and smiled through tears. Her gaze traveled to each and every member of her family, affectionate and passionate. "I wouldn't trade any of you for anything!"

"Fifteen seconds!"

"I love you all," Sinistery said and then pulled her mother Henrietta, her aunt Harietta, her sister Feever, and her brother

Kervantee, into a hug. Sinistery knew that hug was going to be their last one ever. And she knew Kervantee was aware of the same thing. Therefore, they made it count.

"Time's up!" Scrouch announced.

The next thing Sinistery knew, Scrouch's men were dragging her and her brother up the wooden steps to the main part of the platform, boards creaking under her feet. But halfway through, she struggled out of her captor's grip, as did Kervantee, and both of them said simultaneously: "We've got this part ourselves, thanks!"

Then, the siblings walked the remainder of the way to the platform, with confident strides and heads raised impossibly high.

Sinistery saw their aunt looking at them proudly, tears in her eyes, and a faint smile on her face. In the next moment, Sinistery was being escorted by one of the guardsmen to take her place above the wooden logs, getting pinned to the wooden pole with a rope.

Kervantee got served the exact same treatment.

A scorching torch was passed from one of the men to the mayor. He took it with a smile.

Sinistery heard Feever screaming. Then her eye range became crowded by the tall, lurking figure of General Scrouch.

"Sinistery Strangerhenz," he said and Sinistery looked at him curiously – he knew her surname – "you're sentenced to death for practicing witchcraft and satanic rituals, casting curses toward Salem's good citizens, and the murder of an innocent little girl!"

Sinistery Strangerhenz looked Scrouch straight in the eyes, head up high.

"Do you have any last words?" He asked and then stepped out of her eye view.

Sinistery looked at the vast crowd – they had sealed hers and Kervantee's fate, murdering them for crimes none of them committed. "All of you," she smiled devilishly, the most wicked smile finding its way across her rose lips. "I hope your families rot and for you all to burn in the everlasting hell, alongside the corpses of your children!"

Astonished shouts and whispers became audible amongst the crowd. And a barely contained laugh. Feever Strangerhenz's laugh.

"She's a filthy witch!" the crowd screamed. "She's gonna curse us! Burn her at once!"

"Actually," Scrouch said, coming into Sinistery's eye range for the second time, inching the flaming torch closer to the numerous logs beneath Sinistery's feet. "You're the one who's gonna burn in hell!"

The logs lit with incredible speed, one by one. The flames engulfed Sinistery Strangerhenz, killing her gradually, turning her skin to mere ash slowly. She let out an inhumane howl of pain and pure suffering, but soon after her struggles ceased, her spirit having left her body.

~~~~~~~~~~

The sun dipped below the horizon and soon Salem began turning dark. But what was darkest were the two victims at the stake, the life of one of them already snuffed out by Scrouch and the crowd's undying cruelty.

Kervantee Strangerhenz was crying his eyes out and he could see that Feever was doing the same from the front row in the crowd, falling to the ground and kicking it wildly. She had to be stopped by Henrietta and Harietta, because Kervantee supposed she was about to walk up to the platform and kill Scrouch with her bare hands, exposing their secret to Salem.

Then, Kervantee saw one of the other guards passing a second scorching torch to Scrouch, who walked up to him with a wide smile.

"Kervantee Strangerhenz," Scrouch said with a smile, "you're sentenced to death for practicing witchcraft and satanic rituals, the murders of hundreds of sheep, being an accomplice to the murder of an innocent little girl, and let's face it," he laughed audibly, "for being such a faggot!"

Kervantee laughed. "I may be a 'faggot', as you say," he said, "but I'm willing to bet I was getting way more action than you. And I had the truest love in the face of Thomas – and that's something that *you* are never going to get! You wanna know why? Come a little closer!"

Scrouch did so, curiously.

Kervantee whispered in his ear: "Because you're a piece of homophobic, sexist shit!"

"Pretty brave words, coming out of the mouth of a man who is about to die," Scrouch said, retreating.

Kervantee smiled once again and looked at the crowd, his vision not entirely crowded by Scrouch this time. His pecan hair was dampened with sweat and dirt. "My last words for you, *dear citizens*, are simply my wish for your kids to catch diseases and die, taking all your precious animals and you, with them!" Kervantee laughed like a true madman. "Die, citizens of Salem, *die!*"

Kervantee saw the General bringing the torch closer to the wooden logs, beneath his feet.

"You're the one who's gonna die," and then Scrouch lit the logs.

The flames started eating away at Kervantee Strangerhenz, but he didn't stop laughing until he took his last breath.

~~~~~~~~~~

Feever stopped thrashing around and was now sobbing quietly in the arms of Henrietta and Harietta, watching the still burning stakes, the realization dawning on her like an everlasting shadow – Kervantee and Sinistery were gone.

Forever.

~~~~~~~~~~

320

Ahronia was looking at her husband, still standing up on the wooden platform in front of the burning bodies, tears in her eyes and gaze insinuated with contempt. She caught sight of his own gaze and just shook her head, starting to withdraw from the crowd into the now almost dark evening. She had realized that General Scrouch had to be taken out.

For the good of Salem.

~~~~~~~~~~

Sarvit and Mour had also started walking away from the wooden platform and the crowd, when suddenly Feever received a sudden wave of energy from deep within her, and she escaped her relatives' embraces. The grief in her eyes had now been replaced with pure and black malice.

"I will make you pay for what you did to me and my family!" Feever threatened, her teeth clattering in anger. "I will make your descendants feel the same pain you inflicted on Sinistery and Kervantee! I will make sure to do something so vile, that your entire family will not be able to recover for centuries to come!" She had to choose her words wisely, because she was surrounded by Salem's population, including Scrouch. But she thought those two sentences drove the point home.

Sarvit and Mour didn't utter a word.

"Sarvit Fehrenberg and Mour Klauzer, I will make sure to bring you everlasting suffering!" Then she turned to her mother and aunt, whispering in anger, "Let's get out of here! I've got a curse to cast!"

Henrietta and Harietta nodded, and the three women walked away from the town square.

~~~~~~~~~~

The sun had now entirely dipped below the horizon and the darkness descended upon Salem.

"Let's go home," Mour told Sarvit, wanting only to go home and make love to his wife, in a bid to forget the dreadful thing Sarvit and he had done.

Sarvit just nodded, and they, too, began walking away from the crime scene.

The two men now had to live with what they had done forever.

~~~~~~~~~~

The crowd began slowly dissipating, but not before Scrouch addressed them: "That's all for today, dear citizens." He headed toward the wooden steps leading down the platform and the fire that was now gradually dying out. He knew his several guardsmen present would stay and finish putting it out. "Tomorrow we will continue the witch hunt! Good night and stay safe," said Salem's mayor, and alongside the crowd he stepped away from the town square, walking intently toward his office.

Chapter 55

"They could still laugh."

B ack in the present-day the tall emerald portal, which Ameralda had created, opened. Berventy Klauzer, who was holding The Book in her hands, was spat out first, hitting one of the pick-up trucks upon her landing, next to the ruins of the Straightvur library.

Teela Fehrenberg and Kasteron Klauzer were the next in line to fly out of the portal, landing straight next to the library's debris.

"Kasteron!" Berventy screamed, her body slightly aching from the fall, running up to check on her son and reaching him within seconds. "Are you okay?" Then she turned to her son's girlfriend. "What about you, Teela?"

"Yes, Mum, we're fine," said Kasteron and at the same time, Perventia and Pattery Fehrenberg landed next to him.

"This portal is monstrous," Perventia noted, while Pattery offered his hand to help her stand up. "Is it that hard not to throw us out so rudely?"

"I don't know, honey," Pattery said and a second later Pacifika, Klacifia and Kayla appeared from the island's universe, flying out of the emerald portal. They landed next to the library's ruins, a few feet away from the already gathered group.

"I hate this portal," Pacifika said while standing up.

"Are you okay?" Perventia shouted.

"Yeah, just a little bit rough around the edges," the doppelganger Kayla responded.

Berventy saw Kayla looking around the library's ruins with a seemingly disgusted expression on her face. For now, no one suspected Kayla, not even Berventy. But she couldn't deny that there was something odd about the way Kayla had reacted to returning to her native world.

Berventy then turned around to see her son Marisii, and his boyfriend Makio flying out of the portal, and landing on the roof of one of the trucks, all the while their hands linked together. They looked at each other and then at Berventy, who looked back at them. But their hands remained linked.

Brouzun, Morven, and Annora were the last ones to be thrown out. Then the portal closed up.

After the group had regained their footing, they gathered around the pick-up trucks.

"We need to decide what we're going to do now," Berventy said, still holding the precious item.

"What do you mean?" Perventia said, from the spot next to Berventy's.

"Well," Berventy started, "I think I speak for everyone when I say that I'm tired of constant running and hiding. At this point, I consider it best if we found a place, where we could spend a few nights in, to regain our strength for Feever's next visit."

"We can go home," Morven offered, but Berventy gave him a strict glare.

"Absolutely not," she said, "that's the first place Feever would look for us. It's just too soon for us to go back there since the last time. And besides, it would be strategically stupid."

"Okay, okay, sorry for asking," Morven said, raising his hands in defense.

Annora stepped forward.

"You've got something to add?" Berventy looked at the ex-medical nurse meanly.

"I would like to go home."

"Excuse me?"

"Yes, that's exactly what I want," Annora said as if she were convincing herself more than anyone else. "I never asked to be involved in your families' drama. That witch Feever, as you called her, just used me as a pawn to swap the babies."

"You do realize it's your fault that one of my sons is forever lost?" Berventy looked at her angrily, the flames burning in her eyes. "And it's your fault that the boy *I* raised killed his own father, and now hates all of us?"

"It's not my fault Feever hypnotized me," Annora countered. "I'm just a pure mortal human, not a witch like you lot!"

"You leaving us right now is out of the question!" Berventy said. "Feever will continue hunting you – it's what she does!"

"I'm sorry, do I sense worry about me in your voice?" Annora almost laughed. "Just two seconds ago you blamed me for destroying your family, and now you're feigning worry about me?" Annora laughed louder now. "I WAS JUST A STUPID PAWN IN FEEVER'S CONSPIRACY!" she shouted. "The only thing she used me for is to swap the babies! I'm sorry, but I'm not a witch, vampire, or werewolf to resist her hypnosis!"

"Why are you getting angry?" Berventy asked her with a calm tone.

"Because I'm sick of you blaming me for something that's your own fault!" Annora said. "That's your battle, not mine! I *am* going home, and you can't stop me!"

Berventy opened The Book and started flipping through its pages, looking for a spell to use on Annora. When she found a suitable one, she raised her hand threateningly. "Is that so?"

Annora flashed a knife out of her back pocket, pointing it at Berventy. She wondered where she'd taken it from. "I'm serious," she said. "Let me go or I will use it!"

"ENOUGH!" Perventia screamed and stepped forward, between Berventy and Annora. "Berventy, you can't just force her to remain with us if she doesn't want to! That's not who we are and that's not how we deal with stuff – we're not Feever, for god's sake!" Then, Perventia turned to Annora. "If that's what you truly desire, you're free to go. But keep in mind that there's a high possibility of Feever coming after you. And if that happens, we wouldn't be there to help you. You do realize that, right? Are you willing to take that risk?"

"I do. And I am," Annora said, putting the knife back in the pocket, and Berventy lowered her hand and closed The Book. "But I would rather be dead than see another one of your faces ever again. Because of you, hundreds of innocents lost their lives in the hospital – and that's on your conscience!"

Berventy saw her blonde friend nodding in understanding.

Annora fixed her tangled mess of orange-crimson hair. The sun was insinuating her light brown skin tone. "I won't tell anyone what I've seen today. Or in the past couple of days – I've lost track of time," the ex-nurse said. "But if you look for me ever again, I will kill you!"

"Is that all? Or would you like to add another threat?" Berventy smiled bitterly. The gingerbread-haired mother got the sudden impulse to close her hands around Annora's neck and snap it for swapping the babies. But her better judgment knew that she couldn't do that – Annora had been indeed just a pawn in Feever's plan. An innocent, who just happened to be in the wrong place at the wrong time.

"Good luck with the fight against the witch," Annora said and Berventy watched her slowly walk away from all of them, limping with one leg, her clothes half-torn, half-stained with mud and leaves. Her stride seemed exhausted.

Berventy noticed no one saying anything until Annora hid from their lines of sight. Then she heard Perventia swearing, looking at Berventy's dislocated shoulder. Berventy herself had forgotten about it up until now, to a certain extent numb to the pain.

"We could have asked her to check up on your shoulder," Perventia said as if she also had forgotten.

"I'm okay."

"No. No, you're not," Pattery said from behind her and then stepped in her line of sight. "We need to take you to a doctor!"

"I *said* I'm fine," Berventy said through gritted teeth.

"Mum," Marisii joined the conversation, "you need medical help. Let us help you."

Berventy looked at him. Then she looked at all her other sons – Kasteron, Brouzun, and Morven. Lately, she hadn't been spending as much time with them, as she would have liked to. She wanted to hear about their lives – about Marisii's first relationship, about how Kasteron's was going, about Brouzun and Morven as a whole, and what interested and worried them. But there hadn't been any time at all for that.

"Okay." Berventy nodded. "We're going to go somewhere to a hospital." At that, all her children smiled widely. "But after that, I strongly suggest we find a place to spend a few nights at, and even more importantly – to buy new clothes from somewhere because right now we all look like hobos!" She made a joke after all the seriousness and strictness for the past couple of hours, leading from The Island of Lost Hopes to their own universe.

And they all burst out laughing.

It was comforting for them to know that even though after everything they had been through together – after the losses of Tiffany and Brouzenvert and the never-ending battles with Feever – they could still laugh.

Chapter 56

On the road

The Fehrenberg family and the Klauzer family climbed up onto their respective trucks, located a few feet away from the library's ruins. They set a course for the highway, wanting to get as far from the library, and for that matter the hospital, as possible – both carried too many bad memories.

Kayla Fehrenberg – from the island's universe, was sitting behind Perventia in the truck. *I missed you all so much,* Kayla thought, looking at Perventia, who smiled in response from the front passenger seat.

"We missed you too, sweetheart," Perventia touched Kayla's hand with hers gently, "so much!"

Pattery, Klacifia, Teela and Pacifika looked at her uncomprehendingly.

"What?" Perventia said.

"No one's said anything." Kayla smiled regardless. "I thought about something, but I never said it out loud!"

"Honey, are you okay?" Pattery reached out from the driver's seat to grab his wife's hand.

"Weird," she said, faintly smiling at Pattery, "I could swear Kayla said something. Doesn't matter."

Kayla knew Perventia had found her power, even though she didn't know what that power was yet.

But Kayla knew – after all, her birth mother in the parallel universe had the exact same individual power. And what just happened made Kayla aware of the fact that she now had to be extra careful around her 'mother', in order not to be exposed.

~~~~~~~~~~

The two families had stopped in the small parking lot of the nearest hospital they could find, located directly next to the highway, buzzing with the activity of countless other cars and trucks. While Marisii, Brouzun, Morven, and Kasteron had taken their mother inside the hospital for her shoulder to get checked, Perventia, Pattery, Kayla, Klacifia, Pacifika, and Teela had stayed waiting near the trucks. Makio had also tagged along with the Klauzer family.

Berventy was escorted to one of the hospital rooms by a tall, handsome doctor, her family staying behind in the foyer.

"This is going to hurt," the doctor warned and then took hold of Berventy's right shoulder. She was sitting in a huge, long black seat that was elevating her legs, designed for medical check-ups. "You might want to hold onto something."

Berventy couldn't help but laugh slightly at that. She had lost her husband and one of her sons. She had survived two whole battles with Feever and was eagerly fighting to keep the rest of her family alive and well. One twisted, dislocated shoulder didn't even faze her. "Just do it."

The doctor nodded and without any further warning, popped Berventy's shoulder back into place.

It only took a second, but that didn't stop the pain from erupting within her shoulder, making her howl momentarily. Then she got handed some white circular pills for the pain and the doctor began preparing the black sling.

"I never got your name," the doctor said as he was unpackaging the sling.

"Berventy," she said and smiled lightly, "Berventy Klauzer. And yours?"

"That's quite an interesting and unusual name." The doctor returned her smile. "That sounds like the name of a fighter. Are *you* a fighter?"

Berventy had to laugh again. "You haven't the slightest idea."

"I'm Joe," he said, "Joe Smartner."

"It's very nice to meet you, Joe Smartner," she said as Joe was carefully placing her hand inside one part of the sling and slinging the other across her neck and shoulder.

She wasn't flirting with him – Berventy couldn't even *think* romantically about any man other than her deceased husband Brouzenvert. She supposed only a few hours had passed since his death and she couldn't remember when was the last time she got some decent sleep, considering the situation with The Curse and all.

"You're all set," he said and smiled again. "I will give you some medicine that will aid in your recovery."

"Aren't those usually *prescribed* to the patient?"

"That is the protocol, yes," Joe said, "but I like you and I intend on giving them to you straightaway, so you won't have to bother with pharmacies and stuff." He then flashed her another smile.

Was he *flirting* with her? Or was it all in her imagination? Was he just kind and polite to her? Or was there an ulterior motive?

She was pulled out of her reverie when Joe handed her a small ziploc bag, filled with various-colored plastic bottles of pills. "Thank you," she said, taking hold of the bag. "You have no idea what I'm currently going through – your gesture means a lot to me."

"For what it's worth, I'm sincerely sorry for whatever happened to you. And I wish you a speedy recovery."

Berventy could read some indistinct determination, written on Joe Smartner's face, which began turning red. "Are you okay?" Berventy was suddenly worried about the doctor who'd helped her.

"Yeah, I'm fine," the black-haired man said, still in a standing position opposite the sitting Berventy. "What I'm going to say may seem bold and a little ridiculous to you, but…"

Oh, no, Berventy thought, aware of what was soon to follow.

"Do you want to maybe grab dinner sometime?"

Berventy's light facial expression darkened within seconds. The truth was, she didn't want anyone else other than Brouzenvert, and was doubtful she would ever love a man the same way she loved her husband. Joe was a kind man, but he certainly didn't need all of Berventy's family drama. And if he even knew a fraction of what he was getting himself into, he would have run away at full speed. That's why she had to decline – for his sake, *and* hers.

"Look," she started as if she were about to serve some major bad news, "I appreciate your help, I really do! But due to reasons I cannot possibly disclose to you, I would have to decline your offer. Too much emotional baggage comes hand to hand with me, and I can't allow myself to burden you with that!"

"But what if I wanna be burdened?"

"You don't!" Berventy said authoritatively, startling Joe. "Believe me, it's better for the both of us that way." She tightened her grip on the ziploc bag, containing the medication, and headed for the door.

Joe didn't say anything.

But before she left the room and Joe forever, Berventy turned around to him, finding him already looking back at her. "There *is* a woman for you somewhere out there," Berventy assured him, even though she couldn't possibly back that up. "And when you do find her, you two will be very happy together. But that woman is not me

– I already had true love in my life and I lost him!" She decided to share that one small piece of information with Joe, before making her exit.

~~~~~~~~~~

Berventy, Makio, and her four sons walked out of the small hospital and back to the pick-up trucks, where the Fehrenberg family was waiting for them out in the sunshine.

"How did it go?" Perventia asked Berventy.

Better than expected. I got asked out on a date, but I declined. Oh, I also got given some medications, Berventy thought.

But instead, she said: "Wasn't bad."

"You were given medicine?" Perventia looked cheery. "That's great! And what's that about a date?"

Berventy looked at the other woman uncomprehendingly. "Yes, I was given medication," she said, swinging the ziploc bag in front of all the observing eyes demonstratively with her other hand. "But I haven't said anything about any date."

"Is that so?" Perventia's face scrunched up into a frown. "I could swear you just said you've been asked out on a date."

"I didn't say that," Berventy said. "No one's asked me out on a date!" she lied, not understanding how Perventia could have possibly known that. Berventy had just thought about it, never saying it out loud.

"Honey, are you sure you're okay?" Pattery asked. "That's the second time today you've been hearing things no one's said."

"Are you feeling okay, Mom?" Pacifika also asked.

"Of course I am, darling," Perventia assured. "I guess that's caused by all the stress we've all been under. I think we could use one well-deserved break, don't you agree?"

A line of nods followed.

Berventy saw Pattery going to the luggage compartment of his pick-up truck and taking a large paper map out of there. Upon returning, he rolled it out on the black hood of the truck, for everyone to see.

"There's a hotel called Cardiniganin not far from here," he said and then moved a finger up the map. "And next to it there's a shopping center called Primark. They've got a variety of men's and women's clothes."

"That's a good, and as previously mentioned by Berventy, idea," Klacifia said, pointing to her own clothes, and then everybody else's. All of their clothes were torn, burnt, coal stained. "First, we buy the clothes, and then we crash in that hotel, what do you say?"

Another line of nods followed, all the faces wrinkled and slightly muddy.

It didn't take them long to roll the map back up and then climb back onto the trucks, returning to the highway and setting off to better locations than previously explored.

Chapter 57

Shopping

The Fehrenberg and Klauzer families pulled up next to Primark. Family members began filing out of the two trucks. Perventia looked at her husband Pattery, both of them still in their truck. He was looking for something in the glove compartment, between the steering wheel and gear shift.

"*What* are you looking for?"

Pattery pulled out a black leather wallet with a smile. "This!"

The couple then exited the truck and Perventia saw Pattery giving each of his daughters 50 dollars. Then she noticed the notes in the Klauzer boys' hands, and she knew Berventy had already given them money.

"Has anyone shopped in here before?" Pattery asked but they all shook their heads. "Well, this is a really cheap store with quality clothes, so I think you will like it."

Then, both Berventy and Pattery locked the two trucks with two small black remote controls.

Perventia thought her daughter Kayla must have given the remote control to Berventy at some point, even though the truck belonged to her. In the next moment, a string of thoughts coming from Berventy flooded Perventia's mind.

Weird, Berventy thought, *I remember that Kayla always loved driving her truck before. But after we left the library for good and the second hospital she acted as if she'd never seen it before.*

But even though Perventia had heard Berventy's thoughts once again, she decided to keep quiet – Pattery already regarded her as overly tired, and she didn't want to add to his worry.

The two families and Makio headed toward the huge two-floor store, with dark glass windows surrounding every side. Big light blue letters saying *PRIMARK* were built at the middle section where the first and second floors met. The two towering glass doors opened automatically for the families.

"Let's meet back here in three hours," Pattery said when Perventia and the others went inside. "Do you think that's enough time?"

A line of nods and then various footsteps, setting off to different sections of the store.

Perventia decided to stick around with her husband Pattery for a little while and saw Makio enthusiastically grabbing Marisii by the hand and dragging him further into the store.

"Come on," Makio said, "let's go to the men's section – I can't wait to see what you look like in a refined shirt!"

Perventia might have been wrong, especially when Marisii and Makio had gotten so far away from her, but she thought she saw Marisii's face blushing red.

~~~~~~~~~~

Makio and Marisii were standing in front of a big circular sofa in the store, positioned right opposite the lines of men's changing rooms. There was also a tall mirror behind the sofa, so the customers who had booked the room privately could use it. Marisii and Makio hadn't, but the previous booking had been unexpectedly canceled, so the two boys took advantage of that.

Makio handed Marisii one black and one wine-red shirt. "I think you would look killer in both."

"Thank you," Marisii replied with a smile.

A second later Makio was handed a few long-legged pants and pullovers.

"And I think you would look fantastic in that sweater," Marisii said, nodding to the green one with long, white and black stripes.

"Let's try them on," Makio prompted Marisii and watched him as he went into one of the changing rooms, deciding to wait for him to try on his clothes first.

~~~~~~~~~~

Marisii stripped off his black leather jacket, his dirty jeans and shirt, remaining only in his green boxers. There was a mirror in his changing room and for a moment his gaze lingered on his reflection – he looked well, in good shape, but his sleep deprivation could evidently be seen on his face by the dark circles below and around his eyes. Marisii inched toward the mirror, protruding his right shoulder forward intently. The scar from his own bullet directed back at him by Feever from his first encounter with her, was still there. It wasn't big or bad-looking, and Marisii would have never replaced it for anything in the world. But it *was* there, looking back at him as if gazing into his tortured soul.

Marisii decided to snap himself out of it and started thinking about Makio, while he was slipping into the wine-red shirt. He wanted to impress Makio with those clothes – he *liked* him, and he wanted to look good for him. Deciding to mix it up a little bit, he also slipped into a pair of beige pants. Buttoning up the shirt and the pants, Marisii drew back the curtain of the changing room and stepped out.

~~~~~~~~~~

Makio was holding the pants and sweaters Marisii had chosen for him when he saw Marisii and dropped them all on the floor. He stood like that for a moment, mouth gaping wide open, gazing at Marisii in delight, but then he snapped out of it with a smile and a giggle.

"Do you think they look okay on me?" Marisii said, now standing in front of the mirror behind the circular sofa.

"Are you kidding me?" Makio went over to him, looking at the other man in the mirror. "If you go dressed like that out on the street, you will attract all looks – males' and females'!" Makio was absolutely delighted – Marisii looked so sexy and natural in those new clothes. They had stuck to his athletic body in all the right curves and angles, and Makio couldn't resist noting the shape of Marisii's booty in the beige pants, and his chest in the wine-red shirt.

"I don't know," Marisii turned around from all sides, to look at himself. "Don't you think it's a bit much?"

"Much?" Makio couldn't help laughing. He gently took Marisii's right shoulder and turned him over to face him. "Look at me."

Their eyes met on almost the same level, considering Makio was an inch or two shorter than Marisii.

"You look *amazing!*" Makio said. "You're so sexy." He smiled, gladly seeing Marisii's smile following as well.

"You really think so?" Marisii was now inching closer to Makio, the distance between them shortening drastically.

"There's no way to change my mind," Makio smiled playfully. In the next moment, his hands were grasping Marisii's neck, pulling him closer, finding his lips effortlessly, opening them hungrily with his tongue. The kiss went on for a couple of minutes before Makio started making his way over to Marisii's neck, applying a good amount of spit there, enjoying the tingling sensation of Marisii's skin on his lips when he gave him a hickey. Makio knew Marisii had never been in a relationship before, so he wanted Marisii to have some firsts with him in the most beautiful way possible.

"YES!" A moan suddenly escaped Marisii's lips.

That turned on Makio and he, without even realizing it, started unbuttoning Marisii's elegant shirt, sliding a hand along his bare flesh underneath.

Marisii suddenly drew away and Makio felt his hand no longer on Marisii.

"What is it?" Makio was suddenly worried that he had done something wrong, but he also felt a slight disappointment.

"I..." Marisii stuttered. "I..."

And then it hit him – Marisii had never slept with anyone before – girl or boy. Makio covered his mouth with his hands, angry at and disappointed by himself that he had allowed his passion to overcome him, touching Marisii without even considering the option that he maybe wasn't ready for that part of their relationship. After all, they had been together for merely a week.

"I'm so sorry," Makio said, wanting to beat himself up for what he'd done.

"It's not your fault," Marisii said, a note of sadness in his voice. "It's just that I... I've never slept with anyone ... and when I felt your hand on my body, I..."

"Marisii, I'm so, so sorry." Makio pulled him into a tight hug, suddenly afraid he had screwed things up. "I didn't know, and it didn't even cross my mind until now. I shouldn't have done this."

Makio felt Marisii's hand sliding around him, intensifying the hug. The two men stayed in each other's arms for a few minutes, before breaking the embrace.

"Look," Marisii said, his eyes directly rooted on Makio's, "all of this is very new to me. I like kissing you, I like you kissing my neck, but..."

"But you're just not ready for something more?"

Marisii nodded. "Do you hate me now?"

"Hate you?" Makio asked, his eyes widening in shock. "It's like you said – all of this is very new to you. I can't possibly expect you to dive straight into every aspect."

"But I don't want you to think that I'm not attracted to you in that way, or something like this," Marisii's voice almost stuttered. "Quite the opposite! But this is my first relationship ever, so I can't do *it* that soon."

"I understand, Marisii." Makio took Marisii's hands in his gently, as a sign of support. "Really, I do!"

"One day, I would be ready," Marisii said. "Are you willing to wait for me until then?"

"I would wait for you for years if I had to!" Makio smiled and placed one of his hands on Marisii's right cheek. Marisii gripped the hand as if he were holding on to a lifeboat.

"Thank you," Marisii sighed. "Thank you for everything."

Makio smiled once again at the other man – if for now he could only kiss and hug Marisii, if he could only do this with him for eternity, that would have been enough. Simply because he cared deeply about Marisii, and he knew Marisii felt the same way towards him. And *that* was the only thing that mattered.

Marisii looked into Makio's eyes and he looked back into his. The next thing Makio knew, Marisii took him by the neck and closed the space between their lips, biting hungrily as if Makio's lips were the last supper he was ever going to have. Their tongues met and explored one another.

After about 20 minutes, the two men stopped kissing and looked each other in the eyes. Marisii's wine-red shirt still had three of its buttons unbuttoned and he hurried to quickly fix them up.

"If I'm not wrong," Makio said. "We've got more clothes to try on."

"Yes, that is correct." Marisii laughed slightly.

"Now, go back to the changing room and put on the black shirt," Makio almost commanded through laughter and smiles. "I want to see you in it!"

"I listen and obey," Marisii said through laughter and disappeared from Makio's view.

Makio's eyes followed Marisii until he hid behind the curtain of the changing room. Makio liked Marisii and he knew his feelings were mutual. He was happy to have finally found someone who liked him after he had parted ways with his ex, who was emotionally abusing him.

"You deserve the world," Makio whispered ever so slightly, so Marisii could not hear him.

Then he smiled upon seeing Marisii emerging out of the changing room, the black shirt clinging to his toned, on the brink of muscular features. He looked even sexier with the black shirt on than he did with the wine-red one. Makio looked at Marisii in a daze as he fussed whether he looked good with the shirt, observing himself in the designed mirror.

"And I intend to give that to you."

~~~~~~~~~~

Perventia Fehrenberg was browsing through dresses in the females' section, when she felt a sharp pain in her head, dropping the violet-pink dress she was holding in her right hand.

And then he told me he won't go out with me anymore, Perventia heard the thought of a random woman passing by her. The thought echoed loud and clear in her skull as if the random woman had said it loud and clear.

You can't expect him to still be interested in you, considering how big of a slut you are! Perventia heard the thought of the woman, walking next to her, probably a friend of hers. Just as loud and just as clear as the previous one.

Perventia dumped browsing through the dresses entirely and walked with a hurried stride to the exit, wanting to get as far away from all these people as possible – they were too loud and were giving her a massive headache.

I don't want to go to the office again on Monday, Perventia heard the thought of a random man passing by.

The cucumbers have increased in price drastically, a granny's thought struck Perventia's mind, like a flood.

I'm sick of dumb people all around me, another flood of thoughts, this time coming from a teenager Perventia saw walking past.

"SHUT UP!" Perventia shouted. She took her throbbing head in her hands and ran for the exit. The throbbing pain increased by the seconds; the overflowing thoughts wouldn't stop. "JUST SHUT UP!"

Perventia thought, with the little mental capacity she had left for herself, that the customers must have been looking at her in confusion, because she heard a line of random thoughts, such as:

What is the matter with her?

She must be on some kind of major herbs!

Does she even notice that her clothes are dirty and torn? Perventia heard the thought of a woman, before finally emerging from the store out into the open, fresh air hitting her face.

Her headache subsided but to her terror, didn't fade away entirely. Perventia, without giving a damn what people would think of her, screamed on the street. Her lungs were filled to bursting with her out-of-this-world howls, and several onlookers made a point of running away. Then she saw that the power in Primark had suddenly cut off. She could hear murmurs of bewilderment and even panic, coming from inside the store. Only when the blond woman stopped screaming, did the power come back on, several seconds separating the two events.

She stood rooted to her spot for a few seconds, observing the shopping center. Then, Perventia stopped a man, passing her, concentrating her gaze on his lips, waiting to hear something – anything. But he didn't say anything – his lips remained shut.

I'm craving a burger, she heard his thought. But he hadn't uttered a single syllable.

"Excuse me, sir," she said, realizing she had grabbed him by the jacket. She let go. "Are you craving a burger? It seemed to me like you just mentioned it."

"How did you know?" he asked, Perventia sensing the wonderment and confusion in his voice. "I thought about this, but I never said it out loud."

Perventia Fehrenberg smiled, completely ignoring the man, vaguely aware of his departure. She had found her power, but back then, on The Island of Lost Hopes, she didn't know what exactly that power entailed. Now, she did.

Perventia Fehrenberg could read people's minds.

She was a telepath.

And it dawned on her that when she had screamed, the power in Primark had gotten cut off.

Which led her to think that her power was mighty.

Perventia smiled. "Feever, I am ready for you!"

She wasn't going to let that witch take away another one of her precious girls – not this time. Not after she had unlocked her power and could do something.

Chapter 58

Cardiniganin Hotel

Pattery Fehrenberg pulled up his truck at the hotel's vast parking lot. He then turned off the engine, grabbed the keys from the ignition and together with his wife Perventia and his daughters Pacifika, Kayla, Klacifia, and Teela, they emerged from the vehicle. Pattery took a good look at the hotel, shielding his eyes from the afternoon sun – the hotel was a tall, at least 20-floor building, with enormous windows surrounding its every side. At the entrance, there was a red carpet lined up, and the name 'Cardiniganin' was etched into marble with capital metallic letters, just above the entrance's double doors.

Pattery stepped closer to the hotel, his family following close behind. He could spot a long beach on the other side of the hotel, stretching beyond the hotel's perimeter. In the next moment, Pattery heard the squeal of tires and together with his family, turned around to see Berventy pulling up Kayla's truck, and stepping out of it, alongside her sons Brouzun, Morven, Marisii, Kasteron, and Marisii's boyfriend – Makio. The mother seemed to approve of the vastness and spaciousness of the hotel with a nod.

"You guys like what you see so far?" Pattery asked Berventy and her sons when they went to stand in front of them.

"It's beautiful," Berventy responded, her head poised up high, seemingly taking in the tallness of the hotel. "But if it's pricey as much as it is beautiful, we'd better check our wallets."

"Money is not a problem." Pattery noted, who before The Curse began, had a successful career as an adult-fiction fantasy and horror writer. His works were widely popular and critically acclaimed, but he had had to set that part of his life aside, in order to protect those he loved from the wicked witch Feever.

~~~~~~~~~~

"Then I think that this would be a great place to spend a couple of nights," Berventy agreed and then smiled – she was finally going to get some rest from Feever and her curse. Berventy was going to protect her children at all costs but decided that it was probably best to gather her strength for the next battle. Besides, when Brouzenvert had sacrificed his life to allow Pacifika to continue living hers, Berventy had cast the Blood Magic. This kind of magic was providing her family with immunity against Feever for at least three weeks, and something told Berventy that with it, Feever wasn't going to be able to hurt any of her children, or Berventy herself, the next time she came hunting. Berventy's right palm was still healing from the moment she had cut it open, in order to cast the Blood Magic, in addition to her aching, but already healing right shoulder. But Berventy knew she was going to be alright.

~~~~~~~~~~

Perventia Fehrenberg was smiling, from her place next to her husband and in front of her four daughters. She had found her power and was glad she could read people's minds. And she felt like that power could prove useful in the fight against Feever, because in that way Perventia might be able to predict the witch's next move, and maybe – just maybe – she might be able to stop Feever from cold-heartedly killing another one of her family members. Perventia still hadn't told Pattery, or her daughters, the good news, but she was planning to, once they all got settled in the hotel.

"If we all like the place, let's go in then," Pattery suggested.

"Wait a minute," Morven stopped them. "We need to take our new clothes!"

Everyone groaned in response as if they had completely forgotten that their current clothes were torn and beyond dirty, and that they had bought new ones. The crowd made their way back to the two trucks to pick up the shopping bags and then walked back to the hotel's entrance.

Pattery was the first one to reach the double glass doors of the hotel, and they opened automatically for him. He set foot inside and the rest followed him.

The two families were amazed by the quality of the hotel's interior – from the left side, there was a huge winding staircase, leading to the upper floors of the hotel. On the opposite side, four sets of double steel elevator doors could be seen. Right in the center of the lobby on the first floor where the two families were currently situated, there were several expensive-looking sofas, practically shining with vibrant rainbow colors, where the guests of the hotel could sit back with a drink and relax. Next to the sofas, there was a big fountain, with at least a dozen glass ornaments, each of them spitting out water into the small pool below. And that wasn't all. Right behind the fountain and the couches, there was a restaurant, called 'Rizio', a flutter of voices coming out of its widely opened glass doors. And last but not least, right next to the restaurant was the lobby's reception, two women dressed in sophisticated uniforms mixing shades of grey and white, standing behind the counter, probably waiting to greet their brand-new customers.

After the two families stopped marveling at the perfection of the hotel, they all walked toward the reception, with Perventia, Pattery, and Berventy taking the lead a few inches ahead.

"Welcome to the Cardiniganin Hotel," one of the women said, the one with the vibrant bronze hair, a similar shade to Pattery's. She tapped her name tag with a finger and an accompanying smile. "My name is Sydney and I'm the general manager. How can I assist you today?"

"Hello," Pattery smiled politely. "I've come here with my family, and we would like several rooms for a couple of nights."

"You have quite a large family," Sydney noted, her eyes planted on the rest of the crowd. There were 12 of them, including Makio.

Pattery laughed, and for some reason, Perventia didn't like that laugh – it seemed way too forced, way too polite.

"I've also come here with my family," Berventy added with a polite smile.

"Are you here on holiday?" Sydney said as she was typing something on the keyboard of the computer, next to her, now looking at the screen.

"Something along these lines," Pattery said.

"Not really talkative, huh?" Sydney said, still looking at the computer screen.

"Can you hurry it up?" Perventia asked impatiently. "We're all really tired, and we just want to get some rest!"

"We're doing everything we can, ma'am," the other woman, next to Sydney, politely said, long orange hair covering her head, a name tag on her grey-white blouse. "My name is Diana, and I manage the Cardiniganin Hotel, together with my sister Sydney."

"It's a family business," Sydney added with a smile, still not taking her eyes off the screen.

"How many rooms would you like?" Diana inquired.

"One for myself and my wife Perventia," Pattery started.

"One for me," Berventy continued, "one for Brouzun and Morven, one for Kasteron and Teela, one for..." Berventy looked at Marisii, who was holding Makio's hand, whispering something in his ear that no one else could hear. Makio laughed. "One for Marisii and his boyfriend Makio."

"And another room for my three other daughters – Pacifika, Kayla, and Klacifia," Perventia finished the annotations. She was wondering whether to read Diana's thoughts or not. But specifically, she was curious to see what was going on in Sydney's head. The hotel manager was way too polite and Perventia had grown suspicious of such behavior, given her recent adventures with an infamous witch. Perventia also didn't like the way Sydney had looked at Pattery when they first entered the ground floor of the hotel.

"To sum it up, six rooms for 12 people?" Sydney asked and after they nodded, she pressed the right button of the computer mouse she was now holding. Then, she smiled and turned over to them. "How many nights are you planning to stay for?"

"Let's say three and then if we want to stay extra, we will let you know," Pattery said, causing Sydney to smile again.

There it was. That smile, that blush. Perventia had noticed that.

Sydney turned back to the screen, the click of keyboard buttons returning in the air.

Perventia wished she could wipe that smug look off her face. But she was powerless to do so as Sydney smiled once again after a pause of about a few minutes, turning over to Perventia and her accompaniment.

"That's going to be 574 dollars."

"What?" Perventia almost screamed, scandalized. "Is this a five-star hotel or something?"

"Actually, *yes*, it is," Diana confirmed, from behind Sydney, stepping forward. "The Cardiniganin Hotel is one of the most famous hotels in the whole area – every year we get 15,000 guests minimum, each staying for at least a week."

Pattery nodded. It *was* expensive, but even Perventia knew that that was their only option at the moment. Pattery took his credit card out of his wallet and Sydney handed him the PDQ machine.

Perventia concentrated her eyes on Sydney, who was looking at Pattery intently. *That's a tasty catch. Too bad he's married.*

"All good to go," Sydney announced. "You can take out your card now."

Perventia saw Pattery sliding his credit card out of the device, and it took every ounce of self-control she had not to close her hands around Sydney's throat and squeeze.

Diana handed six keys to Pattery. "You're in rooms 78 to 83 on the seventh floor," she said. "We wish you a pleasant stay at the Cardiniganin Hotel. If the need for anything arises, anything at all, we would be right here for you, ready to assist. You can also call us from the phones in your rooms."

We would hardly need yours and your sister's slut services, Perventia thought this time, her facial expression bitter with resentment toward the two sisters, but mainly toward Sydney.

"Thank you," Berventy and Pattery said in sync and then the two families and Makio moved away from the reception area and headed for the elevators, which were going to take them up to the seventh floor, where their new rooms awaited them.

Chapter 59

Meeting at the jacuzzi

Marisii and Makio opened the door of the room they had been placed in – №78.

"Wow," Marisii could only say when he stepped inside the vast space, his Primark shopping bags hanging around one wrist. Marisii looked around the room and established that it definitely matched the reputation Diana had been so fiercely talking about.

At the center of the room, there were two double beds, with neatly arranged white and brown covers, which Marisii concluded were made of silk and cotton when he touched them. At the end of each bed, a few towels of various sizes had been placed. Next to the bed, there was a small wooden desk, a glass transparent bowl resting on its surface, containing small square chocolates and a big greeting card: *'Welcome to the Cardiniganin Hotel'*. Opposite the two beds, the two men could find a huge plasma TV and remote control, and right next to it two towering windows that revealed a beautiful view of the beach below. The curtains were also mixing shades of white and brown, made of cotton and silk.

Behind Marisii, Makio entered the space fully and threw his shopping bag on one of the beds, running off into the bathroom. "Oh my God," he said, emerging out of the bathroom after a minute, holding something in his hand. "They even have some of those small, cute, scented soaps!"

Marisii could make out a tiny red soap in the shape of a circle in Makio's hand. "I see you're enjoying yourself."

"Are you kidding?" Makio chuckled. "This is amazing! I haven't stayed in a five-star hotel before – and the bathroom? Did you see the bathroom? It is so beautiful, refined, and polished, it practically shines!"

Marisii laughed slightly and left his two shopping bags on the floor next to the other bed. He stepped closer to Makio, a wide smile drawn on his face. "You know," Marisii said, his tone playful. "You're awfully cute when you're excited!"

"No more than you!" Makio said with a wink and then gently shoved Marisii with a finger.

Marisii took a hold of his hand and in the next moment moved his gaze to his face. His black-framed glasses were gone, lost on The Island of Lost Hopes, but he didn't look any less attractive without them. Then, Marisii looked deep into Makio's brown eyes, placed his fingers on his neck and pulled him closer, locking their lips together, hungrily inserting his tongue to explore Makio's mouth. Marisii was glad to see Makio offering no resistance and returning his kisses with the same amount of hunger and ferocity.

The room's door was wide open, from when they had entered, but Marisii couldn't care less. He didn't give a damn about who was going to see him with Makio – he just wanted to stay forever in that moment, kissing his boyfriend continuously and passionately.

~~~~~~~~~~

The night fell. Most of the family members were preparing to head to bed. They all needed the rest.

But Pattery Fehrenberg was in the mood to try the hotel's jacuzzi – he had never been in one, and due to all the services of the hotel being included in the package he had paid for, he decided it was time to blow off some steam, literally, and do some thinking. His wife Perventia had already gone off to bed, and he carefully undressed himself and changed into his dark blue swimming shorts, so as not to wake her up. He had bought them at Primark, and he might as well use them. Pattery then took his bath robe and carefully slid out of the room, aiming not to make too much noise, tiptoeing when he walked on the floor with his flip-flops.

Once out of the bedroom, Pattery headed for the elevator, situated at the other end of the spacious corridor, lined with bedroom doors. He had taken a shower earlier, but he thought dipping into the jacuzzi would have a positive effect on him. Pattery stepped inside the elevator cabin and pressed the button, indicating the first floor. The double steel doors closed and within a minute, they opened back up, having delivered him at his desired location. He stepped out of the elevator cabin and walked up to the reception, where he noticed one of the hotel's managers – Sydney. By this time, he had pulled his robe on, but a lot was still revealed of his strong, muscular chest. His muscles were well-defined, but not over the top, his body was hairy, but also not over the top. Add that to his bronze hair and towering, handsome features, and he was bound to spin any woman's head around. However, Pattery was conscious of his neck and face burns, which were substantial, from the time Feever had placed her scorching hand on Pattery's face at the battle in the library. And as much as he wanted to, he couldn't hide them.

"Good evening." Pattery smiled warmly at Sydney, even though it was technically night.

"Good evening to you too," she said playfully in response. "How can I help you?"

Pattery was vaguely aware of her eyes gazing all over his body but chose not to address the matter. "I would like to use the jacuzzi, which, if I'm not mistaken, is situated somewhere outside?"

Sydney laughed. "Someone's read the hotel's leaflet, I see. The jacuzzi is down the corridor over in that direction–" she pointed at a corridor, close to the now-closed restaurant, but then she seemed to decide otherwise and emerged out of the reception through a glass door on her right. "I can show it to you if that would be easier?"

Pattery nodded, and the two of them started walking toward the restaurant. "I believe the price of that is included in the package I paid for?" He wanted to double-check, hence the uncertainty plaguing his voice.

Sydney looked down at his dark blue swimming shorts. "Your package is big indeed!" She laughed in a playful manner.

"Thank you," he smiled. "But I meant the hotel's package."

"Oh, is that so? Silly me!" Sydney slapped herself on the forehead, but her cheeky smile gave away her unseriousness to Pattery. "But yeah, the jacuzzi is included in the package for every single one of you."

"Splendid," Pattery exclaimed and let himself be led to the jacuzzi by the thirsty hotel manager.

The two of them started walking down the long corridor, the roof of which was entirely composed of transparent, expensive-looking glass panes. After the corridor, there was something like a living room area, with a small bar and some stools and couches, but the area was now closed for the public. The corridor continued after that area and a little bit further down were two glass doors. Pattery could vaguely make out the shape of the long jacuzzi beyond them. Sydney opened the door for him, and he stepped out. Pattery saw the jacuzzi, which could fit at least five people, and the water inside it, which wasn't bubbling yet. Next to the jacuzzi, there were also two deck chairs, designed for customers of the hotel to relax on in-between jacuzzi sessions.

"Let me start it for you," she said, and then pulled a small, black remote control out of the pocket of her pants. Pattery saw her pressing a button and then witnessed the water starting to slowly bubble up. "It should be warm and pleasant in just a few minutes and you will be able to go in and relax." Sydney then handed him the remote. "Just in case you want to change the temperature or pressure."

Pattery took the remote control in his right hand. "Thank you for your help."

"I'm always happy to help," she said and Pattery caught her looking at his slightly exposed body again. "I will leave you to it then." And she was heading for the double glass doors when Pattery saw her turning around toward him again. "Who knows, maybe later I could join you."

Sydney winked at him and he laughed – he loved his wife Perventia more than anything and he was never going to cheat on her, but he had to admit it was nice that somebody younger, such as Sydney, was flirting with him. It showed him that he was still attractive even though the years passed by – after all, he had turned 47 just a couple of months ago. He was just two years older than his wife. And yeah, it made him feel better.

Sydney officially left and once she had, Pattery stripped out of his robe, leaving himself only in the dark blue swimming shorts, exposing his muscular, hairy frame. He waited a few minutes for the water to bubble up entirely. Pattery was feeling cheeky, so he removed his swimming shorts and threw them on the discarded dressing gown, next to the deck chairs. Once he was all natural, he slowly stepped into the jacuzzi, immersing himself inside the water and letting it soak him through and through. He couldn't help but moan slightly at the feel of the gentle water against his skin – it was like a silk curtain, massaging his every feature, relaxing the tension that had built up inside his body up until that moment. The bubbles touched every aspect of his light skin, and he liked that. After enjoying the hot water in a standing position for a few minutes, he moved to one of the jacuzzi's edges, where he could relax and prop his elbows up on the armrests. As Pattery was doing that, he exposed his armpit hair in the process. He closed his eyes and let the gentle water continue massaging him.

Pattery must have dozed off because he suddenly opened his eyes in alarm upon hearing someone's footsteps growing nearer. But that alarm quickly went away when he saw his beautiful wife, standing next to the deck chairs, in nothing but her hot-pink bikini, her robe being discarded on the floor on top of his robe and swimming shorts.

"Perventia?" he asked, slightly confused. "Not that I'm not happy to see you, but what are you doing here? I thought you were asleep!"

"I was asleep indeed," Perventia said with a smile and Pattery caught her overlooking his now wet hairy chest, and his whole body. He could practically feel the excitement building up in her gentle, but sometimes dominant limbs. "But then I woke up and you weren't there. And I remembered that the hotel included a jacuzzi in our package, and we're going to spend a substantial amount of time here anyway, so I decided why not? You're not the only one who read the leaflet, you know." She laughed warmly, but also seductively.

That laugh always drove Pattery crazy.

"I guess great minds think alike." Pattery winked at his wife and looked at her body dreamily – when was the last time he had made love to her? Perventia looked so attractive in her low-cut bikini, exposing just the right amount of flesh. And the years hadn't had much effect on her. But he reckoned she would have looked even more attractive with her bikini completely discarded and she herself in his strong, muscular arms.

Pattery could feel an erection forming beneath his hairy navel – he loved his wife endlessly, and he loved having sex with her over and over again. And his 'buddy' certainly approved of that notion. Pattery saw Perventia starting to climb into the jacuzzi but he raised his hand to stop her. "Ah, ah, ah," he smiled at his wife, who was suddenly confused at his reaction, "don't you know the rules of the jacuzzi? You can't come in, dressed!"

Perventia smiled at him as if she weren't amused. "You're adorable." She unclasped her bikini top. "But face it, you *just* made up that rule." Then, Perventia fully removed her bikini, standing fully natural in front of the horny Pattery, whose penis ached to be inside of her. Perventia stepped further into the jacuzzi and giggled, Pattery supposing possibly at the feel of the water against her skin.

When she was in close proximity, he grabbed her off her spot and pulled her closer to him, hungrily and affectionately finding her mouth with his. He hadn't shaved in weeks, but he knew Perventia enjoyed a stubble. "I'm gonna fuck you!" he whispered in her ear, massaging her vagina, making her moan beyond control in the silent night. Pattery knew they both loved dirty talk.

They spent many more moments massaging each other's intimate parts, and kissing passionately, when Pattery pulled Perventia closer to him, positioning her just above him, penetrating her. As a result, two loud moans escaped into the night.

Pattery grabbed a fistful of her blonde hair gently and looked into her eyes. "I love you! I love you more than anything!"

~~~~~~~~~~

Perventia grabbed Pattery's shoulders, holding on for dear life as he was sliding her along the length of his penis, up, and down, up, and down.

"I love you too!" She kissed him by biting at his lower lip fiercely, moving along the rhythm of their well-defined bodies.

In two dozen minutes, when both of them were on the verge of coming, Perventia read Pattery's mind, without meaning to: *You're amazing!*

Perventia smiled.

Her power was working effortlessly, even though she didn't know why she had read her husband's mind without meaning to. But she didn't give it much thought – it must have been the literal heat of the moment.

Even after they had come, the two of them stayed in each other's arms for hours, without uttering a single syllable.

Chapter 60

"I saved you because I think you're worth it."

The empress of The Island of Lost Hopes, Ameralda, had just sent the Klauzer and Fehrenberg families back to their own universe – she thought they had gotten what they came here for, and they had no place on the island, or on this universe, anymore. Ameralda tightened her fists and wanted to scream and shout due to the fact that her rival Feever had stolen one of the vials with the cure – and because of her Brouzenvert Klauzer had died. Ameralda had sworn to take revenge on Feever for meddling in her affairs, in *her* world. Ameralda had been present on this world much longer than Feever – they were both powerful witches, more than capable of acquiring what they wanted. The only difference was that Feever was immortal and Ameralda was mortal. But not like a human-mortal, more as a-thirty-bullets-and-fireballs-and-counting-mortal.

Ameralda was now taking a walk through the jungle of her island, her long and black dress with leaves pinned on it, spilling on the ground as she walked, enjoying its beauty – the jungle, the tall trees, the waterfalls. The island was like heaven – *her heaven.*

She owned it and she was its empress. After all the drama with the two families, Ameralda needed to clear her head, and that's why she was just walking about, thinking about her beauty of an island and how she was going to take revenge on the devious witch.

Suddenly, Ameralda noticed a figure, lying lifelessly on the ground – she realized she had gotten close to the place where she had sent the two families home from. The empress narrowed her eyes and when she recognized who the figure was exactly, she started running toward it at full speed. Ameralda reached the bloodied figure, laying on the leaf-infested ground with a knife stuck deep inside her stomach, within seconds.

"Kayla?" Ameralda asked in confusion.

Kayla Fehrenberg was out of it, her body still, her face drained of all color.

"What the hell?" Ameralda asked herself, kneeling next to the body, remembering vividly how she had sent both of the families through the portal. But then she also recalled how she hadn't stayed until the end, to see everyone off. *Unless*, she thought, *unless someone else went into the other universe in her place*. Ameralda remembered hearing a rumor about Kayla from this universe having lost all her family due to Feever's rampage and being the sole survivor of her invasion. Was it possible that Kayla from this universe had stabbed her twin and then jumped inside the portal, assuming her place in the other universe? After all, Ameralda had left the scene, not seeing the original Kayla *actually* stepping into the portal. It wasn't out of the question that the second Kayla was the reason for the view Ameralda was now witnessing.

Ameralda looked at Kayla again, who was in a dreadful condition. "Let's fix you," Ameralda said, outstretching her right hand toward Kayla, grabbing hers, and then the two of them disappeared from the vast jungle in a cloud of deep emerald smoke.

~~~~~~~~~~

Kayla Fehrenberg 's eyelids fluttered open. The world all around her was blurry and her eyes needed a couple of dozen seconds to adjust and recognize anything. After her vision sharpened, she noticed that she was in something like a large throne room. Kayla looked down below her and saw that she was placed in a bed, composed entirely of leaves and long vines. In front of her bed, there was a path, lined with more emerald leaves. Butterflies and grasshoppers were flying about in the air. The roof of the throne room was also either composed of or covered with leaves. Kayla started getting up, but a female voice stopped her.

"You'd better not do that," Ameralda said from the other end of the room, sitting in what Kayla noticed was a throne. Surprisingly for the atmosphere of the space, Ameralda's throne was black, surrounded by small threads of green silk, which was also composed of leaves. The throne was large and towering, but Kayla saw it fitted Ameralda's frame perfectly, leaving plenty of space above and around her, to accentuate her mighty highness.

"You don't want to open your wound now, do you?" Ameralda asked, and then stood up from her throne in all her majesty. Her long emerald-raven hair was flowing freely in all directions, as Ameralda walked closer to Kayla, clad in her usual long silk-cotton black dress with leaves pinned on it. "How are you feeling?" she said, sitting up on the bed, and Kayla felt her hands on her shoulders, inviting her to lie back down on the bed.

Kayla did exactly that. "Like someone hit me with a hammer," Kayla laughed, but then her stomach wound began throbbing with pain, and she stopped. Her stomach was covered with leaves, which were emanating healing qualities throughout Kayla's system. "What's going on? Why am I still here, on the island?"

"I think you need to tell me that."

Kayla paused for a second, trying to think. "The last thing I remember is you opening the portal and then we started going through it one by one," Kayla started shakily, and as she recalled events, she gradually started remembering how she had ended up here while her family went back home. "Then I bid farewell to the other Kayla." Her eyes widened in shock. "We hugged and then she stabbed me! She just flashed out a knife from somewhere and struck me in the stomach, leaving me there on the ground to die, while she took my place in *my* family!"

"I supposed something along these lines happened," Ameralda said thoughtfully.

"She…" Kayla started moving her limbs in distress. "She even apologized to me for what she'd done, claiming she just wanted to be with her family again and avenge their deaths! What had Feever in this universe done that was so bad for Kaya to wish to kill me, in order to achieve her end goal?"

"Those are just rumors and I'm not even sure they're entirely true, but I heard that her family from this universe was killed by Feever, leaving her as the sole survivor."

"That doesn't excuse her!" Kayla countered suddenly, sitting up in the bed again. "She almost killed me, leaving me to bleed to death!"

"I agree with you," Ameralda said, smiling. "And I know exactly how you feel – betrayed and deceived. That's the exact way I felt when I found out Feever had stolen one of the vials with the cure, so only one of you could be saved. She meddled in my business and I have every intention to meddle in hers!"

"And I want to go back to my universe and show the impostor Kayla that no one messes with me and my family!" Kayla looked once again to her wound, just now noticing that there was also green gel, showing out from beneath the leaves.

"My handiwork. Your wound is healing but you better not make any sudden movements in the next couple of days," Ameralda said and then placed a hand on Kayla's. "And you *will*. But right now, you need to rest. There will be time for reckoning, I assure you!" Ameralda stood from the bed and headed toward the throne again.

But then Kayla stopped her. "Why did you save me?" Kayla asked.

Ameralda turned around toward her. "Excuse me?"

"Why did you save me?" Kayla repeated. "You could have left me to die, but you saved me instead, and you're now taking care of me. The first time I laid eyes on you, I noticed by the way you held yourself and how you spoke, that you weren't one of those people who would do something just out of the goodness of their heart. You gave us the cure and you saved my sister Pacifika because you thought it wasn't fair that Feever stole the cure and because you wanted us away from your kingdom. So, why did you save me? What do you stand to gain from that?"

Kayla noticed Ameralda smiling and then finding her eyes with hers.

"If you were a goddess too, existing since the beginning of time, you would have searched for gain in your every deed too," Ameralda began. "I never do favors, or anything for that matter, without expecting something in return – you guessed that right! You may think that makes me selfish, but even though I've always been only slightly susceptible to harm, that's how I survived all those millions of years. I've known Feever for a long time and I think that she needs to pay for tricking someone who's much higher in the hierarchy than her!"

Kayla was listening to her, not daring to interrupt – Ameralda might have helped her, might have saved her, but Kayla was confident she was capable of altering her decision just as quickly if she wanted to.

"I saved you because I think you're worth it," Ameralda said. "I think you deserve the chance to go back to your own universe and show that impostor, as you called her, that she can't mess with you and your family, as you said." Ameralda started walking away again, but Kayla interrupted her once more.

"Thank you," Kayla said after her. "Without you, I would have been dead!"

But this time Ameralda didn't turn around. "Get some rest," she said. "We will discuss your return back to your world later." And then, without uttering a single additional world, Ameralda walked in the direction of her throne.

Kayla lay back down on the bed, Ameralda's retreating footsteps echoing in her ears. She adjusted her body more comfortably in the emerald bed, pulling up a massive blanket made of leaves, that she only now noticed resting at her feet, over her. Then she adjusted a pillow, made of the same material, below her head, her long caramel hair spilling in all directions, and closed her eyes, her stomach wound slightly hurting. Kayla really needed some rest and decided that she could allow herself not to think about the vile thing her doppelganger had done, for a couple of hours. She closed her eyes, vaguely aware out of the corner of her eye that Ameralda was watching her from the throne. Within minutes, Kayla drifted off to sleep.

Today, Kayla Fehrenberg was recovering.

Tomorrow, Kayla Fehrenberg was going to take her twin down. Whatever it took.

END OF PART I

To keep up with the latest publishing news visit
Georgi Velkov's Facebook page at:

facebook.com/gvelkovwrites

BV - #0012 - 180822 - C0 - 210/148/21 - PB - 9781915338020 - Gloss Lamination